THE THINGS I DO FOR YOU

"A touching novel."
—*Publishers Weekly*

THE PUB ACROSS THE POND

"The ending is as enchanting as the Ireland she describes,
and this is guaranteed to become one of the books
on your shelf that you'll want to read again."
—*Fredericksburg.com*

MY SISTER'S VOICE

"At once a story about love and loss, family and friends,
the world of the hearing and that of the deaf,
My Sister's Voice satisfies on many levels."
—Holly Chamberlin, author of *The Family Beach House*

"Gripping, entertaining and honest. This is a unique,
sincere story about the invisible, unbreakable bonds of
sisterhood that sustain us no matter how far they're buried."
—Cathy Lamb, author of *Henry's Sisters*

"Carter's talent continues to evolve, as evidenced in this solid
offering. The unique spin Carter takes on the familiar theme
of self-discovery gives this a welcome, fresh feeling."
—*Publishers Weekly*

ACCIDENTALLY ENGAGED

"Carter shows she has a knack for creating odd but likable
characters and readers are sure to take notice."
—*Booklist*

She'll Take It

MARY CARTER

KENSINGTON BOOKS
www.kensingtonbooks.com

KENSINGTON BOOKS are published by

Kensington Publishing Corp.
119 West 40th Street
New York, NY 10018

All Kensington titles, imprints, and distributed lines are available at special quantity discounts for bulk purchases for sales promotion, premiums, fund-raising, educational, or institutional use.

Special book excerpts or customized printings can also be created to fit specific needs. For details, write or phone the office of the Kensington Sales Manager: Kensington Publishing Corp., 119 West 40th Street, New York, NY 10018. Attn. Sales Department. Phone: 1-800-221-2647.

Kensington and the K logo Reg. U.S. Pat. & TM Off.

ISBN-13: 978-0-7582-6643-9 (ebook)
ISBN-10: 0-7582-6643-X (ebook)

ISBN-13: 978-1-4967-0635-5
ISBN-10: 1-4967-0635-8
First Kensington Trade Paperback Printing: March 2006

10 9 8 7 6 5 4 3 2

Printed in the United States of America

To my mother,
who loved the book even before she read it.

Acknowledgments

A big thank you to Jim McCarthy and John Scognamiglio for their patience, humor, and advice; Lisa Erbach Vance for taking the time to share some early, helpful thoughts with me; Jerry Cleaver, whose writing course started my novel ball rolling; and thank you to my team of early readers: Corey Lindberg, Tamara Moxham, Jennifer Blatto, Melissa Carter, and Pat Carter. And last but not least, I'd like to thank the friends, who sometimes willingly and sometimes after several glasses of wine, regaled me with their own "sticky fingered" tales.

Contract With Self

I, Melanie Zeitgar, being of sound mind and body (minus fifteen pounds) do solemnly swear:

1. I will never shoplift again. Ever!*

Exceptions: Breakups, weight gain, job losses, crummy auditions, great auditions where you don't get a callback, high Visa bills, cavities, the trauma of using automated telephone menus, surprise visits from stalkers and/or muggers, surprise visits from Mom or Zach, no visits or phone calls from CLOML (Current Love Of My Life)—i.e., Ray—and henceforth any unforeseen tragic bouts of stress.

Chapter

1

Before I steal, I pray. *Saint of Kleptomaniacs, forgive me.* That's all. I don't think it's necessary to waste the Saints' time with lame excuses about how society or New York or your parents are making you do it. They know we're weak, original sin and all that. For me stealing is like love: I'll know it when I see it.

Today it's a beautiful, little lavender bar of soap—a sudsy slice of heaven. It's wrapped in soft purple tissue paper and topped with a white satin bow. I could eat it. I survey the territory. The five-hundred-square-foot boutique is divided into sections, and I am standing in the southeast corner flush against the wall. New Yorkers are slow to come out of their holiday comas, but the late January thaw has ignited early spring fever, and the boutique is crowded and noisy. Decorative hand mirrors are propped like sentinels on the shelves above the soaps, but there are no security cameras.

I pick up one of the hand mirrors and use it to glance at the girl working the register. The crowd obscures my view. This is good news; if I can't see her, she can't see me. My heart begins to tap dance. My fingers tingle. While holding the mirror with my right hand, I covet the bar of soap in my left, holding it like an injured baby bird. Then I set the mirror down, open my purse, and scrounge around until I find my cell phone. I don't need to make a call, but it's an old magician's trick—distraction, distraction, distraction. While removing my phone with my right hand, I open my left and tilt it down toward my purse like a slide. Whee! The bar of soap glides past my fingers and disappears safely inside. I snap the purse shut and linger by the soaps for a few more minutes, smelling the fragrances, pretending to be a normal, ambivalent shopper. "Excuse me." I move away from the woman elbowing her way in. I head toward the door reading the posted sign as I slip out. SHOPLIFTERS WILL BE PROSECUTED. *Only if they're caught,* I think to myself. *Only if they're caught.*

Look at the lights! Look at the people! Can you smell the roasted chestnuts, the soft pretzels, and just a trace of diesel? Look around you, there are so many of us. Tall, short, fat, round, skinny, punk, white, black, Asian, Indian, and klepto. Look at those sweet, pudgy Midwesterners clutching their programs from *The Producers* while juggling their tourist maps and cans of mace. There is no greater place on earth than Manhattan. I could die now. I could die happy right this very minute, my size seven and one-half feet bouncing down the sidewalk, toe to toe with every other New Yorker, squeezing my dreams between theirs, offering them up to this maze of steel, concrete and blazing lights like a sacrificial lamb. I'm a lamb, I'm a lamb, I'm a happy little lamb.

I'm also a good twenty blocks from home, but I decide to walk anyway. In addition to the springlike weather, I'm emanating warmth from deep within, riding the high that always bubbles up in me after a good, clean lift. I walk with a bounce in my step and blow mental kisses to my Saints.

And before you think I'm totally off my rocker, I know I'm interacting with invisible, made-up idols of perfection, but can I help it if I feel the need for daily, Saintly intervention? Some people throw salt over their shoulders, walk around ladders, and knock on wood for luck—I simply call upon the Universe for a little ethereal backup. And although I prefer to find God in the stars instead of a church, I consider myself a vicarious Catholic, and I figure if I'm going to be saddled with random guilt and a healthy fear of my own mortality, I might as well reap a few fringe benefits along the way.

But don't get me wrong—they may be Saints, but they aren't perfect. Case in point, here I am bobbing along, singing their praises while they're clearing the stage for the next act. Ladies and gentlemen, it's only been three blocks, two shoves, four "Spare any change" and one "Hey baby" since I've left the store, but the guilt portion of this morning's program is about to begin. Suddenly, the glorious bar of soap in my purse turns to stone. Its dead weight is like an anchor weighing me down. Ugly thoughts touch down and take off again like flies pestering a horse.

You didn't need a bar of soap. You should wash your mouth out with it when you get home. You could have walked up to the counter and paid for it like a decent human being. Turn around right now and take it back. But I don't. I keep walking downtown. If I make it to the twenties there's no turning back. Just five more blocks and I'm in the safe zone. The safe zone is where I can no longer rationalize going back to the store and the guilt stops. I can take it. I'm an actress, a New Yorker and a vicarious Catholic. I eat guilt for breakfast. It's like a multivitamin; you just have to take it. Guilt is like the gunk that washes to shore at the beach. You don't stop going to the ocean because of the gunk. You just pick out the pretty seashells. It's the yin yang of shoplifting. It comes with the territory. And believe me—by now I've got the territory down.

I don't look like a thief. I'm an attractive young woman. True, I'm clinging onto the last rung of the ladder of my twenties like a bulldog with a stolen bone, but I come from good aging genes, and I figure by the time I'm forty they will have come up with an anti-aging treatment that still allows you to use your facial muscles to do the odd thing like smile now and again without looking like a deranged robot, so I'm trying not to freak out. In all other aspects, I'm a decent citizen. I use sunscreen with an SPF of 15 or higher, I vote, and I buy Girl Scout cookies for my anorexic friends. I get Pap smears once a year, AIDS tests every six months, and I give to the homeless.

In one way my decency makes up for the stealing, but on the other hand, it leaves me very little room to rationalize my habit. I'm neither a pimply faced teenager crumbling under peer pressure to stick heart-shaped lip gloss in my pockets nor a poor mother forced by tragic necessity to swipe a few boxes of generic macaroni for her three starving children. That would be understandable. Forgivable even. The truth is in this tale there are no starving children—not even starving cats or dogs. Likewise, no animals or children have been hurt by my kleptomania, so let's call it a wash.

I do not steal to feed a drug habit. I do not smoke crack cocaine, nor do I pop speed with my morning latte (nonfat, double shot, one Sweet'N Low). I like an occasional glass of wine (Australian Shiraz is always a good choice) or a pint of Guinness now and again, but that's about it. Okay, I have been known to drink to excess on special occasions (birthdays, New Year's, and getting to the subway only to find your ticket is gone and you've only fifty cents in your purse) and I've spent at least three mornings in the past six months swearing and puking and bargaining with the *Saint of Hangovers* that I'll never, ever drink again if he would just (please!) make that ridiculous pounding in my head go away and let me take a sip of water without immediately returning it to the great white throne, but it has absolutely nothing to do with my secret shame.

I'm afraid there are no explanations good enough to explain why I'm a 29-year-old klepto. Except this. I'm in love with ~~my eighth grade history teacher, the captain of the football team, the cute guy who sits in the back of my psych class, the Irish guy from the Tile Bar,~~ ~~a bisexual actor, a Californian Crystal Consultant, a waiter/novelist, waiter/actor/, waiter/painter, waiter/waiter~~ (okay, so he had no ambitions whatsoever, but you should have seen the body on that man)~~, a Wall Street stockbroker, an accountant, a waiter/clown~~ (in my defense he didn't enroll in clown school until after we had slept together)~~, a construction worker, a mortician~~ (don't ask)~~, a~~ (British, Australian, Irish, Russian) ~~tourist, a married man~~ Ray Arbor. Beautiful, wonderful, incredible, there's-just-one-catch Ray.

He's a musician.

I know it's bad, it's wrong, it's foolish, it's trouble—but it is. For those of you who have loved and lost musicians, no explanation is needed. You feel my pain. You know dating a musician is akin to sticking your hand in a roaring fire to save a falling s'more. No matter how delicious it tastes, in the end you're going to get burned.

At some point in the dating scheme you have to ask yourself, "Is he thinking three little words about me, or am I just another groupie?" Ray Arbor and I have been spending every day together for the past three months. Ray's band, Suicide Train, plays in dives all over Manhattan, New Jersey, and Long Island, and I've been a fixture at every show. By the second week of our courtship, I knew I would marry him and live in a trailer with six squalling brats if it meant spending the rest of my life staring into those jade green eyes. The guys in the band are used to women hanging on Ray, and they've started taking bets on how long I'm going to last, so I've doubled my efforts to be nice to them. I told Brett, the drummer, that he reminds me of Bono from U2, when actually with his curly red hair and freckled face, he looks more like a Muppet. I bring scotch and soda to the bass player, Tim, and point out the women in the crowd who I think will sleep with him on the first date. Nine out of ten times I'm right. Jason, the main singer, is the one I haven't succeeded in winning over. He responds to my flirtations with a quiet disdain that leaves me feeling like I just wet my pants in public. I have decided to leave him alone.

Last, Trent, Ray's backup singer, is a pushover. He is a hundred pounds overweight and responds to touch—a hand on the shoulder, a pat on the knee, a peck on the cheek. I'm proud to say that when Trent gets drunk after shows and rants and raves about how evil women are, he never includes me in that category. In summary, Ray and I are having sex four plus times a week, I'm ignoring my closest female friends and sucking up to his, and I regularly shave my legs, highlight my hair, and wax my eyebrows. He has to be in love with me, right?

Then why, why, why has it been six days, three hours, and twenty-four minutes since he's called? The last I heard from him was the day after Trina Wilcox's party. And even though I was blind drunk by the end of it, from what I can remember I looked smashing and it went swimmingly. We even had sex in the coatroom. It's enough to make you insane. It's enough to make you a klepto.

As punishment for stealing the bar of soap, I go home, turn on every light in my place, and stand naked in front of my full-length mirror. My roommate Kim is out so I don't even shut the door. I try to imagine my imperfect body swathed in orange prison garb. It's not so bad. I would look good in orange—especially if I get blond highlights to perk up my roots. I wonder if I'll be propositioned by a prison guard and what the chances are the relationship will last. I imagine myself by the side of the road, picking up trash with a long, sharp stick. The sun would feel good on my cheeks, my highlights would glimmer, and my fellow inmates and prison guard/lover would say, "She's really calmed down.

She's at peace with herself. We've locked up her body but we can't touch her soul." And "Has she lost fifteen pounds or what?"

Here are the facts. You already know I'm twenty-nine and holding. 5'7" (relatively tall, but I'm no giant), I have shoulder-length, dark blond hair, and long, thin arms with freckles. I thank the Saint of Freckles that he marched them up my arms and sprinkled them on my shoulders but left my face alone. I wonder if prior to this lifetime we're given a choice about our appearance as well as our disposition. Did I give up sanity for a freckleless face? I can see Saint Peter prodding me with a white feather pen. "Melanie dear, you must decide. Would you like a face full of freckles or a lifetime supply of Prozac?" I wouldn't have hesitated. "I'll take the Prozac please, and make it a double."

Back to the mirror. Breasts adequate, not too small, not too large (Goldilocks would be proud), hips too big, stomach okay if I suck it in, calves actually very nice, but thighs frustrating beyond belief and constantly in need of hiding as if my entire lower body were a spy. Although I would never resort to liposuction, I do look forward to the day that you can buy your own fat-sucking vacuum right off the shelf and do it yourself in the privacy of your own home. I'm sure the technology is only minutes away. Until then, I'll continue to refer to myself as "voluptuous"—it's much nicer than "needs to lose a few."

My eyes are my best feature; they fluctuate between gray, blue, and green like a mood ring. If I go a few days without eating, I look even better—cheekbones—but a few days after that I binge from all the deprivation, and they puff out again. I really like my feet, but I hate my ass. My feet are petite, and I have a great arch (I could have been a ballet dancer), but my ass is way too big. Ray (My boyfriend? Friend I'm sleeping with? Future husband?) tells me he loves my ass. What kind of man could love this ass? The kind who doesn't have to spend hours trying on a bloody pair of jeans, that's who. Bloody hell. (I picked that up after a week in London. That and *shagging*. Sounds like you're having way more fun. Some of it doesn't work. For example, "Shag you!" Not enough grit. But when it comes to my ass, nothing works like a good "bloody hell." Sod off!)

When I'm done torturing myself, I hide the bar of soap in my bedroom closet. It's the only spot in this room that's not a disaster area. In fact the rest of my room looks like an abstract, post-robbery painting. It's purposeful. My roommate Kim hates a mess, and although I would prefer a nice and tidy space, as long as I keep my room like this she won't dare enter it. The padlock on my closet door would grab Kim's attention like sharks smelling blood. She's a sensitive girl and would think the padlock was because of her and might even accuse me of not trusting her, blah, blah, blah. You know how we are. I would do the same thing. After all, her room is an open book. There are no locks on her closets, and I'm welcome to waltz in anytime I'd like and borrow anything of hers that I can squeeze myself into. So for now I have to put up with my messy room and content myself with a meticulous closet.

On the windowsill next to my closet sits a porcelain clown that my father gave me for my tenth birthday. We were supposed to actually go to the circus that day, but at the eleventh hour my father couldn't get out of work and instead of a night of Lions! Tigers! And Bears! (Oh my!) I got a moody babysitter and a porcelain clown. Now my father is a tour guide who lives a laid-back life in the Florida Keys, but the ten-year-old me is still waiting for an apology. Ironically, I was too young then to be bitter, and I absolutely loved the clown. Now I use it to hide the key to my closet. It just fits underneath his big blue feet. I remove the key now and hold my breath. I relish the anticipation of opening my closet.

The first thing I notice (with a twinge of panic) is that my closet is getting full. I have to hide what I steal or I can't sleep, like an insomniac squirrel. I used to worry that dirt would build up on the objects and attach to my soul, but the nightly dustings have eased that. I place the bar of soap on the bottom shelf next to a package of island coasters (Bahamas! Bermuda! Virgin Islands!), a spanking-new Yankees cap, and six long, twisting beeswax candles. I feel a little bit sick. I didn't really need another bar of soap. I'm a horrible person. That's it. I'm done shoplifting. Besides giving myself an ulcer, I just don't have the closet space. New York apartments are infamously small.

It's a two bedroom that sits right above a sushi restaurant on Thirtieth between Lexington and Third. I used to love sushi. Raw fish no longer touches my lips. The smell of it clings to everything, including my clothes, but the worst part is that it's an open house for cockroaches and mice. They come to us in droves. I shower constantly now and stuff cotton in my ears at night after hearing a story about a woman who had a cockroach crawl into her ear while she slept. It had to be surgically removed. I've missed my alarm going off a few times due to the cotton, but it's worth it to have a bug-free canal.

We don't have a doorman, but we do have Jimmy, a homeless man who sleeps in the hallway. If he's in a good mood he'll open the door for you and flash you a toothless grin. However, if he's had a bad day he'll try and trip you, so you always have to watch your feet in relation to his. He hails from Georgia, but he's lived in New York for the past fifty years. "I'm from Georgia," he said the first day I moved in. I was trying to drag a futon mattress up the stairs, stopping every few seconds to swear and readjust my grip on the monstrous thing. I would like to see the basement of the person who invented the futon. I wouldn't be surprised to see it rigged up with chains, whips, and other sadomasochistic machinations. He either completely ignored the fact that people have to actually move these beasts around or enjoy the thought of the pain it causes.

To add to my frustrations, every friend who had promised to help me move had suddenly been hit with the Moving Virus, and so there I was cursing the Saint of Moves From Hell every time my wet tennis shoes slipped on the stairs. The skies had been crackling with rain and lightning all day. "You want some help with that?" Jimmy asked, taking it over before I even answered. I weakly waved my hand in protest, but he was already tossing it over his shoulders and heading up the stairs. "I used to be a professional mover," he called over his shoulder as I crumpled with relief on the stairs. It had taken me four hours to load the truck from my fifth-floor walk-up in Chelsea. The truck was due back in an hour or I would owe another seventy-five dollars. Jimmy was a lifesaver.

He carried the rest of my things in all by himself. I watched the muscles in his brown skin flex as he effort-lessly heaved my futon, kitchen table, rugs, and television up over his head and ascend three sets of stairs without breaking a sweat. Later I learned it was a cocktail of speed and cocaine that allowed him to do this, but at the time I bought the "professional mover" bit. Over the next few months he would also profess to have been a professional chef, professional swimmer, and professional Boy Scout leader. I give him food and money almost every day, and he uses his spare change to buy Jack Daniels.

Lately, he's taken to announcing me. He stands outside the building, and the minute he spots me heading down the sidewalk, he opens the door to our building, bows grandly, and screams "Melanie ZZZZZZZZZZZeitgar" at the top of his lungs. I don't know why he buzzes the *Z* like that, and I'm ashamed to admit it, but he's embarrassing the hell out of me. I've considered letting him use my shower lately because of his stench, but I think Charlie is the one who should give Jimmy his own apartment complete with a shower. Charlie is our landlord, and Jimmy is the unofficial super. Charlie lives in the apartment building across the street, and it's ten times nicer than ours. They have potted palms and a chandelier in their lobby; we have a broken lightbulb and a plastic container of wheat grass. They also have a real doorman who always smiles, and I've never seen him trip anyone even once.

Sometimes I think I should report Charlie to the NAACP or some other such human rights group, but would that really help Jimmy? Isn't it better for him to have a semiwarm hallway to live in rather than the streets? The day I moved in I gave him a pillow and a blanket to sleep on, but they've subsequently disappeared. I don't understand how he'd rather sleep on bare cement, but it's really not my place to teach him how *not* to be a homeless drunk. I suppose I could protest, move out, raise a stink, but I don't. I have rent control. I like Jimmy but I'm ashamed to admit that sometimes when he smiles at me I have to look away.

Inside our apartment there are problems as well. I can handle the cockroaches (with a little help from my friend the cotton ball), but both Kim and I are terrified of the mice. They mainly hang out in the kitchen section of our pad, and if we stomp on the floor before we enter, they're polite enough to scatter back to their holes. The cockroaches, on the other hand, have no such decency and they're becoming quite bold. I found one on the television the other day watching *The Sopranos*. He was perched on Tony Soprano's right nostril. It was so entertaining we couldn't bring ourselves to kill it. I named him Tony, and I marked the top of his little body with red nail polish. He's the only one we won't squash, poison, or drown. The rest of them are on their own.

Before I go to bed, I play the movie *How I Met Ray*. It

gets five stars, it runs in my head, and I can even watch it without a huge bucket of buttered popcorn. It goes a little something like this:

EXTERIOR—NIGHT—MANHATTAN
CHARACTERS: GIRL (Me)
            MOST BEAUTIFUL MAN EVER
            (Ray)

A beautiful GIRL in her late twenties (twenty-nine is still late twenties) is dejectedly walking the streets of Manhattan after a *lousy* audition for an off-, off-, off-, off-Broadway play. She leaves the audition when the director declares that it will be performed in thong underwear as a ploy to put the audience at ease. GIRL walks out without uttering a word of her two-minute comedic monologue. GIRL decides she will *quit* acting and definitely *quit* waitressing at Beef Boys Bar and Grill where Columbia frat boys come in to check out her ass over pitchers of beer.

Suddenly we hear *music*. It wails from a bar on the corner, a small basement dive distinguishable from a sad basement apartment only by the neon eye that blinks above it. GIRL drops to her knees on the sidewalk and peers in the window.

MOST BEAUTIFUL MAN EVER stands on a rickety stage with a guitar slung around his neck and a harmonica wedged in his full lips. GIRL's heart never stands a chance. She closes her eyes and holds his image. Broad shoulders, shaggy black hair, and since she can't see that well through the dirt and the din, she imagines eyes like soft blue ice (I was wrong about the blue eyes, but jade green is unbelievable too, don't you think?), rough hands, and a mind clear enough to pierce through the clutter of hers. GIRL knows if he makes love like he plays, GIRL is in huge, big trouble. GIRL licks index finger and writes "I Want You" backward in the dirty window. Music stops. Lights dim. MOST BEAUTIFUL MAN EVER looks up, sees GIRL, sees "I Want You," and smiles. The smile says, "Then come and get me." And she does.

THE END (but hopefully just the beginning).

Here's the part of the movie we don't get to see: One month later, lying in bed with him I ask him about this moment, the moment we fell in love at first sight. I trace the dimple in his chin, waiting for his rendition of our magical moment. Ray leans his beautiful head back and looks thoughtful. He squints and says, "I thought you were this girl Clara I was supposed to meet for drinks that night." Regardless, to this day I'd like to thank the *Saint of Neurotic Impulses* that I wrote on the window, and the *Saint of Obscure Skills* that I am, and always have been, an excellent mirror writer. Before I fall asleep, I strike a deal with the *Saint of Kleptomaniacs*. As long as Ray calls tomorrow, I promise not to steal.

Chapter

2

Okay. I'm going to be honest with you. I was born with sneaky fingers. My mother delivered a healthy, eight pound, twenty-two inch, blue-eyed, wailing thief. At the age of two I stole car keys from the babysitter, at four I lifted three jars of Jif peanut butter and a box of plastic knives from Safety Town, and at six I was regularly pilfering chocolate milk for me and a few choice friends. All through junior high and high school, if anyone wanted anything, I was the girl who could get it.

They came to me for condoms, pregnancy kits, Swiss Army knives, makeup, and the occasional vibrator. I charged a flat twenty dollars an item, and by the time I graduated from high school, I had a little over six thousand dollars in shoe boxes under my bed. In every other aspect, I was a good kid. I did what my parents told me, I was kind to the elderly, I got straight As with the occasional B, and I once spent an entire summer painting birdhouses for the mentally ill. Could I help it that I had an uncanny ability to make objects disappear off the shelves and into my pockets without a trace?

And living here is like an alcoholic living in a bar. New York is full of large, anonymous, evil, money-grubbing department stores. I can't feel too guilty ripping them off knowing that we're being ripped off in return. You can bet they're polluting the environment, gauging prices, following black people around the store, and/or have secret factories in underdeveloped countries where starving, grubby children sew glass eyes on teddy bears they'll never get to play with. Just thinking about it makes me want to run to Bloomingdale's and relieve it of a few tubes of lipstick. But first I'm going to listen to my message. You see, what did I tell you? Today is a new day, and the blessed answering machine is blinking. I pray to the *Saint of Men Who Want to Call But Have Suddenly Had All Their Fingers Chopped Up in a Horrible Blending Accident and Finally Decide to Call With a Pencil in Their Mouth*, please, please, please, let it be Ray.

But it's not. It's a message from Jane Greer, the "placement coordinator" at Fifth Avenue Temps. In a gravelly Brooklyn accent she demands to see me in her office tomorrow morning. Jane is intimidating on a good day, but she's never left me a message like this. I have good reason to be afraid; Jane is famous for having a short fuse and a long range. I'm going to need backup. I venture into the living room where Kim is lounging on the couch with her recently painted toenails propped up on several pillows. "Uh-oh," she says when I tell her about the message from Jane. While I wait for her to elaborate, I study her little piggies. They're tangerine orange. It would look hideous on me, but she can get away with it. At six foot one, Kim Minx takes up the entire couch.

Her head is propped on the armrest and her long blond hair cascades down the side. She's flipping through the latest edition of *Vogue*. Despite commercials begging me not to, I do hate her because she's beautiful. I also love her because she's my best friend. Kim and I met eight years ago at an open audition for milk, making it a "cattle call" in more ways than one. This was way before the celebrity milk mustache campaign, and they were in search of a beautiful young ingénue to deliver the line, "Mmm, milk. Does the body good." In typical cattle call fashion, young, eager women were lined up for blocks gripping their headshots and resumes, trying their best to intimidate each other out of the line. They were auditioning the union actors first, so us non-unioners had plenty of time on our hands to do what unemployed actresses did best—feed off each other's insecurities like a production of *A Chorus Line* meets *Lord of the Flies.*

At the time I was enrolled in serious acting classes and considered myself better than the phony, tap dancing divas that surrounded me. I was a method actor, studying at the Village School of Acting, where I was immersed in the practice of Sense Memory. The concept was to bring your real-life experiences to bear in the roles you were playing instead of "pretending" to be someone else. No matter what role you were playing, you simply had to scour your memory for an experience in your past that matched the one your character was immersed in.

For example, if you were playing someone in a fearful situation, you needed to dredge up a fearful memory and simply insert that memory into your scene. More than once I've longed to be the victim of an armed robbery or a carjacking just to ingrain myself with a shot of pure terror. It's brilliant because everything in life becomes fodder for your work as an actress. Aunt Betty died? Use it! Use dead Aunt Betty the next time you need to cry in a scene. Unless you hated Aunt Betty, in which case you could dredge up her hateful memory to make you shake with rage or vibrate with disgust. Did your favorite childhood cat get run over by a truck? Yes it's very sad, it's tragic—but it's golden material! Everybody in my class dredged up these painful, wonderful memories, and we used it to make ourselves laugh, cry, or spew rage all over each other. Acting is the art of the damned, and I was its humble servant.

So while the other actresses were chatting and strutting and bragging, I was scouring my inner soul for my relationship to milk. I knew if I could dredge up a really powerful, painful memory of milk, I would get the part. Problem was, I was lactose intolerant.

Okay, I'm not *exactly* lactose intolerant, I just can't stand the stuff. On the other hand, I had really nice breasts, and I was hoping that would balance out the whole hating milk thing. Unfortunately, as I looked around the sea of cleavage surrounding me, it became apparent that everyone else was banking on their beautiful breasts, and in a fit of inspiration I knew I had until my turn in line to become one with milk. *Mmm, milk. Mmmmmm. Miiillk.* Should I be sexy or coy? Or both. Maybe I could do it with a Russian accent. I was really good at accents. *Da. Milk.* Maybe I should think about milkshakes! I do like a thick, frothy milkshake. *MMM Da Milkshake.* Drop the stupid Russian thing. *Mmmm, milkshakes! Does the body good.* Except they make you fat. Strike that! Don't even think fat or you'll project an aura of fat. Shit, why did I do that? Think skinny, Melanie! *Mmm, skim milk. Does the body good!*

This isn't working. The great acting teacher Uta Hagen would tell me to use the technique of substitution. I don't have to like milk! I just have to substitute something I like and *imagine* it's milk. No—not something I like. Something I love. Something I've *gotta have* for milk. Go deep, Melanie. Yes, that's exactly what I have to do. What shall I use for my substitution?

Chocolate? Sex? Fame? Wait a minute—what if I substitute this very audition for milk? I want to get this part more than I want anything else in the world—so this part will become milk. Yes! I want this part with my very soul, and therefore I want milk with my very soul. God I'm brilliant. *Mmm. Milk. Does the body gooooooood.* Yes, I've got it.

And three hours later I get to say it. "Don't be sexy" the woman coming out of the windowless room whispers to me as I'm about to go in. "They're sick of sexy."

"What?" But she's gone. And she's totally thrown me. I want this job with a passion—I would die without it (and therefore without milk) and how in the world can I be passionate and not sexy? It's just not possible. I am exuding sex right now—I am bathing—make that drowning in sexual milk.

But there's no time to assimilate a nonsexual connection to milk. I was ushered into the room in front of two stern-looking people, a man and a woman bearing clipboards and number two pencils like warriors wielding their swords and shields.

"Say your name for the camera," the man said.

"Melanie Zeitgar."

"Okay—you didn't let me finish." He threw a look to the woman who rolled her eyes and shook her head. I suddenly hated milk again and I started to sweat. "When the little red light goes on you will say your name for the camera, wait two beats and then deliver the line. Okay?"

"Sure." Two beats. Okay that's like counting to two, right? But is it one, two or one Mississippi, two Mississippi? Shit. I wondered if I should ask? Would asking make me appear confident or terrified?

"Miss?"

"MMM DA MILK!" I shouted before I could stop myself.

"Your name is first and then the line—after the little red light," he said impatiently.

"Calm down a little" the woman added. "Take a deep breath."

I smiled and breathed deeply to show how capable I was of following directions.

"Okay red light. When it comes on, speak."

I had the sudden urge to bark like a dog, and the thought

made me giggle. And then I tried to stop giggling and it made me giggle all the more. And then the little red light went on and even though I was laughing so hard I was barking like a seal, I said my name and I delivered the line. And because of my inappropriate laughter, the word *milk* came out more like *mulk*. Mmm, MULK. Does the body gud. Incidentally, had I been drinking milk at the time, it would have been coming out of my nose.

"Can I do that again?" I started to say, but like a roller-coaster you've waited in line for (all freaking day in the scorching sun), the audition had lasted a few rattling moments, plunged downhill at the speed of light, and jerked to an abrupt end. A skinny assistant dressed in black appeared out of nowhere and yanked me out by the elbow. "Next!" the man with the clipboard bellowed as if a straight jacket awaited me in the hall. And as I was being escorted out, I could hear the woman say, "Is it just me or did she sound Russian?"

I immediately hauled my humiliated self to the ladies' room. *Don't worry*, my little voice said, *you can use this humiliation another time.* Do you see how sick we actors are? The thought actually cheered me up a little. And there was Kim Minx at the bathroom sink, crying her eyes out.

At first I thought she was just thinking about a dead childhood pet, but my trained eye quickly realized this was more than a sense memory practice. "Are you okay?" I asked softly. Her watery eyes met mine in the mirror. "Those bastards!" she screamed. "Those fucking milk bastards." She hung her head and really sobbed. Her long blond hair was dangling in the sink. I was about to pat her on the back when she suddenly whirled around and stuck her chest out so that I ended up patting her left breast instead. I quickly took my hand away.

"They think they're not even!" she cried, sticking her chest out even farther. "Are they? Are they even?"

I glanced at her breasts and hesitated. The truth was, the left one did look a little bit bigger than the right. But she was so devastated and distraught that I didn't want to hurt her feelings.

"They said that?" I asked horrified.

"Not exactly," she admitted. "But I know he was thinking it. He turned his head sideways. Sideways. Like this." Kim suddenly dropped her head to the side as if she were a marionette and her neck string had been suddenly severed. I found myself dropping my head sideways in imitation.

"But they're perfect," I said, hoping she wouldn't think I was a lesbian. "I'm sure my boyfriend would love them," I added, just in case my preferences were in question. "How dare he. How dare he turn his head sideways. You're beautiful! You're perfect. I just look at you and I think 'Mmm milk.'" Oh God, now I think I've gone too far. I was just trying to be nice, maybe even make a female friend (actresses are notorious for hating each other and hanging out with their male counterparts instead), and now I definitely sound like I'm coming on to her. But she isn't glaring at me or backing away like I'm a freak; she's smiling.

"Really? You're not just saying that?" she says.

I guess she likes freaks so I continued to lay it on thick. "I'm telling you you're so perfect you make me sick!" I yelled. "You fucking make me sick!"

Her face lit up like a neon sign, and she immediately wiped the tears from her eyes. She flipped her long blond hair back and held out a soft, perfectly manicured hand for me to shake. "Kim Minx."

"Melanie Zeitgar."

"Do you like Mexican food, Melanie Zeitgar?" she asked.

"Love it," I lied.

And so that afternoon Kim and I went out for the first of many margaritas together. Mmm, margaritas. Does the body good. We became fast friends, shopping partners (Kim shopped, I praised and sometimes returned to the stores to steal little tidbits I noticed on my reconnaissance missions), and confidantes. She knows everything about me—except for the bit about stealing, of course. We lost touch for a while when I started classes at NYU, but we've been able to pick up the thread. She was the first person I called when my life exploded on me three years ago, and I was the fourth person she called when she found this great rent-controlled apartment last year. Okay, so the friendship isn't exactly even, but I don't care. She's the only one who couldn't care less about all my little neuroses. But sometimes she can be extremely annoying.

"Uh-oh? What?" I whine.

She turns the page of her magazine before answering. Fashion before friendship. "Tell me what she said again. Exactly."

"'Melanie, I'd like to see you in my office. Can you be here at eight A.M.?'"

"Uh-oh."

"Kim. Stop saying that. Maybe she has a great assignment for me."

"I doubt it. But good luck."

"Do you have to be so honest? Whatever happened to little white lies?"

"Sorry, Mel. You're right. She's going to give you a fabulous job on the Queen Mary. How's that?"

"Insincere."

"I'm sure it's nothing. Just go in there, smile, and agree with everything she says." Kim smiles at me by way of example. I smile back. She shakes her head. "You look like you're in pain." I imagine Ray kissing my neck and smile again. "Whoa, way too happy," Kim says. "Discount smile," she suggests. Kim's favorite thing in the world is a good sale. I imagine stealing a cashmere sweater. "Perfect," Kim says. "That's the smile."

Chapter
3

After several agonizing minutes of smiling, I start frowning. Should I really trust Kim's advice? Kim is a fellow Fifth Avenue Temp. We've been employed through them for years while managing our "creative" careers. For Kim it's modeling, for me, acting. And if you're thinking I'm just another flash in the pan who enrolled in a three-year acting program, guess again. I may be only a mediocre actor, but let me tell you, I had to claw my way to mediocrity, and I think that should count for something. I was only eighteen years old when I announced to my mother that I was leaving Rochester to study at the Village School of Acting, and suffice it to say, she freaked out a bit over it. Two days before I was to leave, I was ambushed intervention style in my living room by my mother, my brother Zachary, and a postcard from my father, on which he had written, "I agree with your mother. Go to college."

After hours of screaming and crying and begging (my brother, Zach), and gnawing nervously on lemon bars (my mother), and mentally shoplifting (me), the three of us struck a bargain. I was granted five years to make my dream of becoming an actress a reality and in exchange I agreed not to touch the money that Aunt Betty had left me for college. If after five years I was not a working actress, then I promised to go back to college with Aunt Betty's money and get a degree so I could get a real job and be just as miserable as everybody else.

And so I spent the ages of eighteen to twenty-three dedicated to perfecting my craft, arming myself to be a triple threat. Technically, a triple threat referred to someone who was an actor/singer/dancer, but since I wasn't really adept at singing or dancing, I decided I'd throw in everything under the sun, hoping that knowing how to do a hundred-plus extracurricular activities in a mediocre manner would at least qualify me—if not as a triple threat—at least a threat in general.

So I took movement lessons, tap dancing lessons, oboe lessons, improvisation for the serious actor, sautéing with a wok, acting for the camera, stage presence, Shakespeare, and even speech classes where I learned at least a hundred tongue twisters to improve my diction. (I am the very model of a major modern general.) I was a rollerblading, sewing, stir-frying ball of fire.

After three years completing my studies (although a true actor never really completes her studies), I leaped out into the world of New York auditions with my head held high (a brief stint at finishing school helped me accomplish this), and I directed every ounce of energy I had to landing a paying acting job. But with the exception of a couple of plays (no pay), offbeat commercials (paid in product; I still have a drawer full of vaginal cream), training videos (free footage of me in a hard hat), and student films (I got to play this really drunk girl who made out with a really drunk guy in his stinky dorm room), I wasn't exactly a working actress.

My only steady paying job had been one summer on tour with a murder mystery dinner theatre where my only line was "I'm hungry." (I'd like to think that my delivery of this line, no matter how short, was a show stealer. "I'm hungry" can have many layers of meaning: think of everything one hungers for—fame, beauty, sex, drugs, rock 'n' roll, along with the occasional Kit Kat bar—and you'll get my drift.)

But that was it, and suddenly my five years were over. So, as promised, at the age of twenty-three I enrolled as a freshman student at NYU. In an effort to please my family I didn't even take a single acting class. I lasted through three years and three different majors, and I may have eventually gotten it together, graduated, and become another human resources manager in a stuffy office who drank gin on her lunch hour and reminisced about her days as an actress if it hadn't been for one memorable night where everything imploded. And as much as I hated thinking about that night, it was a wake-up call, I answered it, and I was out of there. To hell with my promise, I still longed to be an actress.

But I'm still not exactly thriving. In fact, I've spent the last three years waitressing, handing out hot dog flyers dressed as—can you guess?—and temping. I was beginning to think the problem boiled down to this: In acting, your body is your instrument, and my instrument has cellulite.

Just to add to my jealousy, Kim actually gets modeling work while I'm still dragging myself to crummy audition after crummy audition and zippo. I hadn't done anything since my off-, off-, off-, off-Broadway show four months ago. It was about a psychotic killer who joins a convent. I played a nun with nymphomania. I had four lines. Seven, if you counted "Oh God, oh God, oh God" as three. It ran less than a week, and I didn't exactly get paid. In fact, after headshots, rehearsal fees, posters, programs, and mass mailings, it kind of cost me over a thousand dollars.

And then there's the two hundred I spent on the herbal wrap that was supposed to melt away unsightly inches overnight. (It didn't. Instead I smelled like cabbage for the next two days, and everyone kept their distance. Maybe that was the point. The farther away people get from you, the thinner you look!) But it's all right. I put everything on my Visa. I figure I'll have it paid off in ten months. Ten months is nothing. If you're not willing to invest in yourself, how can you expect anyone else to? I would be fine. I just needed a good, long temp assignment. But Jane Greer had been ignoring my calls all week. Until this.

"Well I'm not worried," I lie. "So she wants to see me. It's not like I've done anything wrong." This wasn't exactly true. I'd had a slew of nightmare assignments lately, and it's just possible that on one of them I had a teeny, tiny bit of an attitude. I was processing loan applications for an insurance company, which in itself is enough to make anyone want to slit their throat and write "Save Me" with their blood on the cubicle walls, but for a creative person like me, the job was absolute torture. My immediate supervisor, Tom Spencer, had the nerve to tell me that I'd be a knockout if I would just "lose a little in the caboose." The fact that I was eating a Cinnabon at the time made it all the more humiliating. So it's possible that when the condescending asshole offered me a full-time job, it's just possible, that I told him I'd rather strip naked and hang myself from the bank of fluorescent lights than work for him.

Well, that's what I meant to say—but if memory serves me correct, I think I might have slipped and said, "I'd rather strip naked and hang myself from the bank of fluorescent lights than *sleep with you*." I didn't mean to, but he was giving me a lascivious look, and I was imagining his fat, hairy body lowering onto mine like a net full of dead, wet fish when he offered me the job.

"Well good luck," Kim says again. "Juan's for dinner?"

"You think it's that bad?" Juan's is our favorite Mexican dive around the corner. We go there anytime one of us has a crisis and commiserate with our "Three Musketeers"—

Grease, Salt, and Tequila. Kim stops flipping the pages of *Vogue* and flashes me a discount smile. "Definitely Juan's," I agree, fighting back tears.

She wiggles her toes. "You can borrow something if you'd like."

I nod and head into her room.

Unlike mine, Kim's bedroom is immaculate. It's like a mini Barneys. She has loads of clothes, makeup, and accessories that she gets from photo shoots and sample sales. I could spend days in here. But I know what I want. Her baby blue cashmere sweater. I remove it from the pink silk hanger and cradle it in my arms. Pure bliss. I know what you might be thinking, but you'd be wrong. I have rules about stealing, and I never take from friends or family. Kim's things are safe with me, and I know I'm extremely lucky that she is so generous with her things. It's one of the reasons I put up with living with someone so gorgeous.

I mean really, given the choice I'd much rather have ugly friends. Who wouldn't? The ideal would be to have friends who were attractive enough that guys would approach you in a bar but ugly enough that you're really the one they want to talk to. But with Kim around, I could steal a guy's wallet right out of his back pocket (I hardly ever do, I swear) and he'd be so enamored of her that he wouldn't even be able to pick me out of a lineup the next day. They see Kim and suddenly I'm gone. Poof! Except for Ray. Ray, Ray, Ray, Ray, Ray. Beautiful, wonderful Ray. He's not the least bit interested in Kim. It's one of the reasons I don't regret sleeping with him so soon after we met. (Four hours later to be exact.)

"Oh!" Kim says as I parade past her in the sweater and my black miniskirt.

"Does it look okay?" I ask when I see the funny expression on her face. "Is something wrong?" I crane my head around trying to inspect my ass.

"Your behind looks fine," Kim says. "It's the sweater."

"Not my color?"

"Actually it is. It brings out the blue in your eyes." I wait. "It was a gift from Charles," she says finally. "I haven't even worn it yet." Charles is her latest beau. He's our age and a physicist of all things. The two of them are a walking Kohler commercial—"The perfect combination of beauty and brains." And from the dreamy looks I've seen passing over Kim's face these last few weeks, I'd say I'm not the only one madly in love.

"Maybe I should find something else," I say, sourly disappointed. I really love how beautiful the sweater makes me feel. I was hoping if I wore it, I wouldn't be tempted to steal.

"You can wear it," Kim says finally. "Just be careful."

"I promise," I say. "I'll have it dry-cleaned."

"Good luck," she says again. Does she know she's said this three times already? And by this time, I am starting to believe I will need it.

This is how I die:

FIFTH AVENUE TEMPS

Temporary Assistant: Melanie Zeitgar
Assignment: Insurance Division/Death and Dismember-
              ment Benefits
Duties: Cold calling.
Duration: Three hours
   Hello? May I speak to Mr. or Mrs. Davis? This is Melanie from J.D. Harrold's Life Insurance Division. I've got good news. We're offering you three free months of death and dismemberment insurance. That's right! If you lose a limb or your life in the next three months, we'll pay you or your family accordingly. Fifteen thousand dollars for a finger or a toe, fifty thousand for an arm or a leg, and a whop-

*ping one hundred thousand dollars if you die in an accidental,
tragic way. Hello? Hello?*

Fifth Avenue Temps is situated in midtown Manhattan
just a few blocks away from the main branch of the New
York Public Library. Most mornings I make sure to stop in
front of the library to stare at the pair of stone lions flanking
the entrance. They give me strength and today I really
need it. I stand there for a few minutes gazing into their
cold stone eyes until I feel better. I glance at my watch.
Seven forty-five. I have enough time to get coffee and a
muffin. Then I remember that this is the day I'm supposed
to knock off the pastries and start a healthy eating/exercise
regime, but in light of the situation it will have to be post-
poned. If all goes well with Jane, I can start my healthy
regime tomorrow.

I love the delis in New York. The outdoor buckets of
fresh flowers and arrays of colorful fruits and vegetables are
a shoplifter's dream. It is child's play to swipe an orange or a
kiwi as you float by, and there's no danger of cameras or sensors. However, I hardly ever steal fruit anymore. First of all,
I can't hide fruit in my closet (it's not an Egyptian pyramid
that can mysteriously keep fruit from rotting if placed directly in the center) and second of all, stealing fruit just
doesn't give me as much of a rush. I'll take a bottle of lotion
over a squishy orange any day.

I hesitate at a bouquet of yellow roses. Should I bring
them to Jane? "Just a little something to brighten your day,"
I'll say, waving off her gush of gratitude. Or would she smell
the fear and think I was trying to bribe her? I pick up the
flowers. I put them down. I pick them up again and smell
their faint, powdery scent. I touch a petal ever so slightly. It
floats off and sticks to the palm of my hand. No flowers. I
put them down and enter the deli.

"You break, you buy." She is right behind me, a stout,

dark woman with bushy eyebrows and an intense glare. She shoves the yellow roses at me.

I put my hands up as if at gunpoint. "I don't want them."

She thrusts them toward me again. "You break, you buy."

I head to the counter. She follows. "One regular coffee and a chocolate chip muffin," I say to the man behind the counter.

His eyes slide from me to the yellow roses. The woman speaks to him in rapid tones in a tongue I can't recognize let alone decipher. He speaks back to her and she hands him the roses like the passing of the torch at the opening of the Olympic Games. He rings the roses up along with my coffee and muffin.

"Eighteen dollars."

I dig in my purse and hand him a twenty. I glance behind me to see if I'm still being tailed, but she has already headed off to harass other innocent, flower-sniffing customers.

My right hand drops down to the candy section and my fingers play across them like a Beethoven concerto. I lift candy bars and flick them into my purse with a sleight of hand that would impress any magician. Although I don't quite make up for the twelve dollars the roses cost me, I do manage to swipe two Kit Kat bars, a bag of peanut M&M's (New! Twenty Percent More!), and a box of Chicklets. My diet is indefinitely on hold.

"Chicklet?" I hold the yellow box out like a peace offering.

"No, thanks," Jane says curtly while positioning her soy milk and grapefruit so that they square off with my coffee and chocolate chip muffin. Then she turns back to her computer screen and ignores me. I start to sweat. Five minutes go by. Five whole minutes and she has yet to say anything directly to me. She has answered the phone and talked brightly to the callers, she has smiled at other temps coming in to get their assignments, and for an excruciating twenty seconds she filed her nails. Finally, I pull out the yellow roses and hold them out toward her.

"Just a little something to brighten your day," I squeak.

Jane stops filing her nails and stares at me. She is a pretty girl, born and raised in Brooklyn, Italian descent, and a take-no-prisoners attitude.

"Flowers, Melanie? You brought me flowers?" She jabs a recently filed fingernail at me like it's a self-guided missile and my head its target location. "Get me a vase, will ya? Back there." She throws her arm back and points her fingernail file at the tiny kitchen behind her. Obediently I fetch a vase and arrange the flowers in water while she taps on her keyboard and makes mysterious notes in the margins of her desk calendar. "All right. Let's have a little talk."

She opens her desk drawer, brings out a stack of pink telephone messages, and slams them in front of me. "Do you know why you're here?"

"You have a wonderful assignment for me?" I ask with a nervous laugh. Her answer is a cold stare. I shiver. She picks up the first message and reads it out loud. "Banco de Popular de Puerto Rico." Uh-oh. "What does"—she brings the pink note closer to her face and wrinkles her nose—"*Una cerveza por favor* mean?"

"One beer please," I translate for her.

"I know that," she says in a controlled voice. "Why were you saying it?"

"It was a joke. The woman training me asked if I knew any Spanish."

"She said you wouldn't stop saying it."

"I didn't mean to. She just kept piling work on me, and then she would ask if I needed anything. I was just trying to lighten the mood."

Jane picks up the next message. "Bank of America. They said you spent all afternoon playing solitaire—"

"They didn't give me any work—"

"I'm not finished. They didn't mind the solitaire, but they weren't happy about you screaming 'fuck, fuck, fuck.'"

"It was a really bad hand. Not that I'm excusing it. I'm sorry."

"And last but not least, Tom Spencer from Spencer Insurance said that you propositioned him for sex."

"What?" I leap out of my seat and grab the message. "That's bullshit," I say. "That's total bullshit."

She snaps the message back and accidentally scrapes me with one of her spears. It leaves a trace of white against the back of my hand like an airplane streaking the sky.

"So you didn't say anything about stripping naked and standing on your desk?"

"It's out of context. Totally out of context," I say, flopping back down in my seat and stuffing the rest of the chocolate chip muffin in my mouth. "Have you seen Tom Spencer?" I cry, conjuring up his bald head and enormous gut. "Can you imagine anyone propositioning him for sex?"

Jane surprises me by throwing her head back and belting out a laugh. "All right, all right. I'll give you that one." She wads the message from Tom and flings it across the room. It lands in a potted fern.

"Thank you," I say. "From now on I'll be on my best behavior."

"That's what I was hoping to hear." She picks up an assignment card, jots down an address, and hands it to me.

"Parks and Landon," I read. "A law office?" I perk up immediately. This is definitely good news. She can't be too mad at me if she's sending me to a law office.

"You got it. It's at least a six-week assignment. Maybe more."

I do an incredible job of not screaming. I nod my head like I expected as much. Six weeks as a legal secretary! This was incredible. I start calculating forty hours a week times twenty-five dollars an hour in my head. Or do legal secretaries make more?

"Their file clerk is on maternity leave," Jane says.

I nod and smile, but I'm really wondering why she thinks I care about their file clerk.

"Of course, I can't give you your usual rate," she says. I was right. Legal secretaries make more.

"How much more?" I ask, crossing my fingers that it is at least an extra five bucks an hour. What if it's ten? An extra ten dollars an hour? I can pay off my credit card and maybe even take a little trip. Yes, that's exactly what I'll do. Ray and I could run off to Atlantic City for a weekend. What a perfect excuse for calling him. I conjure up the Saint of Raises. If it is ten dollars an hour more, I'll never steal again.

"Not more. *Less*," Jane hisses. I look around to see who she's talking to now. I hate these new "in your ear" phones. They're so deceiving. It almost looks like she's talking to me. "Melanie, you know that a file clerk isn't going to pay your usual rate," she says.

"I don't understand."

"What don't you understand?"

"Why would the file clerk be paying my rate?" And then the horror hits. "You mean. Me? A file clerk?" I can barely get the words out; they're so heinous, so ill fitting on my tongue. "Jane. I'm an administrative assistant," I say, sitting up as straight as I can and trying to conjure up an administrative air about me. "I'm a legal secretary. Project manager. Um—consultant." I flick out job titles and spit them across her desk like a casino dealer plucking aces from a deck of cards. "Once. Once I was a hospitality agent—for Estee Lauder—but that's just because you were really stuck, remember? And even then you paid my rate. Because she loved me. Estee Lauder loved me," I say, slapping the desk with my hand for emphasis. (To tell you the truth, I'm still not sure if the elderly lady I met in the elevator that day was really Estee Lauder, but she was her age, had an *E* embroidered on her sweater, and smelled like baby powder and dried roses, so it might as well have been her.)

"I've never been a file clerk. Ever. I type ninety-four words a minute, Jane. How many file clerks can do that?" I sit back and fold my arms across my chest. I don't like to brag about my speedy fingers—but a file clerk! Come on!

"I'm sorry. I don't have anything else right now," Jane says, turning away from me again and going back to her computer screen.

"I see," I say, stalling for leverage.

"Maybe if you do well on this assignment," Jane says, letting the thought hang in the air like stale cigarette smoke.

"Jane. Please. Please. I promise you. My best behavior." I clasp my hands in front of her. I've only been here fifteen minutes and she's already reduced me to begging.

"I really need this job filled, Melanie," she says, her jaw set in a stubborn line. I eye the roses and consider taking them back.

"Come on," I say, instead hoping that logic will be the thread that sews this up. "There are a hundred temps who would jump at the chance to do this. Someone less qualified. Send them."

"I've sent four temps already."

"And?"

"This position has proven challenging."

"I can't believe this is happening."

"I'll take you off it as soon as something better comes in."

"One week. And you pay my rate."

"Two weeks and I'll pay you as a receptionist." I sink in

the chair and nod. "They want you there by nine," Jane says.

"Nine o'clock tomorrow," I say. "No problem."

"Nine o'clock today, Melanie." She looks me up and down, and I'm thankful I'm wearing cashmere. "Be sure and dress a little more corporate tomorrow, Melanie," she says, turning back to her computer. Our "little talk" was over. "Don't forget," she says as I am just about out the door, "you have two strikes against you—"

"And you play baseball," I finish. Two weeks as a file clerk. She isn't just playing "baseball," she's choking me financially. But what choice do I have? If she wants me to suck it up and be a file clerk for a few weeks, I'll suck it up. "No worries, I'll be perfect."

"I don't doubt it. Especially with Trina there to watch over you."

I freeze in the doorway. "Trina who?" I say, trying not to betray the fear in my voice. Not Trina Wilcox. Not Trina Wilcox. Please, please, please not Trina Wilcox. I hold my breath. I cross my fingers. I pray to the Saint of People With the Same Names. Please, please, please don't let it be Trina Wilcox.

"Trina Wilcox," Jane says smiling at me. *I've sent four temps. Filling the position has been challenging.* Oh, God. "Do you know Trina?" Jane asks sweetly. I smile and nod but avert my eyes. Jane hates dissension in the ranks. "Is there a problem?" she asks. See what I mean? The woman is a bloodhound.

"No, no. Trina's great," I say with forced enthusiasm.

Jane nods in agreement. "They love her to death over there," she says. "I think they're going to offer her full time."

"Oh."

"Not that she'll take it. I swear her modeling career is

going to take off any day now. I mean, she's perfect looking. An absolute doll."

"I absolutely agree," I say (if by *doll* you too are thinking of Chuckie from the psycho slasher movies). I raise my eyes heavenward and beg the Saint of Evil Women for mercy. Trina Wilcox is friends with Kim. Trina Wilcox is Ray's ex-girlfriend. Trina Wilcox hates my guts.

Chapter

4

Once outside I pour the entire box of Chicklets in my mouth and chew. It makes my jaw ache, but I welcome the pain. Trina Wilcox. The Wicked Witch of the West Side. I should turn around and go home. I should march back in there and tell Jane Greer that I absolutely refuse to work with Trina Wil(suck)cox. I should have taken my roses back when I had the chance.

I walk to the subway venting my complaints out loud like an escaped mental patient. It's okay—the only people in New York who will look you in the eye are talking to themselves too, so no need to worry about looking like a nutter. (Another Britishism I've picked up. My friends wish I had never read *Bridget Jones's Diary*. The only one I can't seem to work into a conversation around here is *gobsmacked*. But give me time, I will.) I should never have agreed to be a file clerk in the first place. What was I thinking? I'm a twenty-nine-year-old file clerk. This isn't how my life is supposed to be going. I'm supposed to be a famous actress with a loft in SoHo and if not a gorgeous husband and baby on the way, then at a least a semiattractive straight boyfriend who has his green card.

You have Ray, a little voice reminds me. Thank God for

that. But it's a little too early to call him my boyfriend, isn't it? My stomach tingles at the thought of it. Maybe he is my boyfriend—but I'm not going to screw it up with labels. We're both adults, enjoying a consensual, sexual relationship. We may be a little off on our expectations concerning consistency of contact, but surely that will work itself out. It's not like I can force the man to call me. I've already left him two voice mails and an e-mail, so obviously the ball is in his court.

Unless he didn't get my messages. Technology is an unpredictable beast. Here I am thinking he's ignoring me when I should be blaming some satellite tower in the middle of god knows where (New Jersey—blame New Jersey!) screwing up my love messages to Ray! Focus, Melanie, I'm sure he received your messages. What are the odds that three out of three were zapped in yesteryear? Maybe I can't control my love life, but I can certainly control my career. Jane had baited me into a game of chicken, and I had veered off the road before the first feather was even swiped. How could I be so stupid?

Maybe I'm worrying for nothing. Maybe Trina doesn't hate me. This will be a chance for us to start fresh and really get to know each other. If she was hard on the other four temps, they must have deserved it. I mean maybe they filed the Z under the As. I would have fired them too. Besides I'm only going to be there for two weeks. Two weeks of perfect behavior and I'll be back in Jane's good graces. I have to think positive. That's it. It's decided. From now on, I'm going to have a positive outlook on life. I'm going to stop stealing, start auditioning, and stop labeling my love life. That's it. That's really all it's going to take to make me happy. I've just been way too obsessed. Relax, Melanie. From now on you're going to have *no expectations*. It's the only way to enjoy life.

I glance at the assignment card. The law office is on 28th

between Park and Madison. I could hop on the Number 1 train to Penn Station and walk a couple of blocks from there. I'll just cut through the garment district and—

Garment district. The words have a psychotropic affect on me. The air around me shifts slightly, and suddenly everything burns just a little bit brighter. God I love shoplifting in the garment district. I could spend hours there staking out my next claim, lovingly running my fingers over beautiful, brand-new sweaters—slipping slim bottles of perfume into my pockets. I could really go for a little "lift" right now. It would make all the stress over Trina Wilcox go away for a while. Tempting thoughts swirl around my brain like a stuck record. *It would balance out the universe. I don't steal enough to hurt anyone's bankroll. I'm not really hurting anyone. Nobody's perfect. Think of all the other horrible things I could be doing instead.* That's true. I don't even drive a car. I'm not one of the millions of people polluting the environment or getting behind the wheel after having a few drinks. And okay, maybe I don't exactly abstain, but last I checked, drunk walking never hurt anyone except maybe the occasional pigeon. And really, how was I to know his little feet were stuck in gum? Besides, he should be grateful that I knocked him down. Otherwise he might have been stuck in that gum all night long.

Hell, I could be a drug addict or a porn star. I'm probably the only actress on the planet who doesn't smoke cigarettes or snort cocaine! Stop it, Melanie. You are through with shoplifting. Get your mind on something else. I whip out my cell phone and call Kim. She'll know whether or not Trina still hates me. I get her voice mail. "Hey Kim. It's me. Call me ASAP. I'm on my way to an assignment and I'll be working with Trina Wilcox. And I know it's silly but—just wondering—is she over the whole Ray and soap dish thing yet?"

I giggle as I hang up the phone. It's ridiculous to think

that she's still upset with me. Isn't it funny the unnecessary stress we put ourselves under? Positive thinking 101 tells us that ninety percent of the things we worry about never come to fruition. There's nothing to fear but fear itself! It's eight-thirty and I'm on my way to an assignment. Okay, so it's a demotion, but I'll do a phenomenal job of filing (filing!) and surely I'll have a new assignment in a matter of days. By next week I'll be out of there. Maybe Trina and I will become great friends. Someday we'll laugh over it. In fact, this is really the beginning of my new life.

There you have it, I'm going to stop stealing. Not because it's that big of a deal, but because it's time to wipe the slate clean and start a whole new life. Do you hear that, Saints? I'm done. From now on, I'm a law-abiding citizen! I pick up my stride and smile. Everything is going to be fine.

Thanks to the *Saint of Trains on Time*, I arrive at Penn Station in a matter of minutes. In fact, I have time for a latte. I shouldn't buy coffee twice in less than an hour, but I didn't even get a chance to drink the other cup, and besides, Starbucks is right across the street. I have plenty of time. Thank you, thank you, thank you, Starbucks! A Venti quad shot nonfat vanilla soy latte. Yes, yes, yes, yes, yes! God I love coffee. Smack! Smooch! I do a little espresso dance. Oh my god. Oh my fucking god. Somebody didn't put the lid on tight enough. I've spilled coffee all over the front of Kim's baby blue cashmere sweater. There is a large dark streak sliding down my left breast like the Oregon Trail. Damn you, Starbucks! Damn you for handing me hot, dark coffee and making me jump up and down with joy. I hate you. I hate you—you big, evil, corporate giant. I am going to sue you! Sue you, sue you, sue you.

I can't show up for work like this. Water isn't helping. The Oregon Trail has turned into Crater Lake. Stained and wet would be perfect if I were going to, say, The Rodeo Bar, but it isn't going to cut it in a law firm. I should go home and change, but I don't have time. On the other hand, if I show up looking like a contestant in a wet T-shirt contest, it's not going to reflect well on me either. Especially with Miss I-hate-you-for-stealing-my-latest-man-toy Wilcox. Imagine Ray being stuck with her. I did them both a favor. Everybody knows that musicians are temperamental and models are narcissistic. It's that genetic recipe that gives birth to future politicians. I was saving them from themselves. But I have to face facts. Even if Trina is over the whole soap dish incident by now, she still wouldn't pass up an opportunity to get me fired.

No. I definitely cannot show up at Parks and Landon looking like this. Then I see a sign with three, beautiful, little words. Well, technically, three huge words in fire engine red. Blow. Out. Prices. Fate has planted a sweet, little department store right in my way. I glance at my watch. It's 8:35 and I'm still a good ten blocks away from the law firm. But I can always hop in a cab. That would leave me fifteen minutes or so to find a pretty scarf to cover my stain. That's it, I'm just going to walk in and steal a scarf. Buy a scarf, buy a scarf, buy a scarf. I throw a prayer to the *Saint of Freudian Slips*—I really meant *buy a scarf*. You'll see. I'm going to walk up to the register and pay for it like a normal human being.

Finding a scarf is not going to be a problem. Getting out of here in fifteen minutes or less is going to be impossible. The place is jam packed. We're talking wall to wall breasts, hips, and stuffed purses laced with a symphony of cheap perfume. Women are juggling the merchandise like carnival junkies and grabbing sales as if stalking the last slab of meat for their starving villagers. It is a study of the disintegration of the human race. It is neither spiritually fulfilling nor feminine nor feminist. It's discount shopping.

The aisles are stacked with ready-made tables and blinking red signs boasting slashed prices. The lines at the regis-

ter trail the entire length of the store. Some of the sales associates are still smiling at their customers despite the line,
but others glare at you as if they have a collection of voodoo
dolls beneath the counter with your DNA. You know the
moment you leave the store, the sales associate is going to
whip out your doll and stab needles in your cushy little
heart or add cellulite to your thighs. The stout white clock
above the counter is moving like a sloth in quicksand on
this day of days, Annual Clearance Day at Brewber's Department Store.

My scarf floats on a hook just above a row of sparkling,
beaded handbags. It's swaying from the breeze of heavy,
sweating bodies and thin, twittering sticks battling one on
one for the goods. This is not a race of the fittest or prettiest
but the quickest. The scarf is me hanging there—vulnera-
ble, beautiful, and alone. It is a light, misty green color and
so, so soft. The perfect soulmate for my cashmere sweater.
Now that I've seen it, I can't imagine wearing this sweater
without it. In fact, after I get the sweater dry-cleaned, I'll
give it back to Kim with the scarf. Really, they were made
for each other. If it were as easy to find a man as it was this
scarf, I would never steal again.

To reach it, however, I have to squeeze past a horde of
teenage savages insulting each other with their best smiles
and high-pitched squeals. ("Like really. Like it looks good
on you. Like, with that flower in the middle, like you hardly
notice how like flat your chest is.") Finally I am close
enough to touch it. It is so soft, so free! But when I reach for
the scarf, instead of its silky grace I feel skin. Scratchy,
fleshy skin that belongs to another woman.

Another woman is holding my scarf. My scarf looks tiny
in her large fleshy arm. Now she is putting my scarf in her
cart. She throws it on her heap like adding salt to a stew and
takes off without so much as a backward glance. "Hey!" I
shout, but she doesn't even turn around. In fact, she's pick-

ing up speed and I have to jog to catch up with her. "Hey!"
I say again.

She makes a left near the bras and panties. She's trying to
lose me! I zigzag around a table of scented candles and cut
her off in front of women's watches. She still hasn't spoken
to me, won't even look at me. I've got her boxed in though;
the only direction she can turn is right, and I'll be damned if
I let that happen. She tries to take the right, but I head her
off at the pass. I reach out with my foot and lodge it underneath the cart, bringing it to a dead squealing stop. She
treats me as if I'm the sun and she'll be blinded if she looks
directly at me. With her head held straight, she slides her
eyes to the right and studies me like a bird of prey.

"Excuse me," she says as if I've done something wrong
and shoves the cart forward with gusto. Even if I want to retract my foot (which I don't) it's too late. It's stuck in the
spokes, and when she pushes the cart, my foot stays in
place, but the rest of my body falls at a ninety-degree angle.
As I hit the floor, I pray to the *Saint of Stupid People Tricks*
that I won't be maimed for life. How can I show up to work
with a peg leg? With detached curiosity, I hear someone
screaming and wish they would stop. Later, I realize it's me.
The pain is bypassing my head and hurling straight out of
my mouth. "Help, help!" I yell. Then, like a Fellini film,
suddenly I'm surrounded by large women with blue eye-
shadow and clown cheeks. We have attracted a crowd of elderly women, and my nemesis is already trying to sway the
jury.

"She put her foot right in my cart. Just jammed it right in
there." The old ladies look from her to me, back to her. I
open my mouth to defend myself but a moan escapes instead. My foot really, really hurts. "What were you thinking?" the fleshy-armed scarf stealer shouts at me. From my
position on the floor I can see her jowls bounce up and
down as she screams. Flicks of spit dangle off her upper lip

threatening to drip on me with the next shake of her head. I throw my arms up to protect my face from her spittle, and I instantly win the sympathy vote.

"Leave her alone!" one woman shouts. "Help her up," another one says.

I'm no dummy; I strike while the iron's hot. "My scarf!" I cry. "That's my scarf." I point dramatically to the top of her heap.

"Your scarf?" the woman says, grabbing my misty green savior and kneading it in her sweaty fingers. "No siree. This here is my scarf." She takes the scarf and sinks it into the depths of her cart. I glance at the crowd. They're starting to frown. They're not sure who to believe. "She's stalking me!" the woman cries. "She's stalking me and my cart. Took her foot and jammed it right in there!"

I don't have a great reply so I start to cry. It comes easy to me these days. Even Tampax commercials make me cry. (You go girl! You go horseback riding!) "It's for my mother," I gasp. "My mother whom I haven't seen in—ten years." I'm wailing now; I'm the antifeminist. I throw a quick apology to the *Saint of Gertrude Stein* not to cancel my membership, but I can't stop now—I'm winning over the grandmothers in the crowd, of which there are many.

Three have knelt down by me—two of them are gingerly removing my ankle from the cart, and a third wipes my tears with a hanky that smells like cinnamon. At his grandmother's nudge, a young boy whips the scarf out of the cart and hands it to me with a shy smile.

"Thank you," I whisper. "Thank you."

The woman with the cart leans down and blasts me with the smell of stale cigarettes. "You little bitch," she says, but we both know I've won.

I remain on the floor with my prized scarf, assuring everyone that I'm fine, I can walk, thank you, and if it's all the same I would just like to get home and wrap the scarf for my dear estranged mom. They help me to my feet, pat me on the back, and slowly depart as I whip out my cell phone whispering, "I'm calling my mom." Some of the old ladies don't want to move on. They're standing around and staring at me, expecting an encore. I point south and yell, "Look, seventy-five percent off!" then resume my fake conversation with my mother as I hobble away in the opposite direction. But even a hobble is more than I can bear.

Ow, ow, ow, ow. Pain, pain, pain, pain, pain. I beam a prayer to the *Saint of Cripples*. Please, please just get me the fuck out of here. I look at the clock. 8:53. Oh God. I look at the line. It's all the way back to the women's restroom. I will never make it in time. This is it. This is the true test of my resolve. I have three choices:

A) I leave now without the scarf, grab a cab, and show up at Parks and Landon in my stained sweater. Trina will tell Jane that I showed up looking like a filthy pig, and I'll be fired.

B) I stand in line to pay for the scarf and show up at Parks and Landon looking gorgeous in my scarf and sweater, but I'm an hour late. Trina tells Jane I'm a slacker who couldn't be punctual even if I had Father Time tattooed on my ass, and I'll be fired.

C) For the sake of my career, I steal the scarf.

Wait just a minute. Wait just a darn minute. I don't *steal* the scarf. I just *borrow* it for a while. Then, after work, I return it. *I promise, I promise, I promise,* I whisper to the Saints.

Sometimes, the best way to steal something is to hide it in plain view. I place the scarf around my neck and arrange it so that it covers the stain. I was right. It's a perfect match. So far I'm not breaking any laws. So far I am simply trying on the merchandise. And there is no law against trying on merchandise, now is there? In fact, legally speaking, the store has to see you remove the object from its location and wait until you've actually left the premises without paying for it before they can approach you. There have been a few times when I've had to drop the merchandise before leaving because I knew I was being tailed.

But there's so much chaos here today that I'm home free. The scarf doesn't even have a sensor on it; they save those for the big-ticket items, like the leather coats. Now I'm simply walking toward the door. Nobody is paying any attention to me. I set my eyes on the door and walk with purpose. I spot a bedraggled sales associate trying to fold a pile of clothes. Each time she succeeds in straightening them, someone comes along and whips one out from the bottom of the stack.

"Excuse me," I say. "What time do you close?"

She doesn't even look me in the eye. "Six," she wails.

"Thank you." Perfect. My day ends at five. I'll have plenty of time to return my borrowed scarf.

By the time I'm outside, my heart is pounding against my chest like aliens beating at the door. I'm a little surprised that I'm still getting the high—given that I'm just borrowing the scarf and all. But it's there. I feel on top of the world. I want to jump up and down and shout, "I'm alive, I'm alive!" but I can barely step on my ankle, let alone jump. Then the laughter descends. I bend over, grab my knees, and howl with laughter. I bend back the other direction and snort and whoop. I let out long, barking HA HA HAs while gasping for air. Women try to shove me out of the way as they pour in and spill out, smacking me with their purses and their bulging Brewber's shopping bags. Each time I'm jostled, pain flares in my ankle like oxygen feeding a fire. I don't care. I don't budge. I laugh until I cry.

Happy tears stream down my face until suddenly, like showers springing from a sunny sky, I'm crying for real. Sobbing, actually, over my prized stolen scarf. Tears fall down my face, my dirty blond hair whips in my eyes from the gust generated from the revolving door, and within seconds a familiar thudding pain settles back in my chest. It's guilt time. "Jesus Christ, no, please let me be happy for just a little while!" I scream at the *Saint of Joy*, but it is too late. Gravity reverses the polarity of my lips, tugs at my throat, and ebbs my beating heart back to a dull ache. I am so engulfed in my own misery that I don't even notice the security guard until his black vinyl sleeves reach for me, his large bushy eyebrows furrowed with concern. He says something to me, perhaps, "Miss, are you all right?" but what I hear is, "You there! Where did you get that scarf?!" And "Stop thief! Backup, I need backup!"

I pull the scarf tightly around my neck, growl like a mother bear protecting her cubs, and bolt across the street. Well, limp actually. Limp, run, limp, run, limp, run. Cars squeal and drivers slam on their horns as I hobble to the curb. Blimey. That was really, really stupid. Pain shoots through my ankle and I buckle under, once again finding myself on the ground with the rest of the world above me. I decide right then and there that I will never beg, borrow, or steal again. Never, ever, ever. It's 8:55. I stick my good leg in the air and wave it around. There's more than one way to hail a cab.

Chapter

5

It's one minute to nine, and I'm waiting for an elevator. Why, why, why can't at least one of the three get here? I know the stairs are good for you and all, and I'll use them after today (it will be my new exercise routine) but I can't climb fifteen stairs in two minutes. Besides, my ankle is still throbbing and if I take the stairs I'll be panting and sweating and Trina will become enraged because she'll think that I've just come from having sex with Ray. I shouldn't have said that. Just the thought of it is getting me all worked up. Until I remember that he hasn't called me in eight days. Come on elevator. I look at my watch. Forty seconds. Come on, come on, come on. Ding. It's here! It's a sign!

I enter the reception area of Parks and Landon and fall in love. It's modest, but so inviting that I would move in tomorrow. It looks more like a funky SoHo loft than a stuffy corporate law office. It is a wide-open area with wood floors, huge windows, and exposed brick behind the reception desk. The walls are painted a deep yellow, giving the place a golden, friendly glow. There are a few oriental rugs scattered about—plush and beautiful against the shiny floor. Potted trees adorn every corner. And then it hits me—I'm on the wrong floor.

This can't be a law firm. Law firms are stuffy and demanding. I've stumbled into a PR firm or an advertising agency. Maybe they'll hire me! Maybe this is where my destiny lies. The Saints knew all along that a creative soul like me doesn't belong in a sterile filing room doing mind-numbing, soul-killing paperwork. I belong in the belly of the creative beast. "Parks and Landon Attorneys-at-Law, how may I direct your call?" My head snaps toward the reception desk. A harried-looking woman in her fifties is standing behind the desk with the phone cradled in her neck. She is holding a stack of papers and has a pen behind each ear. My creative universe disappears. At least it's cool in here, I think as I step up to the desk.

"May I help you?" She is polite, but her tone carries a hint of urgency.

"I'm Melanie Zeitgar," I say, holding out my right hand. "From Fifth Avenue Temps."

"Oh. You are?" It isn't so much the way she says it—she's still polite, but it's the once-over she's giving me with her eyes that makes me feel like I'm naked in the middle of the schoolyard.

"Yes," I say with a bright smile. "I am."

She nods and finally shakes my hand. "Margaret Tomer. I'm a paralegal."

"Nice to meet you, Margaret."

"Likewise. And can I tell you, I'm glad they sent you." I beam. You see? They were going to love me here. "I told them it doesn't look good hiring model after model after model," Margaret continues. "Okay, so the men do like it. Who wouldn't? But they've already got enough to look at. And we get plenty of female clients in here too, and they don't need perfection thrown in their faces every minute. I told them it didn't bode well for Abercrombie & Fitch and it won't bode well for us. I said 'Greg, Steve, enough of the gorgeous models. It's not the real world.' Unless they want

to get a few hot men in here, right? Am I right? Just like
Hooters. I for one would go in for a burger now and again if
they had muscle-ripped men flexing their pecs and wag-
gling their six packs at me, wouldn't you? Welcome. It's
about time we had an average temp in here."

I should be used to this. I live with Kim Minx after all,
the prettiest girl on the planet. But my stomach turns none-
theless, and I feel tears coming to my eyes. I bite the inside
of my mouth and remind myself that I, too, am a beautiful
woman. As far as we "averages" go anyway. Margaret sees
the look on my face and back paddles a bit. "Not that you
aren't a pretty girl. You are dear. You're darling. Remind me.
Are you one of our new paralegals or Steve's new assistant?"
I glance at the names on the wall behind the reception desk.
Greg Parks, Attorney at Law. Steve Landon, Attorney at Law.

"I'm Steve's new assistant," I say without hesitating. Do
you see what a good actress I am? It sounds so truthful that
I believe it myself. Relief floods over me. I'm not a file
clerk. I am never going to be a file clerk. We're all going to
be dead in a hundred years, so who cares if I lie a little along
the way? Besides, bad habits are like a diet. You have to
start fresh in the morning. I had already inhaled a chocolate
chip muffin with 31 grams of fat and stolen a scarf, so what's
a little lie in the mix? Besides, it's not like I'm hurting anyone. Steve obviously needs an assistant, and I'm going to be
the best damn assistant he's ever seen.

"Wonderful. Follow me." Margaret bolts down the hall as
if she's on fire. I have to run to keep up. The pain in my
ankle roars up, and halfway down the dim hallway I stumble over an electric cord.

"Umph." For the third time today, I hit the floor. Margaret
stops and cocks her head toward the ceiling before realizing
that the noise is coming from behind her.

"Are you all right?" she says, staying ten feet ahead of
me.

"Just—an old stage injury," I murmur.

She waits for me to get to my feet and come toward her again. "Are you an actress then?" Margaret asks with a trace of boredom as I limp toward her.

I stir the question around in my mind, playing out the sequence. I'll say yes. She'll ask what I've been in. I'll gloss over the slutty nun business and tell her about the time I played the spurned ex-wife of a mobster. She'll ask if I've ever been on TV or in the movies. I'll have to admit that those are my hands and voice hocking Ginger Root Cream, an organic, vegan, vaginal lubricant. Fireworks of disgust will play out across her face and she'll offer me a pained, sympathetic smile.

"Not anymore," I say. "I'm—" My eyes land on a large stone sculpture in the corner of the office we are passing. It is five feet of twisting black marble with a smooth, round top and diagonal white stripe slashing through the middle like the second hand of a clock. That's the only explanation I have for what comes out of my mouth next. "I'm a clockmaker," I blurt out.

"A clockmaker?" Margaret asks, frowning. "What do you mean?"

Excellent question. "I'm an artist," I say. She waits. "I make clock sculptures," I add. She's still waiting. Didn't that say it all? "It's art," I say slowly, "that tells time." I zap her with an intense, artistic stare.

"That's so unusual," Margaret murmurs, finally looking away.

"Very," I agree.

"Here we are." Margaret stops at a closed door at the end of the hall. I can't wait to see the office I'll be working in. So far all of the offices we've passed have been devoid of personnel. On the one hand, I was wondering where everyone was, but on the other I was relieved. Maybe I'd never even see Trina Wilcox. Maybe I'd be in a huge office with a view of the East River, happily assisting Steve Landon of Parks and Landon. "Everyone is attending Greg's Loss Prevention Workshops today," Margaret says, reading my mind. "He's so popular he has to give a morning and an afternoon workshop. They've been packing them in since his brush with fame last year."

"His brush with fame?" I ask politely, wishing she'd open the door to my new digs. Margaret stops walking and looks at me.

"You know who he is, don't you?" She continues to stare at me expectantly.

"Uh, he's one of the partners?" I say.

Margaret answers my question with a loud laugh. "Well of course, but I was referring to the media blitz he got caught up in last year. Maybe you don't read the newspaper?"

I feel my face burn and count to five in my head in Spanish. "I read the newspaper *daily*," I say. (Actually I only read it on Sundays, skim the headlines the other days of the week, and get the rest on the Internet and CNN, but she doesn't need to be bogged down with the details of my life.) "And of course I wondered if he were the same Greg Parks—"

"He is," Margaret purrs. "Not that he brags about it. In fact he doesn't like us to bring it up at all. He's rather media shy, which is ironic when you think about it. Don't tell anyone I told you, but he's up for a position as a commentator on *Side Court TV*." She's staring at me, waiting for a reaction.

"You don't say," I murmur. I had only watched *Side Court* a couple of times, and it usually bored me out of my mind. Personally, I think sitting on your duff and watching a couple of stiff suits haggle over case law is a flagrant waste of America's favorite guilty pleasure.

"It's between Greg and the woman who successfully prosecuted that deranged midget who was flashing children in the Central Park Zoo," Margaret continues. "Isn't that a thrill?"

"I hardly know what to say," I answer with a discount smile.

"Well it's too bad you'll miss his presentation, but they'll be back this afternoon."

I nod and try to get the image of a midget in a trench coat out of my mind. I really was going to have to start reading the newspaper. So I would probably run into Trina after all. But that's okay. I'm not a file clerk! I am going to have to call Jane the first chance I get and tell her I've been promoted to Steve Landon's assistant. Looks like the Saints aren't going to punish me for stealing the scarf after all. Margaret finally opens the door, and I step grandly over the threshold into my new home.

"Melanie, this is Steve Beck. He's the file lead. He reports directly to Trina Wilcox, who is Steve Landon's assistant."

I can't speak. I am still struggling with the fact that instead of a fancy office with a view of the East River, I am actually standing in a file room. And as file rooms go, it is completely hideous. Whereas the rest of the building has the feel of a SoHo loft, the file room could be in a hospital basement for all of its charm. Tan steel cabinets are shoved against drab white walls like rows of teeth awaiting a root canal. Steve Beck is a short, fat boy with red hair and thick, gold glasses. He is standing behind a card table buried in papers. He barely looks up as his thick fingers continue to sort various papers into mysterious piles while Margaret makes the introductions. Before I can tell her that I was kidding, that I too am a paralegal, she races out of the dungeon, leaving me alone with file boy from hell.

"Get to work," Steve Beck says. He has a high-pitched voice and his nose whistles when he talks. *Well hello to you too.* "You'll have to be a little bit more specific," I say, biting back a hundred insults. "I'm new," I add in case he is a little slow. He sighs, adjusts his gold-rimmed glasses, and grunts and drops to the floor. My first thought is that he's having a heart attack and that I'm going to have to do mouth to mouth on this guy. I took CPR training a couple of years ago and had actually been looking forward to using it. But in all the rescue fantasies I had engaged in over the past couple of years, none of them had involved a rude, nose-whistling, pudgy file clerk.

Just as I start looking around for a piece of plastic to use as a barrier between our lips, he pops back up with a cardboard box sagging in his arms. "You can start with these," he says, lurching across the room and launching the box on me like a hand grenade. I stagger back a few steps as the box hits my chest, and it's a miracle I don't fall for the fourth time today. "Client files," he wheezes. "File them alphabetically, last name first."

"You're kidding me," I say. He answers with a dirty look. "I mean don't they have some type of electronic filing system here?" I ask.

"No."

"Oh. Well, they should."

"They don't. So file them, Goldilocks."

"Excuse me?"

"Look, I don't have time to babysit you. Just do it."

"My name is Melanie."

"Whatever."

I swallow the urge to beat him within an inch of his life. Hell hath no fury like an out-of-work actress and all that. But he isn't worth it. He is already an overweight file clerk with a nasal condition—what more could I do to him? Three hours of filing later, I've had it. My eyes are blurring from staring at tiny typed names, and my hands are aching from hauling overstuffed boxes up and down the dingy rows. Not only am I getting paid less and losing brain cells by the second, it's also hard manual labor. I resolve right here and now that I will start auditioning again. Otherwise I'll be doomed to a life of temping and thieving. Tomorrow, I will get the *Backstage* newspaper, dig my headshots out of the closet, and tweak my resume. I will eat only lean meats and veggies for the next seven days, learn Pilates, and start taking a multivitamin with calcium.

Don't get me wrong, I'm not just about vanity. I know it takes more than a beautiful face and body to be a really great actress. I learned that lesson at a very young age. I was in the third grade and Mrs. Miller had just announced that our class was going to put on a production of *Snow White and the Seven Dwarfs*. The next day we would read a few lines from the script and she would assign roles. In that instance, I knew my destiny. I was born to be Snow White. By the time class ended that day, I had whipped myself into such a frenzy that once home I dressed in rags and went about the house pricking my thumb with my mother's sewing needles, bleeding all over our yellow shag carpet and sobbing "Why can't I be a normal girl?" I think I was getting Cinderella, Sleeping Beauty, Snow White, and Pinocchio all mixed up, but nevertheless for a third grader I was putting on a stunning performance.

So I wasn't at all prepared for the next day when Mrs. Miller announced to the entire third-grade class that Lara Thomas was to play Snow White. I stared at my bandaged, bloodied thumb and turned to stone in my seat.

"And Melanie Zeitgar will play the role of the Wicked Queen."

What? I stared at Mrs. Miller's bright pink mouth, trying to make sense of what she had just said. Me? The Wicked Queen? Somehow I managed to sit there in my seat and not vomit. Somehow I ignored the snickers from Lara and the rest of the girls as they glanced at me to see how I was taking the news. Somehow I managed not to hurt anyone.

Ironically, and again ever the method actress, that afternoon I stole an apple off Mrs. Miller's desk and chewed on it all the way home.

"Why, Melanie darling," my mother said later that evening when I dissolved on the kitchen floor in a puddle of grief and rage, "Snow White is nothing. Anyone can play Snow White. The Wicked Queen is a much bigger part. Without her it would be nothing but some little girl humming and skipping around the stage, and who wants to look at that? Honey, it takes a *real actress* to play the Wicked Queen."

My tears came to an immediate halt as the linoleum floor and I took in this new information. I lifted my head for a moment to see if she were making a joke. She looked pretty serious. And suddenly this incredible feeling of raw, blinding *power* surged through me. Mother is right. *Snow White is nothing*, I thought as a vision of Lara Thomas and her little brown pigtails floated before me. She's nothing. And boy, is she going to be one sorry Snow White.

I had all of my lines memorized by the next day, my real lines, the lines of a real actress. "Lady Pendula," I announced in a booming voice, "shall I wear the red dress or the blue?" Every head in the class snapped to my attention, and Mrs. Miller's bright pink mouth fell open in surprise. I had commanded the stage! And from that day on, Snow White didn't stand a chance. I was the Wicked Queen. I practiced her voice, her walk, her evil cackling when she pretended to be the old witch bringing the apple to (pathetic) Snow White. The kid playing the mirror on the wall actually shook when I talked to him. Snow White was a joke, a pale shivering stick, a pathetic pawn on my stage.

And my glory and reign lasted throughout rehearsals until the opening night, where I was so into my character that in a fit of Queenly rage I hauled off and smacked Snow White clear across the face before either of us knew what hit her. A week later, when I was allowed to come back to school, I was relegated to backstage duty and Lisa Hardy took over my reign as the Wicked Queen. But despite the suspension and the letters of apology, *Dear Lara, I'm reel sorry if I smacked you* (just in case there was any question in anyone's mind if I did or not), and three weeks in a row of no television, I still would have done it all over again. It had been the best night of my life, and from that day forward, I was a real actress.

That's it! Remembering my roots has infused me with a new passion for my craft. I'm going to really throw myself back into the swing of things.

Once I'm thin I'll go on at least five auditions per week. That's only one a day. I can do one a day. I'll work it out so that it replaces my lunch hour. Temp agencies know that we're all struggling actors, so they'll just have to live with it or fire me. Otherwise I am going to die right here next to twelve boxes of expired lawsuits. Steve Beck is boring me to tears. He has allergies, and every few minutes he breaks the silence with a loud, crackly sniff. There is no chance of engaging him in mindless, witty banter. I suddenly yearn for Trina Wilcox, even if she does still hate me. When noon hits, I drop my box with a satisfying thud.

Chapter

6

"Time for lunch," I say happily.

"Not yours," Steve says with a sniff.

"Pardon me?"

"My lunch is noon to one. Yours is one to one-thirty."

"One to one-thirty? You're saying I only get half an hour?"

"That's correct."

"But you get an hour?"

"Right again."

"That's not fair," I stammer.

Steve shrugs. "You didn't start until 9:30. So you get half an hour. Unless you want to stay until 6:30."

"Six-thirty? I go home at five."

"Six."

"Five." I suddenly feel like I'm ten years old arguing with my brother, Zach, over Monopoly. I always thought that the money for any fines you incurred should go in the middle, giving people a fighting chance to win it all back if they land on the Free Parking square. Zach was a stickler that the fines went to the bank. He was a lawyer at thirteen—cheeky little bastard. Except Zach I loved/hated and this guy I hate/hate.

"My temp agency told me that I was to work from nine to five," I say in the haughtiest tone I can muster. "I can deal with lunch at one. But I'll be taking an hour and I'll be leaving at five." There. Take that file boy. Steve picks up a lunch sack and heads to the door while I turn back to my files. We both know I've won that round, so there's no need to rub it in.

"You'll have to take this up with Trina Wilcox," he says from the doorway as he's departing. "I believe you two know each other?" He meets my eyes, and when he sees the look of horror creep into them, he smiles for the first and only time all day.

The minute he leaves I stop working and call Kim again. "Hi, Mel," she says instead of hello. Fucking caller ID. "How did it go with Jane?"

"Didn't you get my message?" I say in a whisper just in case Steve is lurking in the hallway.

"Um. I don't think so," she says.

I roll my eyes. Kim handles questions like a politician up for re-election. "About Trina?"

"Trina?"

"Wilcox," I say. And then I wait. One never knows whether Kim is actually thinking about what you've said or merely parroting your words as a stalling tactic.

"What about her?" she says finally.

"She hates me, doesn't she?" I whine.

"Oh God," Kim says. "You've seen the Web site."

Time stops. I have this nagging feeling that I do not want to know what Kim is talking about. I should just skip it. What do I care if Trina Wilcox hates me? I'm a good person. This isn't about me, it's about her. Sticks and stones. Don't worry, Melanie, in the scheme of things, who really cares? You're supposed to care about cancer and AIDS and terrorists. You're supposed to do your best to be kind to children, animals and the elderly. If you hang up now, I bargain with myself, I'll let you steal something on your lunch hour. It won't count. You'll still take back the scarf at five, but you can take a little something. It will make you feel better.

"What Web site?" I demand. If Kim had been thinking she would have realized I was clueless and stopped there. But in addition to her beauty Kim was blessed with a child-like innocence, and picking up on subtleties was not her forte.

"Trina's Web site," she says again. "And I swear, Melanie—nobody thinks it's funny. I didn't know about it until she showed it to everybody at the Fruit of the Loom audition. But don't worry—she's the one who came off looking bad. Even the banana thought she was a bitch." I pause here, not only because unlike me Kim uses cuss words sparingly and I'm thrown that she's just called Trina a bitch, but for the second time today I have a weird image stuck in my mind. Great. Now I'm thinking about a naked midget and a banana. It served to momentarily distract me from the matter at hand. "Do you hate me for not telling you, Melanie?" Kim says quietly. "I just didn't want you to get hurt. She's just jealous."

I open my mouth to say something but nothing comes out. What is she talking about? Why would I be on a Web site?

"And before you ask," Kim continues, "the answer is no. You don't look that fat in real life."

I slide down the file cabinet and sink to the floor. "I look fat?" I say, trying not to cry. I still don't even know what she's talking about, but anytime anyone says "you don't look that fat in real life"—take it from me—it's never a good thing.

"And I'm not judging you," Kim continues. "Honestly, if that's what you're into—who am I to judge?"

"What? What am I into?"

"I wouldn't have believed it was you except you're wearing my pink diva shirt." Pink diva shirt, pink diva shirt, pink diva shirt. "You can have it by the way. I could never wear it again now."

"Kim—"

"I'm sorry, I didn't mean it that way. I just have too many clothes. You know that—you've seen my closet—"

"Kim, listen—"

"But don't you think it's kind of funny? I mean, you should almost be flattered, it's had like a million hits so far." A million hits? I stare at the ceiling and pray to the *Saint of the Drunk and Stupid* to jog my memory. Pink diva shirt, pink diva shirt, pink diva shirt. Think, think, think. Nothing is coming to mind. I know the shirt. I know Kim has a pink diva shirt. I did borrow it once too, didn't I? When did I, when did I, when did I?

Oh, the night of Trina's party. The famous party where she accused me of stealing her pearl soap dish. The party where Ray and I made our first public appearance as a couple and made love on a pile of coats. Beautiful, magic Ray. How many days has it been since he's called me? Is it eight? Nine? It feels like longer. He'll call. He's a guy. They have to do their caveman thing. It's not personal; it's just what they do. It means he likes me. Just the thought of Ray is restoring peace and balance to the panic that is rolling around in my brain. Who cares about a Web site? I, Melanie Zeitgar, am dating Ray Arbor. Ray. Arbor. Isn't that a beautiful name? Like a sunny field of trees.

"Oh God. You don't think that's why Ray hasn't called you, do you?" Kim asks, setting my sunny field of trees ablaze. "Because of the Web site?"

I've never been hit by a train. As a kid, my brother and I would walk along the railroad tracks near our house picking up smooth blue glass and flattened pennies, listening attentively for the sound of a whistle, anticipating the delicious feel of vibrations on the tracks. Zach would torture me with

stories of kids "just like us" who had been innocently walking the tracks when, blam, here comes the train and there's
nowhere to go and now they're dead. Just like the movie
Stand by Me based on Steven King's short story "The Body,"
every kid secretly dreams of narrowly escaping a speeding
train.

But now that I know the feeling, the fantasy is gone. It's
none other than raw dread. I can feel it in my bones. I'm on
the tracks and the train is coming. I have one last chance to
hide. One last little chance to throw my body flat against
the retaining wall, taste the bitter bite of concrete, feel the
sun on my shoulders for the last time, and most likely pee
my pants as the tracks start to vibrate from the force of steel
hurling toward me at eighty miles an hour. "What is the
Web address?" I groan as the train streaks by. "What's the
fucking Web address?"

Not only am I locked in a tiny room with no windows and
a psycho file boy, I'm also sans computer. I have to see the
Web site. Why in the world would I be on a Web site? I
peek into the hallway. It's as quiet as the desert. I head
down the hallway back toward the reception area and enter
the first office I come across. This is more like it. This office
has gleaming hardwood floors and floor to ceiling windows
with a great view of the Empire State Building. There is a
leather couch and chair, a bamboo coffee table, and a ma-
hogany desk. The walls are adorned with black-and-white
photos of New York City from the twenties to today. I like
the person who lives here and I wish I had more time to
snoop around, but Steve Beck is going to be back from
lunch any minute now. He's the type who will finish ten
minutes early just so he can catch you doing something
wrong, and it's obvious that he's Trina's little pawn.

The computer is right there on the desk. I have yet to
move past the entrance. So far, I'm safe. If anyone came by
now, I'd say I was just admiring the photos from afar. I could

even claim to be a bit of a photographer myself. Aren't we all? The computer may be password protected and it will be a mute point, but I still have to have a story in case someone sees me. Think, Melanie. What is a good excuse? Why would I be snooping around on a computer my first day here? If someone comes in, I'll have to make up some kind of e-mail emergency. It is now or never.

The computer is already logged on and I am relieved to see an AOL icon on the desktop. I sign in as a guest, log in my screen name and password, and within seconds the cursor blinks in the http address line. My hands shake as I type in the Web address, fuming at the title. Shemalediva.com.

I wait another few seconds and then suddenly the entire screen is filled with a picture of the ugliest woman I have ever seen. She is on her knees and her mouth is thrown back in ecstasy. Strangest of all, she looks like she has a large wooden penis. Her hands are wrapped around it and she appears to be masturbating. And, if you're not yet completely horrified—here's the part I really can't swallow. Here's the part that has me bolted to the spot, staring in slack-jawed, nauseating terror. She is me.

Chapter
7

I can't stand. I sink into the leather desk chair and continue to stare at my image. From the looks of my hair, the picture must have been taken toward the end of the evening. I was deliriously drunk and madly in love with Ray. We had just made love in Trina's bedroom under a pile of coats and purses. In fact I had even managed to collect a few post-coital trinkets (a tube of ChapStick, a magnet that said ARE YOU A BITCH OR DO YOU JUST LIVE IN NEW YORK, and a pack of Camel Lights that I later give to an anorexic model).

After we made love, Ray went to get another beer and I ran into my friend Tommy in the dining room. Someone cranked Kiss, and Tommy and I started doing our crazed rocker impressions. I didn't want to be outdone by Tommy, who was gyrating like a tornado in his tight, red leather pants, so I mussed up my hair, fell to my knees and screamed like Keith Richards for a small but appreciative audience. Then someone handed me a large wooden spoon to use as a microphone. And the Kodak moment of the evening ladies and gentlemen, was the moment where I, Melanie Zeitgar, brought the wooden spoon down toward the floor—I'm just singing folks—just doing a little crazed rocker impression, but from the angle at which the picture was taken, it looks like the spoon is sticking directly out of my crotch. It's *my* head thrown back in crazed "ecstasy," *my* mouth splayed wide open, and *my* hands gripping the base of the wooden spoon. My breasts stand out clearly in the camera too, with glittery silver letters spelling out the word DIVA. The caption above the picture reads, PINOCCHIO GIRL PLAYS WITH HER WOODY.

I drop my head into my hands and moan. This is bad. This is really, really bad. How many people have seen this? Kim didn't say millions of hits, did she? Oh my God. What if my mother has seen this? I mean she doesn't usually show an interest in kinky things like wooden she-males, but you hear stories every day of the Internet bringing out the freak in people. And my brother Zach surfs the net all the time. What if he sees it and shows it to her? What about Ray? Had he seen it? Is this why he hasn't called me? I have to get this off the Internet. And then I have to kill Trina Wilcox.

I am so wrapped in my own misery that I forget all about the fact that I am in somebody else's office breaking into their computer on my first day on the job. Had I been thinking straight, I wouldn't have left the offending picture up on the screen while I cried either. But I wasn't thinking about anything but my wooden penis. Maybe Freud was right. Maybe there *is* something about a penis that makes one entirely self-absorbed.

"What the hell?" She's out of breath and leaning in the doorway wearing a beautiful lavender suit and wielding a black leather power briefcase. Trina Wilcox is a dark-haired beauty, poised and lethal. "What are you doing here, Melanie?"

"I work here," I say, scrambling to shut down the Web site. But I hit the wrong button and only manage to minimize it. In a flash Trina is leaning over me, her hair descending like a guillotine between me and my minimized, she-male doppelganger.

"You broke into Greg's computer? Move over." She shoves me out of the way and maximizes the Web page. Once again I stare at the image in horror. Trina's eyes turn on me and I swear I see them glint. She's Lucifer with tinted blue contacts.

"I know you did this," I say, trying to control the anger clawing up my throat.

"Greg's on the phone," Margaret says, popping into the room. "He wants to know if you have the laptop." I jump up and stand in front of Trina so Margaret can't see the screen. "Melanie, what are you doing here?"

I turn toward Trina, who is packing the laptop in her briefcase. "I saw Trina run in here and I thought she might need some help," I say.

"She's going to run this over for me," Trina says, shoving the briefcase in my hands.

What? What was she doing? "I don't think so," I say, holding the briefcase at arms length as if it were a bomb.

"Melanie, I have to finish up a few things here, but Greg and Steve need that PowerPoint presentation pronto. Go." She's now physically shoving me toward the door. I look at Margaret for help.

"You'll get to see his presentation after all," she says smiling. "They were an hour into it when Steve's laptop bit the dust. Am I dating myself? Do the kids still say 'bite the dust'?"

Trina gives me another shove. "Hurry." Margaret takes my arm and escorts me out. Whether it's to save me from Trina or explain further colloquialisms I don't know. I do know that I'm being propelled down the hall toward the elevator.

"The audience is mostly made up of retail management and security personnel," Margaret informs me as if this is somehow helpful.

"I have files waiting," I plead, craning my neck lamely toward the file room.

"There's a town car waiting at the curb," Margaret continues as if I hadn't spoken. "It will take you to the 92nd Street Y. The workshop is in Buttenwieser Hall. Security will direct you. I'll call Greg and tell him you're on your way."

The 92nd Street Y is a renowned Jewish institution that opens its doors to cultural events, literary readings, concerts, performances, authors, and even housing for young men and women of every race and religion. They have a gym, a health care center, and an impressive list of events. In an effort to expand my cultural horizons, I had been meaning to get there for some time but had yet to make it. As the town car zips toward the Upper East Side, I attempt to open the briefcase. Breaking and entering isn't usually my thing, but I had a sick feeling in the pit of my stomach. Why was Trina so quick to send me to the workshop? The briefcase is locked by a combination built into the clasp, and although I pray to the *Saint of MacGyver* for some instant lock-picking brilliance, no bobbie pins or credit cards materialize to help me out.

Before I know it we arrive at our destination. I enter the 92nd Street Y and before I can think of an excuse to flee, a security guard ushers me into an elevator and escorts me to Buttenwieser Hall. I can hear the murmur of a crowd as I approach. The hall is filled to its 200-seat capacity. As I enter, a woman in a navy suit hands me a pile of note cards. "Questions from the audience," she says. "Hand them to Mr. Parks, please." I glance to the front of the room where two men in suits are standing on a small stage near a large screen.

"Mr. Parks," I say to the two men as I near the stage. Both men turn toward me. The largest of the two is a barrel of a man with dark hair and a goatee. He dabs his nose with a hanky and gestures to the other man. Greg Parks turns and nails me with a huge smile. I feel like a butterfly pinned to cardboard, and I try to smile back. There is something familiar about him, but I can't quite place why. Maybe I do read the newspaper. He's certainly easy on the eyes; he's wearing a gray Armani suit with a blue shirt and a black silk tie. But I think more than anything it's his navy eyes that catch me off-guard. After all, what other explanation is there for the instant rush I'm feeling? Besides, he has wavy dark blond hair, and I like men with dark hair, don't I? He's definitely tall and I like tall but—

He's holding out his hand so I switch the briefcase to my left hand and hold out my right for the shake. He laughs for a second before shaking my hand. He has a nice grip. Why is he laughing at me? Then he leans toward me and whispers, "Can I have my briefcase?"

Oh God. "Of course," I say, handing him the briefcase. "Your other laptop bit the dust huh?" I say nervously.

He looks at me for a second and then gestures to an empty chair in front. "Why don't you have a seat?" he says smiling.

I nod and quickly take my seat. I'm still holding the stack of questions from the audience. I don't know whether I should give them to him now or not. He's busy setting up the laptop, and Steve Landon has already left the stage, so I just keep them in my lap. As the laptop is opened, Greg glances to the side of the room and I follow his gaze over to a cameraman standing in the corner setting up a tripod. This must have something to do with the commentator position Margaret mentioned Greg Parks was going after. Sure enough, when the cameraman turns around I note he's wearing a blue badge reading *Side Court TV*.

"Thanks for bearing with us, ladies and gentlemen. This won't take me long. Technology, huh?" Greg says, still plugging things in. The audience laughs politely. Uh-oh. He was going to have to do much better than that if he wanted to be on television. Americans eat boring people alive, even if they are easy on the eyes. As an actress I could give him a few tips for spicing up his act, but it will cost him. I'm growing bored so I start to leaf through the stack of questions in my lap.

How much annual revenue do businesses lose to shoplifting? What? I swallow. *Do stores have a right to ask customers to check their purse at the door?* Huh? Yeah, right, I think. First of all, you'll piss off the nonshoplifters and lose revenue. Second, customers would accuse the stores of snooping through their purses, yakking on their cell phones, and using their lipstick while they're shopping. What a dumb question. Besides, even if you take our purses we still have pockets. I see a dark shadow fall across the note cards. I look up to find Steve Landon hovering over me.

"Are those the questions from the audience?" he says reaching for them.

"Yes," I say, scrambling to arrange them in a neat little pile. "Here you go. Sorry."

"Greg, why don't we take a few questions while you're setting up?"

"Good idea," Greg says. "I'm almost there."

Steve picks up a note card and turns to the audience. "When will they come out with Sensormatic tags that can't be cut with scissors?" he reads. I glance at my purse where my own scissors sit guilty at the bottom along with several said Sensormatic tags. Oh God. What is this? Is this some kind of a sick joke? I glance at the camera again. Am I on Candid Camera? Stop thinking about yourself. This is work. No one is looking at you. "Greg? This is your area of expertise, I'm just your Vanna White today," Steve says good naturedly. The audience laughs. Uh-oh. He's a tad funnier than Greg. Are they competing for the commentator position?

"They have come out with smaller electronic sensors now that aren't as visible to the consumer," Greg says. "But the sales associate has to be able to find it and remove it for the customer without damaging the material. The truth of the matter is, you can never depend on a tag to protect your merchandise. Cameras, security guards, sensor tags, they're all helpful. But they have to work in concert with your employees to successfully catch and prosecute a thief. There's no quick fix, and of course ultimately our goal is to deter theft in the first place. But shoplifters are a pretty smart bunch, and they'll find a way to cut any sensor they come out with. Believe me. Next question?"

"Why did they give Anita Briggs such a lenient sentence? Is it because she's a celebrity?"

I gasp. Greg glances at me before speaking to the audience but I tune him out. Anita Briggs. The actress who walked out of Barneys last year wearing thousands of dollars worth of stolen merchandise. Her arrest was a media blitz. It was all over the—

I do read the newspaper! Greg Parks. The Loss Prevention Consultant who worked with Barneys on her arrest. I feel faint. Water. I need water. I can't breathe. I need to breathe water! Stop thinking of naked midgets with bananas! "Okay, good questions, and we'll get to more after the presentation." I hear the telltale chimes of Windows booting up. Get me some goddamned water! But before I can reach for the pitcher on the table in front of me I'm stopped by a collective gasp from the audience. But it's not until I hear the poised Greg Parks say under his breath quietly, but distinctly, "What the fuck?" that I dare look at the screen.

And there I am, not just one, but multiple pictures of me, Pinocchio Girl, tiled across the large screen. Every ambition I ever had to be an actress dissolves on the spot. Trina Wilcox saved me to the Windows desktop. I never thought my crotch would reach so many people.

Steve Landon stands and kneads his hanky. "Greg?" he says in a shaky voice. "What's this?"

The audience laughs nervously. Greg peers at the screen. "Apparently it's 'Pinocchio Girl,'" he says. The audience roars. The cameraman moves closer. Greg's head snaps to the camera; he had forgotten it was there. The cameraman peers out at him and gives him thumbs up. Greg looks at me, back to the screen and then back to me. "Is that you?" he says.

Oh. My. God. I jump up. "No. It's a question from the audience," I say, waving the note cards. Steve Landon moves toward the screen like he's approaching a tiger's cage. I hold up a card. "The question is—"

"Stand next to me," Greg interrupts.

"What?"

He holds up the tiny microphone attached to his shirt. "I'm sure everybody wants to hear this," he says, eliciting another laugh from the audience. Who knew the man had an inner comedian?

With shaking legs I walk up next to Greg and speak into his tie. "This picture of me was taken at a party," I say, pretending to read from the card. "Although it appears to be— something—uh—*else*—I am simply doing a Keith Richards impression. The wooden spoon"—here I point to the screen—"is supposed to be a microphone." Greg tilts his head and looks at the picture. "I don't have a wooden penis and I'm not a culinary sex freak," I "read" over the laughter, "but someone has plastered this picture of me on a Web site. Is this legal?"

Greg Parks is biting his bottom lip. The cheeky little bastard. He's trying not to laugh. I give him a dirty look. He folds his arms across his chest and moves a few feet away from me. "Interesting question *from the audience*," he says. "Can this *audience member* take legal action against the Web site? Is that the question?"

I nod. "Against the person who sent the picture to the Web site," I clarify. "Like defamation of character or something like that," I say dropping the card. "I'm assuming that's what the audience member wants to know."

"That depends on a few things," Greg says. I wait as he paces in front of the picture. At least he's taking me seriously now. "Does this person know who put the picture on the Web site? An ex-boyfriend maybe?" We hold eye contact. Is he flirting with me?

"I know exactly—I mean *the audience member* knows exactly who did this."

Greg nods again. "Very good," he says. "One more question." He points to the wooden spoon sticking out of my crotch. "If she tells a lie," he asks with a big grin, "does it grow?"

The audience is still roaring when I walk out. I keep my eye on the exit praying to the *Saint of Grace* to get me out of this without further incidence. Everyone is looking at me, but I'm just focusing on the exit. This too shall pass. Tears pool in my eyes and threaten to spill, but I order them to wait. Get out, get out, get out. I make it into the hall. I push the button for the elevator. Okay. I'm in the elevator. This isn't so bad. I press L. I start to cry. Just as the elevator doors are closing, a gray arm reaches through and pries them open. Greg Parks steps into the elevator with me just as the doors start to close and the elevator begins its descent. I try to wipe my tears. Greg reaches the panel and pushes a button, and the elevator lurches to a stop.

"You're crying," he says. "Don't cry." This makes me cry even more. "I'm such a jerk," he says. "Hey, hey please don't cry."

"I can't stop on cue," I say angrily.

"I'm so sorry," he says. "I wasn't trying to hurt you. It was them. They were laughing you know? And I was being filmed for this—work-related thing—and it just—it threw me you know? At first I didn't know how to handle it so I tried a joke and—it worked. So I just—I guess, you know, I usually

can't get them to laugh like that." Oh I know, I thought bit-
terly. "I got carried away. And I swear—what's your name?"
The question stops my tears. "Melanie Zeitgar," I say.

"Melanie," he repeats. "I'm Greg." He holds out his
hand for a real handshake. I compose myself and shake his
hand. He has a nice firm grip; there's nothing clammy about
him.

"Melanie," he says. "I promise—they have no idea that
was your picture. They're all looking around to see which
one of them it is. And don't worry—it's down now. I've got
pictures of tulips up there now or something equally as
manly."

Despite myself I laugh again. "How did you know it was
me?" I say, praying that he doesn't say that I actually look
like the ugly she-male on the screen.

"Your uh—breasts," he says blushing. "The similarity
was uncanny." We both laugh again. "And the look of horror
on your face when you saw the picture," he admits. "I hope
you don't play poker." I wipe my eyes and pray to the *Saint
of Mascara* that mine isn't smeared all over my face.

"Listen, I have to get back in there but—you work for us
now right? You're a temp?"

"Yes," I say. "I'm normally an administrative assistant—"

"Great. Let's continue this conversation later and I'll
help you with your uh—predicament. In the meantime you
should send an e-mail to the Webmaster and ask him to remove the picture. Feel free to name drop our firm. That
should do the trick."

"Thank you," I say. He turns and pushes the Open Door
button on the elevator. "I always get them mixed up," I say.
"That was probably the wrong one."

"No," he says. "It was the right one." He pushes it again.
Nothing happens. He glances at me, laughs nervously, and
pushes the button again. Nada.

"Try pushing another floor," I say, leaning forward and

pushing three. It lights up but the elevator doesn't move. I giggle.

"This isn't funny," Greg says with a nervous laugh.

"No," I agree. "I have to pee." Did I just say that in front of my new boss? I look at him in horror, but he's collapsed against the back wall. At first I think he's feeling around for a trapdoor, but then I notice his shoulders shaking with laughter. Reflexively, laughter spills out of me too, and I have to bite my bottom lip to stop myself from barking like a seal. We're trapped. And I really do have to pee.

Chapter
8

Unlike the movies, neither of us makes a move to rip off our clothes and slam the other against the wall in an awkward yet passionate embrace, and I have to admit I feel a little ripped off. Not that I want to make love to Greg Parks. I'm in love with Ray. But still, why isn't he attacking me? Is it because I mentioned the thing about having to pee? On the other hand we're not stuck in here with a pregnant woman near her due date either, so I guess I should be grateful. And then, as if reading my mind, Greg takes a step toward me, his hand reaching for my breasts. Oh my God. Is this sexual harassment? I'm not actually going to let him feel me up am I?

"I have a boyfriend," I say before he touches me.

His hand stops in mid-trajectory, but his index finger remains pointing toward me. "No," he says in alarm. "I wasn't. It's—your scarf," he says. "The price tag."

Mortified, I look to where he's pointing. Sure enough the price tag is dangling off my scarf.

"I was just. I wasn't—" Greg says flustered, stepping back.

"Oh. Thank you," I say, ripping the price tag off. "I've had this scarf forever, too."

I want to die. We both reach for the emergency phone at the same time and our hands collide on top of the little red phone.

"I'll get it," Greg says.

I remove my hand and step back while Greg talks in clipped tones to a security guard. Within seconds the elevator is moving again, and I can't help but notice that Greg is now standing as far away from me as he can get. When the elevator opens into the lobby, Greg flashes me the peace sign and heads back up to the presentation. Before I know it, I'm back in the town car heading downtown.

"How are you today?" the driver says, looking at me through the rearview mirror. I try a discount smile but I can't even manage 10% off. In less than four hours I've broken into a computer, displayed my crotch on a full-size screen for a couple hundred strangers, and accused my boss of sexual harassment. I think I've earned a lunch. But first I'm going to kill Trina Wilcox.

I find her in the women's bathroom applying blood red lipstick to her snakey mouth. She stops when I enter, and the edges of her lips twitch like a rabbit on cocaine as we stare at each other in the mirror.

"Did Greg get his laptop?" she asks. I tell myself to breathe. "What? Why are you staring at me like that?"

"Greg Parks was mortified in front of a live audience and a cameraman from *Side Court TV*," I begin.

Trina whirls around, her eyes glowing saucers. "A cameraman?" she whispers.

"Didn't you know?" I say. "He was being considered for a position as a commentator and they were at the presentation to get an idea of how he comes across on camera."

Trina swallows. "*Was* being considered?"

"Well I don't know for sure, but how did you think it was going to look when he brought up that picture? Everyone thinks he's a sex freak now."

Trina stumbles backward into the sink. "Oh my God," she says. "I must have—"

"Save it," I say. "You knew perfectly well what you were doing."

"I wasn't trying to get him in trouble," she cries. "Does—does he think I did it?"

"I'm sure after a little investigating he'll find out who is responsible," I say. "He mentioned something about a lawsuit too."

"A lawsuit?"

"Yes, against the person who put my picture on the Web site to begin with. He said something about 'defamation of character.'"

Trina scrounges through her purse and pulls out a pack of cigarettes. I glance at the smoke alarm. She follows my gaze and shoves them back in her purse.

"Look, Melanie," she says, twirling a strand of hair around her finger. "It was probably just a joke. If you want I'll hint around—see if anyone knows anything—see if I can get them to take the picture down."

"Why don't you do that?" I say, making my exit.

"By the way," Trina says, following me down the hall. "I don't think it's professional that you were snooping on Greg Parks's computer and asking him for legal advice your first day on the job."

I stop and clench my fingers.

"I'm sure Jane would agree with me," she adds.

I secretly give her the middle finger and walk faster. "I have to get to lunch," I say.

"Okay," Trina says sweetly. "Will I see you tonight?"

This makes me stop again. "Tonight?"

"Sheila's play. Aren't you going? Ray and I are."

Did she just say she was going to Sheila's play with Ray? I turn around and meet her eyes. They're lit from behind—

glowing like Satan himself, hungry for my reaction. She wants me to pounce on her comment about Ray.

"Sheila's in a play?" I ask pleasantly. "Sheila Hedges?"

"Off-Broadway," Trina says with obvious disappointment that I ignored her comment about Ray. "She's also doing a voice-over for Chevrolet, and she was signed by William Morris. Can you believe it? She's only been out here what—three months? How long have you been here?"

A lead ball bounces around in my gut. "I grew up in New York," I say.

"Upstate wasn't it?" Trina goads. "That's not really what I meant. How long have you been in the city trying to act?" she clarifies.

Trying to act? Trying to act? I pray to the *Saint of Instantaneous Objects* to make a chandelier appear and to the *Saint of Freak Accidents* to bring it crashing down on her pretty little head, but no such luck.

"I've been very busy with my clocks," I say.

"What clocks?" Trina says, the sweetness in her voice cutting out like a cell phone in a tunnel.

"Just an artistic endeavor I've embarked on," I say with a sufficient balance of mystery and snobbery. "Now if you'll excuse me. I have a lunch date." It takes everything I have not to sprint out of the building. If I don't steal something in the next five minutes, I'm going to become physically violent. And I know I said I was done stealing, but in the scheme of things would you rather be a klepto or a violent maniac?

Once I'm out into the fresh (car exhaust, hot dogs, urine, sweat, sewer) air, I feel a little bit calmer. *I'm just going to get something to eat*, I coach myself. I'm not going to think about the humiliation I've just endured, and I'm certainly not going to call Ray. I'm going to go into this deli, grab a plastic container, and fill it with yummy things like deep fried chicken chunks and maybe a little broccoli. Then I'm going to go upstairs, find myself a tiny table, and stuff my face. Only when I've rehearsed what I'd say to the tee—only then will I call Ray and make small, happy talk. Small, happy talk. Such as:

> *Good:* "*Ray. Hello, how are you?*"
> *Bad:* "*Ray. Are you fucking Trina Wilcox?*"
> *Good:* "*Ray. I've been tremendously happy attending to my very busy, fulfilling, athletic, creative life but I've managed to squeeze in a few moments thinking of you and I just wanted to say hello.*"
> *Bad:* "*Please, baby why haven't you called me—I'm thinking of you every waking moment and I'm catatonic without you.*"

See? One must practice these things. Only when we've gotten the small, happy talk out of the way will I venture over the land mine. "Ray, I ran into Trina Wilcox today. You remember, your ex-girlfriend? You're not really going to a play with her tonight (or play with her tonight) are you?" It's honest, to the point. "And by the way, you know that picture of me on Shemalediva.com isn't what it looks like, don't you? I mean you don't think I'm some sort of culinary sex freak, do you?" That one I'm going to have to work on.

Besides the chicken and broccoli, I pick up a few other things. A slice of carrot cake. A bar of caramel and dark chocolate. A thick slice of garlic bread. Fried rice. An egg roll. And I pay for it all. I could have easily slipped the chocolate bar in my pocket too, but I don't. I'm in the throws of tragedy and I'm behaving like a law-abiding citizen. I'm a saint. I stuff myself until I replace my emotional pain with a bellyache. My cell phone rings. I look at caller ID and brace myself. Oh God. What if she's calling because she's seen the Web site?

"Hi, Mom."

"Darling," she says. "What a surprise reaching you for a change." So far so good—I don't detect any trace of "my daughter has become a freak" in her voice. "Any news for me?" she says.

She means—are you gainfully employed. I grit my teeth. "Yes, Mom," I say. "I've started a job at Parks and Landon. It's a law firm." I hold the phone away from my ear as my mother squeals. "Uh-oh," I say, "I'd better go—my lunch is almost over."

"Parks, you say? What's his first name? Did you tell him your brother Zachary is a lawyer too?" I grip the phone like I'm strangling a chicken. My mother could work my brother into any conversation imaginable. I could say, "Mom, I got a part in a Broadway play!" and she'd say, "Didn't Zachary once attend a Broadway play?" Or "Mom, I was bitten by a cobra and I only have an hour left to live," and she'd say, "Zachary once made me a pretty little snake out of pipe cleaners. I still have it somewhere—"

"I have to go, Mom," I say, cutting her off. "I'm extremely busy."

"Call me later, Melanie. I want to hear more about your position. What is the phone number? What's your extension?"

"I'll be right there," I say to the perplexed woman sitting at the next table. "Bye, Mom. Love you."

"Bye, honey. Call me later and tell me about your health plan." On my way out I stop at the condiment stand. I grab a handful of Splenda packets, a fistful of salt, ten packets of mustard, and twelve plastic forks. Outside I grab a lime. I don't know why I take the lime, but it makes me happy. It thumps in my purse as I walk back to work. It's very comforting. It stops me from calling Ray.

The rest of the afternoon goes by without incident. I actually file. And once I get into it, it's not too bad. Mindless, yes. A chimp could do it—yes. But between the pile of food in my stomach and the repetitive nature of the filing, I'm able to induce a comalike state, ignore nose-whistler file boy, and actually get some work done. Before I know it, the day is over. All I want to do is return the scarf as fast as I can so that I can meet Kim at Juan's. Trina corners me before I can escape into the elevator.

"Melanie, I think I found out who posted that picture of you," she says.

"And they're going to take it off?" I ask bluntly, dropping the pretense.

"Maybe," she says. "But I just wanted to ask you again if you know anything about my pearl soap dish. Remember, the one that *somebody* stole from my bathroom the night of my party?"

I stare at her. For a second I hesitate, wondering what kind of perversion allowed her to obsess on a soap dish.

"Trina," I say, conjuring up a tone of maturity and pity, "I don't know why you think I would take your soap dish. I really don't. But I didn't. I swear on my mother's grave I didn't take your soap dish."

"Your mother is still alive, Melanie," Trina hisses.

I shrug. "Her future grave then," I say. "Or yours," I add with a smile, holding her eyes until she looks away.

"It was mother of pearl with a 14 karat gold inlay," she says as if she's talking about a queen's crown instead of a tool used to house soap scum. "It belonged to my grandmother, Melanie. It's extremely valuable."

I clench my skirt in my hands. "I'm sorry to hear that. But I've told you—I don't know anything about it." She doesn't reply, but she doesn't leave either. She's looking me up and down as if she's actually considering frisking me to see if I have the soap dish hidden on my person. I'm gearing up to walk out on her when Margaret Tomer rushes up to me.

"Melanie, I'm glad you haven't left yet. We need you to wait for Airborne Express," she says, sticking a large envelope in my hands. "You can do that can't you?" I look at my watch. It's five-fifteen. If I stay I'll never make it to Brewber's Department Store before they close and I promised the Saints I would return it. Rational or not, I have this feeling that really bad things are going to happen to me if I don't keep my word and return the scarf by six o'clock today.

Whereas some little girls read fairy tales and get all inspired by the romance and the magic, I have been tormented all my life by the punishments. This scarf is ticking, and six is my midnight. If it's not on the shelves by then, I'm a squashed pumpkin. And it's not just that I think I'll lose Ray or gain ten pounds—although that would be bad too—I'm afraid that if I don't take this scarf back I'm going to be a thief for the rest of my life. I'm never going to be able to stop. And I do want to stop. I've had a good run, and my rules have kept me safe so far—but I'm smart enough to know it's a game of odds. If I don't quit now, it's going to take me out.

"If you don't stay then I'll have to ask Trina—and that wouldn't be too nice. Trina has a hot date tonight," Margaret says, winking at me.

"You owe me one too," Trina says, meeting my eyes.

"Of course I'll stay," I say in a pitch a few octaves higher than my normal voice.

"That a girl," Margaret says, shoving an envelope at me. "He should be here any minute now."

Chapter
9

Any minute turns into an hour an a half. I watch my chances of returning the scarf tick away with the second hand of the large black clock above the elevators. By the time I get to the Number 1 train at Penn Station, it's almost 6:30. I squeeze into a seat next to a nun and try not to look at the drunk across from me with his fly open. And if that's not revolting enough, it appears that he isn't wearing any underwear, and I find myself continuously glancing at his penis, wondering exactly which part I'm looking at. I force myself to look above him at the array of posters advertising birth control, AIDS, drug addiction, moisturizer, littering, and the Gap.

Underneath the birth control ad, someone has scribbled "Murdering Cunt" in red paint. I wonder if the nun was doing her rosary and if her presence was a sign from the Saints that they're going to punish me for not returning the scarf. I make a mental note to go to confession. The train screeches to a stop at 42nd Street, and more sardines cram themselves into the can. Something wet and hot spills on my leg—lukewarm coffee. At least I hope it's coffee. I don't even make a move to wipe it off—I can't bring myself to touch it. At least Kim is meeting me at Juan's. I really need the Three Musketeers now. A cell phone starts to ring and suddenly they pop up like fireflies, emerging from the pants, pockets, and bags of busy New Yorkers. To my surprise, even the nun reaches for hers.

It's not until the exposed drunk across from me leans forward and says, "Your hello is running over," that I realize it's mine. He winks at me and smiles as if he knows I've been looking at his penis. By the time I answer the phone, they've hung up. I scroll through the screen, desperately trying to find out who called me. Caller Unknown. It's the story of my life. I wonder if it's Ray. I wonder if I should call him and check. But if it wasn't him, then I've just blown my chance at playing it aloof and mysterious. Bring on the margaritas.

As usual, walking into Juan's Mexican Restaurant immediately makes me happy. Hundreds of colorful sombreros dangle from the ceiling like balloons, and the cement walls are painted a sunny yellow with wide turquoise stripes. Two large cactus plants stand guard near the register, and every tabletop is adorned with cactus salt and pepper shakers wearing little sombreros. But the margaritas are the real reason we love it here. They're as big as your head and bottomless. Even the salsa is laced with tequila. The waiters wear black capes, call you Señorita, and are always smiling. Kim is late as usual. So far I've eaten an entire basket of chips and lifted five sombrero candles and a fork. I'm eyeing the cactus salt and pepper shakers when she walks in.

Every male in spitting distance cranes their neck to get a look at her. All I can do is smile; I read that men like it when you smile. Two waiters and a busboy float down from the ceiling and pull out Kim's chair. Jealousy strikes my throat, and I fight the urge to light her hair on fire with the sombrero candle, but I don't because I am a mature woman. Besides, with my luck, cute firemen would rush to her rescue, tossing me aside like pyromaniac roadkill. Kim flips her hair, smiles, and inspects the empty basket of chips like she's investigating a crime scene. Within seconds, a full one appears in its place.

"Nice scarf," Kim says. "It looks good with my sweater."

I feel one twinge of guilt for the stain that it's hiding and another for not returning it. "Thanks. Margarita?"

She nods and immediately the waiter appears.

"Two margaritas," Kim says, eyeing my recently emptied one. The waiter bows grandly and takes off. "Listen I hope you don't mind but I called Tommy," Kim says. "I think three heads are better than one on this one."

I had already called Kim and filled her in on Trina's bombshell about Ray. If anyone knew how to win a man back it was Kim.

"Where's Charles tonight?" I ask, wondering how many chips I could eat before they attached to my thighs.

Kim sighs. "To tell you truth I'm getting a little bored of him," she says.

I nod sympathetically, but I'm not surprised. Kim goes through boyfriends like I go through underwear. (And yes, I change them daily.)

"I mean the geeky science thing was attractive at first," she says, pondering her situation. "But that's all he ever talks about. Light bending and—particle something or others. I mean, come on—I invite him to parties with scantily dressed models and all he can offer me is a conversation on light bending?"

"How's the sex?" I say, then, "I miss Ray."

"Ugh. Please don't go on again about sex with Ray."

"I'm not going to go on—it's good that's all. Except—" I pause to worship my second margarita, which is being placed in front of me. "Thank you, Señor," I say, batting my eyelashes at the waiter.

"You're welcome, Señoritas," he says to Kim.

"Except what?" Kim says the minute he's gone.

"Nothing. It's just—"

"Spill."

"First tell me how the sex is with Charles."

She shrugs. "It's good," she says.

"Good? Like really good or okay good?"

"Melanie."

"What? I don't want gory details or anything but you don't seem that excited, that's all."

"It's good good. He's just a little too—"

"Big?" I ask, curiosity clinging to my throat like socks to a dryer. I had seen his shoes once in the hallway. Huge, clown feet.

Kim laughs. "I was going to say too gentle. Too sensitive, you know? Like he's afraid of breaking me."

I nod while images of Ray and me having sex on my fire escape flash through my mind.

"Your turn. 'It's just' what?"

"Okay. It's no biggie. He just—he's not that into oral sex I guess."

"He doesn't like blow jobs?" Kim says loudly. Now the men are really looking at her.

"Shh," I say. "No, he's quite enthusiastic about them. It's the reverse that seems to be an issue for him."

"You mean you have to ask him?"

"I mean he's never even made an attempt. Not once."

Kim studies me while finishing her margarita. "You're going to have to guide him then," she says.

"What? My terrain is so confusing he needs a guide?" I say.

Kim giggles.

"Has Charles—"

"Of course."

"So it's weird that—"

"Yes."

"So I'll just have to guide him."

Kim holds up her margarita and we toast. "You could draw a map on your stomach," Kim says. "South Town that way."

We laugh. I giggle. It was good to talk about these things. Really, maybe Ray just needed a little nudge.

"Bring on the tequila!" Tommy shouts from the doorway.

Tommy Vance is a gorgeous, funny, talented model. (Before you ask, I would have but he's gay.) He was the one impersonating Kiss with me the night of the party. But for another ten seconds, it would have been him kneeling on the floor with a wooden penis, and his community wouldn't have thought twice about it. Kim signals a waiter, and this time a pitcher of margaritas appears.

"Are we eating?" Kim asks. The three of us stare at the pitcher and shake our heads no.

"Good," Tommy says. "We're going to get nice and drunk. Now fill me in. What exactly did Trina say?"

Tommy and Kim hate Trina as much as I do, but since they constantly run into each other on modeling jobs they have to hide it. But it doesn't stop them from relishing every drop of gossip they can squeeze out of anyone. "Okay. First she asked me if I was going to Sheila Hedge's play—"

"Sheila Hedge?" Tommy interrupts. "The Canadian with the big melons?"

"Yes," I say. "Anyhow—and then she casually said 'Ray and I are thinking of going.'"

"Are they real or has she had them done?" Tommy interrupts. For a gay man he's way too obsessed about breasts.

"I don't know," I say.

"They're real," Kim says.

We both look at her.

"What? Cynthia Howard got drunk and squeezed them on a dare last Fourth of July."

Tommy nods, satisfied.

"Anyhow," I say with a trace of irritation, "she said she and Ray were going to the play."

"Thinking of going, or going?" Tommy says.

I look at Kim for help.

"We're two drinks ahead of you, Tommy. No talking until you catch up," Kim orders.

"Kim," I plead. "Ray hasn't called me in like ten days. What if he's seen the Web site? What if he's not calling me because he thinks I'm a she-male?"

"She-males are really in right now!" Tommy pipes up. Kim and I corner him with dirty looks. He shrugs and goes back to his margarita. "It's true," he says to the salt and pepper shakers. "They're third. Bisexual women are first, metrosexuals are a close second, and she-males are rounding third! On second thought I think we need some fajitas. Waiter!"

"But what if he hasn't seen it?" Kim says, picking up our conversation. "Then you draw his attention to the Web site unnecessarily."

"But what other explanation is there? We weren't fighting—we had great sex—he called me every day. Every single day for three months. Obviously something is going on."

"Maybe he's gay?" Tommy says hopefully. Tommy thinks every straight man is secretly gay, and there are times when I sadly concur.

"He's not gay," I huff. "He's definitely not gay."

Tommy waves the empty basket of chips in the air. "A commitment-phobe then."

"Say more about that."

"Three months you say? You should check into his past relationships. Do a little digging, and if you find out all of his relationships disintegrated after three months—poof—there you have it. You didn't do anything wrong at all. You're just past your expiration date."

I look to Kim. "How long did he go out with Trina?" I ask. Kim studies the floor. "Kim?"

"Three years."

"Ah-ha! "There's your three. Look, just call him," Tommy says, handing me his cell phone.

I reach for it but Kim grabs it before I can touch it.

"That is relationship suicide. Do you hear me? Call him and it's over."

"Maybe he's just not that into you," Tommy says.

"Tommy!" I yell. "Stop watching Oprah." He shrugs. "Did you even read the book?" I say piously.

"No," Tommy says. "But it's propped up on the back of my commode, and I will get to it right after *Straight Men On Parade*."

I don't know what *Straight Men On Parade* is and I'm not sure I want to, so I skip the snappy comeback.

"Tommy has a point," Kim says. "I mean, first he doesn't call you and then he goes to a play with his ex-girlfriend? I mean, is that the kind of guy you want to be dating?"

I take my straw out of my margarita glass and stick it in the pitcher.

"Well maybe he's not calling because of something Trina said. And maybe she's lying about him going to the play. I mean I should at least find out, shouldn't I? Even if it's over I need closure, don't I? Come on. You guys know how I am about closure."

"Chris Sorenson," Kim and Tommy say, nodding in unison.

"Chris Sorenson!" I yell. "Three hundred and sixty-five fucking days go by and not a peep. I hear nothing from him until New Year's 1999 when I get a collect call from *Moscow* informing me he's married a Russian woman and running her father's dry-cleaning business." I slam the pitcher of margaritas down on the table. "Did we order the fajitas?" I ask.

Four pitchers of margaritas, five basket of chips, and two orders of fajitas later, Kim is struck with a brilliant idea.

"What sis phone number?" she says, playing with the cell phone.

"Whose sis?" I ask.

Kim bursts out laughing. "Hissssssss," she says. "What's his phone number?"

Tommy looks around the room. "Do you see a hottie?" he says.

"Where? Is it the guy in the corner with the black glasses? I was thinking that myself."

"I'm talking about Ray," Kim says loudly. "Melanie, what's his number?"

I stare at her trying to assess her level of drunkenness. "Walk a straight line first," I say, marching the salt and pepper shakers up and down the table.

"You two are a couple of crazy bisexual metrosexuals," Tommy slurs.

"We're not bi or metro, Tommy," I say.

"Plain old hetero," Tommy laments. "Not cool. So not cool."

"Manhattan," Kim says into the phone.

"Kim. What are you doing?"

"Ray. Shit, what'sis last name?"

"Arbor," Tommy says. "Like a sunny field of trees."

I glare at him. He smiles at me.

"Ray Arbor," Kim says into the phone. "Got it." And then she smiles.

It's like watching an artist at work. Kim purrs. She coos. She even concocts a fake cry that sends waiters flying to the table with free fried ice cream. For her. "I'm so sorry to bother you, Ray, but I had to ask you if Melanie's acting any different lately?" Tommy wiggles his eyebrows across the table at me. I cover my mouth with my hand. "Well it's just that—I think my boyfriend Charles is falling in love with her." I start to choke. Kim glares at me.

"Can you speak up?" Kim says over my choking. "I'm on

the subway." This makes me laugh. But I'm still choking so I sound like a motorboat starting up. "Well have you picked up on anything with Melanie? I mean she's spending an inordinate amount of time on her hair, wearing new perfume, and dressing sexier than I've ever seen her. And she's been going out a lot lately, and if it's not with you—I mean, do you think she's losing interest in you?"

I cough into my napkin as happy as a girl choking on her own saliva can be. "Oh, so you've been really busy? I thought maybe you'd broken up because Melanie hasn't even mentioned you. And what with Charles hovering all over her—yeah, give her a call. Feel her up. I mean out." She hangs up just as Tommy and I explode with laughter.

"Feel her up?" Tommy shouts.

"Yes!" I shout.

Ten minutes later, my cell phone rings.

"Don't answer it," Kim whispers as if he can hear me. "Let him leave a message."

Except for the fact that I'm going to have to start dressing sexier and spending an inordinate amount of time on my hair, I'm ecstatic. Kim is a beautiful genius.

Chapter
10

To Whom It May Concern:

Dear Webmaster:

Hey Webmaster:

To: The Webmaster

To: Shemaledivas.com
Attn: Webmaster
From: Parks and Landon Attorneys At Law
To Whom It May Concern:
   We are writing to request the removal of a certain photograph on your Web site. It features a beautiful woman, Melanie Zeitgar, who was innocently impersonating Kiss when her picture was snapped. The spoon in the photograph that you insinuate is a wooden penis is actually a microphone. Melanie does not have a penis. She doesn't even own a set of wooden bowls.

To the Webmaster of Shedivas.com
   I find the photograph of "Pinocchio Girl" offensive and

*misleading. I happen to know that the woman in the picture
has never used kitchen utensils to represent anything other
than—well—kitchen utensils and the occasional microphone
while drunk. Please remove her picture immediately or the
law firm of Parks and Landon will be forced to take action.*
    *P.S. The photograph in question also adds at least ten
pounds to the Melanie we know in real life.*

Dear Shedivas.com:
    *Listen assholes. I was drunk. The spoon is a microphone.
If you don't remove my picture immediately I'm going to slap
you with a lawsuit so fast your freaky little heads will spin.
Sincerely,
Melanie Zeitgar*

Things still in their packages. Round things. Square
things, things in tubes, things in plastic, useful things, silly
things, pointy things—things you could put your eye out
with! As I imagine these things I break out in a little sweat.
That's odd, I think to myself. *Is it hot in here?* I am wearing a
sweater, so I slip it off and hang it about my chair. Much
better. But it's not. My hands feel funny now; a tingling
sensation is running up and down my fingers, and I can't
stop thinking about the drugstore in the lobby of this building. This morning I casually strolled through it, and I can
clearly see the layout in my mind's eye. There are three
cashiers up front, a pharmacy in the back, and a security
camera that scans the middle of the store. The pharmacist
has a good look at the left row and the cashiers face the middle rows, but there is one little neglected corner in the back
right-hand side where it would be very easy to acquire a)
reading glasses, b) a jar of Vaseline, or c) plastic hair clips.
    Automatically, my hand curls around the pocket of my
sweater, and like an accident victim feeling the phantom
limb long after its been cut off, I can actually feel the read-

ing glasses in there, and guess what—there is still plenty of room for the Vaseline and the hair clip. *Stop it*, I tell myself. *You no longer need to steal.* It's true. Ray had left me several messages as of late, and after the third I called him back. He was sweet and funny and apologized like crazy for not calling me lately. I wanted to jump into a cab and into his bed so that I could (among other things) try out my new belly map, but Kim made me wait. So we're all going to see his show next week. It's horrific that I have to wait a week, especially since today is Friday and I don't see why we could-n't see his show *this* week, but Kim insisted it's part of the master plan.

My hand starts to hurt, and I realize that my fingers are still curling around the navy glasses that I'm not going to steal and instead I'm actually digging into the file I'm hold-ing. Unfortunately, I seem to have ripped it a bit. When I ask file boy what I should do about it, he barks at me to get a new folder from the supply cabinet. I look at him ques-tioningly until he silently extends his arm and points in the direction of the next room like the Grim Reaper ordering me off to hell.

Only it's heaven. Ten rows of spanking new ebony sta-plers are parked next to each other like stretch limousines, flanked by crisp white boxes of Bic pens (blue, black, and red ink), surrounded by stacks of bright yellow legal pads and guarded by a wall of genuine black and brown leather binders. I forget all about the file folders as I lean forward and inhale the scent of the supplies. I think I'm going to faint with joy. I'll just take a pen and a legal pad. Surely I need a pad to take notes. Why hasn't anyone offered me one before? And just as I'm about to close the door, I notice a whole other cabinet I've yet to explore.

Glue sticks, rolls of Scotch tape, staples, clips, pencils, erasers, and sticky pads in every color of the rainbow. Everything I need to do a good job. In fact even a leather binder is a necessary accoutrement for an assistant at a law firm. Granted, I wasn't exactly an assistant yet—but it was only a matter of time, wasn't it? I have to force myself to close the cabinets and stroll back to the file room like I'm not on fire. Then I have to wait an excruciating hour (while visions of glue sticks dance in my head) until file boy goes to lunch. As soon as he does, I slip back to the supply room like a kid on Christmas morning.

I should grab one of each, just in case. I commend myself for bringing a large satchel with me and I proceed to put supplies (one of each, just one of each!) in my bag. Finally I remember the file folder, and I grab a few of those too. My bag is starting to sag. Just as I'm throwing another leather binder in my bag, Margaret Tomer walks in.

At first she's smiling so I smile back. Then her eyes slide down to my pregnant satchel and her smile disappears. I hold up the bag. "It's ready," I say.

"I beg your pardon?"

"The bag," I say. "For the children."

"For the children? What children?"

"School PS 47. Anna at the front desk told me we were donating school supplies to them since Mrs. Kragel's third-grade class lost most of theirs in a flood."

"I don't know anything about this." "Oh. Well apparently the janitor left the sink on overnight. Must have been quite a drip."

"I still don't see—"

"It was all over the radio. They were begging local companies to pitch in. Anna told me to fill this bag."

"Anna was a temp, and yesterday was her last day."

"Oh. Then why did she call me and tell me to fill this bag for the children?"

"Why indeed. Did she give you that bag? Is that her bag?" Margaret grabs my bag and starts rifling through it. "Why do the children need leather binders?"

"You don't think. I mean—this isn't for Anna herself is it? Margaret, I believed it was for the children. Anna said she would pick it up and—oh God, I am so stupid."

"Hold your horses. We shouldn't go around accusing her of anything, mind you. There could be children. It just seems a little strange. Doesn't it?" Margaret looks through the bag again.

"I know," I say. "Why don't I call the school and see if there really was a flood. If her story checks out I'll talk with Greg or Steve first to see if they'll authorize us supporting the children. And if her story doesn't pan out—well then I'll let you know and you can take the appropriate action."

Margaret smiles at me. "You're a dear. Just keep this on the down low. We wouldn't want to start any rumors."

I nod respectfully and hold my finger to my lips. "Now what did I come in here for?" Margaret says to the ceiling. Oh. Greg Parks wants to see you in his office." I try not to let the surprise show on my face. I hadn't seen Greg since the incident in the elevator. I nod and start to walk out. "Melanie," Margaret calls after me.

"Yes?"

"Why don't you leave the bag with me. You know. Until we find out about the children."

"Of course," I say and grudgingly hand her my bag.

Greg is sitting at his desk talking on the phone. The nervous feeling in the pit of my stomach takes me by surprise. *It's just because I take my work seriously,* I tell myself. Greg senses me in the doorway, looks up, and gestures for me to come in. "Well, I don't see why not. That's okay. Yes, yes, you can call anytime. Yes, as a matter of fact she's right here." To my surprise Greg hands me his phone. I must look as horrified as I feel, for he says under his breath, "There's that poker face again."

"Hello?" I say into Greg's phone.

"Melanie, dear. I was just having the sweetest chat with

your boss." Oh. My. God. No, no, no. The Saints are going to pay for this one.

"Mother," I say. "Can I call you later this evening?"

"Of course, dear. I really didn't call to speak with you anyway."

"You didn't?"

"I was just introducing myself to Gregory, dear. Why didn't you tell him that Zachary was a lawyer too?"

"I'll talk to you later, Mom."

"He sounds like a wonderful boss, Melanie. I'm sure this is the beginning of wonderful things for you, dear. Oh. I forgot to ask him about the health plan—"

"Bye, Mom." I hang up the phone. Greg is turned around in his chair, and I can see his shoulders shaking. "I am so, so, sorry," I say. "I swear it won't happen again."

He turns around, his face flushed with laughter. "It's okay. It's kind of sweet actually. Except she seems to be under the impression that you're here full time."

"I can explain—"

"As my assistant."

I nod and make hand motions around my head. "She's got his condition," I say.

Trina barges in the office with my satchel. "Melanie, what's this about children in a flood?"

Margaret pops in behind her. "Melanie, the clock in the lobby is off by fifteen minutes. Do you think you could fix it?"

"Margaret," Greg admonishes. "I'm sure fixing clocks is not in Melanie's job description. Call the custodial staff."

"But she's a clockmaker," Margaret explains. "Or do you prefer Clock Sculptor dear? She makes art that tells time," she murmurs reverently.

"Is that right?" Greg says. "That sounds fascinating."

"Fascinating," Trina repeats. The three of them stare at me as if expecting me to break into song and dance.

"I can't fix the clock, Margaret," I stammer. "I create the art," I explain, "and leave the inner workings of my clocks to—uh—the Swiss."

Trina folds her arms across her chest and glares at me, Margaret cocks her head and Greg slightly raises one eyebrow in my direction.

"I'm going to go call about the children," I say, grabbing my satchel from Trina and hightailing it down the hall.

I spend the rest of the day filing and sketching clocks. Before I know it I have a flower clock, a ghost clock, a staple clock, a yellow sticky pad clock, a blue sticky pad clock, a glue gun clock, and a metrosexual clock. I'm doing everything I can to drown out the voice in my head chanting glasses, glasses, glasses. I know I'd take the one on the top left with the navy rims. I look at my metrosexual clock and think *I'm a thief and a pervert.* And when five o'clock hits I have every intention of just heading home. But who doesn't need something from the drugstore? I mean, can you honestly think of one time in your life where you had all the supplies you needed? Razors, aspirin, makeup, gum, tampons, deodorant, rubber bands, water guns—the list of necessities is endless. And it's right downstairs. Incredibly convenient. It would be a crime not to take advantage of it.

CONTRACT WITH SELF

I, Melanie Zeitgar, being of sound mind and body (minus twelve pounds) do solemnly swear:
1. I will never shoplift again!!!!!!!!!!!!!!!!!!!!!!!!!!!!!!!!*

*Exceptions: Research has shown that filing all day in a dark room may cause a Vitamin D deficiency that can lead to momentary lapses in judgment.

Chapter

11

As soon as I exit the drugstore and arrive safely at the next corner, I pull the navy glasses out of my pocket and notice that the ends are crushed. I blame myself; I'm usually very selective in what I steal. But the pharmacist was rounding the corner just as I reached for the glasses, and I didn't have time to examine them as carefully as I should have. Some thieves will steal things just to turn around and take the object back to the store for the cash. This works especially well if they've purchased one and stolen one. They go back into the store with the receipt from the one they've purchased, say they've changed their minds and walk out with cash. But I wasn't that type of thief. I was never after money—I just wanted the object.

If I had to force myself to analyze it further, that's probably not the truth either. I wanted the thrill of the lift. But it wasn't as thrilling when the darn things were defective. Cheap piece of plastic. No wonder I steal things. These aren't worth more than two bucks let alone $16.99. Melanie, that's not the point. *Take them back*, my little voice says. As if confirming my decision, my satchel full of supplies grows heavier on my shoulders. I might have ended up going back for more than I originally stated. So maybe now it *was* stealing. I didn't exactly ask anyone if I could take three leather binders, (okay four, but one I really was going to use at work), two staplers, twenty sticky pads, twelve rolls of Scotch tape, four glue sticks, nine erasers, and a handful of pens now did I? And if I needed them for work, why was I bringing them home? Because I don't have a desk, that's why. But I should not have taken these glasses. I turn around and march back to the store.

The same two women are behind the registers. One is scratching off a lotto ticket, and the other is picking at her purple nails. I stand at the counter and study the packs of gum like they were the LSATs. I can't return the glasses because first of all they're damaged and second of all, despite the defect, I can't bear to part with them. What I plan to do is pay for them like a normal person! Casually, I slip a twenty dollar bill out of my purse, set it on the counter, and sidle away. Outside I feel a new kind of thrill run through me. Not only did I pay for the glasses—but I overpaid. $16.99 plus tax—well okay, I didn't overpay by much, but I was definitely going to even out my karma!

"Miss. Miss!" I hear someone yell four blocks later. I just crossed Park and Forty-forth and am headed toward Lexington when she catches up with me. She is a thin middle-age Latino woman who is obviously not used to running. She is gasping for breath and her cheeks are flushed from the exertion. I note the chewed purple nail polish and the Rite Aid pin. "You drop your money," she says, clutching a sweaty twenty in her brown hands and flashing me her yellow teeth. "I bring. You see?" She holds the twenty out like an hors d'oeuvres tray at a fancy restaurant. When I don't make a move toward it, she grabs my hands and stuffs the twenty in them.

"Are you kidding me?" I say. What is the world coming to if you can't count on basic things like dishonesty in Manhattan? Out of hundreds of thousands of nefarious salesclerks, I had to get the one who would run four blocks to return a dropped Jackson? What kind of rotten luck is that? She pats my hand and then taps my cheek like I'm a naughty puppy. *"Gracias,"* I say, wanting to throw up. Her smile grows until I can see silver flashing from within.

"My good deed for the day, no?" she says beaming.

"Sí," I say. "Reward?" I hold the twenty back toward her. She throws her head back and laughs. Then she pinches my cheek. Really fucking hard.

"Bye-bye," she says, trotting off happily as I stand miserably clutching the slimy twenty in my guilty hands.

It's Friday night and I'm dying to go to Ray's show. Kim went to see her mother, Maura Minx who lives on the Upper West Side where she spends her weekends scouting out potential husbands. Kim's mother is a knockout, a cookie-cutter version of Kim with just a few more chips. She had Kim when she was only fifteen, and she tries to be more of a friend than a mother. Kim invited me to go along with her but the truth is, one Minx at a time is my limit. But now I'm wondering if I should have taken her up on it. Taking the supplies hasn't made me feel any better and paying for the glasses was a bust. I can't stop thinking about Ray. Did he go out with Trina last night? They probably made love too. Get your mind on other things, Melanie. You can't control Ray's penis. Quick, use self-help jargon to keep self from going insane. Imagine a door in your mind. All you need to do to keep out unwanted thoughts (like Ray eating out Trina right now) is to close the door. It's not working. Tell yourself you are closing the door. Close the door! Bolt the door! Push a huge dresser in front of the bloody door.

The door is not working. Okay don't think about him, think about you. This is New York City, the entertainment capital of the world. I am an intelligent, beautiful, young woman. I don't have to stay in on a Friday night feeling sorry for myself. Manhattan is my playground. I'm going to go out and have an adventure. But first I have to shave my legs.

A half an hour later when I'm rubbing lotion on my shaved and bloody legs, I've changed my mind. I am definitely not going to go to a bar. But a nice round of healthy, anonymous sex might be just what I need right now. Maybe I'm having trouble playing hard to get with Ray because he's the last person I had sex with. Everyone knows you can't get over someone if they're the last person you had sex with. That's what I need. Anonymous last-person sex. I don't want to know anything about him. I don't want to even say hello. I just want to fall into bed in someone else's room with nice underwear (mine) and soft lighting (theirs). I just want to have wordless, nameless, passionate sex. With condoms.

Oh God, I have to go back to condoms. I finally went on the pill for Ray. We went through our sexual histories and grilled each other about recent tests, and we came up clean so we had stopped using condoms. Oh God that sucks. This is totally, totally not fair. I should just have sex with Ray. Ha ha. Could I? I mean I could, physically I could, we could. Would he? Of course he would, wouldn't he? Wouldn't he? Oh my God, I mean it's bad enough he didn't call me for a week and he's possibly sleeping with the Wicked Witch of the West Side—but does he not even want to have sex with me? Calm down. He would. He would. You are not going to have sex with Ray. Stop it. I mean it. Really. I am not going to have sex with Ray. I am going to have sex with a condom and a stranger. Okay good. Call Kim, see what she thinks. She's not answering. Now what? I have on really nice underwear and I've shaved but I'm still just sitting here. It's ten o'clock. It's ten-thirty. Maybe Kim will answer now. She doesn't.

Okay so I'll go to a bar. Maybe a nice little Irish pub. I'm

not going just to pick up a man, I'm going because it's a
Friday night and I don't want to sit here staring at my
closet. In fact, it's a social decision. I should bring something to do so I don't look like I'm going there just to get
laid. What should I bring? A book? Pathetic. Who brings a
book to a bar? Me. Mostly when I'm traveling. Or feigning
traveling. I could bring clay and sculpt. Too messy. A camera! I could photograph drunks and prospective bedmates!
I can see it now:

"What's your name?"

"Melanie Zeitgar"

"What do you do?"

"I'm a freelance photographer." Smile! Snap! Hmm,
or—

"What's your name?"

"What's in a name?" Too cheesy. "Call me Mel."

"What do you do, Mel?"

"I sculpt." Get closer to the truth. "I read. I cry. I call my
ex and hang up when I hear his voice. I steal. I call again. I
rip the phone out of the wall and march outside in my flan-
nel dog pajamas and throw the phone in the dumpster. I sit
on the curb near the dumpster and cry some more. My ass
gets wet because some idiot threw his beer on the curb and
I'm the lucky spider who sat down beside her. I imagine a
large vacuum sucking all of the cellulite out of my thighs.
What do you do?"

On second thought, I think I'll just stay home and watch
the tellie. What's on? *Sex and the City*. Perfect. I'll just watch
thinner, richer, cuter, more fashionable New York women
having sex and in an alternate Manhattan universe. Some
days that's as good as it gets.

Chapter
12

Saturday mornings are for sleeping in. Everyone knows this. Even if you didn't get laid the night before, Saturdays are a marvelous thing. I usually sleep until nine, pull on whatever jeans and T-shirt are lying on my floor, and go in search of a latte and a newspaper. Maybe I'll have breakfast at Moon Glow Diner where you can gaze at an aquarium full of neon fish and eat French toast for $2.99. Or I can grab a latte and egg sandwich at the corner diner. Your options are endless on a New York Saturday morning.

Today I am going to get the headshots out of my closet and I'm going to pick up the *Backstage* newspaper. I'm a little bit behind since it's already Saturday and the edition came out last Wednesday, but at least it's a start. I'll see if there are any auditions on Monday and I'll force myself to go. It's occurred to me that if I want to be a working actress, I need to network. I need to surround myself with talented, working actors. And here is where I want to scream at the *Saint of Stubbing Your Toe on the Door When Opportunity Knocks*, because I was once only inches away from two very famous actors, and instead of finding a way to use their connections and fame to boost my own stalled career like any idiot would have done, I choked.

I was standing on a sidewalk next to a private supper club at nine o'clock at night wearing spiked high heels and a full-body sandwich board that read: ASK ME WHAT VENUS DID TO MARS. I had answered an ad in the *Backstage* calling for an actress to do promotions for an upcoming film. It paid $75 for three hours' worth of work and guaranteed you exposure to actors, directors, and agents. They had left out the bit about wearing a humiliating, heavy sandwich board in front of the rich and famous, but I was getting paid, and so far I didn't have a clue who any of these people were anyway.

And they were just as happy to ignore me. In fact, they were more than ignoring me, they were walking around me and looking at me sideways the way you would a drunken lunatic with a jar of change. Blocks earlier, as I waddled my way toward the supper club (I didn't want to waste my $75 on a taxi so I had walked forty blocks instead), I noticed a guy standing underneath a storefront smoking a cigarette. I knew him from somewhere. I stopped and stared at him, trying to place him. He puffed on his cigarette, tilted his head at me, and smiled.

"Village School of Acting," I said to him.

"What?"

"I know you from somewhere. Did you go to the Village School of Acting?"

He smiled politely and shook his head. I shrugged (not easy to do when you're wearing a sandwich board) and asked if he ever did any temping.

"No, not really."

"I swear I know you from somewhere," I said, shaking my finger at him.

He looked me up and down and said, "What did Venus do to Mars?"

"I don't have a fucking clue," I answered honestly. He laughed, and for a moment I laughed along with him. He had a nice face, but I was suddenly afraid that I knew him from my stint at the psyche ward and I wanted to get out of there before he recognized me. I mean, maybe he thought I was wearing this sandwich board because I was still a nutter.

Before running away, I offered him a promotional flyer, which he turned down, and asked him if I could bum a cigarette. I was in my smoking phase then, and I figured if you're going to be a sandwich board, you might as well be a smoking one. But then the guy had the nerve to say that he would give me a cigarette only if I could tell him what Venus did to Mars.

"I'm an actress," I huffed. "If you wanted to know so bad you'd take one of my fliers and go see the goddamn movie." I'm not usually such a bitch, but walking forty blocks in stilettos and fifty pounds of plywood had a way of putting a girl in a foul humor. I threw my head back and stalked off as gracefully as I could under the circumstances.

Just ahead, I saw the entrance to the supper club where a line of beautifully dressed, famous, happy people were waiting to get in. I positioned myself near the end of line, wearing my sandwich board, holding my fliers. I had yet to see anyone famous, but any one of them could be a writer, a director, or an agent! I smiled. I wished this bloody sandwich board showed more of my body. Nobody wanted a flyer. I was still stewing about the jerk in the alley, who, I guess if I was honest, hadn't really done anything wrong. He had a nice smile too. But he could have taken a flier— and for all I know he was an ex-nutter himself. But I was starting to wonder if maybe I *should* know what Venus did to Mars. Why didn't I think to ask? I guess I could make something up, but what if these people went to the film based on my review and it was about something totally different. Oh. My. God. What if it's a porno flick?

My mind was launched into a sudden, pornographic panic, when suddenly, there he was—Kiefer Sutherland, in the flesh, whisking past me, making his way to the front of the line. And although this was the big break I had been waiting for, I suddenly wanted to die. Please don't see me, please don't see me, please don't see me. And since he was already at the front of the line, I believed the Saints were going to spare me. And then it happened.

In slow motion he turned around, leaned past the people in line behind him, commanding all of their attention, and looked me directly in the eye with a big grin. "What *did* Venus do to Mars?" he asked as if he knew it was a porno flick. I opened my mouth and squeaked. And then the mysterious redhead from blocks earlier, or Eric Stoltz, as I had now realized him to be, brushed past me and joined Kiefer at the front of the line, but not before tossing me a cigarette and winking. To this day I regret that I didn't get them to autograph my sandwich board and I didn't keep the cigarette Eric threw to me. If I had, I could have at least sold it on eBay.

Instead I burned the sandwich board in an alley while smoking and fuming that I didn't have a quick monologue about Venus and Mars at the ready. I could have stunned the crowd with my stunning acting abilities, and Kiefer and Eric would have whisked me inside making me the newest member of the Brat Pack. But no, instead of jumping on my fifteen minutes of fame and reciting a brilliant, eloquent, dramatic rendition of WHAT VENUS DID TO MARS, I squeaked. It sent me on a twenty-one-day nonstop stealing binge, and to this day I can't even think of our solar system without lamenting the unfairness of it all.

The trip down memory lane has deflated me and I need a pick-me-up. Maybe I'll take a trip to Strand Bookstore and wander around the East Village. But first I need a latte. There's no sense in ruining a beautiful Saturday with ghosts of acting jobs past. I'm going to tackle the day with a sense of freedom and optimism!

I'm kneeling in a confessional. My beautiful Saturday

plans didn't work out so well. I got the latte all right and then went to the Strand, but I ended up stuffing *Your Karma, Your Self* down my pants. Then I set the alarm off—which was quite a shock considering I didn't even realize they had an alarm. Luckily, there were three of us going out at the same time and I'm the only one who stuck around when the employee stomped out to see what was going on. I held my arms up and opened my purse, and when the search didn't reveal anything I pointed down the other street toward the other two. "You'll have to run after them if you're going to catch them," I told him. I was sorely disappointed when he didn't.

"I'm not a religious freak," I say.

"I see," Father Lorry replies.

"If I had to categorize myself, I'd say I was a vicarious Catholic."

There is silence.

"What is a vicarious Catholic?" he says at last.

I sit back and try to relax. "Well," I explain, "I don't go to church and I don't believe in hell—except here on earth—but I really like the Saints." There is no immediate reply, so I wait.

Is he judging me? They aren't supposed to do that, are they? Then again, they aren't supposed to touch altar boys either, and we all know how that one is going. "I've never done this before, Father. Should I call you Father?" I squeak. Through the wire mesh window I can see his black robe and his head of salt and pepper hair trimmed at the edges. He is bent toward me, listening.

"Call me Father Lorry," he says at last.

"I really like the Saints," I say again, relieved he's still talking to me. "I pray to them all the time." This seems to peak his interest.

"Which ones do you like?" he asks.

"Well," I say, stalling for time, "there's Saint Anthony. I

pray to him whenever I lose anything. Like keys or phone numbers. Oh, and one time he helped me find my purse—that was a really good save because I had just cashed a check and was loaded." Just as I think he's warming up to me, silence descends once again. "That's all I can come up with right now," I say defensively.

"I see," he says again.

I start to feel like this isn't going well. Does he think I'm greedy?

"I don't just pray for things or money, I pray for people too. Like once Ray couldn't find his guitar pick right before a show and I prayed for him." There, that should show him that I think of others too.

"I see," he says.

Does he know he's said this like twelve times already? Is this a real priest or have I reached a recording?

"It may not sound like much to you Father, but it was his lucky pick. Ray can't play without his lucky pick. So I prayed to Saint Anthony and lo and behold I found the pick in—" I stop, suddenly remembering where I found the pick. It wasn't lost at all. I had stolen it and put it in my underwear because I was trying to talk to Ray and he wouldn't stop strumming. Ray hated to play without his pick, so it was an effective maneuver. Not as effective as I would like, since I wanted him to remove it with his tongue.

Now why didn't he take me up on that? Because he was focused on his music, that's why. I mean that's the only reason. What other reason could there be? Obviously he was tempted to remove it with his tongue, wasn't he? And he did eventually retrieve the pick, and okay he used his hand instead and even though it wasn't my first choice it did the trick, didn't it? In fact it really, really did the trick, and the memory is making me squirm. Oh my God, I'm not supposed to get sexually excited in the middle of confession am I? Or am I? Am I supposed to confess that I'm getting turned on? No way. I'm not confessing that. Besides it's not confession getting me all worked up, it's thinking about Ray's hand going after the damn pick. Father Lorry doesn't want all the gory details, does he?

Or does he? Is this how they get their kicks? I should change the subject. Think about something else. Think about anything else. Pray to the *Saint of Disgusting Thoughts* to distract you. Think about getting the flu. War. Overflowing outhouses. Severed limbs. Okay, okay it's working. I'm not at all turned on now. "I even prayed to him when I lost my virginity," I hear myself say. Oh. My. God. Did I just say that to a priest? Melanie—I remind myself—that's strictly a bar joke. I hear a shuffling noise and wonder if he's trying to move even farther away from me. "And uh—Saint uh—Michael. Isn't there a Saint Michael?" I squeak. I'm drowning here Father, throw me a bone!

Do you mean Saint Michael the Archangel?" Father Lorry asks.

"Of course," I say as if I had heard of him.

"The Saint of Thieves," Father Lorry says.

"I see." I start to cough. "May I have some water please?" Why did he mention thieves? Is it possible God knows everything I've done and is taunting me through Father Lorry? Maybe this is where I die, choking on my own saliva, before I can absolve my sins. What happens then? Does it count that I was about to confess?

"Of course my dear. Wait here," Father Lorry says. He opens the door to the confessional, and I listen to his shoes clomp down the hall. My first instinct is to run, to get out of this hot box, but I'm frozen to my spot.

I wonder how many Hail Marys he would dole out if I told him everything. I wonder if he's ever coming back. Maybe he thinks I'm insane. Has he listened to so many confessions he can peg the crazy ones in a matter of seconds? Just as I've convinced myself that he's calling the police or scrounging about for a straight jacket, I hear the familiar clomp coming toward me and a few seconds later he opens the window and hands me a glass of water. "Thank you, Father," I say.

For a moment I wonder what it would be like if he were my dad and I was his daughter stopping by on the way to school. Would I have to confess all my deeds, every day? Jesus, that would be draining. Then I remember priests can't marry. Maybe it's for the best. I wanted to ask him if he thought the whole celibacy thing had perverted his sexual drive, but we were there to talk about me, not him. The water tasted stale. "Is this holy or regular?" I ask.

Again, I'm greeted by a thick, dark silence, and just as I'm about to write Father Lorry off as a dud, he laughs. He has a deep, comforting laugh, and it relaxes me. "To tell you the truth, Father, I don't really know the names of all the Saints. I kind of make them up as I go along and then pray to them. Is that okay?"

"God hears all of our prayers, dear."

"Well thanks, this has been great."

"Is there anything you'd like to confess, my dear?"

I'm addicted to love. I say "fuck" three plus times a day. I'm twenty-nine and I don't know what to do with my life. I'm jealous of my brother. I haven't voted for two years. The last time I went to the dentist I stole a water pick. I talk to cockroaches. Three years ago I spent two weeks in a psyche ward for taking a Bic razor to my wrists. I have cellulite on my thighs. My left breast is slightly larger than my right. Sometimes I shave my eyebrows because I'm too lazy to pluck. I have a hundred and eighty-eight stolen objects in my closet and I'm afraid that if I stop stealing I'll die.

"Not today, Father, I think I'm good."

Chapter
13

"Melanie, it's your mother. I just wanted to remind you about dinner on Saturday. Make sure you bring a gift, darling. Corinne wouldn't say anything of course, but it's the right thing to do. I'd also like to Clear The Plates with you—if it weren't for you, we'd be bringing the boys. I wanted to bring them anyway, but Richard said we need to give you some time. Don't tell him I mentioned it because it will make him anxious. Richard is on new medication. I don't think it's as strong as the one you're on, but there's no need for you to mention it. We can't wait to see you and—I have a little surprise for you too, darling. Bye-bye."

I stare at the answering machine while violent thoughts cascade through my brain like a slot machine from hell. Knife! Gun! Bomb! Who does she think she is? My mother, Rene, had become a royal pain in the ass ever since my dad left her and she dropped the second *e* off her name. She lives in New Haven, Connecticut, in a two-story brick house with her new husband, Richard, and his five Bichon Frises, that is, "the boys." Last Thanksgiving, Mom set up a kiddie table for the boys so they could dine next to us, gobbling turkey parts from little placemats in the shape of bones. "Mother," I made the mistake of saying as I stared at the drooling beasts, "do they have to be in the same room?"

My mother shot a "didn't I tell you" look to Richard and ran her hands through her new hair. It was short, choppy, and furniture polish red. The ends stood straight out, and she looked radioactive, as if touching a single strand could zap you into yesteryear. I kind of liked the funky cut but it didn't fit her personality. "Melanie, we know you're having a hard time adjusting to my new marriage," my mother said as I glared at the boys.

I put my fork down and stood my ground. "That's not true, Mom," I said in a reasonable tone.

"You refuse to accept the fact that Richard and the boys are family," my mother continued, blowing past my incredible show of maturity. "You always do this, Melanie. God forbid, if anyone in this family finds a little happiness, you've got to go and stir up some drama. I warned you about a career in acting so please, please don't make a scene in front of Richard and the boys."

I looked to my brother Zach and Corinne for support. They buried themselves in their sweet potatoes and fussed with my niece and nephew. I knew Corinne didn't want dogs at the table either; she barely let her children sit with us. But she was a coward and wasn't going to say a word. Richard didn't say a word either, but a flush rose in his cheeks as he grabbed another buttered roll from the turkey-shaped basket Corinne had weaved by hand.

"I don't have a problem with Richard," I said, smiling at Richard with clenched teeth, "but *the boys* are *dogs*, Mother. They're dogs!" I suppose a tiny bit of my anger was decades old; Mother had never let *us* have a dog growing up. I was glaring at Zachary now; *he* was the one who went on a three-day hunger strike the time a stray mutt followed him home and Mom and Dad refused to let us keep him. They said they drove him to a "farm" where he would be very happy. Then Mom started to cry, and I immediately melted into a puddle of guilt. Richard scooped the boys up in his arms. They squirmed and yipped, turkey giblets hanging from their whiskers. Corinne put her face close to her plate and started shoveling like it was a driveway buried in snow, and Zachary shook his head at me. "Let's just give Melanie some time," Richard said as Mom sobbed across the table. "When she's ready, we'll Clear The Plates."

Richard is a marriage therapist and is writing a book on marriage called *Clearing The Plates*. It is supposed to be a friendly way to "get rid of the dirty plates between you and your spouse." When everyone has "Cleared The Plates" then it's time to "Set The Table." If you asked me, it was just an excuse to hurl insults at the other person in such a way that they looked like the bad guy if they tried to defend themselves. It was genius really, but it didn't make it any less annoying. I think his real expertise on marriage stems from experience—he has five ex-wives. I've often wondered if he acquired one Bichon Frise per marriage and that's why there are five of them, but I've yet to work up the nerve to ask.

A certain amount of the blame for the descent of the Zeitgars has to go to my father and his exodus to the Florida Keys where he asked my mother for a divorce via a postcard with a dancing starfish. Zach, who had just graduated from Cornell University, took over my father's law practice and went from twenty-five to fifty overnight. Last year he and Corinne packed up their SUV and moved to Connecticut, just three houses away from "Rene," Richard, and the boys. Zach said it was so my mother could be closer to her grandchildren, Zachary Junior, five, and "little Corinne," three. I think it's because he's a mama's boy. They live in a two-story brick house with a manicured lawn and a territorial view of Target. It's a nice house, but it's been severely abused by my sister-in-law, Corinne.

The house has been beaten with ribbons, hearts, dolls, pastel color schemes, and extensive stenciling. I bring sleek interior decorating magazines with me every time I visit just so I can imagine what the living room could look like without the pink glass bowls filled with dinner mints, beaded pillows proudly displaying the American flag, and crocheted teddy bears staring at you from the mantle. If the shiny wood floors and simple white couches in the magazines fail to calm me down and I start hyperventilating, then I have to conjure up the *Saint of Frank Lloyd Wright* and we feel the pain together.

The kids are cute but my nephew, Zachary Junior, is way too astute for his age. Last week on the phone he actually asked me what a "psyche ward" was. At first I gave him the benefit of the doubt, even though my heart was galloping like the winner of the Kentucky Derby.

"Where did you hear that word, Zachary?" I asked.

"Aunt Melanie, it's two words, not one," Zachary Junior answered in a voice way too condescending for a five-year-old. Bloody pretentious snobs the lot of them.

"You got me—two words. Where did you hear them?" I prodded while he hemmed and hawed.

"Daddy," he said finally when I told him I'd bring him taffy if he told me.

"What exactly did Daddy say?" I asked in a singsong voice as if I were as happy as a clam. (Are clams really happy? I made a mental note to conduct a study.)

Zachary picked up on my mood and said in a loud, cheerful voice, "He said if you didn't get your act together you were destined for another stint in the psyche ward."

Had to hand it to the kid, he handled those big words like a pro. I have every intention of clawing my brother's eyes out the next time I see him. But first, I have to get a birthday gift for Corinne.

Manhattan Kitchens, nestled on Park Avenue and Twenty-first, is one of my favorite overpriced culinary boutiques. They're snobby with a capital S, and it's always a pleasure to steal from them. I know I promised I wouldn't steal anymore, but this is an exception. Zach had no business telling a five-year-old his Aunt Melanie did a stint in the psyche ward and knowing Mr. "I've-never-even-had-a-past-due-library-book-perfect" was about to house a stolen item in his kitchen was more pleasure than I could bear.

Today the store is really crowded, which is always a good thing. But I didn't count on the cameras and sensors. When were those put in? I pick up a porcelain gravy boat and feel it up. Sure enough the tag on the bottom is lumpy. I almost laugh out loud. What genius thought of this? Let's put a sensor in the price tag. Thieves will never think of removing it. I hang around the pots and pans for a while, just to see if anyone accidentally trips off the alarm and how it is handled. You'd be surprised how many times they go buggy, beeping every few seconds. A few false alarms and most store clerks will wave everyone through with a tension headache and an apologetic smile. While I wait, an associate sneaks up and asks me if I need any help. I pretend to be seriously into the nonstick pans and give him a perturbed look. It works; he slinks off to help someone with the new Mega Toasters.

Like a game of Shoplifting Twister, I rub the tag off the gravy boat with my left hand while pretending to be shopping with my right. I move my foot over the pieces of shredded tag and shuffle in behind a woman who is so obese no one will notice me standing behind her. Slipping out the door would be possible if I had one of their shopping bags. That way, if the alarm did go off, I'd look innocent and hold up my bag as if I paid for it—then pray they wouldn't badger me for the receipt. "It's a gift," I'd say as I pawed through my purse, totally exasperated until they waved me on. But how was I going to get a bag? They were only giving them to those who made purchases. I could make a purchase and get a bag, but I refused to. The store was so expensive! Not that I didn't have the money, it was just the principle of the thing. Who in their right mind would pay eighty-two dollars for a gravy boat?

Someone touches me on the elbow, and I almost drop the gravy boat. It's the sneaky sale associate again.

"Careful," he whines. "You break it, you buy it. Would you like a basket?" He shoves a silver bin at me.

"No thank you," I say, pushing it back and shaking my auburn wig. "I wouldn't want to scratch it."

In a flash the gravy boat is out of my hands. "Of course you wouldn't. We'll just keep it safe and sound until you're ready." With that, he and my gravy boat sail away.

I circle the store until the sales clerk busies himself with another customer, and then I head back to the gravy boats where I proceed to take another one. This time I hover behind a stack of teapots while removing the tag. I hide there until a woman with a baby stroller wheels to the front of the line and starts arguing with the cashier about the price of refrigerator magnets. I thank the *Saint of Stressed-Out Moms* for the distraction and sneak up behind her as if I'm a fellow want-to-be-mom with a ticking womb.

As I'm goo-ing and gaa-ing at the baby, I carefully slip the gravy boat into the little storage basket at the back of the stroller. Genius really, that those suckers have so much storage room! But then I have to wait for her to leave, which takes forever, and really tries my patience. I mean, how long can you look at cutlery without going stark-raving mad?

Meanwhile, the twerpy sales associate keeps looking at me. Every few seconds he holds the other gravy boat up and waves it at me like it's a doggie treat. I have to get out of here. I slip out the door and wait. It takes the young mother twenty-five minutes to emerge, but when she does, I follow her. She's walking at a pretty fast clip, and just when I think I've lost my gravy boat, she stops at the corner and I'm able to make my move. I pretend to drop my purse and while I'm bent down to pick it up I simply grab the gravy boat out of the stroller without her even noticing. You know, people really should pay more attention to what is going on around them.

"Oh my. What a beautiful gravy boat," Corinne gushes. "Manhattan Kitchens. But they're so expensive." You can tell she's impressed; her face is cherry red. Corinne is in a constant state of blushing and apologizing as if an invisible piece of toilet paper were permanently stuck to her behind. She has beautiful, milky white skin but drab mousy brown hair that hangs past her shoulders. I hinted around once about taking her to get her hair cut and styled, but she quickly told me she "had no time for vanity." Then she smiled and said, "You would understand if you had children."

I stewed on this for a long time. Why didn't she say "You will understand *when* you have children"? Is she assuming I'll never have children? Does she think I'm an unfit mother because I highlight my hair? She has big Bambi brown eyes and a small eyetooth that stands out against a row of otherwise perfectly shaped choppers. I constantly find myself wanting to cap it. More than once I've stopped myself from telling her to get it done. Once I suggested it to Zach and he had a fit.

"I love my wife exactly the way she is," he said to me in a huff. "Do you get that? Exactly." I guess that means I shouldn't mention exercise or a wardrobe change either.

Corinne wears pastel polyester suits. Today she is in a soft yellow suit with huge yellow buttons. The top button is missing, and she's replaced it with a gold angel pin. I mean, it's just down right cruel no one says anything to her. If Kim is religious, Corinne is a fanatic. I always leave family gatherings with bruises on my shins because my brother Zach has to kick me under the table every time I say something inappropriate. I guess he's afraid if Corinne blushes once too often she'll overheat and blow. She's still gushing over the gravy boat, hanging onto it like it is Noah's Ark. It's not as satisfying as I thought it would be.

Chapter
14

I've been at Zach's for twenty minutes now and I know something is up. Everyone is being incredibly nice. Mom and Richard didn't bring "the boys," and Zach hasn't once asked me about my future plans. Even Corinne and the kids are tolerable and there are only three pink ribbons on little Corinne's head (usually the kid is so loaded down with ribbons I'm surprised she can hold her head up straight) and to top it off, Zachary Junior has yet to make another mention of my "stint in the psyche ward." Maybe I love my family after all!

From now on, they will treat me like an adult and we will pass brief but pleasant visits, say once every six months. Then Corinne asks if I would like a drink, and that's when I know something is drastically wrong. You see, Corinne doesn't drink alcoholic beverages and Zach hates it when anyone wants to drink wine before we sit down to the table. But when I say, yes, I'd like a glass of Chardonnay, everyone just smiles at my request. I smile back—the kind of smile you would give your captors if you've been kidnapped and chained to a post.

"So," my mother says, clasping her hands to her chest. "How is the law firm, Melanie?"

I continue smiling and sip my wine while everyone waits for my reply. "It's wonderful," I say. "My boss is an amazing man. He even donated school supplies to the children of School PS 47 when they were caught in a flood."

"What do you mean?" Richard asks. "Were they on an expedition?"

"No," I say. "The janitor left their sink running." Richard looks like he's about to ask me another question, so I'm gearing up to launch into a description of my flexible, affordable health plan when the doorbell rings.

"Melanie, would you mind getting that?" Mom says with a look of pure contentment.

"Sure," I say and walk to the front door like a lamb to the slaughter.

"Surprise!" he says.

Greg Parks is on the doorstep holding three red roses and a bottle of wine. He looks incredibly handsome in black dress pants, a maroon sweater, and a black leather jacket. I look down at my jeans and T-shirt and curse the *Saint of Rebelling Against Your Mother* that I didn't follow her advice and wear something nice.

"Don't just stand there with the door open, Melanie, let the man in," my mother urges.

"Come in," I say, obediently standing aside. The moment we step in, my mother rushes him like a linebacker.

"Oh, aren't you sweet," she gushes, taking the bottle of wine. "Isn't this a lovely surprise?" she adds, linking arms with me.

I pray to the *Saint of Orphans* to crash through the roof and whisk me away to my real mother. Instead the old one grips my arm tighter and whirls me around to face Greg Parks. I smile and wrench my arm away from my mother.

"Lovely," I say. "How did this come to be?"

I try to catch Greg's eye so that he knows how mortified I

am, but my mother has hustled him into the living room where she's taking the leather coat off his back.

"I just thought it would be nice to meet the man my daughter talks so much about," my mother says.

Kill me God. Kill me now.

"We're so proud of her," she continues, taking the roses and handing them to me.

"Uh, there's one for each of you," Greg says.

"Did you know she types ninety words a minute?" my mother replies, taking two of the roses out of my hands.

"Ninety-five words a minute," I correct. Good God, have I really sunk to bragging about my typing skills in front of my mother's captive?

"Ninety-five words a minute?" Greg asks incredulously. "With how many errors?"

"Zero," I shoot back. I could tell he didn't believe me. It was everything I could do not to let the stubborn streak in me take over and march us all to Zach's office where I could show off my speedy fingers. Instead, I pour myself another glass of wine.

We sit stiffly around the table like pegs in wooden holes. Richard leads us in grace and of course thanks God for "the boys." It was everything I could do not to dump the pot roast in his lap. My mission was to stay quiet, stuff my face, and catch the next train to Manhattan. I pretend not to notice Greg staring at me from across the table.

"Do you have any of Melanie's clocks here?" Greg asks Zachary when there's a lull in the conversation. Everyone stares at me. I looked vaguely around the room, and everyone else follows suit. I shrug and shake my head slightly.

"Clocks?" my mother says loudly. "Did you say clocks?"

Greg looks to me for help. I make a cutting motion across my throat and he nods. "I'm sorry. That's not exactly the term I should be using is it?" My mother's left eye begins to twitch. "What do you call them, Melanie?" Greg continues. "Sculptures? Is that right? Art that tells time."

"They haven't seen the sculptures we were discussing the other day," I say quickly.

"I've seen them," little Corinne pipes up.

"Have not," Zachary Junior blasts her.

"Have too," she sings louder. She starts to pound her spoon on her plate. "Have too, have too, have too."

"Young lady, do you want a time out?" Corinne hisses under her breath.

"Melanie, what sculptures are we talking about here?" Zach asks. Zach never misses an opportunity to show off his vast knowledge of any topic. Conversations with him turn into a trivia game. The blah, blah, blah was built in blah blah blah at the turn of the century.

"Artists never talk about their work until they're ready," I say vaguely, hoping it will be enough to choke the conversation.

"What artists?" Richard asks.

"What clocks?" my mother echoes.

It is getting hot in here. I try subterfuge one more time. "Greg has a sculpture in his office," I say slowly. I'm still receiving blank, attentive stares. Why don't they pay this much attention to me when I want them to? "I told him his sculpture reminds me of my clocks," I conclude. "Mom, can you pass me the green beans?"

Several agonizing seconds go by. Corinne is the first one to nod like it makes sense.

"I see," Richard adds. My mother smiles at Greg and then focuses on her plate like she's a scientist unraveling the secret of DNA. Zach is the only one who continues to stare at me, waiting for clarification.

"We think it's wonderful what you've done for the children," my mother says loudly. Greg, startled, looks over at Zachary Junior and little Corinne. I giggle.

"Was the janitor fired?" Richard says suddenly.

"I don't think so," I say to Richard. "More wine?" I ask Greg.

"Please," he says helplessly.

"Did you know Melanie's also an actress?" my mother volunteers after another round of awkward silence. Zach snorts. He's never supported my ambitions to be an actress, ever.

"Really, an actress?" Greg says with admiration. "I think that's great. Not everyone has the courage to follow their dreams. That says a lot about you."

My mother erupts in laughter. "Oh, Melanie always does exactly what she wants," she says. "Just like her father."

I can't believe she just compared me to Dad. Did I run off to Florida and dump her for tan, skinny women and peel-and-eat shrimp?

"Not that there's anything wrong with that," she continues. "I've always tried to support Melanie's dreams. But it's not like she's making her living as an actress."

"Still, she's doing it and you have to admire that," Greg says.

"Oh, it's not her fault," Mom says. "They want extremely thin women in the movies these days. My children tend to be a little on the heavy side." Zach and I glance at each other and we both push our plates slightly away. "Don't get me wrong—Melanie's a beautiful girl—it's the standards I tell you. The standards are too high. It's a losing battle. That's why we're so happy she's in your firm now. Do you have a career ladder for Melanie, Mr. Parks? Because I've always encouraged her to take night classes. I suppose she could even take one of those on-line classes. I don't really understand how they work and I'm quite suspicious of them, but at this point we'll take whatever we can get."

This is how I die. Large blocks of ice crash down from the ceiling impaling me with a million frozen shards. Blood gushes from my heart like a geyser drowning the happy little dinner party. My mother screams, Corinne covers her eyes, and Zachary Junior shouts "Cool!"

"Melanie looks thin enough to me," I hear Greg say. I could jump him right here and now for saying that. And I would too—except it would send Corinne into a therapeutic frenzy—Zachary Junior and little Corinne would have to be whisked away to a private institution in the country and subjected to years of vigorous psychotherapy and horseback riding just to drive out the memory of slutty Aunt Melanie. "Have you been in anything I might have seen?" Greg asks.

I was still imagining the kids in the psyche ward, finger painting depictions of lewd sexual acts in front of tense psychiatrists.

"Melanie, Earth to Melanie, did you hear what Greg asked?" Zach says as if I'm one of his children.

I stare at Zach while counting to ten in my head in Spanish. Then, I pointedly look at his forehead. Whisps of gray hair hang over his unibrow. I silently thank the *Saint of Healthy Hair* for skipping me in the early gray category, and the *Saint of Separate Eyebrows* for spacing mine appropriately above my eyes with skin in between them.

"I'm sorry—Greg—what did you say?" I say with a frozen smile. My mother clears her throat. It's her way of reprimanding us in public. She's been clearing her throat at me for twenty-nine years. I wonder if she'll eventually lose her vocal chords. One could only hope.

"I was just wondering if you'd been in anything I might have seen." He looks genuinely interested, but now I want him gone. I want all of them gone but my mother, who I want to nail down to the table until she explains exactly what she meant by, "Melanie always does what she wants, just like her father"—although I know she would slip away from my question like an eel in handcuffs. I tilt my head as if I'm considering his question and hold up my index finger.

"One second please," I say with a frozen entrée smile.

"Mom," I turn toward her. "What do you mean, I'm 'just like my father'?"

Mom sighs loudly and sets down her fork. "Oh Melanie, don't start with me. It was just something to say."

Zach kicks me underneath the table. "Tell Greg what shows you've done," he pleads.

I'm still staring at Mom, but she has that vice-grip look on her face; I'm not going to pry anything else from her in front of all these people.

"Yes Melanie, tell me," Greg says again. "Have I seen you in anything?"

I put my fork down and stare at his biceps. "I'm not sure you would have seen me in anything," I begin. "What bars do you hang out in?" We hold eyes for a moment. I can tell from his stare and the gleam in his eye that he knows I'm bluffing and he's more than happy to play along.

My mother clears her throat again. "Melanie," she titters. "Remember this is a birthday party."

"The children, don't forget the children are here," Corinne whines.

"I've done mostly off-, off-Broadway stuff and a few low-budget films," I say, dismissing the subject.

"Like what?" Greg prods.

What is this, twenty questions? Why weren't we badgering the birthday girl instead? "Let's see. I played a whore in an Edward Albee play last year," I announce. I should stop while I'm ahead, but I can't help it—my anger has caught up to my head. How could they invite my boss to dinner? This is humiliating. My anger is churning around like a pig on a spit.

"What's a whore?" little Corinne asks in a singsong voice.

"Look at the lovely gravy boat Melanie bought me," Corinne says, holding it up with shaking hands.

"*Everything in the Garden,*" Greg says out of the blue, slapping the table. All eyes turn expectantly toward him, but he's looking at me. I have to admit, I'm impressed. I hadn't taken him for a theatre buff. "That's the name of the play, isn't it?" he adds with a huge grin.

I nod my head and stuff more pot roast in my mouth.

"That sounds familiar," my mother says.

"It should. That's the play I was in last year," I sulk.

"No, it's not darling, the play was about a garden—and uh—the things that grow in it. That's what you said."

"I said no such thing, Mother. You just assumed it from the title." None of them came to the play either but I refrained from saying so.

"So it's not about a garden?" my mother persists.

"No. It's about housewives who become whores," I say pleasantly. In actuality it's a brilliant play, and I feel a bit guilty that I'm making it sound more like a pay-per-view movie than a work of art, but this is war.

"Whore, whore, whore," little Corinne sings while dipping her fingers into the gravy boat.

"Well I wish I could have seen you," Greg says.

I don't reply. Even though he's studying me like I'm an insect in a jar, I feel sorry for him. It's not his fault I'm being launched on him like a love rocket. I can tell my mother has visions of me marrying him and buying a Victorian house on their block. Ray would have never received this type of red carpet treatment. The words hurl through my head and fall out of my mouth before I can stop them.

"Fond of whores are you?" I say to Greg.

"Melanie Ann, enough!" my mother yells.

Greg looks a bit startled, but I have to hand it to the guy, he recovers well.

"I would say I'm fond of interesting dynamics, Ms. Zeitgar," he says, poking his fork in the air toward me. For a moment it feels like he and I are the only ones in the room. We stare at each other. I don't know if he's putting me in my place or coming on to me. What really bothers me is that I'm not sure which one I would prefer. Corinne drags the dinner conversation back to child-appropriate topics, and although I appear to be listening, I'm thinking about Ray. How would he have handled it if I had thrown something like that on him at a dinner party?

Someone kicks me under the table. I'm ready to throw a dirty look at Zach, but it's Junior. Like father like son. I look at him and he mouths something at me. What? I mouth back. I can see his little lips moving but I have no idea what the kid is saying. Greg leans across the table and whispers, "What is a whore?" When he sees the look on my face, he lets out a low, seductive laugh that stretches to eternity and back. "His question," he says, throwing his head toward Zach Junior and winking at me. I want to die.

"How do you know so much about the theatre?" Richard asks Greg during Neapolitan ice cream and ladyfingers. "Do you attend regularly?" We had just finished a hearty round of happy birthday, and I'd be able to leave in less than an hour. *Do you attend regularly*, I repeat in my head. I hate how Richard talks. He behaves as if he were an actor reciting a script, covering for the rest of us who were constantly missing our cues and flubbing our lines. What in the world does my mother see in this man? And if she likes Greg Parks (which she obviously does from the way she's smiling at him and nervously glancing at me) and hates Ray—my beautiful, creative Ray—then I don't need to think twice about it. Ray is definitely the way to go.

Not that there was ever any doubt. Not that I'm thinking about Greg in any romantic sense, mind you. I'm not. Even if he is easy on the eyes. Besides, he's a stuffy, wealthy lawyer. I'm a creative, starving artist. Although at the moment I'm quite full largely due to the fact that I had shoved dinner into my mouth like a contestant on Fear Factor. I can't help it. My family stresses me out, and stress makes

me eat like a banshee. *I'm going to take up smoking*, I think as
I stir my ice cream into soup.

"I have to admit, I don't go to shows as often as I'd like,"
Greg says, looking at me. "How often do you go to shows,
Melanie?" Shame rises in my cheeks. Because you see—
the answer would be—never. It's horrid I know. I live in
Manhattan—just a short subway ride away from "Broadway!"
and I am after all an actress. I *talk* about going to shows, I
make lists about going to shows, I vaguely suggest that perhaps I'm going to go to shows—but somehow I never get
around to actually going.

In fact, somehow I always end up going to bars instead.
So by all rights, I should be a bartender. That way I could
impress everyone with how well I know my craft. I could
laugh huskily and say, "If you want a good Irish pub try
Murphy's on Second, but if you're in the mood for a cellar
and a night of whipping then try Pussies on Bleeker." I
shrug and mumble something about being too busy studying my craft to attend any shows as of late.

"Greg's all too familiar with the actor types, aren't you
Greg?" Zach bellows, leaning in toward Greg and wiggling
his unibrow. "You know what I'm talking about," he says.

"Do I know what you're talking about, dear?" my mother
asks. Richard smiles at my mother and gives her an air kiss.
I'm stuffed, but the gesture drives me to shove another ladyfinger in my mouth.

"Greg helped catch Anita Briggs," Zach brags. One
should never inhale with their mouth full. I realize this a
microsecond too late and even shoot a prayer to the *Saint of
Failing to Deflect Controversial Topics With Your Mouth Full* to
save me, but it's too late. A ladyfinger lodges in my startled
windpipe, and I am choking to death. Instead of my life
flashing before my eyes, I see everything I have ever stolen
parade through my head one at a time and wave good-bye
like a funeral procession on acid. I think I even see what re-

sembles a tunnel (unless it was the kaleidoscope I had taken last year from the gift shop at the Hayden Planetarium), but before I can enter it, someone is lifting me out of my chair and wrapping their arms around my waist. I look down at my stomach and recognize the maroon sweater. Greg Parks is giving me the Heimlich while everyone else at the table remains rooted to their seats, mouths open in horror.

Chapter

15

The ladyfinger flies out of my mouth after the third thrust. By now, little Corinne is crying, and her mother hustles her and Zachary Junior away from the table.

"I want to see, I want to see!" Zachary Junior yells as she drags them away. Greg is rubbing my back, and I'm wondering where the cookie had landed. Mother and Richard are hovering around as if there's going to be an encore. My mother barks at Zach to boil some water as if I had just spit up a baby. I try to tell them I'm fine, but my voice comes out as a wheeze. My throat is killing me. Greg is still rubbing my back. I turn and face him.

"Thank you," I whisper. And then I throw my arms around him. I'm not trying to be intimate, but the man did just save my life. He surprises me by pulling me in tightly and holding me. After a minute I start to think this has to be weird (especially since it doesn't feel weird) and I pull back. "You're quite welcome," he whispers as he lets me go.

Since spewing a ladyfinger across the room was a dessert killer, we retire to the living room for tea and coffee. Just as Corinne is passing around the cream and sugar, Richard pushes the button again.

"So who is this Anita Briggs and why were you chasing her?" he says.

I swallow my mouthful of tea as quickly as possible and then place the cup as far away from me as it can go. Maybe I had finally found a diet that would work—the choking diet. Zachary is laughing up a storm, and I'm starting to get pissed off, until I realize he's laughing at Richard.

"Nobody was chasing her," he says, slapping his knee.

"He caught her shoplifting," Zach says. I can see from the glint in his eyes that Greg wants to laugh at Richard too, but he's way too polite.

"I didn't actually catch her stealing myself," Greg clarifies. "She had stolen from the store once before—a pair of sunglasses I think—but the security guards were afraid of apprehending her. They didn't want the negative publicity unless they were a hundred percent sure the charges would stick. So I helped them come up with a foolproof plan in case she came in again. Which she did—the very next day. This time she took a lot more than a pair of sunglasses, and she was arrested on the spot."

Mom and Richard look like they've just landed on Mars. They're nodding with blank stares and looking at each other for help.

"The actress," Zach says, exasperated his news has fallen on clueless elders. "The really hot actress."

Mom and Richard remain pleasant, but blank. Even I'm exasperated.

"Come on," I urge. "It was in every news report, magazine, and newspaper in the country."

My mother tilts her head one way and Richard the other. They are starting to take on mannerisms of the boys.

"What has she been in?" Richard asks politely.

"I know who she is," Corinne says loudly. We turn in surprise. Corinne usually speaks in whispers.

"She's a sinner. Imagine breaking one of the Lord's Ten

Commandments and then lying about it on national television!" Her face is scarlet red and she's clutching the handle
of her hand-painted rose teacup like it's a hand grenade.

"She walked out of Barneys with thousands of dollars
worth of merchandise," Zach explains to Richard and Mom,
still trying to get them to remember like they were amnesia
victims and he was their long-lost son. "She piled clothes
on her body and then just walked out the door. That girl
wanted to get caught," he said, giving up on Mom and
Richard and turning to Greg. I silently agreed with him.
About her. I certainly didn't want to get caught. Anita
Briggs had taken the art form of shoplifting and flaunted it
in front of the Saints. It was an insult to the rest of us.

"Well why in the world do they do it if they want to get
caught?" my mother says.

"Because they're sick in the head," Richard pipes in.
"They've never Cleared The Plates. Imagine years and
years of stuck-on food."

And that image, ladies and gentlemen, is Step Two in
"How to Use Your Annoying Family to Lose Weight."

"Was she high on drugs?" my mother asks, deftly cutting
off Richard's monologue about stuck-on food.

"Daddy why don't you put a video in for little Corinne
and Zachary?" Corinne squeals to my brother at the mention of the word *drugs*. Zach dutifully removes the children
from the room.

"She wasn't on drugs," I find myself saying. "She was
careless, that's all."

Corinne's teacup shakes in her hands. "Careless?" she
says. "She was careless? Melanie, really. The girl is a common criminal. A low-life thief!"

"But she barely got a slap on the wrist, didn't she?" I ask
Greg, ignoring Corinne.

"Yes," Greg admits. "It's kind of a sore spot with me," he

adds. "I think the judge was easy on her because of her celebrity status."

"She wasn't punished?" my mother asks with a *tsk-tsk*.

"She had to return everything to the store and pay some hefty fines," Greg answers, "but otherwise she got off with probation and community service. There are people doing three to five years for less."

I swallow hard. "Three to five years? For shoplifting?" I ask casually.

Greg nods. "Easy. Especially if they're repeat offenders."

I hold my tea with my pinky out and look around to see if anyone else is as horrified as I am. Nope. They all seem quite calm. They have no problem with a klepto doing five years. "That seems a little harsh," I say at last.

"I can see why you would think that," Greg says diplomatically to me before turning to Corinne. "And I can see why you feel she's a common criminal, but in her defense she's an addict—plain and simple."

"What did I say?" Richard says. "Drug addicts."

Greg shakes his head. "No, no. I don't mean drug addicts. I mean she's addicted to shoplifting."

"I don't see how you could be addicted to stealing," my mother says.

For once I agree with her. "Yes. That's ridiculous," I say with a little more passion than I intended. "Are you saying they're like alcoholics?"

"Or drug addicts or gamblers or overeaters. Yes, Melanie, that's exactly what I'm saying. They get a high from stealing. And like any other disease, it will continue to get worse until they hit bottom—in most cases that means one or two arrests down the line. How else would you explain someone like Anita Briggs? She's beautiful, famous, and wealthy. There's no reasonable explanation for her to steal. If she's not an addict, what is she?"

"It's not the first time either," Zach adds. "I read she's been stealing for years."

"Of course she has," Greg says. "It's rare someone is caught their first time." Greg looks at me and I look away. This conversation is starting to piss me off. "I'm not asking you feel sorry for them," Greg says, mistaking the look on my face for pity. "It's not an excuse. People who have that affliction should get help. They know they're sick and they should get help instead of taking things that don't belong to them. They also suffer from an inflated sense of entitlement."

"Exactly," Zach says smugly.

"Entitlement? I don't—" I stop myself just in time. Thank you *Saint of Keeping Your Mouth Shut*, thank you. I almost said, "I don't feel entitled." Do I? What does that even mean? Sure I feel entitled to the things everyone else has. You know, the pursuit of happiness and all that crap.

"I say lock them away and throw away the key," Zach says.

"Lock them away and throw away the key?" I repeat. "You are so intolerant." My mother clears her throat, and Corinne puts her hand protectively on Zach's arm.

"Why am I intolerant? They're the ones breaking the law," Zach says sanctimoniously.

"I agree," my mother chimes in. "And this girl, this Miss Briggs—she's exactly the type I tried to warn you about, Melanie. Those actor types and their lack of morals. You don't take what doesn't belong to you, period. She must have had an absolutely horrid mother, that's all I can say."

I bite my tongue until it bleeds.

The conversation eventually changes, but I don't hear a word anyone says the rest of the evening. I stew over Greg's comments. Addicts. Addicted to shoplifting. I had never heard of anything so insane in my entire life. I, for one, was not addicted to stealing. I was just good at it. And isn't it a waste not to use the talents you're born with? Some people spend their lives catching alligators and wrapping snakes around their necks. Now that's crazy. One could say they have an inflated sense of entitlement. What gives them the right to crawl into a swamp and wrestle reptiles?

Or construction workers. How about their inflated sense of entitlement? Who said we had the right to rip up the earth and build skyscrapers? Pollute the skies with exhaust fumes? Fill up our land with garbage? What about grave-yards? Some people have to live in tiny apartments with mice and cockroaches and doormen who trip them while dead people have acres and acres of manicured lawns adorned with flowers and trees. Now that I think about it—lawyers have the biggest sense of entitlement of all of us. Prosecuting people to the "fullest extent of the law" be-cause some founding father somewhere got a little happy with his quill pen and started making up rules for the rest of us.

Besides, if you're stupid enough to walk into a store, put items on your body in front of the camera, and then waltz past the security guards, then yes—you want to get caught. But entitled? An addict? Give me a bloody break. It's gobs-macking. (Doesn't quite fit there, does it? Can you say *gobs-macking* or is *gobsmacked* the only form of the word?) And okay—there is a little bit of a high associated with steal-ing—the thrill of the chase, the elevated heartbeat—the rush of endorphins after a close lift. It's orgasmic at times, but not addictive. And okay, nobody is satisfied with just one orgasm in their life, so it's repetitive too.

But lots of things are repetitive without being addictive. Maybe I was unique. After all, I had rules. The things I took didn't hurt anyone. I had never taken anything worth more than $100. Okay, so it would get pretty steep if added up the total of everything over the years—but it's not like I've taken all of that from one person. $100 or less per inci-

dent. Usually much less than that. Yes, Greg Parks was definitely talking about a different breed of thieves. The stupid
ones, the ones without any humility or respect for the art of
shoplifting. Besides, I had the Saints on my side. And of
course, the main difference was that I could stop stealing
any time I wanted.

Greg Parks stays for another half an hour and then politely takes his leave. The rest of my family mysteriously
disappears, leaving the two of us standing alone by the door.
"Thanks again," I say. "For saving my life."

"Any time," Greg says, walking toward me until we're
close enough to kiss. I back up. He notices my retreat and
takes a step back himself. "Say," he says, "why are you in
the file room if you can type ninety-five words a minute?"

"The temp agency was desperate," I tell him. "Nobody
wants to work under Trina Wilcox." I realize as soon as it's
out of my mouth that it's a risky thing to say. Maybe he likes
Trina. They could be sleeping together for all I know. I note
with detached curiosity that I don't like the idea of the two
of them together. But Greg doesn't look offended, in fact he
laughs. "I can see that," he says. "But still—maybe we can
find a better place for you. Have lunch with me Monday
and we can discuss the possibilities. All right?"

"All right," I say, matching his smile. "And thanks. I'm
sorry I uh—didn't clear up my mother's understanding of
my—uh—current position." He smiles at me again. "Don't
be," he says, moving toward me again. "It made for a very
amusing dinner."

With that he plants a kiss on my cheek and then disappears out the door. I stay another two hours out of duty and
guilt, trying to make up for the choking and the whole business about whores. I even help Corinne do the dishes, and I
tell Mom and Richard I would be willing to babysit the
boys sometime. Mother takes out her faux red leather calendar and books me on the spot. Bloody barking hell.

Chapter
16

T his is how I die. On a porch in a rocking chair on a crisp autumn day. The sun is hovering low in the sky, leaking red and orange spikes into the horizon. The scent of baking bread wraps around me like a warm blanket. My arms stretch, become wings, and suddenly I'm flying above the earth, touring the mountains and oceans at heavenly speed. I can go wherever I wish. Look, down there, a café in Paris. The warm, turquoise waters of Greece. A roof terrace in Italy, that's me with the flowing white dress and glass of Merlot. I'm dancing. I twirl in midflight, my bird body twisting horizontally like egg beaters held straight out.

I think of those I loved and am leaving behind, broken hearted. I imagine my mother crying into her Connecticut chili, the contest only a week away. Her tears mix with the jalapeños leaving a salty reminder that her only daughter is dead. My father gives me a funeral at sea from his boat, Second Chance. *The twenty-one-year-old he's screwing has tears in her eyes. Could be for me, could be from the wind. My brother Zach writes my eulogy in his SUV while Corinne drives them to the American History Museum. (For children must not play for the sake of fun alone, good God, they must be immersed with educational activities or they'll be directionless underachievers like poor dead Aunt Melanie.)*

Last, I picture Ray learning of my demise, and I want it to kill him. He falls to his knees, shakes with grief, and howls with regret. His body trembles so violently it causes the floor to shake like an earthquake. Neatly stacked porcelain dishes fall from the shelves and crash into a million shattered pieces next to Ray. He's gazing at a picture he took of me in Central Park where my lips are soft and the lens is his love. Groaning, he rolls on the floor, and the shattered glass cuts a million tiny marks into his skin. He kisses my picture, begs me for forgiveness, and dies from regret as the blood slowly drains out of his luscious, muscular body.

I don't care about global warming. I don't care that I lose more little black socks per year than middle-age men lose hair. I don't care that my thighs have cellulite. I don't care that my bank account has more stretch marks than the Woman Who Lived in a Shoe. I don't care because there is no space left in my head for anything but joy. Joy, joy, joy! Tonight is the night we go to Ray's show.

But first I have to find something to wear. Kim and Tommy are going directly from a fashion show so I'm on my own. I spend the next hour trying on everything in Kim's closet. I finally settle on a low-cut green leotard that Ray loves. He says it makes me look like a cat about to pounce. I wear my tightest pair of black jeans and long black boots, carefully apply my makeup and tease my hair into a semi-curled state. Then I throw on my leather jacket, add a soft beaded choker around my neck, and dab vanilla oil on my neck, wrists, and cleavage. Men love women who smell like baked goods.

There's already a small line of people at the Cave. The bouncer, perched on a wooden stool at the door, is about two hundred and fifty pounds and looks like he hasn't shaved in a decade. He has a cigarette hanging out of his mouth and a black bandanna wrapped around his huge head. He's not smiling. I was hoping I would run into one of the band members out here so I could sneak in without paying. Just as I'm contemplating picking someone's pocket, Kim and Tommy show up looking fucking gorgeous. The bouncer straightens up his huge frame, touches his bandanna nervously and waves at us. "Evening," he says grinning at Kim. "Come on up."

We push past the rest of the pissed-off crowd and arrive at the door. Kim puts her hand on the bouncer's shoulder and purrs. "We're with Suicide Train," she says to him in a soft voice. The bouncer's nostrils flare and either he is pulsing his biceps or his tattoos have learned to jump up and down on their own. He opens his mouth in a large grin, giving us a glimpse of his gold fillings.

"By all means," he says, waving us in without the cover.

"Thank you," Kim gushes. I grab her arm and yank her inside. We have an hour to get drunk and somehow make Kim look like shit.

"Why are we doing this again?" Kim says a few minutes later. The three of us are standing in a dimly lit unisex bathroom. Tommy is more than willing to help me dress down Kim, but we haven't quite convinced her. She's playing with the rubber band and thick black glasses I have just handed her. "I said, why are we doing this again?" she whines.

"Metrosexual," Tommy says.

I glare at him. "Because I can't have you meeting the band like you look now," I say, wiping off her lipstick with toilet paper. "I just can't. You're too pretty."

Kim sighs and puts on the glasses while I tie her hair back. "Better?" she asks.

I button the top few buttons of her blouse. "We're getting there," I say.

We sit toward the back, which is Kim's idea. "You don't want to seem eager or clingy," she says.

"But what if he doesn't see me at all?" I protest. "It's dark in here. Shouldn't we move a tad closer?" *Like the first fucking row?*

"Believe me, they'll see you," she says. "You're with us, remember?"

Kim and Tommy chat away while I try to breathe and look sexy. Tommy is complaining about his boyfriend, Rob. "He's suddenly into colored condoms," he says, stirring his rum and coke.

"What's wrong with that?" I ask, wringing my hands and willing the opening band off stage. I can't wait to see Ray!

"Depends on the color," Tommy says. "Green, okay. It says 'go.' It says horny. Black, wonderful. The black stallion. But *red*? It says Santa. It says stop. It's just wrong."

"Little Red Riding Hood," Kim giggles.

"Exactly," Tommy says, sucking on his straw. Then his eyes bug out and he wiggles his eyebrows at me. But I'm so intent on watching the opening band leave the stage that I don't see him coming. As I'm draining my second White Russian, I feel a hand on my shoulder.

"Melanie?" he says. Keep it cool, keep it cool, keep it cool.

"Ray. Hi there." I look into his eyes and melt.

"Well 'hi there' yourself. This is great." This is great. He sounds like he really, really means it. Then Ray turns to Kim. "Hi Kim," he says. "You look different."

But he doesn't mean 'different' in a bad way, ladies and gentlemen. In fact, I don't like the way he's looking at her one bit.

Please, please make her do something disgusting, I silently beg the *Saint of Unexpected Bodily Noises*. But no such luck. In fact, she holds out her hand to him and now they're practically holding hands. *Let go of her freaking hand.* Then Kim takes her free hands and removes the heavy black band. Her long blond hair cascades down like a waterfall of beauty.

"Wish I could stay," Ray says to her. "But we have to warm up. You'll be here later?" he says, mesmerized by her hair. Kim takes off her glasses and sets them on the table. If he doesn't let go of her hand, I'm smashing it. On three. Uno, dos,—thank God, he let go. Or did she pull away?

"We'll be here," I say, edging my hand close to his. He pats it. Kim kicks me under the table. She's giving me a look. "Uh, maybe we'll be here," I add. "We're uh—playing it by ear."

Ray winks at me. "I gotcha. I'll check with you on break then. Deal?" he says smiling.

I melt again. "Deal," I say.

The minute he walks away, I tear into Kim. "Did he pull his hand away first or did you?" I demand.

"What?" she says, gazing in Ray's general direction.

"You two were practically holding hands," I insist.

"You're exaggerating," she says, playing with her hair.

I hand her the tie and the glasses. I look to Tommy for support. He picks them up and puts them back on her and then ties her hair back again, although he doesn't wrap it quite as tight as I would have and she still looks sexy. I notice the buttons on her blouse have mysteriously popped open too.

"Now tell me," I grill. "Did it feel like he was trying to be polite, or did it feel like he was trying to hold your hand?"

"Melanie, get a grip," Kim says. "You sound like a crazy person."

Notice she didn't really answer the question, but I let it drop.

"So, what do you think?" I say when several minutes have gone by and she still hasn't said a word.

"I can see why you fell for him so hard," she says.

My head snaps in her direction. She has a dreamy look on her face. "Don't tell me you're in love with him now," I say. I know how insanely jealous I sound and I don't care. My worst fear has always been that Kim was the one who had been meant to fall in love with Ray and I had interceded with fate's grand plan.

"I just mean—he's really cute," she says, avoiding my eyes.

"You think he's out of my league," I say, reading her mind.

"She didn't say that," Tommy says quickly.

I wait but she still doesn't look at me. "Fine, it's on the record. She didn't say it. I'm asking her. Kim, do you think he's out of my league?"

Kim shifts in her chair and looks at the air above my head. "Of course not," she says.

"Really?" I beg.

"Melanie, you're a beautiful woman. You're funny—"

I stop her. Funny is not what you want to hear when the man you're in love with is as beautiful as Ray. "I'm funny?" I say disgustedly.

"And smart," Kim continues. "I mean you could use a little more self-confidence, but other than that you're great."

I finish my third drink in a single swallow.

"What about beautiful? Am I beautiful?" I demand.

She puts her hands on mine and smiles. "You're very attractive," she says.

"Very attractive," Tommy echoes.

Very attractive? Bloody word dodgers, I think to myself.

"I think I'm going to need help," I admit at last.

"Then that's what you're going to get," she says.

Kim's plan is simple. All I have to do is dance with as many good-looking men as I can while the man of my dreams stands feet away watching. Piece of cake. Except nobody wants to dance with me, they want to dance with Kim. My plan to dull her up isn't fooling anyone. In fact it is backfiring—igniting the Librarian Turns Into Raving Slut fantasy most men harbor.

"You should have brought Charles. He's supposed to be madly in love with me, remember?"

"Doesn't matter," Kim whispers back when I whine this to her during our third dance. Once again, she has the good-looking partner and I have the leftover. "It's working anyway. Don't you dare look, but I swear Ray hasn't taken his eyes off you."

This makes me so happy that I actually smile at the pale, hairy-armed man I am dancing with. He takes it as an invitation to move in closer and puts his hand on the small of my back. Just as his hairy knuckles inch toward my ass, the song ends so I don't have to stomp on his foot with my boot after all. I drag Kim away from her leech and steer us to the bar. It is just the two of us now since Tommy has left us for a hipper, metrosexual bar in Chelsea.

"Tell me everything. Was he really looking at me? Really, really?"

"I swear, Mel," Kim yells across the music. "He's watching you like a hawk. This is going to be easier than I thought."

I squeal. "You are the best friend ever," I say. My tongue is starting to feel heavy. I can't remember being happier than this ever. "I love him, Kim. I really, really love him."

"I know you do," Kim says. "That's why we're leaving."

I didn't think anything could sober me up, but that sure did. What does she mean, *we're leaving*? I wasn't going anywhere. Really, she'd have to kill me and drag me out of here by my hair. I am drunk, happy, and minutes away from sucking face with the love of my life. "No way," I say. "Go if you'd like, but I'm staying." She tries to argue with me but the band is on break and I am already making my way toward him. It's crowded and I'm forced to push giggling girls and drunks out of the way so I can get a clear view of Ray.

I notice with some irritation that he seems to be singing to a gaggle of girls to my left. They're playing one of my favorites, "Only For You." Ray had helped write the song and he sang the lead on it. So of course it's normal that a ton of women are drooling on him—he's gorgeous and he has an amazing voice. But it doesn't mean anything. It's a show. It's like if I were in a play and my character had to kiss another guy or have stage sex with another guy. It's an act. If only he weren't so good at it. He finally catches my eye during the second refrain, and one smile from him is enough to melt me. I smile back. He plays his heart out and, like that, my world is back in balance. Ray is mine. I dance.

Jason is the first to approach me on the break. I smile at him and to my shock he smiles back and gives me a hug. "We've missed you around here," he says.

"Me too," I say, stunned he's talking to me let alone touching me. Then Trent is by my side lifting me in another hug. "Hey there, handsome!" I shout. He blushes.

Tim slaps me on the ass and brings his beer breath next to my ear. "So which of these babes want a little Tim action tonight?" he says.

I laugh and scan the crowd. "That one," I say, pointing to a woman in the corner sucking on her straw. "Definitely that one." And then there is Ray.

He grabs my belt buckle from behind and pulls me in toward him, wrapping his strong arms around me. I'm the envy of every woman in the place and I love it. I turn and throw my arms around him—inhaling him. He's wearing a dark blue T-shirt that makes his eyes sparkle. He smells incredible. His face has a tiny bit of stubble, which drives me wild. I reach up and touch his face. "I forgot," he says with a deep laugh. "Stubble drives you wild, doesn't it?"

"Mmm hmm," I say, going in for a kiss. Pre-Ray I was anti-PDA. I thought couples who made out in public were disgusting. I dig my fingers into his curly dark hair and press myself against him. We kiss shamelessly, passionately. He pulls back first and grins.

"Missed me?" he asks boyishly.

"Maybe," I say mysteriously.

"Want to come back to my place tonight?" he asks.

"Try and stop me," I answer. Okay, okay, I know. Believe me I know. I'm supposed to play hard to get. I'm supposed to be happy and aloof. I'm supposed to jog with lipstick or some shit. I don't know. I don't care. You try kissing that man and then not going home with him. You try playing hard to get when you can't get enough.

Jason and Trent wedge between Ray and me just as I'm going in for another kiss. "Who's your friend?" Jason asks, pointing to Kim who is making a beeline for me.

"What, her?" I reply like I'm surprised.

Tim grins ear to ear. "She's hot," he says.

"Yeah," Jason says. "You practically shot your load on stage."

I fume silently. Oh well. They could have her. As long as Ray was mine, they could all have her. "She's a lesbian," I say and watch as Jason and Trent fall over themselves to get next to her. "And a librarian!" I shout after them.

Kim is trying to get my attention but I ignore her. There is no way she's getting me to leave so she might as well stop gesturing like that. I shamelessly throw myself back in Ray's arms. I step back to gaze lovingly into his eyes. But instead of gazing lovingly back at me, he's looking over my shoulder. I feel a chill run down my spine.

"Happy birthday Ray," a voice from behind me sings. Ding dong the witch isn't really dead. Turns out she's just been biding her time, waiting for the sequel.

Chapter
17

She's holding a glittering silver package adorned with a red bow. Ray has to take his hands off me in order to accept it. "Trina," I say, turning to face her. "Ray's birthday is in July."

"No, it's not. It's today. Isn't it, baby?" Baby? Baby? Did she just call my man baby?

"I wish you wouldn't do this," Ray says to her. Well that's a little more like it.

"Ray," I say, "your birthday is in July, right?"

I know he told me it was in July because I'm a big birthday person. I already had a half dozen ideas in mind for it. He said he wasn't happy about turning 35 so I was going to do something crazy like take him on a hot air balloon ride or fly us to Paris. Okay, maybe not Paris, but the point is I was thinking big.

"Okay, it's today," Ray admits.

"Ray," I say. "I wish you would have told me," I say, trying to sound casual. "Happy birthday."

"Thanks."

"Aren't you going to open your gift?" Trina flirts.

"Later, okay?" Ray answers. "I have to get back on stage."

Kim comes to my side. "I tried to warn you," she whispers.

"Kimberly," Trina says. "It's so good to see you. I was just going to tell Melanie not to feel so bad. Only Ray's closest friends know when his real birthday is."

"Will you excuse us for a minute?" Kim says. She drags me away before I have time to claw Trina's eyes out. She pulls me into a corner. "Melanie," she says. "Do you trust me?"

I glance at her before answering. "Yes?" I ask.

"Good. Listen to me. We have to leave right now. Do you understand me? Right now."

"But it's his birthday," I argue.

"Even better," Kim says. "You have to play this cool."

"But I already told him I'd go home with him." Kim clocks me on top of the head. "Ow."

"Trust me. Let's go."

"I should at least say good-bye—" But Kim is pulling me out the door, leaving Trina all alone with her prey. I argue with Kim in the cab all the way back, but she insists that Ray is going to be so obsessed with where I went that he wasn't going to pay any attention to Trina. I highly doubted it, but I had to admit that Kim was much better at playing these kinds of games. Still, I was bummed. I didn't even get a chance to try out my belly map let alone see Ray in his birthday suit. If Kim was wrong about this I was going to have to kill her.

She gets to live. Kim gets to live! Ray called me the very next day and *made a date* with me for next Saturday. Before you say "big whoop" let me give you the date. February 14th. That's right. Ray and I have a date on Valentine's Day. The thought keeps me sailing through Monday. Greg Parks was going to be out for the week, and Margaret was going around whispering that it was because he got the commentator position. "They're going through test runs as we speak," she says. "You know, just to get him comfortable in front of the camera."

"His girlfriend must be thrilled," I say casually.

"His girlfriend?" Margaret says.

"Doesn't he have one?" I ask with a crack in my voice.

"Oh, he dates" she says. "A handsome man like that. But there hasn't been anyone serious since he broke up with—oh, what was her name? The Miller Lite girl."

"The Miller Lite girl?" I squeak.

"Yes," Margaret says. "You know the one who was plastered all over Times Square in her little white bikini. But they broke up about six months ago. Why do you ask? You don't have a little crush on him do you?"

"No," I say defensively. "I have an incredible boyfriend. He's in a band."

Margaret gives me a look, and I slink off to the file room. But I find myself thinking about Greg at odd times of the day, and I'm seized by this unreasonable urge to break into his apartment and check his fridge for Miller Lites. Not that I begrudged him a girlfriend. He should be dating someone. Everyone should be as happy as I am with Ray.

CONTRACT WITH SELF

I, Melanie Zeitgar, being of sound mind and body (minus five and a half pounds), do solemnly swear:

1. I will never steal from a mom and pop store.
2. I will never steal items worth over $100.
3. I will never steal from the same place twice.

*No Exceptions!

Contracts are guidelines. Everyone knows rules are meant to be broken. And I have good reasons for breaking mine. First of all, next Saturday is Valentine's Day. Second of all, since I missed Ray's birthday, he deserves something really nice. He deserves something he really wants. He deserves the watch on page four of the catalog underneath my pillow. He saw it in the window of a jewelry store we passed by on our second date and stopped to admire it. He's going to be gobsmacked that I remembered.

The small store is just around the corner from Grand Central Station. I've been passing by it quite frequently the past week and I've just happened to notice that on most days there is only one woman manning the store. It would probably be easy to slip in and out of there with the plan I've come up with. But the watch is worth way more than the hundred dollar limit I've set for myself. Try eighteen-hundred dollars. Which explains why I've spent all morning shaking and pacing and bargaining with the Saints. I am a woman who follows the rules, and so far my rules have kept me safe.

I'll just go to the jewelry store have a little look. That's all. I'll just look and that will be that. Maybe I'll put it on layaway. I could give it to him in July—as a joke. Not that the watch would be a joke, but the fact that from now on we will celebrate his birthday in July. It will become one of our favorite in-jokes. And this watch will mark the occasion.

It sits in the center of a glass case reflecting silver rays of light like a metallic starfish. *Rays*, I think. For Ray. I'm simple like that sometimes. I press up against the counter, tilt my head down, and allow my long black hair to fall all around me on the glass. I twirl a strand of it around my index finger and wiggle my bright blue fingernails. "I'd like to see this," I say, tapping on the space directly above the watch. The sales woman behind the counter throws me a tight smile and holds up her index finger. She is in the middle of a phone call. Perfect. I clear my throat and tap again. Click, click, click, click, click. I predict it will only take a few seconds to annoy her, but she doesn't even look up.

"I'm in a hurry," I say finally in a haughty voice.

"I'll be right with you," she answers through clenched teeth.

"Could you just—" I point to the watch and then to the phone. "At the same time?" She sighs and purses her lips. "Could you hold a moment please?" she says into the phone. She sets the phone down and approaches with a set of keys. "Which one?" she says in a belittling tone.

"The Omega Seamaster. In the center."

Another sigh, a tiny click, and the lock is sprung. She sets the box in front of me and glares. "Anything else?" she threatens.

"No," I say pleasantly, "I need to find his wrist measurements. It's in here somewhere."

I started digging through my large purse, hoping she'll go back to her phone call. It takes her a moment—she's studying my fingernails. She is a small woman with frosted hair perfectly bobbed around her pointy face. Her own nails are smooth with a clear polish. She wouldn't be caught dead with blue fingernails. She is probably in her late fifties, but she obviously still works at it and she could easily pass for her early forties. Unfortunately for her, she has a long sharp nose, like a bird's beak. I flash my wrist so that she gets a good look at my tattoo, a bright red butterfly. She takes her time getting back to the phone, keeping her eye on me all the while. I stare back into her eyes and beam my pearly whites at her until she looks away. New Yorkers hate it when you smile at them in public.

I pick up my watch and hold it in my hands. It is beautiful. The silver is a glorious mixture of soft and heavy, like a metallic down comforter. Its face is middle-of-the-ocean blue. I want to shrink myself, dive in, and swim away. This is the watch Pierce Brosnan wore in one of the Bond movies, and even though I always thought Connery was a much better Bond, I certainly wouldn't kick Brosnan out of bed. And if this watch was good enough for him, it was good enough for Ray. Not that any of this would matter to Ray; he would love the watch for other reasons, like the fact that I gave it to him.

The phone call is going to end soon. It's now or never. I glance at the security camera in the corner, stare at the little red light, and dare it to see the real me through my disguise. I take the replacement box out of my purse and quickly switch it with the Omega. I freeze. I thought I had memorized the color of the box perfectly, but I was about a half a shade off. They were both gray, but the original box was December-morning-chance-of-snow, and the replacement was January-afternoon-rain-is-on-the-way. How could I have been so stupid? I curse the *Saint of Crayons* for coming up with so many shades. *Get out*, I plead with myself. *Go, go, go.* But I don't budge. I stare at the boxes until they blur into one. I hate sloppy work.

"I have to go," I hear her say. The mixture of curiosity and concern in her voice jerks me back to reality. She is starting to sense that something is amiss. She can probably smell trouble with that long nose of hers. *Follow the nose, it always knows!* Why, why, why do childhood commercials hit me in moments of crisis? Move Melanie, move! I snap the replacement box shut as she comes toward me. "What time do you open tomorrow?" I ask as I back toward the door.

"Ten A.M." she says, eyeing the box.

"Right. Thanks then. I'll be back."

I'd always wanted to say that. I could hear her report to the police. "Raven hair, bright blue fingernails, a butterfly tattoo—and she said something. What was it? Oh, that's right—'I'll be back.'" The cops would shift; look at each other in concern. One would raise his hand to his hat before leaning forward to ask, "She said—*I'll be back*?" Yes. Just like Arnold. A shadow of a smile escapes my lips as I hit the door, but it evaporates when the alarm sounds, loud and long, wailing after me like wolves baying at the moon.

Chapter
18

A few blocks later, I can hear her heels clicking on the sidewalk as she runs after me. I can't believe it. I hadn't pegged this middle-age bird woman as a chaser. She has a good set of lungs too. "Stop, stop!" she screams. I am half a block ahead of her, but she has the energy of the righteous. Like anyone obsessed with their hobby, I wonder if she has left the store abandoned and unlocked. People less scrupulous than I might be in there right now stealing a ton of loot. I wouldn't do that of course. I have rules.

Yes, and you just broke one of them, my little voice says. I brush it off. Okay, they're more like guidelines and everybody knows guidelines have flexibility. I had a very good reason for stealing the watch, and it's not like I'll ever take anything like this again. I want to look back and see where she is, but pure terror keeps me moving straight ahead. This is a pricey item, and if I'm caught with it I won't get off with just a little warning, that's for sure. I pray to the *Saint of Running in Heels* that hers will catch on a sewer grate, forcing her to give up the chase. Then suddenly, there he is ahead of me, a policeman on a bicycle.

He is perched at the curb, writing furiously in a little black notebook. I wonder what he's writing. *Must stop ring-*

ing little bell, it's making it impossible to catch criminals. I wonder if he ever wants to have children, and if so, does he know all about the crotch-on-bicycle = low-sperm-count thing? I don't have time to be a decent person and warn him; I have to get out of sight before she catches up with him. He isn't much on his own, but he might summon help. I could probably take on him and bird woman, but what good would I be against a swarm of policemen on bicycles, all ringing their little bells?

I run blindly, my watch banging around inside my bag. I can't help myself, I just have to look behind me, and that's when it happens. I slam into a group of tourists stagnating on the sidewalk. There are about fifteen of them tangled up in maps, digital cameras, and cans of mace. Despite the mild weather, they're stuffed into winter jackets and crammed in so close to each other that they have created a human bouncy hut. The harder I try to push through, the higher I bounce.

Their tour guide is a pretty blonde in her twenties, and she's obviously an amateur because she's not anywhere near as aggressive as she needs to be with this group. They are chattering amongst themselves while she desperately tries to speak loud enough for them to hear her.

"Can't hear you," an old man in front of me shouts to her as he waves his hanky.

"She said watch out for pickpockets," I whisper, handing him his wallet. "You must have dropped it," I add, winking at him. His eyes widen when he takes his wallet in his wrinkled hands, and he breaks into a smile when he discovers his cash is still intact. He's even more in awe when I refuse the twenty dollar reward. "Close your ears," I warn him as I put my fingers in my mouth. In junior high school I was crowned "The Whistle Queen of Upstate New York." Although I no longer held the title, I still had the talent.

I let out a piercing whistle, and the crowed immediately hushes and parts enough for me to slip through. Even the policeman on the bicycle glances over. "They're all yours,"

I said to the grateful guide. My euphoria doesn't last long.
The bird woman is still on my tail. While I was slogging
through the tourists, she had gone around them, cutting off
my lead. I had to hand it to her, she was persistent. She
must be the owner of the shop; sales associates wouldn't
chase thieves for minimum wage.

But what I really wanted to know was what kind of heels
those were that allowed her to sprint three blocks without
collapsing in pain, but there wasn't time for that kind of chit-
chat. I don't realize she's behind me until she reaches up
and grabs my hair, yanking off my long black wig. I commend
myself for having the foresight to wear it and use her surprise
to my advantage. While she stands staring at the mass of black
curls in her hands, I run faster then I've ever run in my life.

I don't stop until I reach Times Square a couple of blocks
away. By the time I make the descent to the subway, I have
already peeled off six blue nails, and by the time the downtown Number 1 arrives, I've managed to scrape off one wing
of my butterfly "tattoo." The train is crowded and I have to
do a little shoving to snag an end seat, but it's worth it. I love
end seats—you're guaranteed to have only one crazed New
Yorker sitting next to you as opposed to being sandwiched
between two. I close my eyes and exhale. That was close.

Now that I'm safe, I can relax and review every moment
of the heist. My heartbeat is finally slowing down and endorphins are swarming through my body. I have a one thousand eight hundred and ninety-nine dollar watch in my
purse. I should feel guilty. I should march right down to
NYU and register for classes. I could declare a major and actually finish school this time without slitting my wrists. I
should do it. I should make one positive step toward changing my life. And I will. I'll do it. Just not today.

Kim is out when I get home, but she's left me a note.
Tiffany's tomorrow? At first I think I should resist the tempta-
tion, but then I realize it's perfect timing. I've just stolen a

watch that is so over my stealing limit that, technically, I should lay off shoplifting for at least a couple of months. They say it takes twenty-one days for something to become a habit, so by the end of the month I'll be cured! Tiffany's here I come!

I hide the watch underneath my pillow. I have six days until Valentine's Day. Six days until I see the look of surprise and joy on Ray's face when I place the watch on his beautiful, strong wrist. As I fall asleep, I thank the Saints for my narrow escape and I vow never to steal again. Tiffany's tomorrow. I'm sure it will be a breeze.

"Bedding, silks, and candleholders," the elevator operator announces as the doors open onto the third floor of Tiffany's. Stepping out onto the third floor is like hanging over the edge of a cliff on a pristine summer day. Unlike the first floor where the merchandise is locked, boxed, and behind glass, the third floor is wide-open territory. "Melanie, move," Kim says, pushing me out of the elevator. *Don't look at the bins, keep your hands to your side, breathe.* Oh God. Am I breaking out into hives? I feel like I'm breaking into hives. I examine my arms while Kim stops to admire a silk pillow. She casually picks it up and squeezes it before setting it down and walking away.

"How can you do that?" I say out loud.

"How can I do what?" Kim asks.

I'm still standing by her rejected pillow. My hand reaches out to feel its pink shine, but I yank it away just in time. *If you don't touch it, you can't steal it.*

"Aren't these beautiful?" Kim cries, holding up a stained-glass night-light. "Just look at these colors," she croons.

"And it's small enough to fit in your pocket," I add longingly.

"Why in the world would you want it to fit in your pocket?" Kim asks.

It was getting a little warm in here. I was hoping it was a

rhetorical question, but she was still staring at me, waiting for answer. "Backpacking," I finally manage to squeak out.

"What is wrong with you?" Kim demands moments later as we peruse the linens.

"What do you mean?"

"You're sweating," she says, staring at my forehead.

It's true. Little beads of sweat are breaking out all over my body. I have to get out of here right now. "I—I need a drink," I lie.

Kim grabs me by the hand. "I don't believe it," she says. "I know what's wrong with you."

My heart starts tripping like a kid with his shoes untied and my sweat gathers more force. I'm about to be outed. She's going to ask me straight up if I'm a klepto and I'm going to confess. I'm almost looking forward to it. You can only play Russian roulette so long before the bullet pierces your skull.

"What?" I squeak.

"You're an alcoholic, aren't you?" Kim says.

I almost crumple with relief. But I note a tiny part of me is disappointed. "Maybe a little one," I say to her.

"Okay then," Kim says. "We'll just go for one."

Or twelve I tell myself. Or twelve.

The week before V-Day goes by in a blur. It doesn't even bother me that Greg Parks doesn't stop in to see me, because Steve Beck comes down with a cold and he's out all week so I have the file room all to myself! I use the freedom to daydream. This was the last week of love ambiguity that I'd ever have to face. After Saturday I'll know exactly where Ray and I stand. I haven't seen him since the show, but that is all about to change. Before I know it, it is Friday night. V-Day is twenty-four hours away and counting. So when the phone rings, I practically jump for it.

"I just want to see what time you'll be here, darling," my mother sings.

My thoughts slow down like the second hand of a clock. "Time?" I say.

"Yes, darling, you're sitting for the boys this weekend. You didn't forget, did you?"

Oh shit. Shit, shit, shit, shit, shit. *Saint of Excuses* to the rescue! I sneeze. "No, no, I didn't forget," I say in a muffled tone. "I just hope they won't catch my cold." Mom and Richard are germ freaks.

"Oh God," my mother says. "Richard!" I hear her yelling. "Richard, she has a cold—do you have a fever?"

I touch my forehead. "I'm a little warm," I say huskily. "I'll be fine Mom, don't worry." I let loose a hacking cough. "Don't worry about me and the boys. They'll be fine. As long as I don't have to touch them," I add. I really am a horrible daughter.

"Not touch them! You have to touch them, darling. That's how they feel love. No, no, I'm sorry. We're going to have to make alternative arrangements."

Thank you, thank you, thank you!

"Are you sure?" I say, suppressing another cough. "I was really looking forward to it."

"Some other time, dear," my mother says. For good measure I sniffle. I hang up and look toward the heavens. I was going to owe the Saints big time for this. I try not to feel too bad. I would make it up to Mom and Richard. In fact, I'll ring them tomorrow and reschedule for next weekend. Besides, tomorrow is Valentine's Day. A woman can't spend Valentine's Day with dogs! As I'm drifting off to sleep with Ray's new watch underneath my pillow, I throw a quick prayer to the *Saint of Boyfriends on Valentine's Day*. It's been a long time since I've bagged one at this time of the year, and tomorrow I'm finally going to find out which rung of the commitment ladder we're perched on. Thank you *Saint Valentine*! What a wonderful, perfect, romantic, beautiful little holiday!

Chapter
19

What a worthless, despicable, vomit-inducing holiday. I'd like to rip every fucking Hallmark card to shreds and smash every single box of stupid, little, goo-filled hearts. Well, maybe I'll save a few. If ever there was an excuse to stuff your face with chocolate, this would be it. *Why me*, I pray to the *Saint of Commitment-phobic Men*. Why me?

CONTRACT WITH SELF

I, Melanie Zeitgar, being of sound mind and body (minus seven pounds), do solemnly swear: I will never steal again.*

Exceptions: If it is Valentine's Day and the love of my life has broken my heart and humiliated me in a public place, then the above is null and void and I may steal whatever I wish wherever I please.

Let's rewind, shall we?

V-Day 11:30 A.M., Central Park West

I manage to convince Ray to meet me at the boathouse by the fountain at noon. This in itself is quite a feat, since he usually sleeps until one. He acquiesces when I get tears in my eyes and say, "I guess I'll go it alone." It's one of the perks of my brief acting career—I can cry on cue.

It is an electric morning and you can literally feel a charge in the air. New York is alive, and whether your pockets are being picked or stroked, the magic of the city shoots through you like heroin on a hot fudge sundae. The sun has lured dozens of love-starved New Yorkers and tourists into the park. They spread blankets on Sheep's Meadow, sprawl themselves on steps and benches with interlocking knees, and splash in the fountain. It is a rollerblading, jogging, snogging, hot dog slurping, Frisbee throwing, guitar-playing love fest. I feel high, and for once I don't even have the urge to steal. This is it, V-Day, the day I will finally have a clue as to how Ray Arbor really feels about me.

For the big "love reveal" I have "purchased" (stolen) a lightweight tan blazer with huge pockets. In my right pocket, I have the romantic gift—the Omega Seamaster. If Ray is going to gush love at me, I have it on the ready. In my left pocket, however, I have a lighthearted gift. This is in case he has a lighthearted gift for me, or worst possible scenario, he forgets it's Valentine's Day. In that case, my gift will serve as a gentle reminder he has fucked up big-time but at the same time say, "Hey, I'm a girl with a sense of humor," and how much can you infer from a funny card and a Sweet Tart that says "Bite Me"?

I pace back and forth in front of the boathouse trying to memorize which pocket holds which gift. It may seem simple to remember your right from your left, but one look in Ray's eyes fluster me to the point of stupidity and therefore a heavy review session is a must. Left pocket, L for lighthearted. Shit, I should have used left, L for love. Don't confuse the issue, Melanie. Right pocket, R for romantic. Romantic, romantic, romantic. I long to see the watch on his muscular wrist. I also hope it will help him be a little bit more on time, but it's purely an added benefit.

My reverie is distracted by five young black boys in tuxedos rollerblading to an electric version of "The Love Boat" theme. It's as the crowd cheers and parts that I see them. Roses. Hundreds of them, marching toward me. Although his face is obscured (by a hundred red roses), I recognize Ray's faded Levis and worn brown loafers peeking out from behind them. Even his gait is unique; Ray doesn't walk, he strolls. There is no doubt the man I love is the one behind the mass of roses. My God, I have never seen so many roses. He needs a cart to bring them to me! I thank the *Saint of Men Who Give Flowers* and wipe a tear from my eye. Right, for romantic on the ready!

At this point, women are staring. Jealousy is tattooed to their drooling lips as they throw contemptuous looks to their lovers with their sad single red roses. I am thrilled to the point of sexual excitement. We are going to fuck the minute we get back to my place. The roses will cover every square inch of us. Watch out New York, we're soulmates! Ray is going to become famous and we're going to live in the Dakota. Every morning I'll walk along Central Park West and pick up bagels and raspberries at the nearest market. Ray will brew coffee in his briefs, and our doorman will harbor a secret crush on me. He will smell nice, have all his teeth, and never, ever trip me. I'll wear velvet tops and size 6 jeans. I'll start making my own jewelry. Julia Roberts will discover my necklaces and become my best friend. Our penthouse will face the park, and every morning we'll look out and remember this moment—the moment we made our love official—the moment our lives began.

In a fury of love, I whip out the Omega Seamaster and the card declaring my Love, Love, Love and thrust it at Ray just as he steps out from behind the cart of roses. He steps out from behind the cart of roses, behind the man who is pushing the cart of roses—Ray without even a single red rose. He grins at me and rams me with a pin that says I'M HORNY. Before I can retract the watch and the love you, love you, love you card, he grabs them out of my hands, wraps me in a bear hug, and spins me around. I try to grab the card and watch out of his hands, but I am too dizzy and it is too late. Meanwhile, the man with the cart of a hundred roses stops and pegs us as an easy target. He grins at Ray and wiggles his mustache at me.

"A rose for your lady?" he pipes in a thick Indian accent.

"No thanks," Ray quips, turning his back on him.

"But it's Valentine's Day," the rose peddler continues. "I'll bet the pretty lady would like a rose. Would you like a rose, pretty lady?"

Ray looks at me. *No, I'd like the whole freaking cart you idiot,* I think while smiling and rolling my eyes like it's a ridiculous question.

Ray steps forward to take charge of the situation. "We don't let Hallmark dictate our relationship, buddy. She doesn't need a rose just because it's the fourteenth of February. I give her roses when I feel like it."

(Which, so far, would be never.)

"Leave us alone and find some other sucker who worships the God of Advertising, Consumerism, and Love shoved down their throats at $3.50 a card!"

And then he says five little words that instantly turns my blood to dry ice.

"We are barely even dating," he spits out, looking at me for confirmation.

I know he's expecting me to nod and look appropriately riled at the suggestion that we're a couple, but, barring the last two weeks, I'm too busy running a slideshow through my head of all the sex we've had the past four months. Apparently it's been "nondating" sex.

"Looks like she thinks you are dating," the peddler says

in a singsong voice, pointing to the large card and shiny red package in Ray's hand. I have to hand it to the rose peddler, he's quick. Ray hadn't even noticed what was in his hand.

That's when a Sesame Street book from my childhood, *The Monster at the End of This Book*, flashes through my mind. All through it, Grover pleads with you not to turn the page. "Please, please, please don't turn the page, didn't you hear me? There's a Monster at the End of This Book." I become Grover pleading with Ray and the Universe and the *Saint of Humiliated Women* not to open the card. God, please no! Don't do it! He's doing it. He's opening the card while the rose peddler sneers at him. No, no, no. It's too late. He's seen "I Love You" not only sprawled in big red letters by evil, corporate Hallmark, but worse—written in indelible ink by none other than yours truly, Melanie Zeitgar, who has died a death of a million paper cuts to the heart before Ray has even opened the stolen eighteen-hundred-dollar Omega Seamaster watch.

"Melanie," he says quietly. "Wow." We are sitting on the steps near the fountain, away from the rose peddler, away from the roses. Ray had to physically drag me over here because I had been too humiliated to move. "Wow," is the first thing he's said in five excruciating minutes. He hasn't even taken the watch out of the box. I am quietly wracking my brain for a way to make this okay. How do I turn this into a casual thing? But it's not casual. I love Ray, don't I? I've spent many dazed and confused years on an assembly line of lukewarm dates—and I've finally found someone who really captures my attention.

Okay, we aren't perfect, but everyone knows relationships are like ill-fitting albeit beautiful shoes. You can still walk in them and love them even if they're not a perfect fit. You run the risk that you'll never grow into them, and there's a chance they'll cripple you for life. Or maybe they're great to dance in, but long walks are out. Or long walks are in, but dancing is out. Or you can go ahead and do everything in them but you'll have big, gaping, bleeding blisters the next day.

Perhaps you'll develop a bunion. And then the pretty shoes will fade and scuff as the years go by, and no matter how hard you polish them you can never restore them to their pristine just-out-of-the-box state. So now, not only do they hurt like hell, but they're starting to fall apart. And that's okay. With Ray I knew all of that and I still wanted to be with him. But now I've blown it. I showed Ray how much I love him and so far all he's said is "Wow." And let me tell you—it isn't a good wow. It's the kind of "wow" you would utter if you had just seen a tornado in Ohio suck an entire herd of cows into its vortex. "Melanie, I don't know what to say to you right now."

"Ray," I say. And then I do something really, really stupid. I know the *Saint of Women Who Chase Men* aren't paying the slightest bit of attention to me when I say this, for if they are they would be striking me down with a bolt of lightning. "It's okay if you don't feel the same right now," I hear myself say. "It's no big deal."

He takes my face in his hands. "You're a wonderful woman," he says. Oh shit. "Any guy would be crazy to have you." No. No, no, no, no, no. Not any guy. Please, not the "any guy" speech. "You see, I'm in a place in my life where—"

Do you really need to hear the rest of this? Because I don't. I stop listening and focus on a tiny ladybug crawling along the step near my shoe. At first I love her for her tiny red body and bearings of good luck, but then I start to wonder if she is here for Ray—like maybe she's his good luck sign that he's getting rid of me. And then I hate her, and I lift my shoe to squash her. But I can't do it. My foot freezes a few inches above her. And it's not just because ladybugs are cute—they shouldn't even be called ladybugs, they should be called, "buttons" or something that equally discourages squashing. But that's not why I spare her. She lives because of my ambivalence.

While my foot is poised in midsquash position, I consider what the ramifications would be if the *Saint of Ladybugs* had sent her to me as a sign that Ray would change his mind. If that were the case and I killed her, that would be some bad mojo. And before I work my way back to her being an evil messenger of doom, she's already gone. I will not cry, I will not cry, I will not cry. I bite my lip and nod like I understand every word Ray is saying. Suddenly he stops talking and plants a kiss on my cheek. "Look, I'm sorry but I have to go. I think we should just cool it for a while, you know?" I nod and am still nodding when he disappears up the steps and around the bend.

I sit for another fifteen minutes and then I run up the stairs from the fountain and head toward the east side of the park, away from our phantom penthouse in the Dakota. Who wants to live in a place where John Lennon was shot anyway? I run and keep running until I end up at the carousel. To my surprise it is running, colorful bobbing horses whirling around to piped-in carnival music. I pay six bucks and pick a bright blue horse—forget the white ones with their lame-ass Prince Charmings galloping in to save the day. Why don't they ever show you the part where the prince gets one whiff of commitment and shrivels into oblivion? Bloody hell. I'll ride my own damn horse. I ride the carousel three times and wander around in case Ray changes his mind and comes looking for me, but he never does. I make my way back to the west side of the park in case he's waiting for me. He's not. On my way home I do what any humiliated woman would do on Valentine's Day. I steal three boxes of chocolate hearts and a quart of vodka. I'm never going to speak to Saint Valentine again.

Chapter
20

I would have preferred a Jehovah's Witness. Instead, I find Zach standing outside my door jostling a stack of college catalogues. "Only ten percent of noncollege graduates ever make over fifty thousand dollars a year," he says when I peer into the hallway.

"Hello, Zach," I say. "What a nice surprise." My head is pounding from the vodka and my mouth tastes like pennies.

"Ten percent. And get this—of those that do make over fifty thousand a year, half of those at least have an associates degree."

"Would you like to come in?"

Zach glances into my apartment like a soldier scanning for land mines. "Is she here?" Corinne doesn't like my brother hanging around my model friends—especially Kim.

"Not yet," I say. "But she'll probably stumble in any minute in last night's little outfit," I add just to see him sweat.

"Let's go somewhere, Mel," he says. "We need to talk."

I take him to the India House on Second Avenue and get the tongue-lashing of my life over Naan bread and Tandoori chicken. We make it through the buffet line and he waits until I've taken a few bites before he rips into me.

"We think you should be doing better by now, Mel," he says.

"Who is *we?*" I reply, soothing myself with a mouthful of curried potatoes.

Zach hesitates and twists two colored straws into a modern art sculpture while I wait. "If you must know, all of us. Mom, Richard, Corinne—"

"Corinne? What right does she have to weigh in on my life?"

"She simply agreed you're an intelligent woman who—who—"

"Who what?"

"Who should have, you know, a degree—or a job."

I grab the straw sculpture out of his pristine hands and throw it on the table. "She doesn't know me! Who the hell does she think she is?" (I like Corinne too, except for the fact that she has bad taste in men.)

"She's my wife," Zach retorts. "Who the hell do you think she is?" He slams his fist on the table, catapulting his straw sculpture onto the Christmas lights that hang in the India House year-round. I stare at the twisted mass of blinking red and green lights reflecting early Christmas cheer on my brother's salt and pepper head and have visions of stabbing him to death with a fork.

"You have no right to judge me," I say. "Any of you. Besides, there's nothing wrong with working in a law firm."

"As an assistant?"

"Something wrong with that?"

"Is that what you really want? Because don't kid yourself with the title—you're just a glorified secretary."

I start ripping my napkin into little pieces, which is what I always do when I'm stressed. Why can't he just once visit me like I'm a normal human being instead of a beater car in need of a serious tune-up? Why do I have to put up with his constant lectures? My own father doesn't even lecture me like this. Granted, he hardly ever talks to me at all anymore, but I know if he were here he would be a lot nicer than Zach.

"Melanie. I just want you to have a good life. You know that right?"

I soften slightly. Poor Zach, he feels so responsible for everyone. Maybe he is a lousy father replacement, but it's kind of sweet that he tries.

"I have a good life," I say, forcing a smile. I start shredding the napkin faster and faster and eye the teapot in the center of the table. It's gold with an exotic woman belly dancer etched into it. It's also the perfect size to slip into a large jacket pocket or a purse. Just thinking about it calms me down a bit. I pour more hot water for myself and then for Zach. It will be much easier to steal if it's empty.

"When are you going back to college?" Zach says, sliding the comment into the conversation like a waiter clearing the salad plates.

"Mind your own business," I say with a sulk.

"Look. I understand you went through a hard time," Zach says puffing himself out—priming up for the kill.

And this is where I completely lose it. Because he's very close to a button that could cause a catastrophic reaction if pushed. And I don't care who I have to take down with me—that's not going to happen. Holier-than-thou Zach Zeitgar is walking over a land mine.

"You understand what?" I dare him to say. My voice carries with it a clear warning, and Zach looks away without answering. "Let's just change the subject, Zach. Okay?"

And just when I think we've come to an understanding, Zach slips back into the conversation through the back door. "Does Ray know about your stint in the psyche ward?" he says.

I have a new appreciation for deer in headlights. The paralyzing beams, the frozen limbs. He needs no fist slamming, since silence descends like a guilty verdict, casual dinner conversation screeches to a halt, and all eyes in the India House land on me like fleas on an old dog. My fork hovers halfway between my plate and my mouth, my eyes drift up and to the right, and déjà vu washes over me like oily gloves. He doesn't know that Ray and I are no longer dating, but the comment slices me anyway.

"That was a long time ago, Zach," I say like a ball of yarn unraveling. I shut my eyes, trying to ignore the phantom ache across my left wrist. Elements of the evening tumble through my mind like an old movie.

I'm running in the rain back to my dorm as fast as I can. I yank off my shirt and grab the razor. I don't give myself time to think, I just slice. Blood is gushing out of my wrist so I instinctively grab a hand towel hanging near the sink— a festive bright red towel with a vibrant green Christmas tree—for it was that happy, happy time of year. I press it against my wound while pure terror races through my veins. *What did I do, what did I do, what did I just do?* I stumble into the hallway toward the pay phone, still clutching the razor, dripping a trail of blood. I'm going to call 911. I call Zach instead.

"Don't worry, Zach," I say, snapping out of the memory, "I'm taking my Prozac." Actually I had stopped taking it right after I met Ray, but Zach didn't need to know that. Besides, I didn't need it anymore. I was over all of that. Zach bit his bottom lip while I reached for another napkin.

"Look," Zach says like he's gearing up for a closing argument. "I understand—"

"You don't understand a goddamn thing!" I shout, leaping to my feet. "Not one goddamn thing."

"You tried to kill yourself!"

(It was a Bic. Double blade. As I said, I made the slice before I could think it through, deep and quick across my left wrist.)

"I'm a different person now, Zach. Why can't you just be happy for me?"

"Because I'm the one you run to when everything falls to pieces." I push away from the table. "Melanie," Zach says, "I just want you to be okay." And he means it, I know he does. But something in me snaps, and rage spews out of my mouth like a shaken soda can. I hate myself but I can't stop. I'm Dr. Jekyll and Mr. Hyde. I'm the Grinch. I'm Sybil. I'm Satan. I'm every Iraqi on the Most Wanted Deck of Cards. The shame from that evening is invading my body, and it's all because of Zach. He just had to bring that up, didn't he? He just had to wait for this Sunday, the day after I've been dumped by the man I love, and tear me to ribbons. Hot, raging tears fill my eyes and spill down my cheeks.

"I hate you," I sob.

"Melanie," Zach says, stung. He's trying to reason with me—he's probably willing to drop the whole subject by now and I should just stop—I know I should stop, but blind rage keeps me going.

"I hate you and your perfect little wife and your perfect fucking kids." (How, how, how can I say that about my niece and nephew? I love them. What's wrong with me?) "I'm a failure okay? I'm a fucking failure—but at least I'm not you. Even Dad had the good sense to get the hell away from this family."

"Melanie—"

"Look at you. You're so steeped in your own miserable life that you come after me? I may not be making a hundred and fifty thousand dollars a year, but at least I'm alive. You're a walking zombie. Your whole family is so stiff it's like you've sealed them in Saran Wrap. Your son talks like he's a forty-year-old professor, and little Corinne is so bogged down in ribbons it's a wonder she can even hold her head up."

"That's enough—"

"And your wife—"

"I said that's enough—"

"Corinne is like a Stepford wife without the nice body."

"How dare you—"

"Her entire life is catering to you. So why don't you try to change them and *leave me the fuck alone.*"

The waiter sidles up to our table and presents us with the bill. He puts his finger to his mouth and shakes his head indicating I'm to shut up. I'm definitely taking the teapot. Zach pays the bill while I wrestle with my alligator of shame and try to think of a way to take it all back. We go outside and stand in the rain. I can't stop crying.

"I'm sorry," I whisper.

"Me too," Zach says, and to my surprise he puts his arms around me and hugs me.

"You have no reason to be sorry," I say, breaking the hug.

Zach looks at me for a long time. "I'm sorry that—you know—well I don't know. You won't talk to me. But something happened to you. Right? I mean it couldn't have just been the stress of school. You were a good student in high school—so what was it? Come on, Melanie—talk to me."

I want to stop crying. I want to throw my arms him again. I want to beg him for forgiveness.

"Why?" Zach says again. "Why did you do it?"

"Fuck off!" I say, shutting out the memory. "Just fuck off." And then (it's always good to know where the limit is) Zach shakes his head and walks out on me without as much as a backward glance.

I rub the teapot underneath my coat as I watch him go— its lingering heat is comforting on my belly and a million wishes float through my mind until one lands softly on the tip of my nose like a butterfly—it's the one I wish for more than anything else but never talk about—the one that lives in the back of my closet, the one partially responsible for driving my fingers to take, take, take—the one that wakes me up at night with an angry cry—it's the one that gets away—the one I don't speak of—the one I want to kill. I rub and rub but the genie never shows, and even the Saints are silent on my long walk home.

Chapter
21

T his is how I die. Walking along a high bridge eating buttered toast. My purse is ringing. My hands slip violently through my belongings searching for my cell phone. When I finally retrieve it, I squeeze it so hard it slips right through my butterfingers and flies over the bridge. I don't even hesitate. I jump off the bridge after the phone shouting, "Hello, hello, hello? Can you hear me now? Baby, can you hear me?" But instead of an earful of love, I get a mouthful of water as I plunge into the murky depths below. My last thought before my lungs fill with water is that I'll need to change my calling plan to roaming.

Despite Kim and Tommy's best efforts to cheer me up (and fatten me up), I'm still morose over my breakup with Ray and my subsequent fight with Zach. Even though I sent him and Corinne a family pass to the American History Museum and have apologized to him a million times, I still feel horrible about it. Then I told him it was that time of the month, which was a lie, but I think it made us both feel a little bit better about it. And so it's no surprise that when Greg Parks pops his head in the file room to see me the next Monday, I'm not very friendly toward him.

"How about getting out of here for the rest of the afternoon?" he says with a devilish smile.

"What's the catch?" I say sullenly.

"Does it matter?" he replies.

"No. I'll get my purse."

Greg looks snappy in a tan suit with a light blue shirt. He is carrying a briefcase and has a long black coat thrown over his arm. I'm suddenly extremely self-conscious in my drab brown skirt and cream-colored sweater. Images of Trina's trendy suits flash through my mind. I'll have to do a little clothes shopping next weekend. Did you hear that? I said shopping. And despite my mute telephone, I have maintained my anti-klepto streak. Ha! I was going shopping next week. Shopping. Now all I had to do was visualize walking up to the counter and paying for something like a normal human being. It's not logical, but the thought makes me a little nauseous.

"Are you okay?" Greg says, stepping toward me. I nod and move back. We're on Park Avenue, and Greg is trying to hail a cab. I still don't know where we're going and I don't care. Anything is better than filing. "Bloomingdale's," Greg says to the driver and I gasp. Greg laughs.

"Shopping?" I say. "We're going shopping?"

It's too early, I tell myself. I can't do it yet. Greg mistakes the anxiety in my voice for excitement and laughs even harder. Even the cab driver joins in, until I give him a dirty look.

"No, we're not going shopping. We're giving a training to the security guards at Bloomingdale's on loss prevention." I nod while visions of lipstick, scarves, and small purses float through my head.

"Can I ask you a question?" I say after a moment.

"Shoot," he says.

"Did you get the position on *Side Court TV*?"

Greg laughs, and I can't help but notice how kind nice his eyes are when he smiles. "Margaret running off at the mouth?"

"You could say that."

"Well I don't know yet, but I think I'm close. They're going to have another cameraman there today. It's between me and a female attorney with much better legs."

"I wouldn't worry about that," I say. "They hardly ever show their legs on that show."

"You're a fan then?" Greg asks.

I feel my face flush. I'd only started watching it after Margaret mentioned that Greg was up for the position. "I watch now and then," I say casually. "Mostly I'm working on my clocks."

Greg scoots closer to me. "You know I'd really like to hear more about that," he says.

Great. Me and my big mouth.

"What do you need me to do today?" I say, changing the subject.

"Nothing too difficult," Greg says with a wave of his hand. "Pass out handouts, things like that." I bite my lip, the phrase "nothing too difficult" caught in my throat. "What?" Greg says watching me intensely.

"Nothing," I say, then swallow and look out the window.

"No," Greg says. "That was definitely something. Tell me."

What was with this man? I turn to say something sarcastic, but I'm trapped by his piercing eyes.

"Well," I say honestly. "I didn't like the "nothing too difficult" bit. I told you—I'm more than just a file clerk. In fact, I could give a training on loss prevention."

Greg looks at me for a while and then turns and looks out the window. "I'm sorry if you thought I was implying that you couldn't," he says. "I just don't need much help on this—that's all."

"Then why am I here?" I demand, regretting it the second it's out of my mouth. Besides the fact that this man is my boss—if I didn't watch it he'd send me right back to the file room. Let's see. File room. Bloomingdale's. File room. Bloomingdale's. A monkey could figure that one out. "I'm sorry," I say. "I didn't mean it."

To my surprise Greg laughs again.

"What?" I say, my defenses popping back up.

"You're a horrible liar, Zeitgar," he says smugly. "I'm sorry? That's just the point! You're not sorry. So why act like it?"

I bite my lip again and scan the floor of the cab for pennies.

He puts his hand on my chin and turns me to face him. "I *like* that about you, Melanie. Haven't you figured that out by now?"

There is a crack in his voice, and our eyes lock way beyond the culturally appropriate three seconds. It's more like ten. I know because I'm holding my breath. I look away first and wonder how much he would like me if he knew the real me. The answer is not at all.

"Welcome back, shoppers," Greg says to the twelve Bloomingdale's security guards sitting around the sterile conference room. Nobody laughs so I laugh for them. It's a tough crowd. "First of all, let me introduce Bob." He turns to the cameraman in the corner. "Not to worry, he's here to watch me, not you." Again nobody laughs. Bob gives a weak little wave. "As you remember," Greg continues, "last week we covered employee thefts. Everybody's favorite subject, right?" He is greeted with thick, hostile stares. "Well," he says clearing his throat. "Today we're going to talk about nonemployee thefts. Shoplifters."

I shiver, but luckily no one seems to notice. The woman to my left removes her glasses, puts them on the table in front of her, and then places her hand over her eyes as if she can't even bear to look at him. "Last week I surveyed the store and found that you could use a few more signs," Greg lectures. "You need more in the dressing rooms and a few

more by the exits as well. Signs, cameras, sensors, mirrors.
All very important deterrents. But you—the security guard—
can go a long way in preventing a shoplifter. How, you ask?"
They hadn't, but politely nobody draws attention to that little fact.

"Talk to each and every person who comes into your
area," Greg lectures. "Make eye contact. Say hello. Pay
careful attention to the people who won't look you in the
eye. Also look for people with baggy clothes—and people
who are loaded down with shopping bags." Greg is speaking quickly now, as if trying to outrun their boredom. As an
actress I could have given him a few tips on jazzing up the
presentation, but he made it clear I was just a paper pusher.
As if reading my mind, Greg hands me a stack of papers to
pass out. I dutifully hand each zombie/security guard a
handout.

Ten Secrets Shoplifters Don't Want You To Know
1. They will rarely make eye contact with you. They
   want to be in and out without being noticed.
2. They will often be wearing baggy or layered
   clothes.
3. They may try to bring more garments in the fitting
   rooms than is allowed.
4. They—

I didn't mean to do it. I swear. I forget I'm sitting at the
front of the table where everyone can see me. I forget I am
supposed to be Greg's "assistant." Most of all, I forget that
nobody in here is accusing me of being a thief. But somewhere along the line, I start overheating. I can feel pressure
building up under my arms and a flush rise to the surface of
my face. My hands are shaking slightly, and I am suddenly,
inexplicably angry. These stereotypes are ridiculous. And
dangerous. Teenagers wear baggy clothes all the time.

Does that mean they were now going to be under automatic suspicion? And what about people who were shy, huh? Just because they don't want to make eye contact they're a thief? Ridiculous. I make eye contact with employees all the time. In fact they were the ones who were usually looking elsewhere. Chatting on the phone, reading, plucking nonexistent lint off the merchandise, gossiping. I could steal twelve tubes of lipstick while looking them in the eye. It was simply a slight of hand. In fact the friendlier I was, the less they would suspect me.

The security guards notice what I'm doing first. It starts when a heavyset woman in the back with curly black hair giggles. She turns and whispers something to the redheaded man sitting next to her, and they both look at me and laugh. Soon the whole table is snickering. At first, Greg beams. He thinks they're finally "getting him." Then he glances at me, and it's not until Bob zooms in with his camera and Greg's gaze drops to my hands that I realize what I've done. Tiny shreds of paper are scattered on the table in front of me. I am tearing Greg's handout to pieces.

My hands freeze mid-tear as I ponder the best course of action. Everyone is staring. I have to do something. "Confetti!" I shout, throwing it up in the air. Greg's mouth drops open, as do most of security guards' mouths. I jump up. "Are any of you paying attention to this?" I say, circling the table like a shark. "Or do you think you know it all already?" Heads turn and bob in every direction. The employees look wildly around for help like trapped animals.

"Melanie?" Greg says, stepping toward me.

"This man is a genius," I continue, shooting him a "back off" look. Bob has taken the camera off the tripod, and he's now following me on foot. It's too late to turn back now.

"I want to ask each and every one of you something, and I want you to be honest." I pause again and look around. "How many of you are bored to death?" I ask. Silence.

Then a few giggles. Finally a woman in the back holds up her hand. "I'm bored," she admits. I point to her handout. "Then rip it up," I say.

"Melanie?" Greg tries again.

I ignore him.

"Rip it up?" the woman repeats.

"Yes," I confirm. "I want anyone who is bored—anyone who has heard this crap a million times—to take their handout and rip it up."

Some of the guards reach for their handout and hold it at the ready, but nobody makes a tear.

"Now!" I shout. "Do it now."

"All right!" one man yells, and he begins to rip up his paper.

"That's it," I encourage. "Tear it to shreds!" Papers start ripping all around the table. We are having our own ticker tape parade. Greg has retreated to the back wall where he is standing with his arms crossed. He's not a happy man, but there is no turning back now. "Throw it. Throw it!" I shout. Paper swirls around us like snowflakes. It's our own winter wonderland, and soon every single handout is ripped to shreds. "So what's the point?" I say when most of the paper has settled down. "Why are we doing this?" Again nobody answers, but this time at least they're listening.

The woman who had covered her eyes is feeling around the table for her glasses. "My glasses," she says. "Has anyone seen my glasses?"

"Are they under the table?" I ask. She and a fellow coworker look under the table.

"They were sitting right here," she says. "They're brand new."

I walk around the table as several of the guards search for the glasses. "Right here?" I ask her, pointing to the table space in front of her. "In plain sight?"

The woman curls her fist and puts it near her mouth. "Yes, they were right here," she says. "I swear."

I point to the security guard sitting next to her. "Did you take her glasses?" I demand.

"Of course not," he says.

I turn on someone else. "How about you," I say, "you're sitting right across from her. Did you see anyone take her glasses?"

"No," the large black woman says carefully. "I thought she was wearing them."

I nod. "Who else thought she was wearing them?" I say. Greg's arms are still crossed defensively against his chest, but like the twelve guards, every fiber of his being is paying attention to me. A few hands shoot up in answer to my question. "Who noticed she wasn't wearing them?" I ask. The woman herself and a man next to her raise their hands. I point to him. "Now why would you notice something like that?" I ask him.

"Because she has nice eyes," he says, smiling. "I remember noticing her glasses when I first sat down—and thinking she has nice eyes—so when she took them off—"

"When she took them off," I finish for him, "it stuck in your mind."

"Exactly," the man says.

"So why can't you tell us where they are now?" I ask.

He shrugs.

"Is it because you were bored?" I prompt. "Distracted?"

He laughs. "All of the above," he says. I pace back and forth, gathering up speed. "Twelve security guards who know it all," I say. "Twelve of you bored to death—heard it all before—there's nothing this man can teach you, right?" I acknowledge Greg with a jerk of my thumb. "But not one of you can tell us what happened to this woman's glasses? How can that be? They were sitting right here—in plain sight—she swears to it." Several heads around the table drop, and people shift uncomfortably.

"And that, ladies and gentlemen, is the genius of Greg Parks," I say, pointing to him. I walk over to Greg and take the final intact handout from him. He has the look of a wounded animal that wants to trust you but is in too much pain, but I can't pay any attention to that now. "This isn't anything you haven't heard already," I say, waving the handout. "But this isn't the problem!" I shout. I reach into my blazer and pull out the glasses. Murmurs ripple around the table. I hold the glasses up in the air. "I am not the problem," I say, waving the glasses in front of them before handing them back to the grateful employee. I walk a few steps toward Greg and then wheel around and point at them.

"You are the problem. You're bored. You're distracted. You're making assumptions." I pick up the handout again. "Sure some thieves might wear baggy clothes—or carry multiple packages—but does that mean you take your eyes off the ones who don't? Anyone, anytime, anywhere. That's all you have to remember. It could be anyone, anytime, anywhere." I point to the glasses. "It could be me," I say. "It could be you."

Bob is the first one to clap. It's a bit muffled because he's trying to hold the camera at the same time, but soon the Bloomingdale's employees join in. I'm stunned. They like me. They really, really like me. I turn to Greg. He's looking the other way.

It's alarmingly quiet on the way back to the office. Greg and I travel down the elevator, through Cosmetics, past Menswear, and out to Lexington Avenue without a single word. After such applause I thought he'd be pleased. They were congratulating us and shaking our hands and vowing to have us back again. Bob was smiling! And this is the thanks I get? We're in a cab going six blocks or so back to the office and he's sitting in the front seat instead of back with me. Nobody sits in the front seat of a cab. I want to say something to him, but everything I practice in my head sounds wrong. Besides, he should be thanking me. I saved him in there. When we arrive at Parks and Landon, Greg pays the fare and waltzes into the building without as much as a backward glance. I run to catch up with him, and we ride the elevator up to the twenty-second floor without making eye contact. The silence is deafening.

"Greg," I say when he heads into his office without turning around. "Can I talk to you?"

"I think you've done enough talking for today. Don't you, Melanie?"

"Please. I'm sorry. You see it's a nervous habit—"

"No need to explain," Greg says, straightening up his desk with a vengeance. "You're a creative person. An actress. You thought you'd have a little fun at my expense."

"No, it's not like that. I—"

"You what?" He comes toward me. "You shredded my presentation in front of my clients. In front of the camera."

"I know."

"Why?" It's an excellent question, and Greg is really waiting for an answer. He's still looking at me like a wounded animal.

"I don't know. I—I just rip things when I get nervous. I didn't even know I was doing it." I move toward Greg. He doesn't step back. It's progress I think, and then he looks to the doorway.

"Is everything all right?" Trina calls from behind. "Shouldn't you be in the file room, Melanie?"

I look to Greg to shut her up. He turns away from me and goes back to his desk.

"Side Court is on line 1," Trina says.

Greg looks at me, and although it's slight, I catch it. Greg had looked at me and flinched.

"Melanie, I don't have anything else right now so you'll just have to stick it out," Jane Greer says when I call and ask her to take me off this assignment. "I'll let you know if something else comes up." It was the "if" that sent my warning bells clanging. She didn't say "when," she said "if." She was lying, and I could smell it. Dr. Phil says "You teach people how to treat you." I was teaching Jane Greer that I was a pushover. No more. It was time I laid down the law.

"Listen, Jane. You're not treating me fairly and you know it. I'm a highly skilled administrative assistant. I type ninety-five words a minute. I did you a huge favor taking this lame job for two weeks, and I've had it. I am not, nor will I be ever again, a file clerk. I'd rather be a cashier at the Quality Food Mart than stay here filing one more bloody minute."

Chapter
22

This is how I die. Jumping from a diving board on a warm summer day. I'm thin and tan and my legs are perfectly straight, pointing toward the sky while my head and hands reach for the water. Moments later I hit, but instead of the cool wet grip of the water, I feel crackly soft edges of a million $100 bills. I fold into them, gathering piles to my breast, inhaling the luxurious scent of instant wealth. That's the last thing I remember—pure joy—and then the sun dies.

Its rays are blocked by a figure standing on the diving board. It's a cat burglar from New Jersey. We stare at each other, and I'm just about to suggest a little romp in the dough when he pulls out a .22. (Could be a .21.) I'm still marveling at his baby blues when he cocks the pistol and a shot rings out. My last thought just before the bullet pierces my brain is that he's going to have a hell of a time getting my gray matter off all these Ben Franklins.

I have to be at the Quality Food Barf every morning at 6:00 A.M. I have to scan Cheez Whiz and Miracle Whip and fungus creams. I have to wear an orange and brown smock with a yellow pin that reads IF I DON'T SMILE, IT'S FREE!! I've only been here a week, but I'm only two scans away from seeing Jesus in a tortilla. I have to find another job, but I still can't go back to temping. After Jane Greer refused to give into my ultimatum (i.e., she hung up on me) I called her back and told her to forget it, that I was going to be touring Europe with my one-woman show. It was March. I wasn't due back until the end of summer.

I hadn't heard a word from Greg Parks. Not that I wanted to. But I did have moments (fleeting, of course) when I wondered what he thought when I didn't show up for work the next day. Or the next. I'm sure he didn't think a thing of it. They probably had a party to celebrate my absence. Psycho file boy and Wicked Witch of the West Side must have been beside themselves with joy. I, on the other hand, am the living dead.

"You look hung over," Murray yells at me the minute he shuffles in the Out door. Murray is the world's oldest bag boy and a self-proclaimed pervert. I don a fake smile and tilt my head. The first I learned from my mother, the latter from my childhood dog Sonny.

"Good morning to you too, Murray," I say civilly. He doesn't blink or move as he advances toward me with hairy outstretched arms. He is constantly trying to sneak a touch or a hug. I know you're supposed to be nice to the elderly, but I draw the line at dirty old men. I turn away and try to look busy. Since I have already punched in and counted my drawer, that leaves putting on cherry lip smack and turning my obnoxious yellow pin upside down.

"What is a pretty young thing like you doing here anyway?" Murray says. "I've got a granddaughter your age, and she works at a public relations firm. Pays $75,000. She doesn't even have tits like yours."

"That's nice, Murray. I have to open." I hurry away from him just as the corner of my upper left lip begins to twitch. Anxiety rising, I relieve some stress by pounding a roll of quarters on the counter. Murray approaches and begins talking to my aforementioned tits.

"I hear they're going to be hiring an A.M. manager when Hon Li goes off to grad school," he drools. "You should apply. The A.M. manager gets to open on Saturday. I open on Saturday."

I make the mistake of glancing up at him, and he winks at me suggestively. Hon Li is the only person in here I like, and I feel a stab of jealousy. "Hon Li is going to grad school?" I say more to myself than to Murray.

"Gonna study biomechanics," Murray answers. "Columbia University," he adds.

"I see."

"Bio-mech-an-ics. People like you and me don't even know what that means! I'm right, am I right?"

"I have to open, Murray."

"I'm right. Luckily there's this joint for people like you and me."

"This is a temporary job for me, Murray."

"That's what I said. Twenty years ago." He shuffles away chuckling.

I throw mental darts at his backside as I review the trajectory of my life. Who am I? An actress and a thief. Not a grocery clerk! This is just a temporary stop on my way to fame. Everyone needs a story of their struggles. Maybe I'll even confess my secret habit to the tabloids years from now when it's all behind me.

In fact, having a secret shame probably makes me a better actress. And although I try to keep my kleptomania and my thespian activities separate, there was at least one occasion in which there was a blurring of the lines. But I couldn't help it, and you would have done the same thing if you had to spend five minutes under the (hairy) thumb of Director Jeffrey Gray.

It was a nonpaying independent play staged in a video arcade in Hoboken, New Jersey. We could only rehearse after midnight when the racing and beatings and shootings had finished and the kids dragged their clawed hands and blurry eyes home for the night.

The play—written, produced, directed and ruined by Director Jeffrey Gray—was called *Stuff*. There were only four actors in the show—two materialistic young couples, secretly lusting after each other's stuff. The first act dealt with the accumulation of the couple's stuff, crotch-grabbing raving monologues from the men, and tearful confessions from the women in their skimpy lingerie. I was thrilled to be a part of it all. That is until Director Jeffrey Gray started throwing the stuff.

The first item to fly across stage during the middle of a lukewarm rehearsal was a silk potted plant. My character was in the middle of confessing her secret desire to put a fireman's pole in the middle of their living room when it whizzed by. At first, I tried to stay in character, noticed the plant and ad libbed, "There's certainly some breeze in here," like the consummate professional I am, and continued my monologue.

"I know it sounds crazy, Darren, but I want that pole to go through the middle of our bed and I want to slide down it and onto you each every morning of every day for the rest of our lives."

I was staring lustily into "my husband's" eyes when a lampshade struck me on the side of the head.

"What the fuck?" I said, breaking character.

"I'm not feeling it," Jeffrey shouted, leaping onto the stage and hopping around. "You're not making me feel it." And then all hell broke loose. He started throwing every single prop on the stage as I ducked for cover. "You have to desire the pole, Melanie!" he said with a rotary phone perched in his left hand. "Do you? Do you desire the pole?" I hid behind the couch as the phone was hurled like a football. "That's a wrap," Jeffrey said when there was nothing left to throw.

Actors and directors are emotional people. We all know that. You have to be moody and intense to be in this profession, and that night as I lay in bed, I realized that Director Jeffrey Gray was actually a passionate genius and that he recognized in me a smoldering, slumbering talent, one that could only be nurtured by having a prop or two thrown at my head. I had inspired insanity in him—and what actress could ask for more? I was going to throw myself into this role and live up to his every expectation.

The next day a wooden owl actually nicked my ear.

The day after that the gun struck me in the crotch. (If you see a gun in Act 1, it had better go off by Act 3!)

The third and final day a box of Wheaties hit me in the ass.

On the fourth day the props were gone.

I actually saw Jeffrey reach for a phantom throw pillow and go through the motions of hurling it toward me. He hesitated, cocked his head like a cocker spaniel, and pawed for the pillow again. Then his intense, beady eyes raked over the bare stage, which fifteen minutes ago had been crammed with stuff. I held my head as straight as I could with a gun down my pants and two lemons stuffed in my bra. In my mind's eye I could see every single place in the arcade where I had stashed his stuff. He should have never given us a fifteen-minute break. He and I held eyes like wild animals circling a wagon train, and I smiled.

"It's genius, Jeffrey, that you've decided our stuff should be symbolic manifestations rather than physical things."

Director Jeffrey Gray stared at me for a very long time.

"Thank you," he said.

"No, thank you," I answered. "I'm really starting to feel it."

My trip down memory lane rejuvenates me and puts me into a zenlike scanning zone. Before I know it, two hours have flown by and a man's hand is pushing a jar of olives toward me. It's a very nice hand. "Did you find everything you were looking for today?" I say politely.

He holds my eyes. "I found exactly what I was looking for," he says.

"I'm glad. Although I find it strange you had to come all the way to Brooklyn for a jar of olives. Too many martini parties in Manhattan?"

He laughs, and despite my wish to stay an ice queen, I join in.

"I couldn't find an olive branch, so this was the best I could do," Greg says, extending the jar of olives toward me.

"I would have preferred a chocolate bar," I say, taking the jar of olives.

"I'll remember that for next time," he says.

I'm trying to pretend that I don't tingle at the mention of a "next time," but I'm soon distracted anyway. The line is starting to pile up behind him. There is a little old lady with three cans of Friskies and a bag of peanuts and behind her a nervous-looking man in his twenties with a carton of cigarettes and behind him a housewife with a screaming toddler and a heaping cart of frozen entrees. Oh joy. "I have customers," I say quietly.

"I know," Greg says. "What time is your break?"

I meet him at a deli down the street and we sit by the window with cups of coffee. "How did you know I was here?" I ask after we finish the small talk. (Would you like coffee?/yes please/black?/cream one sugar/so—Quality Food Mart huh?/It's just until my clocks take off.)

"That's another reason I should apologize," Greg says in answer to my question. "I'm afraid I called your temp agency." Uh-oh. "And for some reason they thought you were in Europe doing a one-woman show."

I roll my eyes. "That's Jane for you," I say dismissing it. "She gets us all mixed up."

"That's what Trina said," Greg continues. "She insisted you couldn't be in a one-woman show—so I asked Trina if she could help me out. She got me in touch with your roommate Kim and *voilà*! I found the mysterious Melanie Zeitgar."

"I'm surprised you didn't just call my mother," I say sarcastically and watch in horror as he turns several shades of red in under a second. "You didn't," I say.

"I didn't," he confirms. "She called me."

I groan. "Not again."

Greg nods. "I'm afraid so."

"What did she want now?"

"She said she was putting together a calendar and wanted to know my birthday." I hung my head. "She didn't know you were no longer with working for me either. So I guess that's the third apology I owe you."

I drain the rest of my coffee and experience a sick enjoyment from the scalding that ensues.

"You should probably call them," Greg says sheepishly. "She was a little nervous when I asked if your clocks were taking off. I get the feeling they're not very supportive of your work. That's why they were so quiet when I brought it up at dinner too, huh?"

I nod and start to crush the paper coffee cup. Greg glances at me and I immediately flush, remembering the day I ripped up his presentation. "Look—"

"Listen—" we say at the same time.

"Okay, I'll look and you listen," Greg says, leering at me.

"Stop it," I say swatting him. "Listen—"

"Look—" We stop, laugh.

Greg gestures to me. "Ladies first," he says.

"I'm sorry about your presentation," I say. "I didn't mean to ruin it."

"Melanie, I overreacted. You were right. My presentation was a little—dry."

"No it's not—"

"Melanie."

"Okay. A little."

"And I should be thanking you."

"Thanking me?"

"Melanie, they loved it."

"They did?" I have to admit, a feeling of pride washes over me. They loved it. They loved me.

"I got the commentator position," Greg announces.

"That's great." I grab his hand. "Congratulations."

He's smiling at me and I'm smiling and him and he's yet to let go of my hand. In fact, he's putting his other hand over mine, sandwiching my little hand between his two very nice hands.

"I'm filming my first slot today. We're on live at 5:00. I suppose you'll be working then."

"I'll get my roommate to tape it," I say. "That's so great."

"You're great," Greg says. "That business about the glasses. I didn't even see you take them. I was like—what the hell is she doing—and then *wham*—here come the glasses out of your pocket. Risky. Risky little move, Zeitgar. How on earth did you do it without anyone noticing?" (Practice, practice, practice.)

"I just saw an opportunity and ran with it," I say.

The conversation is making me a little nervous so I casually try to pull my hand away, but Greg clamps down harder and won't let me go. "Melanie help me understand something here."

Uh-oh. I hope we're off the subject of my amazing, sneaky fingers. "Yes?"

"File clerk? Grocery clerk? Look, I'm not trying to insult anyone doing those jobs but—I just think you're capable of so much more."

This time I do manage to yank my hand away. "The file clerk was a favor to my agency. Nobody else wanted to work with the Wicked Witch."

"Who?"

"Trina," I say and then stop. Uh-oh. Did I just make a really big faux pas? Greg looks seriously pissed off. Oh God, maybe he really likes her. "I'm sorry," I say. "That wasn't very nice of me. Trina's great—it's just that—what? What are you laughing at?"

Greg pounds the table. "I love it when you lie," he says. "Your whole face gives you away." I swat him. "Really," he teases. "You should have seen the look." I glare at him.

"I did wonder why we were going through so many temps," he continues, ignoring my glare. "I thought maybe Steve Beck was putting the moves on all the girls." The thought of needy little Steve Beck putting the moves on me makes me laugh, and Greg joins in. We're laughing so hard that we're drawing dirty looks from nearby patrons. I don't care. I can't remember the last time I laughed so much. "Okay, so that explains the file clerk job," Greg says, "but what about this." He gestures to my obnoxious IF I DON'T SMILE, IT'S FREE! pin. "Why are you working at the Quality Food Mart?"

"Because of my clocks," I say. "I needed more time to work on them and since this job doesn't require much of me I've really been able to crank up my creativity." I don't like lying to Greg, but I can't help it. I really like the way he looks at me when I talk about my clocks. It's my moment to shine. Besides, I'll probably never see him again anyway, so why not leave him thinking I'm a creative genius. But maybe he doesn't think that. In fact I'm not sure he's even listening to me. He's still staring at my lips.

"I have a confession," he says.

Every nerve ending in my body comes to life. As long as they're not mine, I love confessions.

"I'm glad you're no longer working for me," Greg says.

What? Here I am miserable that I don't get to brush by him in the hall anymore or stare into his beautiful office, but he's thrilled I'm gone. Why did he have to tell me that? I bite my lips self-consciously. He reaches up and touches my mouth with his index finger.

"Don't," he says softly. I stop biting my lip, but he keeps his finger right where it is and then ever so gently begins trailing his finger along my upper lip and then my lower, tickling them softly like he's painting them. "I'm glad you're not working for me because now this is no longer sexual harassment."

"What's no longer—"

"Shut up, Zeitgar." Greg puts both of his hands behind my head, pulls me toward him, and kisses me. It is a full-on, fourth-gear kiss. Our mouths fit together perfectly, and even though it's new and exciting, it's also feels as if I have been kissing him all of my life. I could stay here and kiss him forever. I would have too, except for the fact that he's suddenly yanked himself away and is hopping up and down yelling, "Jesus. Hot. Hot." For a split vanity second I'm flattered, and then I notice the huge coffee stain on his crotch.

"Oh God!" I say as he hops around. "What can I do?"

"I'm just going to go to the little boys' room," he says, deflecting my hand as I reach toward his crotch with a napkin.

"Oh. Good plan." But I have to admit I'm disappointed. It was looking forward to squeezing the Charmin. Good God. I was going to have to change my underwear.

Since I have to get back to work and Greg has to go home and change his pants, our little make out session has officially been rained out. He walks me back to work holding his briefcase in front of his crotch. "I almost forgot," he says as we're in front of the store. "They're having a little party for me next Saturday to celebrate my new anchor position. I was hoping you could make it."

I take a few minutes to look like I'm considering in while inside I'm jumping up and down for joy. An invitation within seconds of kissing. This is very, very good.

"Next Saturday?" I say, pretending to ponder my social calendar. "I'll try my best."

"Great," he says, then kisses me on the cheek. "My place, eight o'clock." I'm about to say that I don't know where he lives when he hands me a business card with his address and phone number written on the back. Oh yeah. He's into me.

Chapter
23

The rest of the afternoon I'm on cloud nine. Even Murray doesn't bother me. So when my last customer of the day slides a small box toward me with shaking hands, I'm so caught in fantasy land (Greg and I are married and I've just told him I'm pregnant with twin boys) I don't even look up at her. I scan the item and throw it in a plastic bag. It's not until I say "Fifteen ninety-nine" that I make eye contact. She is a tiny thing with stringy brown hair and big hazel eyes. "What?" she says in a wavering voice that sounds like a flute warming up. "Fifteen ninety-nine," I repeat, turning the green digital numbers on my register toward her.

"Oh." She pours a pocket full of change on the counter and starts to separate it into piles of nickels, dimes, and pennies. Her fingernails are chewed beyond recognition. It is then that I glance in the bag and see the small square box. On the front is a picture of a woman holding up a plastic pee stick with an unbridled look of joy. The young girl before me wears none of the same anticipatory glee on her face as she counts her sweaty coins. She stops in the middle of counting and looks at me. "I didn't know how much they cost," she whispers.

It hits me like a brick—she never even considered stealing it. She has a sweat suit on too; her pockets would have hidden the box no problem. Murray and I were the only ones in the store—I was obviously not on the prowl for thieves, and Murray was in the back alphabetizing soup. A mixture of guilt and shame washes over me. I make a mental note to go back to confession. I take the box and quickly stuff it in the front pocket of her jacket. "Go," I say.

"Hey!" she cries. "What are you doing?"

I give her a look. Was she really that dense?

"Go," I whisper again, looking around.

"I'm not going to just take it!" she screams. "Who do you think I am?" She reaches in her pocket and waves the box at me accusingly. Just then, J.D. walks in the front door.

"Listen," I say to the girl, "you misunderstood me."

She plants her hand on her hip and waves the box again. "You put it in my pocket," she insists. J.D. looks my way.

"Morning," he says.

The girl looks at him and then back at me. "Maybe I should tell your manager about our little misunderstanding," she threatens. "You think just because I might be knocked up I'm a thief too?"

I have to do damage control quick. "Of course not," I say. "I'm paying for it. That's all."

"Why? Do I look like I want your pity? I don't want your pity. I just want . . ." She starts crying and her nail-bitten fingers curl up like claws. "I don't know what I want," she sputters.

"It's my fault," I say, patting her hand. "I don't pity you," I continue. "Look, did I smile at you?" I ask her. She looks at me as if I've gone mad. I turn my obnoxious yellow pin right side up so she can read it.

"Um—no?" she answers.

"I didn't think so," I say, ripping the receipt off the register and putting the pregnancy kit in a plastic bag. "If I don't smile, it's free!" I repeat, smiling.

She grabs the bag. "Thank you." She scurries away, leaving me three dollars and fifteen cents in neat little piles. I pocket it and cancel the transaction.

Doing a good deed for that girl felt good. Not smiling felt great. In fact, it made work kind of fun! What if I don't smile all day? People will get free groceries, I'll have fun and the time will fly! Hoorah! I'm not going to smile at a soul all day. In fact, I might as well scowl just so people really get what's going on.

Three hours later, J.D. Pinkett leads me to his office (a crate and card table in the back room next to the "Jane" and "John") and shoves a form my way with a crooked index finger.

"You're firing me?"

"You've had twenty complaints in the last hour."

I play with the dust on the table, stalling for time. "But they got free groceries," I say at last. J.D. pounds his fist on the little table. The legs bow out like a fawn standing for the first time, and the pen I'm holding smears all the way across the table.

"You're not supposed to give away free groceries!" J.D. yells. "That's going to come out of your paycheck."

"That's not fair. I couldn't smile. I have weak lip syndrome."

"Weak lip syndrome?"

"Yes. It affects the lip muscles. They become so weak it's physically painful to smile. That's discrimination you know! You can't discriminate against the weak lipped!"

"Does this syndrome also affect your attitude?"

Was this a rhetorical question? I pray to the *Saint of Divine Quips* for a snappy comeback, but nothing great comes to me. It makes me wonder if the Saints are on a continuous coffee break.

"Huh?" I manage instead.

"You told Bill Sorrenson his twelve-year-old son was in here buying condoms—"

"Which he was—"

"And you made Liliah Jones cry—"

"Well she is a little young for dentures—"

"You told Sarah Grimes that her husband was having an affair!"

"Why else would he buy champagne and lobster in the middle of a Wednesday afternoon?" It was all an act of course. As an actress, I couldn't just "not smile." I had to invent a character who couldn't smile, a character devastated by the state of the human condition. What are a few insults when you're getting free groceries? I'm constantly insulted, and I get zippo in return.

"What kind of person are you?" J.D. yells at me.

That one kind of stops me. Because normally, I'm a very kind person. In fact, I'm usually extremely sensitive to other people. I just didn't know what I was missing being so damn nice all the time.

"What's this?" I say, looking at the form in front of me, craning my neck to read upside down.

"Policy and procedure," J.D. says, pushing it an inch closer as if that will help the acrobatic angle at which I had to read. "Just in case you're thinking of going to the competition, it guarantees you'll protect our trade secrets," he adds. The competition? Does he think I'm going to make a beeline to the 7-Eleven? J.D. stares at me, squinting behind his thick black glasses, while I examine the form. He belches. "'Scuze me," he says, when I give him a dirty look. I sign my name, Melanie Zeitgar with the flourish and confidence of the unemployed.

"I won't be staying in groceries," I say, waiting for a response. Surely there would be some pleading, some words of encouragement, something along the lines of "Well, up until today, you were the best scanner we ever had and we hate to lose you but we knew we'd outgrow a talented girl like you" speech. Come on! But he just stares at me and I stare back at him until there is no choice. It's either kiss him or look away.

I look away and scan the edge of the table for dust. Good God, I am going to cry. No! I will not cry. I'm crying over a job as a grocery clerk? Jesus, no. Please no. I pray to the Saint of Dry Eyes and bite my lip. J.D. reaches over and pats my hand. I yank it away. "Do you want me to mail your last check?"

"Sure. No."

"No?"

"I'll pick it up." Or will I? Come back to this dump that won't even spring for a lousy good-bye cake from the bakery five feet away? Good luck, Mel. We'll miss you, Melanie. Kiss my ass. "Mail it."

"Mail it?" His pen bops up and down like the head of a jack-in-the-box. He adjusts his glasses and nods, demonstrating his condolence for my mental state, his patience for my neurosis. When I don't answer right away he leans forward and glares at me like a driver stuck in ten miles of traffic. I stand. *That's it, look tall.*

"Mail it. Definitely mail it," I say confidently. I should be waltzing out the door about now, but I continue to stand. My feet are stuck. I want to kick his crate out from underneath him. "Is that it?" I demand as if he were holding me there. *Please say something. Don't let me leave like this.* J.D. nods and points to the door. I feel like a jilted lover. On my way out I steal a can of Pringles, a pack of AA batteries, and a NutRageous bar. Once again I am a jobless, clockless thief.

I go to Central Park, sit on the bench, and daydream about shoplifting. I see myself taking the glowing blue topaz ring in Tiffany's, sliding my hands over imaginary cashmere sweaters, and quickly slipping Manolo Blahnik shoes into my oversized Gucci bag (also stolen). When I'm finished mentally shoplifting, I fantasize about taking things out of people's pockets as they walk by. I sit and wonder what secrets people have tucked away.

Does the man in the gray suit buying *Muscle Magazine* have a Kit Kat in his pocket or a business card for a call girl? Does the woman with the little black glasses on the bench next to me see a therapist? If not, she needs to—she's been crying for the last fifteen minutes. Or is she a plain clothes cop pretending to be living a subatomic life, changing colors under the surface like the autumn leaves in the west end of the park? And what am I thinking going out with Greg Parks? He helps prosecute shoplifters, Melanie. Do the math. Would he be smiling at you like that if he knew you were a klepto?

Not that he has to find out. I can just quit now and no one will ever know the difference. I lay the can of Pringles and pack of batteries on the bench. (I've already eaten the NutRageous bar.) There. I'm through shoplifting, and now I can date whomever I like.

I take the subway to Grand Central and wander around the lobby, stopping to stare at the large green clock hanging in the center of the station. It has huge brass hands and elegant roman numerals against a cream background. At night the face lights up. I imagine myself putting the pieces together and having an opening to celebrate my clock. I wonder what kind of clock I would make if I were given the gig to replace it. I picture a shoe clock—high heels clicking around the face like Cinderella. At the stroke of midnight, the ruby shoes would rub together and run off. I giggle to myself, silently laughing until I notice the man who was circling the clock and talking to himself has stopped to give me a wary look. When you frighten homeless, crazy people, it's time to get a grip.

Chapter
24

"Why are you smiling like that?" Kim is on the living room floor doing Pilates. I turn on the television. "Do you have to watch now?" Kim says. "I'm supposed to tune out the world and focus on my core."

"Are you sure you wouldn't rather watch my new boy-friend?" I sing. Kim stops scissoring her legs and sits up.

"Your new what?" she says.

"What time is it?" I say, turning on the television and flipping through the channels until I get to *Side Court*. And there he is. The camera likes Greg as much as I do. He is sitting at a table next to a pretty blonde. "Thanks again to today's guests and thanks to my new partner, Greg Parks, attorney and Loss Prevention Consultant. That's our show for today. Tune in next week when we'll be taking your calls live. I'm Deborah Green."

"I'm Greg Parks."

"We're *Side Court Live*."

"I missed it," I whined.

"Greg Parks? That's your old boss, right?" Kim asks, pulling her leg into the air.

"Old boss who just kissed me *and* asked me out for next Saturday."

Her leg stops moving. "Get out. Tell me everything."

I flop on the couch and hug the pillows. I start talking. It's a long time before I stop.

"Your boyfriend has nice digs," Tommy says to me as the cab pulls in front of the brownstone at Seventy-second and Riverside Drive.

"Don't call him my boyfriend in front of anyone," I warn him for the third time.

"Why again?" Kim says. "What's the big secret?"

"Look we've had one kiss, okay? I don't want to scare him off. Besides I don't want to give Trina Wilcox any more ammunition. So just act normal." Tommy rolls his eyes and gives me an air kiss.

I would know it was Greg's place even if he weren't standing in the living room and pictures of him weren't propped up on a little table in the hallway. It has the same welcoming feeling as his office. First of all, it is the type of space most people would kill for in Manhattan. It is an older brick building with old-world charm, dark wood floors and massive arched doorways. I stand in Greg's entry admiring the crown molding, high ceilings, and large windows looking out over Riverside Park. Ray's place had been like a college dorm, and I'm reminded again that I'm dating a man. After rolling their eyes at my warning for them not to drink too much, Kim and Tommy immediately go into social mode and start to mingle.

I note nervously that there are at least sixty people in here, including Deborah Green, Greg's co-anchor on *Side Court*. I spot Greg across the room talking to Steve Landon and Margaret Tomer, but I refrain from rushing him like a linebacker. My plan is to get a drink and mingle. I'll wait for Greg to come to me.

"It's quite a place, isn't it?" I turn to find Deborah Green next to me. I'm halfway through a martini and making eye contact with Greg across the room. I turn to Deborah, who I'm annoyed to find, is just as pretty in person as she looks on television.

"It certainly is," I say, looking around wondering if Greg is still watching me.

"I'm Deborah," she says, holding her hand out to me.

"I know," I say. "I'm a big fan." She laughs. She has a nice handshake. I glance at her smooth, ringless hand. "Is your husband here?" I ask hopefully.

"Oh, I'm not married," she says cheerfully.

"Of course," I say. "You have such an exciting career. You're probably not looking to be saddled with a husband and a couple of kids."

"I want three. Kids, not husbands. I just want one of those." She laughs gaily. I swallow the rest of my martini. "It's so hard to meet men in this city who aren't intimidated by my success." She's looking in Greg's direction.

"And yet you probably want to meet someone who has a completely different career," I say. "Imagine dating someone just like you. How boring would that be!" Her smile fades slightly. "Oh. I don't mean *you're* boring. I just meant— you know—it would be boring if you were dating—say— Greg Parks."

"Oh, I don't think that would be boring. Inappropriate perhaps, but not boring." She laughs again. "How do you know Greg?"

"Oh. I worked with him on a few presentations," I say. "Nice to meet you, will you please excuse me? There's a crab-stuffed mushroom over there with my name on it."

"Having a good time?" he says from behind me.

"You have a beautiful place," I say, turning to face him.

"You fit right in," Greg says.

"I caught the tail end of your show yesterday," I say. "You were great. And that Deborah. She's a beautiful woman." What am I doing? Now I'm going to sound insecure. Of course I am insecure, but I don't have to advertise it now, do I? But Greg is laughing. He moves a step closer to me.

"She is," he says. "But I've got my eye on a sexy artist." For a moment I'm thrown. I forget all about my imaginary clocks.

"Who?" I say harshly. Greg lets out a loud laugh. Oh. "Ha ha," I say. "Just kidding. You mean me. Right?"

Greg laughs again and then leans in and kisses me. I immediately pull away.

"What's wrong?" he says, searching my eyes.

"Someone might see us," I say.

"So?"

"So, I mean, don't you want to—you know—keep this quiet for now?"

"No. Do you?" He steps even closer. I giggle again. "It's not like you work for me anymore," Greg says. "So what's the problem?"

"No problem," I say. "It's just—this is so new—and you're in the public eye now, you know?"

"God I never even thought of that. I mean, I was in the public eye for the Anita Briggs thing—but that was just for a few months." He hasn't tried to kiss me again but we're still standing so close you could barely pass a straw between our bodies. "You might have a point."

"I definitely have a point," I say.

"Okay, Zeitgar," Greg says. "We can wait and see how this goes. But if it goes the way I hope, I'm not going to hide you for long." Oh God. And now he's doing the staring thing again. You know, the staring thing that makes me want to rip off his clothes and ravish him. "So we're sneaking around is that it?" he says in a low, sexy voice.

"Can you do that?" I flirt.

"With pleasure" he says. And sure enough, I feel his hand sneak around and land on my ass.

"Greg, there you are." Trina grabs his arm and practically

glues her breasts to the side of his body. "Melanie," she says. "I'm surprised to see you here. Did you know there was a rumor going around that you ran off to Europe to do a one-woman show? I'll have to call Jane and tell her it's not true. Because here you are. In the flesh."

I narrow my eyes. Was it just me or did she look at my thighs when she said that? "Here I am," I say. "Oh Greg," I add. "I have something for you," I say, taking the small package out of my purse and handing it to him. "Just to congratulate you."

"That's very kind of you," he says. I smile at Trina while Greg opens the box. He whistles when he opens it. "This is a beautiful watch," he says.

"I'm glad you like it. A client of mine gave it to me after I made a clock sculpture for his jewelry store. I couldn't think of a better person to give it to."

I can't help but be thrilled when Greg removes the watch he's wearing and replaces it with the Omega Seamaster. "Where is the jewelry shop?" he asks. "I'd love to go see your sculpture."

"Yes, where is it Melanie?" Trina echoes.

Oh shit. I pray to the *Saint of Removing Foot From Mouth*. Clean up on aisle three!

"Well unfortunately he went out of business. That's why he gave me the watch."

"He commissioned you to do a sculpture and then he went out of business?" Trina grilled.

"Yes, he did," I say. "He put a lot of money into renovating the place, but unfortunately he just couldn't make it work."

"Well what about your sculpture? Does he still have it?" Greg asks.

"Oh yes. He liked it so much he decided to keep it for his personal collection."

"God, I can't wait to see your work," Greg says. Trina's head snaps toward him and her eyes narrow.

"Will you two excuse me," I say. "There's a shrimp cocktail across the room with my name on it."

"Oh my gay God. Is he sexy or what?" I take a sip of the martini that really had my name on it and smile at Tommy.

"I think so," I say.

"So why are you letting the Wicked Witch crawl down his throat?" he says, poking me in the back.

"Ow. Stop it. Because I'm playing it cool," I say. "Besides, now that I'm dating a man and not a boy I don't have to worry about him falling for the likes of Trina." As soon as I say it, I realize it's true. Greg is a man. He's mature, funny, honest. He's perfect! "Will you excuse me, Tommy? There's an olive tray over there with my name on it."

The bathroom door is closed so I stand in the hall and wait. When I passed Greg in the living room he was talking to Deborah, but as I squeezed by his hand snaked out and held mine for a second so my jealousy was subdued. I'm in fantasy land (Greg and I are honeymooning in the South Pacific) when Trina walks out of the bathroom. I try to ignore her and shut myself in the bathroom, but she blocks my way. "Not so fast," she says. "We need to talk."

"I need to use the restroom," I say. "Would you please move?"

"You're kidding yourself if you think you can get Greg to notice you by throwing around expensive gifts."

"It was given to me—"

"By someone who bought one of your *clocks*. I just find it interesting that nobody has ever seen any of these clocks. In fact I think you're a liar. I wonder what Greg would say about you stealing my soap dish? Huh? Why don't I go over there right now and ask him what type of person would do that?"

"Shut up."

"Excuse me?"

"You heard me. I've told you a million times I had noth-ing to do with the disappearance of your soap dish. It's so ridiculous it's laughable. So if you want to go over there and make a deal of it to Greg, be my guest. Now get the fuck out of my way. I've had three martinis and I have to pee." But she's still not moving, and despite the adrenaline run-ning through my body, I'm not sure I'd win the wrestling match.

"Ray said the drawers in your kitchen are overflowing with brand-new things." I freeze. I had caught him going through them once early in our dating career. I had stashed a few things in there because my closet was getting too full. He had pulled out a stapler and a vibrator.

"What's all this?" he had asked.

"We're just prepared," I said, taking the items out of his hand and shoving them back in the drawers.

"For what?" he asked. "An office party or an orgy?"

"All right, look," I told him, lowering my voice. "I'll tell you the truth. It's Kim. She's an impulse shopper."

A woman hurries down the hall toward us, snapping me out of the memory. Trina moves over, but before I can make it into the bathroom, the woman cuts right in. I was going to have to do a little concentrating and a lot of squeezing to stave off the *Saint of Peeing Your Pants*. Damn Trina Wil(work for)cox.

"Leave me alone," I hiss at her.

"I'll give you until Friday to return my soap dish, Melanie," she warns as she walks away.

"And what if I don't have it?" I yell after her. She stops and turns to look me in the eye.

"Then you're going to wish you did," she says.

* * *

"Melanie. Hey. Melanie, where are you going?" I'm out of his place and halfway down the hall. I told Kim and Tommy that I was leaving but I insisted they stay and enjoy themselves. After all Kim was in the living room nose to nose with a good-looking cameraman, and Tommy was conducting an impromptu wine and cheese tasting in the kitchen. But after my run-in with Trina I felt like I was going to break out in hives. In fact the strangest thing happened to me in the bathroom—I had an overwhelming urge to take Greg's soap dish. It was the run-in with Trina—I had never even considered stealing soap dishes until she planted the stupid idea in my head. But of course I couldn't take his soap dish—it's a soap dish for God's sakes. Besides, I'm done stealing. I chose Greg, remember?

But the thought of never stealing again is making me a little nervous. Okay it's making me a lot nervous, and I don't know if this is a panic attack or what, but suddenly I feel really dizzy and I can't breathe. I'll just go home and steal something from myself. That should do the trick. Or I'll imagine myself taking something. That's it. Don't they say your brain doesn't know the difference between what it experiences and what it imagines? Oh God. Why didn't I think of that when I took the little wooden penguin from Greg's side table? I've never stolen from a friend before. Damn Trina Wilcox, this is all her fault. I'm going to have to return the penguin. Greg doesn't deserve this. I'm going to confess everything to him right now and graciously let him out of the relationship.

"I'm sorry," I say, pushing the button for the elevator. "I have to go."

He grabs my hand and pulls me around. "Hey. You're crying. Melanie, what's wrong?"

"My allergies are acting up, that's all—"

"Liar. Look at me. What is it?"

I like you, I say silently. I never thought a guy like you would fall for me. I'm a liar. I'm a klepto. You deserve so much better. If you stay with me I'm going to ruin your life.

"I'm just disappointed," I say.

"In me?" he asks quickly.

"No. No are you kidding?" I touch my forehead. "I'm disappointed because I really wanted to stay and I'm afraid I'm getting a migraine."

"Do you want to lay down in my bed?"

Yes. I want to roll naked in your bed. With Wesson Oil. And handcuffs.

"Thank you but I need to find a quiet place. I'm just going to go home." He looks so concerned that I decide not to make him any more miserable tonight. I step forward and kiss him. It was just going to be a little kiss, but it's like getting caught up in a wave. Passion overtakes us, and before I know it he has me against the wall, and if I do say so myself it's a little embarrassing how carried away we're getting. I mean, for a girl with a fake migraine, I'm doing pretty well. Looking back I must have heard her heels on the floor, after all the hallways in Greg's building are tiled. But she has to politely clear her throat—we're blocking the elevator buttons. Greg pulls back first and smiles at Deborah Green, who is looking at me with one eyebrow raised.

Needless to say, minutes later when the two of us are alone in the elevator, it's somewhat uncomfortable. We descend six floors in silence. It's not until the elevators open into the lobby and I think I'm going to get away with it that she says, "Doesn't seem so boring now, does he?" And. "Wait, you dropped your—penguin?"

Chapter
25

*T*his is how I die. On a gray cardboard table after a poker game. I'm the only female player, surrounded by burly, beer-drinking, cigar-smoking, betting men. I lay a royal flush on the table, and chaos erupts. The biggest of the three, Jerry D, reaches across the table and grabs me by the collar of my stolen cashmere turtleneck. "You cheating bitch," he growls, "that's your fifth royal flush." I smile, a smile that radiates victory. I'm still smiling when I see the knife, sharp and shiny. I can see my reflection in the blade. I look damn good in this turtleneck. Then the knife pierces my heart and my blood spurts across the table, splattering the cards, sticking to their beards, and drowning my royal flush in red. But I die smiling. I die a winner.

Okay. So I've had a few setbacks this week. In fact today I've stolen from three different stores. I took a butter knife from Fred Meyers, a porcelain clown from Bartells and a two-hundred-dollar butterfly pillow from the Silk Emporium. And yes, I snuck it out under my belly with a large coat on top. I guess my clock is ticking. Little did I know, all of them were.

Three times in one day, Melanie, I scold myself on the way home. Tomorrow you're going to march over to Fifth Avenue Temps and admit to Jane you were never in a one-woman show. Trina's already told her as much, so lying is out of the question. I could bring her chocolates and beg for a new assignment. Once I had a job again I wouldn't be so anxious. Greg had been calling me all week, and although I had been religiously watching *Side Court Live*, I had yet to call him back. It's not that I didn't want to talk to him, but I've decided I'd rather leave him thinking I'm a creative artist than date him and let him discover I'm a neurotic klepto. Kim is trying to call me, but my cell phone is beeping low battery. At least she's home. Maybe I can talk her into the Three Musketeers. *I have everything under control. Things are going to be just fine.* I had forgotten all about Trina's warning.

So I'm shocked to find her sitting in my living room with Greg Parks and a strange man. "There she is," Kim says, pointing to me with false bravado. It's meant to warn me, but against what I haven't had time to figure out. I'm trying not to stare at Greg because he looks downright sexy sprawled on our Ikea couch. His legs are spread apart—a far cry from the composure he normally displays. It hits me on a sexual level. I can feel my clitoris come to life. I bite my lip and turn away in case he can sense my reaction. From the way he's staring at me it may be too late.

Maybe I shouldn't be too quick to break up with Greg. After all, I still haven't had last-person sex. This is not a good thing. So what about it? Should Greg Parks be my last-person sex? Before I have time to steal another glance at him and assess his last-person-sex potential, the stranger in our midst stands.

I peg him to be in his early forties. He's sporting a soft gray suit and is disgustingly tan. House in the Hamptons type. Tommy walks out of the kitchen with a tray of cheese and crackers. "There she is," he parrots with the same forced enthusiasm with which Kim greeted me.

"What's going on?" I say, forcing my lips to spread into a smile.

The tan man stretches out his hand and opens his mouth, revealing perfect laser white teeth. "Your ears must be burning," he says. "I'm Josh Hannigan."

I absentmindedly rub my ear while stepping forward to shake his hand. It's firm, yet soft. He's never done a day of manual work in his life. "Nice to meet you," I say, politely clueless.

"Trina's told me all about you," he says. He still hasn't let go of my hand. Should I take mine away first? Is there a hand-shaking hand disengaging societal norm that I'm not aware of? Isn't handshaking usually quick? Now he's patting my hand. Am I supposed to pat his hand now? I can't take it anymore and I pull my hand away. That's when I notice Kim. Her eyeballs are going crazy trying to catch my attention.

I slide my eyes over to Trina. She has a huge shit-eating grin on her face. Greg Parks is smiling too, but his seems friendly. I start to feel queasy, and I'm suddenly very conscious of the fact that I have a pillow under my coat. I yank it out in front of four pair of eyes. "Baby shower game," I say laughingly. Kim gives me a look. I'm going to have some explaining to do. Thank God I dropped the butter knife and the porcelain clown on Broadway.

"Won't you sit down?" Josh Hannigan says, gesturing to an open chair. As odd as it is to have a stranger treat you like a guest in your own home, I sit like a good little girl. Kim is still trying to bore subliminal messages into my brain with her eyes. I shoot her a dirty look. When nobody speaks I swallow and cross my legs. Why did Tommy have to put the plate of cheese out of my reach?

"So," I say with a nervous laugh. "You're probably wondering why we're all here. I know I sure am." One side of the Ikea couch erupts in laughter. It's Greg. He has a great laugh. I appreciate the audience, and his last-person-sex potential goes up exponentially. I throw him a grateful glance and he holds my gaze until I look away.

"Let me get right to the point," Josh Hannigan begins. "First I have to tell you that you're lucky to have a friend in Trina Wilcox." A pinball rolls around in my gut. For the first time since I entered this den of lions, I dare myself to look at Trina. She meets my gaze head on as if she's been waiting for it. She's smiling. In fact she looks downright thrilled. She's also sporting a Donna Karan pantsuit that makes her look thin, which she already is, so it's just ludicrously redundant. I turn back to Josh Hannigan.

"Oh, Trina is something all right," I say. "What is she up to now?"

"Melanie," Trina pipes in. "Can you believe *the* Josh Hannigan is sitting in your living room? You must be bursting." *The* Josh Hannigan. *The* Josh Hannigan. My eyes drift up and to the right. I glance at Kim. She taps her watch.

"It's—about time," I stammer. The right side of the Ikea couch erupts in melodious laughter again. After a moment *the* Josh Hannigan himself joins in with a slightly less melodious laugh of his own. Kim glares at me and moves her eyes to the far wall. I follow her glance to a cuckoo clock I bought at an estate sale. It doesn't chime anymore because I ripped the head off the bird one night while waiting for Ray to call. Every hour on the hour its headless bird body continued to taunt me that he wasn't going to call. The bird deserved it. Was Kim trying to tell me I was about to get my head ripped off here?

"I have all the time in the world," Josh Hannigan is saying. "In fact I was hoping you would take us to your studio." I was still smiling and nodding. He might as well have been an alien saying "Take me to your leader."

"My studio?" I repeat.

"Yes," Josh Hannigan says. "I don't usually do this—but Trina has been so insistent that I see your clocks."

"You're kidding," flies out of my mouth before I can stop it. Trina laughs with glee.

"I'm sure you know what an honor this is, Melanie," she says. "Don't all new artists dream to be noticed by the Hannigan Galleries?" Hannigan Galleries. Hannigan Galleries. That does sound familiar.

"Of course," I murmur.

"I love the look on your face," Greg says happily. Does this man know sounding like a naïve Boy Scout chips away at his chances at last-person sex?

"Well?" Hannigan says. Now that the formalities are over, he's all business. "I only have one opening left for my new artist feature of the winter show. And of course there are no guarantees you'll even make the first cut. But again— Trina has been very persuasive." Josh Hannigan turns his smile on Trina. They exchange a lingering look giving me a good indication as to what those "persuasions" entail. I can't believe the woman is willing to whore herself out just to get back at me. So be it. Two could play this little game. Trina Wilcox was not going to get the better of me. If nothing else, I could out act her any day of the week.

"I'm flattered," I say, stalling for time. "But I must admit I'm a little confused. Trina has never seen my work," I say, looking directly at her again. "She's taking quite a risk."

"Risk is what drives me," Hannigan says, bouncing a wedge of pepper jack cheese in the air like it's a sailboat flailing in the ocean. "Shall we go?"

"Right now?" I squeak.

"Is there a problem?" Trina asks. She stares at me while I flounder. She is setting me up like a croquet set on an English lawn. I take a deep breath and conjure up one of my old acting teachers, Junie Wilder. She was a frail woman in her sixties with hair as black as night and large red glasses that would be incredibly fashionable even today. She was always hunched over her metal folding chair with a Kool cigarette wedged in the left corner of her mouth. Actors feared her. They also adored her. Every time you finished a scene, there would be a horrible moment of breath-holding frozen silence as thirty pairs of frightened eyes fastened on Junie Wilder, watching as she pondered your worth as an actor and—by association—a human being.

Once she deemed you'd suffered enough, Junie would shift in her chair, exhale cigarette smoke out of the right side of her mouth, and say in a gravelly voice, "I don't believe you." I spent the year desperately trying to make Junie Wilder *believe* me. Today I was going to have to deliver a performance worthy of that believing. My motivation is simple. If I really were a clock maker and a famous gallery owner wanted to see my work, I'd be thrilled. I would be honored. "This is incredible," I say with emotion. "I'm thrilled. This is quite an honor, Mr. Hannigan—"

"Call me Josh."

"Josh. This is a dream come true."

"I can't promise anything," Josh says, crossing his legs.

"It's an honor just to be nominated," I say idiotically.

"So," Trina sings. "Why don't you take us to your studio?"

Take us to your studio. I nod and smile. I pray to the *Saint of Meteorites* to send one crashing through the ceiling. Trina stands, and Greg and Josh followed suit. Kim, Tommy, and I continue to sit.

"Melanie's very shy about showing her work," Kim ventures. I smile gratefully. Everyone should have friends who are willing to lie for them.

"Melanie's clocks are amazing," Tommy says, not to be outdone. "I've seen several of her pieces."

Shut up, Tommy, I plead silently. Shut up.

"You have?" Trina demands. Her shit-eating grin is now gone.

"Of course," Tommy lies. "They're incredible. They make me think," he adds, tapping his forehead dramatically. "Not that they're not also aesthetically pleasing. They are. They're beautiful. And functional."

Okay Tommy. That's enough.

"Some chime," he continues. "Some," he folds his arms and chews on his lip, "don't," he concludes. Well done.

"You see," Josh Hannigan says brightly. "You have a following already. That kind of talent excites me. Shall we go?"

"Yes. Shall we?" Trina sings.

I spring out of my seat. "Yes, let's go," I say with as much enthusiasm as I can muster. "As long as nobody minds a trek to New Jersey," I shout. "I know it's not as trendy as a Manhattan studio," I continue, "but the locals in Keansburg really love to have artists in their midst. You know, it kind of takes the sting out of the smells and sounds of the factory. Of course I have to warn you, my section used to be a meat-packing plant, so it gets a little chilly in there. Not to mention the smell. But it helps the inner workings of my clocks if it's a little cool. And with all the energy you'll burn trying to keep warm you won't even notice the smell. Are you driving Josh, or should we just hop a bus? If you let me drive, we can make in an hour tops."

Josh Hannigan glances at his watch.

"Unless you'd rather just have a look at my portfolio," I add politely. "We could meet for dinner and go over my work."

"Now that's a woman who knows business," Josh says. "I'd love to have dinner and go over your portfolio. We'll save the trek to—Keansburg, did you say? Another time."

"Why don't we all meet at my place?" Greg chimes in. "I've been dying for an excuse to entertain."

"You just had a huge party last week," Tommy points out.

"And there's still plenty of food left over," Greg says. Tommy wrinkles his nose.

"Sounds great," I say, hoping nobody will notice that my voice is cracking like a prepubescent boy.

"Perfect," Josh says, heading for the door. "See you tonight, Melanie," he says over his shoulder. "I can't wait to see those clocks."

Josh Hannigan takes his leave, but Trina and Greg remain rooted to our living room floor. Trina is obviously not happy about the turn of events.

"Josh Hannigan is an extremely influential man," she says. "He's not someone you want to play with."

"What are you talking about?" Greg asks.

I find his naiveté endearing and repulsive at the same time.

"He wouldn't take kindly to being played for a fool. If there's anything you'd like to confess, I'd do it now," Trina continues, ignoring Greg. "Before it's too late."

"There is something," I say pleasantly.

"I thought so," Trina says, sitting down. "What is it?"

I smile. "I have to confess I never thought you'd be willing to help me out like this," I admit. "I don't know how to thank you. I really think this is going to be my big break. Now if you'll excuse me," I say to her gaping face, "I have work to do." I excuse myself and make a dramatic exit into my room, but not before I hear Greg exclaim, "Hey, I have a penguin exactly like this."

When I venture out half an hour later, I find Greg still taking up residence on our couch. There is no sign of Trina, but Kim is perched on the other side of Greg, yakking away in a giggly voice. Not just any giggly voice either. This was her man-catching voice. "You're still here," I say to Greg while glaring at Kim.

"It's my fault," Kim giggles. "I begged him to tell me about *Side Court TV*."

"Kim tells me you've been watching the show," Greg says.

"Absolutely," I say. "You're doing great."

"Do you mean it? Because if I'm not, give it to me. I love her honesty," he says, turning to Kim. "Melanie tells it like it is. It's so refreshing."

"Like an icy peppermint patty on a windy tundra," Tommy says from the kitchen.

"Do I get a sneak peak at your portfolio?" Greg teases me.

"I'd like to take a look too," Kim says.

"Me three!" Tommy yells from the kitchen.

"No sneak peaks," I say. "We'll see you tonight Greg. I'm kind of in work mode right now."

"Are you sure?" Greg says. "I thought I could stay and give you a ride over."

"I'll keep him company," Kim says, sliding onto the couch.

I want to yank her blonde hair until she's bald. Friend or not, I'm not leaving the best last-person-sex candidate I've ever had alone with her. "Please. I'll never be able to focus if I know you're out here," I say to Greg in my sexiest voice. It works. His face lights up and he even blushes.

"Okay. Get to work, sculptress. I'll see you soon."

I kiss him passionately in front of a dumbstruck Tommy and Kim. I take advantage of their shock by ushering Greg out the door and then locking myself in my room before I have to answer any questions. I glance at my watch. I have four hours to put together a portfolio. I pray to the *Saint of Putting Off Your Homework Until the Night Before*. Help me, I beg. Help me.

Chapter

26

I owe my life to Adobe Photoshop. I carefully copy pictures of clocks from the Internet and save them to wonderful, beautiful, glorious Photoshop. So far I have a grandfather clock, a large round Ikea clock, a square clock, and a cuckoo clock (head intact). I plan on using these prototypes and, with a little help from my friend Photoshop, creating at least three different designs for each type, giving me a total of twelve clocks.

Kim and Tommy are in the kitchen playing with the blender when I hurry in to show them my first Photoshop clock sculpture.

"Hmm," Tommy says, sucking on a mudslide. "Do you really think that's going to work?"

I don't answer—I'm stung. I love the picture. I had taken the large round Ikea clock and painted the inside red and the outer rim orange.

"I call it Fire Clock," I say proudly. "Do you think I should find a picture of a hunky fireman and paste him at noon?" I add.

"Definitely," Tommy says, lighting up. "Definitely." He smiles at me and then glances at Kim. They share a pitiful glance that you would accept from siblings taking care of a psychotic aunt.

"You go ahead and do that," Kim says. "We're going to stay in here and get really drunk."

The hours fly by. I was really getting into this. I had the Fire Clock with a hunky half-naked fireman at noon, a Cinderella clock with a pair of high heels that I envisioned tapping together at midnight, an Eiffel Tower clock, a tie-dye clock, a coffee table clock, a clock with steel pipes arranged underneath it like stairs, a clock where the hands were flowers, a cuckoo clock with a barking dog instead of a bird, a pair of clocks—one male, one female—like the symbols on a public restroom, a tango clock, and an art deco clock. God I was good.

"Hmm," Tommy slurs as he turns the pages of my portfolio.

"They're great," Kim shouts. She always shouts when she's drunk.

"What do you think?" I press Tommy. He cocks his head and stares at them again.

"They don't look real," he finally admits.

"That's just because you know I did it in Photoshop," I sulk.

"I know. You should make some kind of studio background," Kim shouts.

"I see what you mean," I say. "Hold that thought."

So it's back to the cutting screen. I find pictures of an artist showcase with concrete floors and a black cloth background. I superimpose my clocks onto the background and once again print twelve copies in different sizes. Just for fun, I print a few in black and white. Despite the criticism from the drunken peanut gallery, I think I'm in business.

"We're pissed," Kim says, interrupting my work.

"I know," I reply.

"You'll be too drunk to go to dinner," I admonish.

"She doesn't mean pissed drunk," Tommy laughs. "Although we're that too. She means pissed, pissed off. We're pissed off!" he slurs.

I take my hand off the mouse and swivel my chair to face them. "Okay," I say slowly. "What are you so pissed off about?"

"You!" Kim yells. "You haven't even thanked us for sticking our necks out for you."

"Yeah," Tommy chimes in. "Why are we lying for you?"

"Because you're my friends?" I suggest.

"Don't you forget it," Kim shouts at me.

"I won't," I say and turn back to the computer. Tommy puts his foot on my chair and whirls me around again.

"Not so fast, Missy," he drawls. "You have some s'plainin' to do."

"Yeah," Kim joins in. "Why does Trina think you're a clockmaker?"

"You explain something to me first," I say. "Why did you assume I wasn't?"

"Huh?" Tommy says. "You two just assumed I must have lied to Trina about the clocks, right? You didn't even consider the alternative?"

"What alternative?" Tommy asks.

"That I'm a clockmaker," I retort. "I could be, you know."

"I think I'd know if you'd been trekking out to a meat-packing plant in New Jersey to make clocks," Kim says. "Wouldn't I? I mean we're friends, aren't we? You tell me everything, don't you?"

I pray to the *Saint of Little White Lies* before answering. "You're right," I say, reaching out for Kim's hand. "Of course I tell you everything."

"But you didn't tell me this business about the clocks?" Kim counters.

"What else haven't you told us?" Tommy asks.

"Nothing," I assure them. "It's just a little white lie that got out of hand that's all," I say. "If you're pissed at anyone you should be pissed at Trina. She's the one making a whole mess of it."

"Then what about *this*?" Kim says, whipping out my stolen silk pillow.

"What?" I say, stalling for time. I'm waiting for her to nail me on the baby shower comment, but instead she says. "It's a two-hundred-dollar pillow, Melanie."

"Mama Mia!" Tommy says. I really wish he would stop attending Broadway musicals.

"So what?" I say. "I decided to splurge."

"With what?" Kim says, shaking the pillow at me. "You still owe me seven hundred dollars for the rent."

"I'm still expecting checks from Fifth Avenue and the Food Mart," I say.

"But Melanie," Kim protests, "if you're so broke—"

"I charged it okay? It's for you."

"What?" Kim looks horrified.

I feel bad, but it doesn't stop me from going on. "Didn't you wonder why I was sneaking it in under my coat?" I say.

"I wondered," Tommy says helpfully.

"It's for me?" Kim says, straightening it out from the shaking she had given it. "It's beautiful."

"I guess I could have just asked for a cash advance from my credit card instead of buying it," I say. "But I intend on paying you back everything I owe you, and in the meantime—I wanted to thank you."

"I'm so sorry," Kim says. "Tommy, we owe her an apology."

Uh-oh. I glance over at Tommy who is gesturing wildly at Kim to shut up.

"We have to tell you something but you have to promise you won't get mad at us," Kim continues.

I sigh. I hate this type of setup. "Ask away," I say, crossing my fingers underneath the desk.

"Promise first," she demands.

"I promise I won't get mad," I lie.

A moment goes by. Kim and Tommy look at each other. Finally, Tommy nods his support. "We were starting to think you stole Trina's pearl soap dish," Kim says, looking me in the eye. I look at the floor. I look at the beheaded cuckoo clock. I fold my arms. "You're mad," Kim says. "You promised."

"I'm not mad," I answer in my mother's voice. "I'm just very disappointed."

"You did lie about the clocks," Tommy says quietly. "And Trina's convinced."

"So you believe her," I say coldly. "You believe Trina Wilcox over me."

"We didn't say that," Kim says. "But the truth is—we've never even asked you. Maybe it was a stupid prank, you know. You were pretty drunk the night of the party."

"Maybe you don't even remember taking it," Tommy adds. "Maybe we could look for it."

I propel myself out of my chair and throw my arms up in the air. "Why don't you frisk me," I shout. "Maybe I'm hiding the soap dish on my person. Better yet—let's search the house. Where could it be?" I march over to the couch and start pulling off the cushions. "Everything ends up hiding in the couch cushions," I say dramatically. "Maybe the soap dish is under here."

"Melanie," Kim says.

"No, no, no," I continue. "You two take the kitchen. We're going to turn over every inch of this place until we find that soap dish!"

"Stop it," Kim says. "Just stop. Look, Melanie. Why don't you just buy her another soap dish? Tell her you're sorry she thinks you stole it and you want to bury the hatchet. I mean, keep the price tag on it and all so she'll know you just went out and bought another one—but at least she'll know you're making a sincere effort."

"Why do you care so much about her soap dish?" I yell.

"I don't," Kim says. "But Melanie, you don't know Trina like we do. Once she digs her claws into something she doesn't stop until she scratches it to bits. And right now, she's got her claws into you!"

"You're like a scratching post!" Tommy chimes in, scratching the air with his hands and arching his back.

"Where am I supposed to buy another soap dish?" I shout. "She said it's a family heirloom. Besides, if I buy her a new one it's like admitting I stole it. And in case my sarcasm flew right by you—let me tell you—just this once in no uncertain terms. *I did not steal her pearl soap dish.* I don't know why she thinks I did—but obviously if she could prove it she would have by now. And you should be horrified—absolutely horrified—your friend is being accused of such a ridiculous thing. It's a soap dish for God's sakes. Maybe if she were accusing me of stealing something of real value I'd be a little more forgiving. But a fucking scum-filled soap dish? She has some nerve."

"We're sorry," Kim says. "Mudslide?"

I shake my head, gather my clock pictures, and disappear into my room. Tommy and Kim stand outside the door for a few minutes murmuring encouraging words, but I ignore them. I'm too busy imagining all the ways in which I could kill Trina Wilcox with a mother of pearl soap dish.

Tommy and Kim are passed out in the living room by the time I sneak out of the house for Greg's dinner. I drape blankets on them and feel a twinge of guilt when I notice Kim is hugging her new silk pillow. I silently vow to make it up to her by really buying her something in the near future. I have my clock pictures arranged in a thin black photo album; it is the closest approximation of a portfolio I could come up with in this amount of time.

I put on a black cocktail dress that accentuates my breasts and hide my hips and thighs underneath a black spandex body shaper. It takes me twenty minutes to pull them on, and they make me walk like a nutcracker, but they're worth it for the good three inches they suck in. I'd have to find a way to stand most of the evening however, since sitting would be extremely uncomfortable. I resent thin women every time I pull them on, and the resentment makes me want to eat a dozen Krispy Kreme donuts. I guess I still have a ways to go on that front. But the results in the mirror are that of a beautiful, artistic woman. No one will ever know that underneath the façade lies a curvy thief. I step out the door to hail a cab.

Jimmy whistles at me as I step outside. "Thanks, Jimmy," I say smiling, wishing he would go away. I don't want to answer a million questions about where I'm going and I don't want to have to think about how long it's probably been (if ever) that Jimmy has cleaned up, dressed up, and gone out for the evening. I don't know why the world is so unfair and I don't know what to do about it. But Jimmy is smiling anyway, and he doesn't seem to be fixating on his plight the way I am—in fact his grin is ear to ear. "You lookin' good Ms. ZZZZZZZZeitgar. You lookin' real good."

"Thanks, Jimmy," I say again. "It's just a business thing."

As I'm making a mental note to bring him home dinner, a large white limo pulls up to the curb. "That your ride?" Jimmy asks, heading to the passenger door.

"No," I say, reaching out to stop him.

But Jimmy goes straight to the door and pulls it open. The back seat is empty except for a dozen roses lying on the black leather seat. "Melanie Zeitgar?" the driver says.

Jimmy winks at me and motions for me to get in.

"Are you sure this is for me?" I ask the driver.

Jimmy pats his pocket. "It better be. Your boyfriend gave me a Ben Franklin just to open your door."

"My boyfriend?"

"Tall blond guy. Real style. Don't screw this one up," he adds with a wink. I slide across the cool leather seats while Jimmy shuts the door. For a moment I allowed myself to enjoy it. For a moment I pretend I deserve it.

By the time I reach Greg's Upper West Side digs, I am thirty minutes late. The door to his place is propped open and I step inside.

"I suspected as much," I hear Trina Wilcox say. "Some people even think Melanie is making up this whole business about clocks."

"Now why would she do that?" Greg shoots back. From my vantage point in the hall, I can see Greg and Trina sitting opposite each other on his couch drinking martinis. Trina has her legs crossed and she's hiked up her dress as far as she can without being completely naked.

"Melanie has always been—shall we say—the wild card of the group. I'm not saying she's pathological or anything—and I'm sorry to say this—but she isn't always truthful. In fact—oh, never mind, I shouldn't say anything."

"You might as well," Greg prods. "Finish what you start."

Trina doesn't need any more encouragement. "She claims to be an actress but she's never in anything—"

"Wasn't she in *Everything in the Garden*," Greg interjects. I could kiss him.

Trina furrows her brow and ignores him. "She tags along with Kim everywhere she goes—and she's a bit of a man chaser."

"Oh really?"

"A friend of mine went out on a couple of dates with her. He says she became a little stalkerish."

It takes everything I have not to storm in there, throw myself on her, and pummel her to death. I have to hold onto a side table in the hall to keep myself back.

"And then there's the night of my party," Trina says.

"I hope you aren't going to bring up the picture of her and the spoon thing again," Greg chuckles. "She blames you for that, you know."

"Which is ludicrous," Trina says. "A lot of people think she staged the picture herself for the attention. I'm telling you she's not stable. No, I'm afraid she may have taken something of mine. Something very valuable."

"That's a pretty serious accusation," Greg says. "If you're spreading that kind of statement—"

I wait for Trina to elaborate about her precious soap dish, but to my surprise she cuts him off.

"Never mind," she says "I'm just saying I'm not surprised she's standing us up—"

I am just about to break up this little "trash Melanie" party when I notice Trina's purse sitting on the console table beside me.

Chapter
27

I don't steal anything from her purse. Shame on you if that's what you're thinking. But I do take a little peek, and her cell phone is right on top. It is turned on and I simply it off. Then I slip into the hall and make a phone call of my own before making my entrance.

"Trina," I say a few minutes later, bursting in the room. "You're here."

Trina looks at me like the Grinch caught stuffing the tree up the chimney. "Of course, I'm here, Melanie," she says like she's just swallowed a snake. "We were starting to wonder where you were."

"I wasn't," Greg says coming over and planting a kiss on my cheek. As usual he smells incredible. He's wearing dark navy pants and a light blue shirt that really brings out his blue gray eyes. I try not to stare at him. "You look incredible," he says, openly staring at me. I beam, and it takes all the maturity I have not to stick my tongue out at Trina. "What would you like to drink?"

"Surprise me," I say, holding up my portfolio. "I have reason to celebrate."

"Are those your clocks?" Greg asks, excitedly flipping Trina a small glance. She looks away. "Kim's been trying to reach you on your cell phone," I say, turning to Trina. "In fact you're the reason I'm late." Greg, who is halfway to the kitchen, stops to listen. Josh Hannigan enters from the opposite side of the room. "I guess your manager has been trying to reach you all evening," I continue. "Something about a last minute photo shoot. I guess the model they had hired has food poisoning and can't make it—"

"But I have my cell phone with me, Melanie," Trina says. "No one has called. Greg, did you hear my phone ring?"

Greg shakes his head.

"All I know is that Kim called me in a panic saying that your manager has started calling her. Maybe your phone is turned off."

"My phone is not turned off," Trina huffs. "I'll show you." She marches into the hallway and grabs her Prada purse. There is a moment of silence as she pulls her cell phone out and stares at it.

"Oh," she says. "Did you touch my phone?" she asks Josh.

"Why on earth would I touch your phone, darling?" he says with a trace of annoyance.

She bites her lip and turns the phone back on. "I'll check the call log," she says. We all wait while she frantically pushes buttons on the phone. "My manger hasn't called," she says. "Just one unknown caller."

"Maybe that's him," Greg suggests.

"Her," Trina corrects. "And this came in hours ago." She tosses her phone back in her purse. "Besides, Melanie— why would that make you half an hour late? I warned you not to blow this. Josh Hannigan is a very busy man. It's not polite—" She is interrupted by her cell phone playing "Fur Elise." She gives me a dirty look before answering. She knows this is my fault somehow but just can't quite put it together for the jury. I smile and catch Greg watching me like a hawk. I turn back to eavesdrop on Trina's call. "Hello? Hi Kim. You're kidding. Yes she did—but—but I don't have any calls from—no, no, I don't want you to do it. If they asked for me, they asked for me. I'm sure they won't mind if I leave. Okay. I'm going to call for a town car—call me in ten with the address, okay?"

Trina snaps her cell phone shut and rushes up to Josh. "You can handle this alone, right? It seems there's a fashion show—not an audition, Melanie—and one of the runway models has a huge zit—not food poisoning, Melanie—this makes much more sense. My manager wouldn't even bother calling me—it's the director of the fashion show. Anyhow, I'd better run—it's the easiest money, and sometimes they let you keep the outfit too. I'm sure you can check out Melanie's *portfolio* without me." And just like that, the Wicked Witch of the West Side is off. I send a quick prayer of gratitude to the *Saint of Friends Who Lie For You*. Kim Minx had definitely won immunity.

Greg brings me a dirty martini. "Are you hungry?" he says, standing inches away from me. "I'm good in the kitchen," he adds when I don't answer right away.

"I'm sure you are," I flirt. "But I'm too nervous to eat." The funny thing is—I'm telling the truth. A part of me is dying to see what Josh Hannigan thinks of my clocks. I have to admit, I'm pretty proud of what I had come up with. If I'm chosen for the opening, I can figure out a way to make the actual clocks, can't I? I could certainly come up with something. Maybe my days of temping are over. Maybe all the lies I've told are going to come to fruition! I'll be an overnight success. Ray and Trina will be devastated by my talent, and Ray will grovel, he'll literally beg me to come back to him. I'll say no, of course, but that won't stop me from relishing a little groveling.

"I can't wait to see your work," Greg says. "If they're half as beautiful—" He doesn't get to finish the sentence. Josh plops himself down on Greg's soft leather sofa and claps his hands like a bossy seal.

"Let's get started!" he commands.

Now that Trina is gone he's all business. I glance at Greg to see if he was saying what I thought he was saying just a moment ago. Was he calling me beautiful? Either I had misunderstood or Josh had broken the spell, for Greg is now seated in a matching leather chair, no longer even looking at me. I sit down next to Josh and gingerly hand him my portfolio.

The silence that follows while he turns the pages of my portfolio is excruciating. Greg and I lock eyes, and he motions for me to breathe. I empty the martini and hold it up. Greg suppresses a laugh and whisks my empty glass into the kitchen. Twenty seconds later I am holding a new one. He is definitely going to be my last-person sex. Maybe even tonight. Josh is going through my portfolio a second time. I take this as a good sign, but if he doesn't say something soon I am going to bust. I cross and uncross my legs. I breathe. I take another sip of my martini. If I wasn't mistaken, this one is a little stronger, and I ponder the possibility that Greg is trying to get me drunk. I sneak another peek at him. He is watching Josh with the same intensity that I was. Finally, Josh Hannigan closes the portfolio and sets it on his knees.

"Melanie," he says after a dramatic pause, "is this truly your best work?"

His tone is that of a teacher speaking to a naughty student. I can see the proverbial red pen hanging above my work waiting to scratch it to pieces with its bloodlike ink. I am suddenly, inexplicably hurt and defensive of my made-up work.

"I picked out my favorite pieces for you, Mr. Hannigan," I say politely.

"I don't begrudge your pieces might have an audience,"

Hannigan says. "But my gallery certainly isn't the place for them."

To my horror, I feel tears forming in my eyes. I bite my lip and nod.

"Maybe you can suggest another forum," Greg says softly to Josh Hannigan. I detect a warning in Greg's voice—he doesn't want Josh to hurt my feelings, and this makes me want to cry even more. "Perhaps—Kmart?" Hannigan says.

I leap to my feet.

"Kmart?" I cry. "You must be joking."

Josh stands as well. "I wish I was," he says. "Your pieces are amateur at best—at worst they are a commercial hoax—something you'd find at Kmart for the kids to take back to their dorms. Frankly, I'm shocked you would waste my time with this dribble. You are no artist, my dear. Unless of course you add the word *con*."

I stand there like a mute fish—mouth open, fins fluttering, eyes tearing.

"You've no right to talk to her like that," Greg says. "Art is subjective."

Josh hands Greg my portfolio. "It is indeed, Mr. Parks. And judging from your works of art—you and I share the same taste. Why don't you tell me what you think of her *work*."

I grab my portfolio from Greg just in case he's tempted to look at it and hug it to my chest. I couldn't take any more criticism at the moment.

"What's the matter? You don't want his opinion?" Josh badgers me. "Artists must have thick skin if they're to survive."

"Even if her work was not my taste," Greg interrupts, "I would never speak down to her the way you just did. Quite frankly, I'd rather have a hundred of her worst pieces of art than one of your best. Now do you need me to hold open the door for you or can you manage to squeeze your big head out all by yourself?"

"How about another martini?" Greg asks the minute Josh leaves. He bounds toward the kitchen before I can even answer. It's strange. Josh Hannigan was right. I am a con artist. I even conned myself. I almost believed I was really a clockmaker. Why else am I so hurt? I'm pathological—there are no clocks and I am no artist! I wanted Josh Hannigan to see something behind my Photoshop clocks; I wanted him to see my soul. I wanted somebody to finally validate that I had something special to give. I wanted someone to tell me I'm not just taking up space in this crazy world, this rotating planet, this insane island of Manhattan. I wanted to be someone.

My whole life I've felt five steps behind the ones who've "made it." Sometimes I think I'd rather be like my college roommate, Jo Ella, who was perfectly content to look pretty, paint her toenails, and read fashion magazines. She didn't sweat about what she wanted to "be" when she grew up. She didn't have little pinpricks of anxiety that she wasn't doing enough with her life—she didn't keep checklists—there was no "to do" list. She didn't continuously start another diet, another life improvement plan, another self-help book, tape, or hypnosis program. And the bitch of it is, she seemed perfectly content. And me? I'm controlled by fear.

Fear. And it's not fear of failure—it's fear of happiness. I don't think I'd know what to do with it if I had it. It's not that I'm a walking rain cloud either—I'm just moody. Introspective, impulsive, adventurous—intense. How can I be all of these things and not be an artist? Sometimes I'm extremely positive. But happy? Happy as in—content? Just the thought of it makes me nervous. This is why I need something—like bad boys like Ray or clocks or a good clean lift to carry me through the dark periods. I just need enough to make it to the next day and the next and the next. Until. Until I'm no longer here. I'll be in the big out there where I imagine everyone will be able to see how incredible I am without requiring proof. My life has been like a perpetual drivers ed course and I still can't parallel park.

Not that I'm too sure what the afterlife is like. Maybe it's just like earth, in which case I'd better start doing something with my life. I can't believe I'm thinking about all this crap. I haven't indulged in this type of introspection since—well, since my "stint in the psyche ward." Do you see how long it's taking Greg to make my drink?

"I made this one a little stronger," he says, finally entering the room and handing it to me. "I didn't think you'd mind." And then he gives me one of those earth-shattering smiles. God, this man is good looking. And funny. And successful. And bright. And he has good taste in furnishings. He's everything I'm not. Which is why this is never going to work out. But that doesn't mean we can't have last-person sex. And I can't think of a better night than tonight. He sits next to me on the couch and we toast. He smells so good all the time, and before I can censor myself I blurt out, "What is that cologne you wear?"

For a moment, he's taken aback. I rewind my comment in my mind and realize it sounded less like a come-on and more like an interrogation. "I love it," I say quickly. "You always smell so good." He's turning a little bit red now and hasn't moved back toward me. I'm an idiot. "Sorry," I say. "I have a thing about smells." I have a thing about smells? Who says that? This is why I'm a twenty-nine-year-old grocery clerk. I'm an idiot. "Good martini," I say, changing the subject. Greg puts his drink down on the coffee table (shiny bamboo), leans back on the couch, and turns toward me. I realize I've never seen him like this: relaxed, unprofessional. "You should put that on a coaster," I say. "It's a beautiful table."

"Thank you. You're right I probably should, but I'm too stubborn."

"Too stubborn to use a coaster?"

"Exactly," he says.

I don't know what to say so I take another sip of the martini. This really is strong. He's definitely trying to get me tipsy. "Okay, I give," I say. "What do you have against coasters?"

"They remind me of my childhood," he says playfully.

"Beaten by coasters, were you?" I say happily. The martini is giving me a warm, floaty feeling. Greg laughs, which makes me float even higher. I would tell him he has a nice laugh, but I don't want another compliment fiasco so I keep my mouth shut.

"Not quite," he says, still chuckling. "But my mother was a neat freak. Plastic on the couches, china we couldn't use—she even wrapped our toothbrushes in Saran Wrap."

"You're kidding," I giggle.

"I'm not," he says. Then, "I love your laugh."

I feel my face flush, and a warm feeling buzzes over me like a swarm of bees. "Thanks," I say. I love yours too, I add silently. "So you won't use coasters because you're still rebelling against your mother?"

"Exactly. I still have dreams where I rip off all the plastic in the house. And of course we were never allowed to have a dog. God forbid. I've always wanted a dog."

"Why don't you get one now?"

"I've thought about it, but I'm hardly ever here." We stop talking and stare at each other. I want to jump him right here and now but the *Saint of Women Who Chase Men and the Men Who Flee From Them* stops me and instead I get up to examine a large black-and-white photo on the wall. It is a night scene of Times Square in the 1940s. The picture was taken from above, looking down on boxy black cars, men in long coats walking hand in hand with women in pillbox hats, and taxis lined up in front of the theatres waiting for the Saturday night show to let out. At least I imagine it to be Saturday night, for the photograph gives off the sense of life and excitement you can only get from a Saturday night in Manhattan.

"Like it?" Greg asks, coming up behind me.

"I do," I say, my voice catching in my throat. He is so close that if I back up even an inch, we will be touching. I can feel my breath quicken, and every nerve in my body is on edge with anticipation.

"Do you see the dog in the corner?" Greg asks.

"Where?"

His arm shoots around my waist as he points to a corner of the photo. Sure enough, sitting on the steps of a deli is a dog lost in the shadows.

"See," Greg says. "I have a dog after all."

"That's great," I say.

He pulls his hand back, trailing it gently across my hip as he does. "It is, isn't it?" he asks. His voice is softer, slower and his breath is labored. I give up all hesitation and step back and into him. His arms immediately circle my waist, and I rest my arms on top of his. We stand there like this looking at long-ago New York from the New York of now. And finally (finally), he kisses my neck. I lean my head back to give him full access. I love how strong his hands are and how firm his lips feel as they trace along my neck. There's nothing worse than mushy lips. But his are perfect. I spin around and we lean into the kiss at the same time. While we kiss he maneuvers me to the right of the photograph and gently pushes me against the wall.

He puts his hands on either side of me and pulls back. We hold eye contact. I had forgotten how intimate it could be to look into someone eyes like this. We make out like our life depends on it. Then he takes my hand and leads me away from the wall. Last-person sex here I come! So you can imagine my surprise when he takes me to the front door. For a split second I think he wants to do it in the hallway, and I'm more than willing to oblige. But instead of pushing me on the floor and pouncing on me, he opens the front door.

"You're showing me out?" I squeak.

"I have to," Greg says. "I'm sorry."

Oh *Saint of Getting Me All Hot and Bothered and Showing Me the Door*, you must be joking. What is this? A cold feeling prickles over me like ice being poured into a hot bath. "I need my purse and—portfolio," I say, stumbling back to the living room.

I will not cry, I will not cry, I will not cry. Maybe Trina put him up to this. Maybe this was one big joke. Let's humiliate Melanie's clocks and withhold last-person sex. That will show her. I grab my purse and portfolio and will my hands not to shake. I focus on the front door and walk toward it with my head held up, trying not to wobble, begging the *Saint of Tears* to keep mine at bay at least until I'm past the doorman and well into the streets.

"Thanks for the martinis," I say in a fake bright tone. Just open the door, just open the door. I reach for it, but Greg's hand shoots out and shuts it.

"Hey," he says. "Look at me."

I can't. I was doing so well not crying—but the dam wasn't going to hold if I had to look at him.

"Look," I say, staring at his door. "You made a mistake. It happens. Let's just forget all about it."

"Is that what you think? That mid-kiss I changed my mind about you and now I'm throwing you out?"

"Well isn't that exactly what you're doing?" I say.

He turns me around to face him and gives me a little kiss on the nose. *I'm not a fucking Eskimo*, I want to say but don't.

"I'm sorry to cut us off like that," he says. "But it's a good thing. If you stay—we're going to wind up in bed."

Well of course—that's usually where last-person sex takes place. Although there are a number of spots in this great pad that we could use. It doesn't have to be the bed-room. I still didn't understand the problem.

"And?" I say, looking at his lips.

He groans and kisses me again. The doorknob is jammed into the small of my back, but I don't care. "I want to take it slow with you," he says, pulling back again.

"Then make love to me slowly," I tease. He bites my neck in response. "Fast is good too," I groan.

He laughs again. "No. We're waiting. We haven't even been on a proper date yet."

"You fixed me several nice martinis," I say. "And your place is much nicer than most bars I've been in."

He laughs. "I mean it, Melanie. I want to do this right. How about Friday night? We finish taping the show at five, so let's say seven?"

I search my brain for an excuse. I open my mouth to protest. Then I shut it. Because it dawns on me that this is a very adult way to handle this. It dawns on me that he really likes me and wants to treat me like a lady instead of a horny teenager. Ray would have never behaved this well—neither would eighty percent of the men in Manhattan. (I'm betting the percentage is higher but I don't want to sound bitter so let's just stick with eighty and give the other twenty percent the benefit of the doubt.)

"I'll take that as a yes," Greg says. "And I'd like to see that some day," he adds, pointing to my portfolio. "When you're ready."

I open my mouth to tell him there are no clocks—that it was all a plot to get even with Trina—but then decide against it. I'll tell him later. I don't want anything to ruin our moment. Greg walks me out to the street where the limo is waiting to take me home. The red roses are still here. I gather them in my arms, lean back in the seat, and replay my kisses with Greg all the way home.

Chapter

28

T *his is how I die. Babysitting the boys. They escape from my mother's yard and sneak in an open window at the house next door. I run across the driveway and peer in. All five of them are inside Mrs. Halliday's house, somersaulting over a suede couch, leaving little dirty paw prints everywhere. One of them sinks his teeth into a couch pillow and starts whipping it around like a dead chicken. "Bad dog. Bad dog!" I scream from the window. He stops for a moment and looks me dead in the eye before returning to his pillow massacre. Fuck you bitch, he says with his eyes. Fuck you. To my horror a second dog sinks his teeth into pillow number two. "No! Bad dogs!" I scream into the window. "Bad dogs! Down. Get down." It's no use; the canines from hell aren't paying any attention to little old me. I'm going to have to crawl in through the window and stop them before they start licking her good china.*

I drag a couple of trash bins underneath the window and crawl on top of them. They wobble (like Weebles) but they don't fall down. Must work out more, I think as I struggle to pull my body up over the windowsill. I'm halfway through when the window slams down on my ass. The dogs parade toward my dangling torso, their little butts wagging in ecstasy at my plight. I reach my hand in and try to swipe at them, but my fingers barely graze them. I flail my

legs and arch my back like a seal in an effort to open the window.
I'm trying not to give the dogs the satisfaction of seeing me cry, but
it's too late. Large tears of humiliation form in my eyes, distorting
my vision and making the boys look like white, fuzzy ghosts.

"Help!" I yell into the house. "Is anybody home?" Then I see the
mess. Drawers are overturned, silverware is splayed all over the
floor like a metallic jigsaw puzzle, and broken glass forms a glit-
tering, jagged path to the kitchen. Suddenly I love the boys like they
were my own and I'm afraid for their safety. "Shh," I whisper.
"Shhh." Remarkably (as if feeling my newfound love) they stop yip-
ping, lie down at the foot of the window, and look up at me like
kindergarteners at story time. But I don't have time to read them a
story. If the burglar is still in the house, surely he's heard us by now.

"Go get the phone, boys. Get me the phone!" One of them yawns
(as if to say "this story sucks") but none of them budge. The only
sound is the ticking of a clock above the mantle. I realize it's my
Fire Clock, and I swell with pride. Then I hear footsteps from
above. The boys start yipping again, running in circles like rhyth-
mic witch dogs. A drum beats inside my chest as the footsteps near.
Thud, thud, thud, down the stairs. Someone is whistling. A mo-
ment later, a large figure appears at the foot of the stairs.

He is dressed head to toe in black, and several bulging pillow-
cases are slung over his shoulder. In his left hand he is carrying a
large, emerald sword. The boys barrel toward him in a frenzy,
tripping over each other to be the first to reach him. Bloody dumb
dogs sucking up to a cat burglar. The whistling stops, and the cat
burglar leans over and pats each one of the dogs on the head. It's as
he's standing back up that our eyes connect across the mangled
floor. I try not to look into his eyes, but I can't help but notice—he's
the best-looking thief I've ever seen. He has an incredible body and
piercing blue eyes that stare out from beneath his black ski mask. I
can't help but imagine his gloved hands dragging along my stom-
ach down toward—

"Well what do we have here." He says it as a statement, but at
the same time he's searching my eyes as if for an answer. His voice

is muffled but pleasantly deep. "Please," I croak. "I didn't know you were here. I just came for my dogs," I say, lowering my eyes again. He looks at the dogs and then back at me. Then he looks toward the kitchen. "Why didn't you just use the back door?" he says. I look to where he points, and damn if the back door isn't wide open. "So that's how they got in," I say, and he laughs. I laugh too, and despite the fact that I have to pee like a racehorse and I may soon have my throat cut by a burglar with a sword, I'm feeling pretty giddy. "What's your name?" he asks as if we've just met in a bar.

"Melanie Zeitgar," I say, remembering from somewhere you're less likely to be killed if they know you have a name. But, Jesus, did I have to give him my real one? "Melanie Zeitgar," he repeats. "What's yours?" I try. He laughs again. "Funny," he says. "I steal too," I hear myself saying. Now why the bloody hell did I say that? Am I flirting? What the hell is the matter with me? He looks at me for a few moments and then laughs. "Sorry but we're not hiring at the moment," he says. I can't see his face but I know he's smiling underneath the mask. "Oh, I don't do houses," I reply. "Shoplifting is my thing."

I don't know how he takes this. His back is to me now. He's heading toward the back door. He stops short of exiting. "Crime doesn't pay," he says good naturedly. "Then why do you do it?" I call after him, wishing he wouldn't leave. He doesn't turn back around, but his shoulders lift in a shrug. "Because I can," he says at last. Then he gives me a wave over his shoulder. "Well, good luck to you, Melanie Zeitgar," he says. And then just as he reaches the door, he suddenly whirls around, points the emerald sword toward my heart, and charges. My last thought before I'm skewered like a pig is that he never even asked for my phone number. The next day Jane Greer from Fifth Avenue Temps reads about my death in the New York Times. *The headline screams, "Melanie Zeitgar Murdered By Cat Burglar While Dog Sitting." "I knew it," she whispers to no one in particular. "I knew that bitch was never in a one-woman show."*

I should have never picked up the phone. First of all, it was the middle of the day and I should have been pounding the pavement looking for work. Instead I was lying on the couch with a latte, watching *Side Court* and circling audition possibilities in *Backstage*. There was a small part of me fantasizing about my upcoming date with Greg—but I was trying to keep it at bay. After all, I reminded myself, this was going to lead to nothing more than last-person sex. "Hello," I say distractedly into the phone. Judge Jeannie was coming on next and I didn't want to miss it. She was the hottest new thing on Court TV. She was much racier than Judge Judy but classier than Jerry Springer. I figured I might as well watch some trash television, otherwise what's the point of being unemployed?

"Melanie?" Oh no. Now why didn't she show up on caller ID? "Uh, hi, Mom," I say. "I was just running out the door."

"What happened to your job at the law firm, Melanie?"

"Mom, I can't talk about that right now—"

"What did you do?" she demands. I squeeze the phone as tight as I can. She always assumes I'm the one at fault. Unlike a court of law, in my family I was guilty until proven innocent. "I didn't do anything, Mother," I say.

"So you still work there? Because Zachary told me—"

"It was a temp assignment, Mom. It ended. That's all." There is silence at the other end of the phone. Talking to Mom was like dropping a penny down a long, dark well and waiting painfully for it to hit bottom.

"I thought this one was permanent," my mother says in her all-knowing voice.

"Well it wasn't," I snap. "I'm sorry," I say after another long moment of silence. "I'm just as frustrated as you are, Mom. I'm going to call the temp agency today and see if they have another assignment for me." Lies, lies, and more lies! Unless my one-woman show was canceled. Maybe

Europeans weren't ready for the razor sharp wit of Melanie Zeitgar. Maybe— "Well I have a job for you," my mother says. Oh no. "I don't need—"

"We need you to babysit the boys this weekend. Richard and I are going to a retreat in the Catskills," she says.

I groan. "This is not a good week—"

"Melanie, I need you this weekend. You promised you'd babysit the boys for us. You need to get out of that city anyway. It will be a nice little break for you. You can take some time and think about your future. Maybe you'd like to see Dr. Phillips while you're here?"

I bang the phone on the end table five times. "Sorry, Mom," I say, "there's something wrong with this phone."

Dr. Phillips was my counselor during my stay at the psychiatric hospital in an undisclosed Connecticut location. This was years ago, mind you—but I was never going to live it down.

"I ran into him the other day," my mother lies. "He said he'd like to see you again—just to catch up—see how you're doing."

"I don't need to see Dr. Phillips, Mother," I say through clenched teeth. "I have unemployment problems—not psychiatric problems." Her silence conveys her disagreement. I could tell her I have a date with Greg Parks on Friday night and she would fall all over herself to find someone else to watch the boys. Worse yet, she may even invite him to spend the weekend with me. I would never be able to have last-person sex with Greg with my mother involved. "I'll be there Friday," I say in the end. It was the only way to end the conversation.

The boys were born with silver bones in their mouths. They were only to drink bottled Evian water. They were fed at seven, noon, and six; brushed at one and three; and bathed before bed. Playtime was at nine, three, and five. I was to take them for three walks and one wagon ride. I study the list while my mother runs around throwing things into her suitcase at high speed. Richard is waiting out in the car with the engine running. Mom quickly kisses me on each cheek. "Phone numbers are on the fridge. We'll see you by Tuesday at the latest," she says, scurrying across the kitchen floor toward the door to the garage. It takes me forever to react.

"Tuesday?" I say before she makes her escape. "I thought it was just until Sunday." From the look on her face, she had anticipated my reaction and has practiced her reaction in the mirror. It was definitely a fake surprised look, eyebrows tilted slightly up, mouth open at the perfect angle. Her expression is a perfect mix of silly-me-I-forgot-to-tell-you and how-can-you-be-so-selfish?

"Is there a problem?" she says with a forced smile as if I were an impolite houseguest. "Do you have plans? A job interview perhaps?" I open my mouth to tell her I needed to work on my clocks, but of course there were no clocks and didn't need to make things worse by bringing up the fake ones.

"No problem," I say. "I'm just worried about the boys. Have they ever been apart from you for that long?"

Her face softens and she wiggles her fingers at me. "Just follow the list. I'm sure they'll be in good hands," she says unconvinced. And with that, I'm left alone with the boys.

The dogs are running in mad circles around my ankles. Five of them. Jesus. Why didn't they just make it six and have a canine Brady Bunch? Yip, yip, yip. They are chasing each other through my pant legs—as one goes under, another goes around—and I receive several nips from the excited bystanders. Should I take them out into the yard? It wasn't fenced, but surely they wouldn't run away. Or would they? I realize I don't know anything about these buggers or how to care for them. Did I need to take them on a leash? I couldn't believe my mother hadn't left me better instructions.

"Who wants to go outside?" I say in my best baby voice. I figured I'd venture out a few steps onto the lawn and see how close they stuck to me before searching for their leashes. They all had color-coded collars, and I reviewed all five names. Julius, red. Hamlet, blue. Richard, yellow. Malvolio, green. Skylark, orange. I didn't know which was which. "Hamlet!" I yell as a test. All five dogs bounce toward me, yip, yip, yip.

I sit on the front porch and watch them play. They sniff hedges, pee on flower beds, and dig like mad fiends in the dirt. Mom was right about one thing. It felt good to be in the suburbs, breathing fresh air. I indulge myself in a fantasy about Greg. I wonder what our life would be like if he and I married, moved to the suburbs, and had kids. Maybe even that dog he's always wanted. I can't believe it, we haven't even been on our first official date and I'm planning our wedding. But I can't help it. My stomach is tingling at the thought of our unborn children. God they would be beautiful. I close my eyes as the boys tumble all over the yard.

Maybe I could convince Greg to come out and spend Sunday night here. I like the thought of the two of us playing house, parenting the dogs. It would be good practice for us! I would be playful and spoil them; he would be gentle, yet firm. We would make up games and run around the yard until we exhausted ourselves. That night we'd curl up in front of a fire with the dogs and smile at each other with satisfaction. "You're going to make an incredible mother," Greg would say. We'd kiss. "And you're going to make an amazing father," I'd say. "What are we waiting for?" the Greg of my imagination says. "Let's practice." I giggle, eyes still closed, sunshine kissing my cheeks.

Greg, Greg, Greg. Greg with whom I have a date at seven o'clock tonight. Which means I'll have to be on the five o'clock train. I have it all figured out. I would simply sneak the boys onto the train (they're small) and take them back to the city. We'd spend the weekend at my place. Kim was off on some modeling gig (bitch) so they'd have the run of the house. I hug my knees and take a deep breath. I have a mess of butterflies in my stomach at the thought of seeing Greg again. I stretch and open my eyes. The boys are gone.

"Hamlet? Julius? Richard the Third?" I run around the yard peering in bushes. "Skylark? Come on, boys, come on." I can't believe I've only been here a few hours and I've lost them. I'm going to have to canvas the neighborhood with fliers and post their pictures on milk cartons. I pray to the *Saint of Lost Dogs* for help. Please, please just let me find them. I'll love them like they're my own. Just as I'm about to really freak out, I see a flash of white out of the corner of my eye. It's coming from the driveway. The boys are lined up in front of the garage like little toy soldiers. Mom and Richard left the Honda for me. The boys want to go for a ride. I run up and hug them one by one. Thank you, thank you, thank you. "Want to go for a ride, boys?" Yip, yip, yip. I didn't screw anything up. "Let's go. Let's go get a treat."

The women at Petco go crazy gushing over the boys. They take turns picking them up, kissing them, and then passing them down the line. It's fun to be so popular, and I'm actually having fun shopping for them. I didn't plan on stealing anything, honest. But I've dressed the boys in little matching outfits that Corinne made them, and can I help it that their little pockets are perfect hiding places for biscuits, rawhide bones, and plastic Shrek chew toys? Three of the dogs are in the cart, two of them in my arms. I place goodies in their pockets without even thinking about it. I'm working fast and furious, my stress building as their little outfits start to bulge.

That's enough, Melanie, I tell myself. I need a large carrying crate to take them back to the city in. It won't fit in their pockets so that I will have to buy. And since I'll be paying for something, it's more like getting a discount than stealing. Besides, the biscuits are complimentary, aren't they? I lift the large crate into the grocery cart. I push it up near the register and gather the boys in my arms. I'll take them to the car first and come back in to pay for the crate. They wiggle in my arms as I walk out the door.

"Excuse me. Miss. Stop right there." Suddenly the manager of Petco is standing in front of me, blocking me from the car. The boys start to squirm, and Hamlet jumps out of my arms. The manager picks him up. I'm about to thank him when he starts unzipping Hamlet's pocket. He holds up a rawhide bone and shakes it at me like he's ringing a bell. "I think you'd better come with me," he says.

Chapter
29

The cramped little office smells like Lysol and dog biscuits. The manager and his assistant are going through each of the boy's pocket and laying the items on the desk. I watch in horror from my metal chair. "Listen," I say. "It's not what it looks like." The assistant manger shakes his head and points to a closed-circuit television on the wall. "We saw everything," he says. "Save your excuses for the police."

"No," I say. "I left my cart by the register. I was going out to the car to get my purse." I point helplessly toward the parking lot. "I was just going out to pay. I swear."

"You concealed items on the dogs and walked out of the store without paying," the manager says. "That's stealing."

"I couldn't leave the boys alone. I told you. I had to get my purse out of the car." The assistant manager doesn't look up from his notepad where he's writing the items down one by one. "My cart is out there by the register," I plead. "There's a blue carrying crate in it." The manager bites his lip. "I'm just watching them for my mother. She shops here all the time. I swear to you, sir—I was just going out to the car to get my purse." The assistant manager stops counting and looks at me. "How much?" the manager asks. "Twenty-two and some change" he says. The manager folds his arms. "Let's say you're telling the truth about your purse," he says. "Why were you hiding items in their coats?"

"I wanted to see how much I could fit. I'm taking them to the city for the week and I needed to know how much I could fit in their coats," I say. "I had to make sure I wasn't overstuffing them. It took me forever to make their little outfits, and I wouldn't want their pockets busting at the seam, you know?" Neither manager is smiling but no one has reached for the phone to call the police, so I continue. "I'll prove it to you," I plead. "Come with me to the car. My purse is in the glove compartment." It is true too. I had taken my credit card out of my wallet and put it in my pocket. I left the purse in the glove compartment so I could have my hands free for the boys. "Let me get my purse and pay for everything. I swear. This is a huge misunderstanding."

"Okay," the manager says finally. "Let's go out to the car. If your purse is there we'll work something out. If not, I'm calling the police."

"Thank you."

"Thank you," I say again. We've been to the car and just like I told him, my purse was in the glove compartment. Now we're standing at the register where I've charged everything to my credit card. I had to bend down as if I were tying my shoe so that he wouldn't notice me pulling my credit card out of my pocket. "Consider yourself warned," the manager says. "If a mistake like this happens again, we're calling the police."

"I understand. Believe me, it will never happen again."

Oh. My. God. Who would've thought five little dogs could weigh so much? These crates should come with wheels. By the time I get onto the train (they were covered in a sheet just in case anyone wanted to question whether or not you were allowed to travel with five Bichon Frises in one carrying case) I am exhausted. My arms are killing me, and I can't wait to sit down. But I needed three empty seats for me and the boys, and the train is packed. After a fruitless search, I'm forced to stake out a corner of the floor near the bathrooms. I put the crate down and sit on it. Now that I'm safe I have time to think about what just happened.

I just got caught stealing. It was terrifying. It was humiliating. It was exactly what I needed. It's hard to imagine that it would take something so embarrassing to make you really sit up and take notice—but this was definitely a good thing. I think I'm cured. All these years without being caught had made me complacent. The Saints were showing me what fate awaited me if I didn't stop. Maybe I could have Greg after all. He'll never even need to know that I'm an ex-klepto. Yes, this was definitely a good thing. I lay back and close my eyes with relief.

The boys, who had been perfectly content with their new Shrek chew toys a minute ago, are getting restless. It begins with a faint scraping sound. Then I hear a whine. Then a little yip. Finally, a full-out bark. I kneel down by the crate and stick my finger through the holes. "Shh," I say. My finger is immediately licked and then bitten. "Ow." I yank my hand back and throw in a few cookies. Mom owed me big time. By the time we reach Penn Station, I've fed them the entire bag of cookies just to keep them quiet. After a while I was able to time when the conductor would walk by, and a few seconds before his appearance, I'd throw in more cookies. So, except for a few dirty looks from passengers sitting near us, we got by unscathed. But by the time we are in a taxi heading for my place it's already 5:30. I would only have forty-five minutes or so to get ready for my date. It soon became obvious I'd have to take them on a little potty walk when we got home—the boys were stinking up the cab. To his credit the taxi driver didn't mention the smell; he simply rolled down his window.

"It's not me," I say. "It's the dogs." I can tell he doesn't believe me; he doesn't even turn around. The dog are farting like they're marines who have just eaten a mess of chili cheese dogs. I'm sure the Saints are punishing me for trying to steal their biscuits. By the time we get to my place, all four cab windows are rolled all the way down. I tip the taxi driver an extra five bucks, and I can see him spraying a can of air freshener in the cab as he peels away, swearing under his breath. I glance at my watch again. It is rush hour and it had taken us fifteen minutes just to cross the park. It was now 5:55. I just didn't have time for this. I couldn't walk the dogs and get ready for my date. Luckily I knew just who to ask for help.

I find him across the street rummaging through a trash can. "How would you like to earn fifty dollars?" I say.

"Your boyfriend needs me to open your car doors again?" he answers without looking up from the garbage. "I charge a hundred for that." He chuckles at himself and then turned to face me. "What can I do for you, doll?" he says.

"Do you like dogs?" I ask.

Jimmy is thrilled to take the five little monsters for a walk around the block. He's less thrilled when I hand him a fistfull of plastic bags and tell him he has to pick up their poop or risk the fifty bucks I'm offering him (and then some) on a city ticket if he doesn't. "Fifty dollars you say?" he says, looking at the plastic bags in his hand. "I used to be a professional dog walker and that sounds kind of low."

"Okay sixty," I say. "But that's my final offer." He sighs and, with a fistful of leashes and bags, takes off with the boys.

Tavern on the Green is a New York institution and I'm a virgin! I can't count the number of times I've stared longingly from Central Park at the lucky diners inside, wishing it was me in there being wined and dined by a handsome man. I have to hold my tongue to keep from squealing when I read the menu. I don't want to come across as greedy by ordering the most expensive item, but then again if I order the least expensive dish it's like implying I think he's a cheapskate. "Order anything you'd like," Greg says, reading my mind.

"I'd like you on a stick," I refrain from saying. I was known for saying obnoxious things on first dates. It was usually due to fear, but it didn't make it any less repulsive. So this time I was censoring myself big-time.

If only we could pause the incredible moments of life and fast-forward through the rest. If we could, the first half of this dinner would go down in history as the most romantic, alive, beautiful evening ever. I wish I were a surgeon capable of surgically removing the first half of the evening from the second. I wish I were a chef who could pick out the rotting bits, throw them away, and serve the rest with a sprig of alfalfa. Greg had ordered a really nice bottle of wine and several appetizers. We had shrimp cocktails, brie, and crackers. Greg asked me about my father, and I talked about him for the first time in a long time. I admitted he had changed so dramatically after I had graduated from high school that sometimes it felt as if our father had died. Greg noted that change is a type of death, and I thought he was extremely profound. Then he said that maybe I could make more of an effort to have a relationship with my father, and I thought he was extremely annoying. But I forgave him because he understood my silence meant I didn't want to talk about it and he gently steered the conversation on to other topics.

I asked him about his family. He told me he had four younger sisters and they all live in California. His parents lived in Santa Barbara, two sisters lived in L.A. (actor/waiters), and two lived in San Francisco (lesbian computer genius and wife and mother). I read once that you'll know how a guy would treat his wife based on his relationship with his mother so I listened carefully for hidden resentments, neediness, bitterness, or other weirdness, but he spoke about her with love and confidence. It soon became clear that Greg Parks was the perfect man.

So you can see why I completely freaked out. What did he see in me? Why wasn't he after a woman who had it all together? He could have a lawyer, a doctor, or a beautiful seismologist. This city was crawling with beautiful, successful women. Maybe I was just a diversion. Or maybe he was intimidated by strong, successful women. Maybe he was a chauvinist. You see how I started to ruin the evening? And then in the middle of my nasty thoughts he has to go and say, "You have no idea how beautiful you are, do you?" And then he gets up to go to the restroom.

I wonder if things would have been different if I had waited until the end of evening. I could have waited for dessert. Yes, I could have at least waited until our dinner plates were being bussed, and no one would have been the wiser. But Greg left the table while I was in the midst of a mini-freak-out session and I did it without thinking. So the next thing I know, Greg is back at the table and our meals have arrived. That's when I realize the error of my ways. Greg's eyes are roaming the table. He looks at his baked potato, pondering his next move. His beautiful arm shoots up, and in an instant the man in black and white is by his side. "Sir?"

"We need salt and pepper," Greg says. The waiter nods and slides his eyes across the table and then toward me. I meet his gaze defiantly. This was Tavern on the Green after all, and we were the patrons. The waiter's gaze drops to my purse. Oh no.

"Sir," the waiter says to Greg, "I distinctly remember placing the salt and pepper shakers on your table five minutes before you arrived."

Greg's brows crease even further, and he scans the table again. "Well I don't see them, do you?" Greg asks. The waiter looks at my purse again. I clamp my hand over it and look down at my silverware. Thank God I didn't take anything else. How in the world did he see me? I had been extremely quick, even stealthlike, while performing the removal. Damn career waiters. They're way too vigilant.

"Maybe something happened to them," the waiter says. "Maybe she knows."

Greg follows his gaze to me and throws his napkin on the table. "Just what are you suggesting?" he asks, his voice raising a notch. A few heads turn our way. "I think you had better bring us a set of salt and pepper shakers and your manager," Greg continues.

"Maybe they fell," I say, maneuvering to look under the table.

Greg grabs my arm and stops me. "Your manners are appalling," Greg says to the waiter, whose face is now the color of a beet, but to his credit he's standing his ground. "I've been coming to this establishment for the past six years and I have never encountered service so rude."

"Is there a problem, sir?" another voice pops up. He is dressed in the same tux but is older and carries himself more authority.

"Yes, there is," Greg says. "I simply asked this gentleman for salt and pepper."

The older man does the same sweep of our table with his eyes minus giving me evil eye. "Of course, sir," he says. "I'm so sorry. Right away."

And that should be the end of it. Greg's posture relaxes, and the older man turns to retrieve the salt and pepper. But the younger man's hand shoots out, he points a long, manicured index finger directly at me, and he says in a loud voice, "They're in her purse."

Greg stands and throws down his napkin. The manager swiftly pulls the young waiter out of the way, speaks to him in low harsh tones, and propels him out of sight. Then he bows slightly to Greg. "Apologies, sir. I'll get you salt and pepper right away." Greg nods but remains standing. I want to shout at him to sit down, I want to dump the salt and pepper shakers out of my purse and pretend they had fallen to the floor, and most of all I want to stand up and throw my arms around Greg for standing up for me. But the biggest urge I have is to run out and never come back.

We get our salt and pepper, but the rest of the dinner is strained. Another waiter is assigned to our table and our dinner is on the house, but the light, airy mood is gone. Greg is sullen and withdrawn. Being an intelligent man, I know he has to be wondering why the waiter accused me of stealing the salt and pepper shakers. He doesn't come out and ask me, but he's on full alert. After dessert the manager approaches to offer his apologies again. The waiter who was so rude to us, he tells us, has been let go. "Thank you," Greg says. I feel like shit. "I'm so sorry, Melanie," he says to me on the way out. "I wanted this evening to be special."

I give him my best smile and lightly touch his arm. "It's not your fault," I say. "The first half was wonderful." He is holding the door open for me; we are stepping out onto the brick patio. He suggests a walk in the park before going home. In the end, some might say what happens next was purposeful. Some may say I wanted to be caught. It's a lie. I'm a klutz. It's that sad and that simple.

I trip in the doorway and land facedown on the brick patio. The recently fired waiter steps over me and shouts "See, see" as my purse tumbles out of my hands and snaps open. The sleek, silver salt and pepper shakers spin out from the depths of my purse and roll downhill like a wagon detaching from its horses. They travel underneath tiled patio tables, between Manolo Blahnik heels and Prada purses, rolling until they reach the edge of the brick patio floor and land in the dirt beside a large oak tree where a squirrel stops to sniff them.

I continue to lie facedown on the warm bricks, listening to the murmurs of the nearby diners as they gather around the vindicated waiter who is shouting, "I told you. I told you she stole them." All the while, the outdoor lights of Tavern on the Green bathe our chaotic little scene in a warm, romantic glow. Sometimes losing your virginity isn't what it's cracked up to be.

"I'm sorry," I say for the third time to the rehired waiter. He rolls his eyes and smirks at the manager. We are standing at the register and the young waiter is grasping the salt and pepper shakers in his hands like they're the Holy Grail.

"I'll just return these to the table," he says as he flounces away.

The older host hands Greg our bill. "I'll get it," I say, reaching for my purse.

"That won't be necessary," Greg says, taking the bill.

I reach for it anyway. "Please," I croak. "It's the least I can do."

The manager looks back and forth between us.

"Melanie," Greg says in a low whisper.

I back off. Humiliating him worse was not going to help matters. I was dying to know if they had charged us for the salt and pepper shakers (because if so, weren't we entitled to them?) but there was no way I could ask, and Greg was just handing the bill back with a credit card, so it was too late to peek.

"I assume we won't have this problem again?" the manager says, looking at me. I shake my head. We're quickly shown the door. I was hoping Greg would still want to take that walk in Central Park, but he was heading out to the street. He hails a cab, and by the time I reach him, one is waiting. Greg opens the door and gestures for me to get in. I do so, scooting over to give him room beside me. Greg leans in, gives the driver a twenty dollar bill, and shuts the door. Before I know it, the cab door is closed and I'm headed home alone. I turn around and look back. Greg is already gone.

Chapter
30

Jimmy is waiting on the steps with all five dogs curled up in his lap sleeping. If I wasn't so miserable I would have thought it the cutest thing in the world. I sit down next to him.

"How did it go?" I whisper.

Jimmy smiles and looks lovingly at the dogs. "They like me," he says happily.

I nod and bite back tears. "We should go in," I say.

Jimmy looks up at me, clearly appalled at the idea.

"We can't wake them now. I've been sitting here forty-five minutes not movin'. No. They need their sleep." And so we sit.

After another half an hour, the dogs wake and Jimmy reluctantly lets me take them inside. "How about tomorrow?" Jimmy asks. "Should I walk them tomorrow?"

"Why not?" I say. "I'm sure they'd love it." Jimmy flashes me a grin and is gone. I head to my room. All I want to do is throw myself on the bed and pull the covers over my head. I kick off my shoes, throw my purse in the corner of the room, and dive in. I'm never coming out.

* * *

She would have made a terrible thief. First of all, she's wearing high heels, and even in my half-asleep state (the other half of me never did go to sleep; it tossed and turned and tortured me with thoughts of Greg and what he thinks of me now) I hear her clicking across my floor and I smell her perfume. Kim is a perfume addict; you can smell her a mile away. I never know exactly what she's wearing because she changes scents constantly, but you can count on it being new and expensive. Tommy is clomping after her, and as if their secret mission wasn't botched enough, here comes the dogs. All five of the dogs trip into the room after them with high-pitched yips. "Oh, they're so cute," Tommy squeals.

"What the hell is going on?" I say, snapping on the bedroom light.

"You're home," Kim says. "I thought you were on a date."

"What are you doing?" I ask again, but this time it's a rhetorical question. My closet glows behind them like a lighthouse beacon. "How dare you!" I say throwing off the covers and jumping out of bed. Kim is holding something behind her back. I'm sure it's the key to my closet.

"How dare I?" Kim repeats. "How dare *I*?"

"What the hell are you doing sneaking into my room?"

"You come into my room all the time," Kim says.

I'm surprised at how hurt and angry she sounds, given she's the one breaking and entering.

"I don't sneak in when you're sleeping," I retort.

"I told you I thought you were out," Kim says.

"And that gives you the right to go through my closet?" I yell.

"Your closet?" Kim says.

"Just give me the clown," I say, holding out my hand.

"What clown?" Kim cries.

"Kim, just show me what's behind your back."

Kim brings her hands out into the open. She's holding

her baby blue cashmere sweater. The one I spilled coffee on and was supposed to dry-clean. I had forgotten all about it. I had left it lying on the floor with the rest of my mess. My stomach drops. "Oh," I say. "Oh. I'm sorry. I'm so sorry, Kim."

"You're sorry?" Kim says in a deathly quiet voice. "You promised to be careful with this—"

"I know. I know—"

"How could you?"

"I just forgot, Kim. I was going to get it dry-cleaned." Kim turns and heads out of my room. "I'll pay for the sweater, Kim. I'll get it dry-cleaned and I'll pay for it. There's a scarf that goes with it—somewhere." Kim suddenly stops and turns back around. "Kim, please," I say. "Please let me explain." Instead of answering she walks over to my closet and peers at it. She lifts the padlock and looks at me questioningly. What do I say? What is there to explain? That I'm a horrible friend? That all I care about is my next lift? That my closet is filled with a hundred and eighty-eight stolen objects?

"You take my things and trash them—you lie to me—you do nothing but talk about yourself—but locking your closet?"

"I don't lock it because of you," I plead.

"Bull!" Kim yells. "We're the only two people who live here. Why else would you lock it?"

It's a secret. I'm so ashamed. I steal everything I can get my hands on. Help me.

"See!" Kim cries. "You're not even denying it. You don't trust me, do you?"

And there's nothing left to say.

"Obviously not," I say.

We stare at each other. Kim looks like she's going to cry. Tommy gives me a sad look and leads Kim out by the arm. I slam the door shut and throw myself on the bed. This time I don't even pretend to sleep. This time I just cry.

* * *

"I don't understand why you took them to the city in the first place," my mother repeats.

"I told you," I say. "I had things to do. I still have things to do. Jimmy is going to bring the dogs back on the train, okay?"

She takes another long slice of silence and sighs again. "Does this have anything to do with a job?" she asks when the allotted guilt time has passed.

I take a deep breath. I knew the question would come and I knew exactly what I planned on saying. *It's none of your fucking business.* "Yes," I say. "It does. Wish me luck."

Three hours later I'm standing outside storage unit #128 at U-STORE-IT in Hoboken, New Jersey, with twelve boxes, two suitcases, and a backpack. I had to take a cab all the way here, and the fare alone cost more than the storage unit for six months, but at least the closet is empty and my things are safe. Fortunately, the units are like mini-garages and mine is only three-fourths full, so after I have the boxes neatly stacked in the corner, there is plenty of room to stretch out and sleep. It's a little cold in here because I have to keep the garage door cracked so I won't suffocate. I throw on a sweater from my suitcase and wrap myself in a blanket. I'll survive the night.

As I lie on my back on the concrete floor listening to water drip and trying to make out shadows in the dark, a tear slides down the side of my face. *Who am I?* my little voice asks. This is why I'm always so busy, always moving, always preoccupied, never thinking. I'm trying to barricade this silent, probing question from entering the recesses of my mind. Because I don't like the answer. *A thief, a thief, a thief* is what I am. It's not who I had set out to become. It doesn't feel like me, or rather it feels like a dead, third leg dragging me down. How did this all start? I blink, breathe into the floor, and let the memory come.

I'm eight years old. My brother Zach has just turned twelve, and the house is filled with noisy, stinky boys whom I desperately want to impress. Only nobody is paying attention to me. Not even my parents or Aunt Betty, my father's older sister who is visiting from Texas. I've never been to Texas, and I want to ask her if she has a horse and why she's not wearing a cowboy hat and boots, but she's not paying attention to me either. All day everyone has been huddled around Zach and his stupid, prized moon rock.

It didn't look that exciting to me, a dumb old black rock with a lot of holes in it, but he had won it in a national science contest and everyone was acting like it was the second coming. Of course I didn't think of it in those terms then, I just knew that a stupid old rock was getting way more attention than little old me. Besides sticking other kids' toys in my pockets as a toddler, I hadn't yet been bitten by the klepto bug. It was pure chance that the ice cream man drove by, pure chance that Zach didn't see me hiding in the bushes near their fort, and pure greed that made him drop that rock on the grass and run toward the seductive song of the ice cream man.

Leaving me alone.

With the rock.

At first I just crawled over to it and stared. Then I gently lifted it up and looked at it in the sunlight. This rock was on the moon, I thought. So what? I still didn't think it was worth all the fuss. I took the rock into the kitchen where my mother and Aunty Betty were poring over magazines and drinking tea. Neither of them looked up. I took the rock into the living room where the television was blasting football and my father sat with his feet propped up on the coffee table. He didn't look at me either. I felt like the girl on the moon. I brought the rock into my bedroom and put it under my pillow. I'd go down and ask Zach nicely if I could play with him. If he said yes, I'd give him the rock back.

They were in the front yard punching each other and wolfing down ice cream. "Hey!" I yelled. One of the boys looked over and stuck his tongue out at me. I spotted Zach in a headlock with his friend Brett. I walked over, leaned down to the ground where Zach's head was dangling, and tried to talk to him. "Hey!" I said again. "Show me your fort."

"Go away, nerd!" Zach yelled, and the rest of the boys laughed.

"Let's go look at your rock!" I said, ignoring the insult.

"Go away, dufus!" he yelled, breaking out of the head-lock and running away from me. They all piled on bikes and sped away. He was never going to get his rock back.

But of course I knew my parents would make me give it back. I went back into the kitchen and injected myself between my mother and Aunt Betty and waited for the axe to fall. Several times I thought about putting the rock back, but another plan was forming in my mind. Maybe I'd be the one to find it! That's it. While everyone scoured the yard looking for it, I'd pretend to help. When and only when Zach started to cry, would I pretend to find the rock. Then they'd pay attention to me. Then they'd let me in their stupid fort. I'd be the star of the family.

And one hour later, after having to endure listening to my mother and Aunt Betty cluck over chicken recipes, the moment finally came. A scream that could be heard blocks away suddenly pierced through the quiet of our tiny kitchen. Zach screamed like a girl. Even my father catapulted himself off the couch, running out the door after Mom and Aunt Betty to see what in the world was making my brother sound like a wounded animal. I ran out after them, tripping on the stairs and scraping my knee on the deck, but I was too excited to whine. Let the search for the rock begin!

I was the last one to reach the fort. Several boys were kicking the dirt and pawing through bushes while Dad, Mom, and Aunt Betty stood around Zach, who had tears pouring down his face. I slipped up next to him. "What's going on?" I said. "Lost something?"

"You took it!" Zach screamed, grabbing me by the arm. "Give it back."

Stunned, I froze as he shook my shoulders. Oh no. This isn't fair. He wasn't supposed to guess it was me. I slid my eyes toward my parents, waiting for my punishment.

"Zachary, keep your hands to yourself," my mother admonished.

"And apologize at once," my father added.

What? My mouth opened in total surprise. So did Zach's, but he dropped his hands obediently.

"I know she took it," he whined. "When we were getting ice cream."

"She was in the kitchen with us," my mother said. "I'm waiting for that apology," my dad added, putting his arms on my shoulder.

"Where is it?" Zach yelled, turning to me.

My father stepped toward Zach. "Apologize or go to your room."

Zach kicked the dirt angrily. "I'm sorry," he mumbled.

"That's okay," I said. "I can help you find it," I added.

"See?" Zach raged, jumping up and down. "I told you— she stole it!"

"That's it," my father said. "Go to your room."

"But—"

"Now."

I had to sit down on the grass and catch my breath as Zach stalked off to his room. My parents had defended me. They sent Zach to his room. On his *birthday*. It was too much for my little brain to take in. I had my first taste of the thrill of "the take," and although I couldn't help feeling bad for Zach, another feeling was edging its way in, pushing out the guilt and laying the groundwork for a long love affair with what I would start to call "the taking." The feeling was pure, unadulterated power. And I was positively swooning in its wake.

I waited two weeks and then left Zach's moon rock out in the driveway one Saturday morning as we followed my father out to the car for a trip to the hardware store. "Well look what we have here," my father said, picking up the moon rock and tossing it to Zach, who again screamed like a girl and accused me of having something to do with its disappearance all over again. But I could care less. I was too busy gripping my Barbie backpack and shaking with sick excitement over what I had decided to do.

You see, I hated going to the hardware store. But my mother had discovered something she called "me time," and so every Saturday we were forced to follow my father into these horrible stores with lumber and nails and lightbulbs and other things too hideous and dirty to mention. I usually sulked all the way there and all the way back. But this morning I was dying to go. This morning I was going to see if my superpowers would work on more than a rock. This morning I was going to practice "the taking" at the hardware store.

I followed my father and Zach up and down aisle eleven, dragging my purple backpack along the dusty concrete floor. My heart was beating so loud I had to look around to see if anyone else could hear it. *No one sees me*, I thought. *I am a superhero. I have the power to take.* With my new, laser-like eyes and lightning-quick fingers, I scanned the bottom shelves as I walked, and the moment I spotted the pile of shiny, crystal doorknobs, I shook with love. I had been practicing for this all week in my room, taking objects off my toy shelf and dropping them into my backpack until I had it down to three seconds start to finish. I was ready for the real thing.

Dad and Zach had already rounded the next corner, not once glancing back at me. A man with overalls was behind me, but he was facing the other shelves. It was now or never. I dropped to my scabbed knees, grabbed a doorknob, and held it in the same fist as my backpack as I walked. I looked over at the man whose head was bent down. No one could see me. I quickly dropped the doorknob in the backpack and sped up to find my father. My suspicions had been confirmed. I had the gift for "the taking."

By the end of that year I was stealing two items a month and hiding them under my bed. At age thirteen I began showing off for a few select friends, and a small but appreciative group of girls had begun to gather around me, admiring me, inviting me out, begging me to pass on my special powers.

And even when I started lying awake with massive headaches and a queasy stomach, I couldn't bring myself to stop. I waited, instead, to get caught. I imagined all sorts of scenarios about how it might happen. In some daydreams, I sobbed and begged for forgiveness; in others I fought like a wild animal while a dozen cops dragged me away in handcuffs and took me to jail. But until then I continued to steal.

Then one day when I was struggling to get my books out of my overstuffed locker (I couldn't fit any more objects underneath my bed and I had begun selling a few things here and there to friends), my high school guidance counselor, Mr. Clements, happened by as a waterfall of stolen objects careened out of my locker and spilled onto the floor. My parents were called in, and we all sat in his little office and stared at the desktop where the counselor had arranged every single item for my parents to see. My mother gasped.

"She's a compulsive shopper," she cried, clutching my father's arm.

"Is this where your babysitting money goes?" my father yelled, picking up a vibrator.

"I've always wanted a neck massager," I said, quickly taking it out of his hands and hiding it underneath a box of Tide.

"You think she's *buying* all of these things?" the counselor asked incredulously, picking up a set of plastic straws and a package of lip gloss. He stared at me, daring me to fess up. "Melanie? Are you telling us you *purchased* all these items?"

"I'm afraid so," I said, breaking eye contact with him and turning to my parents. "I'm sorry, Mom. I'm sorry, Dad. I can't help it. Money just—burns a hole in my pocket," I said, borrowing from a favorite phrase of my father.

"Mr. and Mrs. Zeitgar," the counselor said, slowly looking between them, "have you considered the possibility that Melanie may be a compulsive *shoplifter?*" My mother cried out and dug her nails into my father. The two of them sprang out of their seats like they had been ejected.

"That's preposterous!" my father boomed. "Do you know what I do for a living?"

"Yes, Mr. Zeitgar—"

"I'm a lawyer," my father said, gathering himself up. "My children have a deep and abiding respect for the law, Mr. Clements."

"Perhaps she could show us the receipts," Mr. Clements started to say, but my father cut him off at the pass.

"I've already told you my daughter would never break the law. And unless you want an up-close-and-personal lesson in the law then I'd strongly suggest you stop lobbying false accusations against Melanie and curtail any further damaging and prejudicial remarks."

"Yes, curtail yourself," echoed my mother, who always needed to hide behind someone else to stand up for herself. "However, we thank you for bringing our daughter's *shopping* problem to our attention."

My father nodded curtly to the counselor and took me by the arm. "We're cutting off your allowance," he said sternly as he guided me out of the room. "And you'll hand over all your babysitting money to us for the next three months."

I nodded my assent, not daring to look back and see what I assumed was a dumbstruck look on Mr. Clements's face. Denial is a family affair.

Chapter

31

I'm having a nightmare. "No, no, no!" I'm screaming inside my head. I wake up in a sweat. It takes me a few minutes to remember that I'm sleeping in a storage unit in New Jersey and another minute to remember why. I turn over, touch the side of my nearest box, and feel a sense of calm wash over me. I wonder which objects are in this one. All of the items in my boxes are brand new, everything is still in its original packaging, and every object has a story.

A long time ago I divided my objects into three categories: Throwaways, Gifts, and Sacrifices. Throwaways are the items I allow myself to use. Lipstick, food, office supplies. Gifts are the things I steal for other people (bags of coffee from Starbucks, candles, wallets, gravy boats), and Sacrifices are the ones I never allow myself to open. The objects in this storage unit are all sacrifices. Don't get me wrong, I'd love to rip into them and use them; I'd love to light the scented candles, wrap myself in the cashmere scarf, and write with the Japanese quill. But I won't. The stories behind them deserve to be honored. The thought of returning them causes me physical pain, as if I would be abandoning one of my children.

The stories call to me now as I caress the box. I remember the package of bathing salts I acquired after a particularly horrendous Visa bill, the silk pajamas I took the summer I gained ten pounds, the hand-dipped candles the time the saleslady was rude to my mother, the set of chopsticks the night I was followed by two guys on the Lower East Side, and the cashmere scarf I stole the day after I had a one-night stand with the guy from the Rebar. We didn't use a condom, and I lifted it while waiting for the results of my AIDS test. Every object has a story. Every one of them I've earned like medals in a war.

Just thinking about them isn't enough. I need to touch them. I lift the top box from the pile and open it. Touching each item is like flipping through a photo album, each package invoking a memory, a need, a longing. I stop when I reach the brilliant topaz ring I lifted from a holiday sale at Nordstrom. It's beautiful, but I'll never wear it. My stomach tightens when I hold it; this is one story I don't like remembering. This is the button I don't like pushed.

It was winter break and my third year at NYU. They talked about the party for months; it was going to take place on an entire floor of an apartment building in Hell's Kitchen. Merry Christmas, Happy New Year, and ho, ho, ho. It was going to be *the* place to be—the party they would talk about for years to come. I went with my roommate Jo Ella, and since we planned on getting as trashed as possible, we made an agreement we would take a cab home together and we would go whenever one of us wanted to leave. But she hooked up with some guy, and when it was time to go home, I couldn't find her.

I remember vodka. A lot of vodka. I stumbled around the party looking for her. Someone tells me she's gone. And then, there he is. I don't know his name—he was sober, and his shirt was pink. He had not been at our party—I learn later that he lives in the building and drives a Porsche. That's all I'll ever find out about the man in the pink shirt.

And who would ever think to be afraid of a man in a pink oxford shirt? I've given up on Jo Ella and I'm searching for my purse when he materializes in front of me. *No, I'm sorry I wouldn't like another drink. Can't you see that I can't walk a straight line?* I walk out of the party and stagger to the elevator.

Where are all my friends? They're too drunk to notice or maybe they think I know the man in the pink shirt. Either way he's followed me out into the hall and guided me past the elevators. "I have to go," I slur. "I have to get a cab."

"We can call from in here," he says, unlocking an apartment door down the hall and pushing me inside. The rest I remember in close-ups as if I'm watching a film. Close-up on his telephone. It's white and it's sitting right there on a little end table. I'm sobering up now; even swimming in vodka my brain is sending out faint warning signals. Don't take candy from strangers, never hitchhike, and beware of helpful neighbors. I don't scream. Why don't I scream? Would things have been different? But I know why I don't scream, and the reason haunts me to this day. I don't scream because I don't trust myself. I don't trust my trusty little voice who is warning me of danger. I listen to the man in the pink shirt and ignore my voice. The man in the pink shirt is still pretending he wants to help me call a cab. What does my voice know? She's drunk and unreliable.

I'm so sorry, voice. I'm very, very sorry. If I could replay the evening, I would scream. I would start screaming in the hall before we reached his apartment, and if he still managed to get me to his door, I would fight like a wildcat. But even drunk, the one thing I always learned from my mother—one thing I could not fight against back then—the mantra of little girls everywhere—"be polite." Don't make a fuss. Don't make a scene. The phone is right here. It's white. It sits on a desk. He's just being nice. He's going to let me use his phone. I pick it up. His hand closes over mine and he puts it down.

The film jumps here, and suddenly I find myself upstairs, lying in his bed. I'm not sure how I got up here. The ceiling is spinning and somewhere a fan is blowing. My shirt and bra are already on the floor, and now he's taking off my jeans and then my panties. I can smell a trace of my own urine. I am ashamed. *Wear clean underwear in case you're in an accident.* Then I realize that maybe he thinks I want this. I tell him no. He doesn't stop. Now I do scream. He clamps his hand over my mouth and then pulls it away. "Go ahead," he says. "I like it when you scream." I try to fight him, but he's way too strong. It's happening, and after a while I stop fighting it. I don't even pray to the Saints. I just pray for it to be over. And then it is.

My shame doubles now. In another replay I would run out of his apartment as fast as I could. I would wait for him to fall asleep and then pull on my clothes and get the hell out of there. Instead, I pass out. I sleep next to him all night long. When I wake it's light outside. He's still sleeping. I quietly fetch my clothing off the floor piece by piece, roll my underwear up in a ball, and stick them in my jeans. I'll end up burning them in the dorm. I don't call the cops. I don't tell anyone. As far as I'm concerned, it's my fault for getting so drunk. But I don't forget it. I dream about silent white phones and missing cabs. I see him on top of me, in me, above me. And then I start to look for him. Is that him behind me in line at the deli? Is he lurking in the alley? Who is that sitting in the third row of my Algebra class? I spend more time in bed. I stop going to parties and bars altogether. I miss a few classes. And then I miss my period. And it's nothing in the scheme of things. There are billions of stories like mine in this concrete jungle. At least I'm alive. I get an early term abortion and wait for the results of

my AIDS test. It's negative, but there's no relief. My night-
mares continue, and I unofficially drop out of school. I sleep
with the light on; I steal the topaz ring. It doesn't cure me,
but it makes everything burn just a little bit brighter. People
want to know why I steal; I want to know why they don't.

Only the salve doesn't last long. And one night when I
can't take looking over my shoulder anymore, I pick up a
dull Bic razor and start slicing. I call Zach, and he drives me
to the hospital. And this is my chance—with Dr. Phillips to
really heal. To get real with myself. And there's no doubt
that my stint in the psyche ward helps me—it does—but I
never tell anyone about the man in the pink shirt or my
kleptomania. I think I was waiting for someone to catch me.
I assumed a trained psychiatrist would be able to see right
through me. I especially thought they were going to figure
it out when all the Band-Aids and sutures and potato chip
packets started disappearing from the floor, but they never
did.

And even though I confessed most of my childhood trau-
mas to Dr. Phillip (I talked nonstop about Zach and Mom
and Richard and the boys and my father—after all I had to
blame my problems on someone didn't I?), I don't say anything about my kleptomania. I like the feeling of having a
secret. It makes me feel strong; it makes me feel safe. But
now I seem to be losing my grip. Now the highs aren't last-
ing very long, and the lows are reminiscent of that dark time
years ago. I'm slipping up. Of course the salt and pepper
shakers weren't worth losing Greg. But I don't know what
to do.

Do I turn myself in? Do I go to therapy again? I can't
even face Kim. She'll never forgive me for lying to her, and
if I live with her again where will I hide my things? I could
stop stealing of course, and I will—I will someday. But
today, I still want to steal.

A part of me fears it's the only way I'll ever know power.

It's the only thing I have to place between me and obscurity. I started stealing because I thought I had been granted a superpower, and I've continued because I've never found anything to replace it that gives me the same sense of mastery and belonging. I know it's sick—I belong with the outlaws, but at least I belong. I've failed at absolutely everything I've ever tried to do in my life. Relationships, school, temping, acting, and now I've failed my best friend and my new, wonderful, amazing boyfriend. I'm a failure at everything except stealing, and I know no one would ever understand me if I told them that for me, stealing like feels like an old friend. A sick, perverted friend who comes and goes like a boyfriend you just can't kick out of bed, but a friend nevertheless.

And even though it's eating me inside out, I don't want to give up the one thing in the world that I happen to have a knack for. The truth—which I've been fighting all morning in this musty, dark storage tank—is this: I've been taking things all my life because I'm trying to fill myself up, trying to take back everything I feel the world is taking from me. But I'm a bottomless pit and I take and I take and I take and I'm never full. I'm always wanting, always reaching, always waiting my turn. But I stopped waiting to take my turn the day I stole the doorknob in the hardware store, and I've been "stealing" my turn ever since. I'm the invisible girl, the law-breaking girl, the obscure girl, the girl on the moon.

I've fallen down the rabbit hole and broken every fingernail trying to claw my way back up. But like many others before me who've taken the wrong turn, I just keep going in circles and I don't know how to go straight. I've been doing this so long—I've gone so far off the path—I don't think I can ever get back.

In fact, I've been fighting the urge to steal all morning and I'm losing the battle.

I don't want to face anyone ever again, and it's making me want to take a huge canvas bag into the nearest store and stuff it with items. Luckily, I can't do that because it's the middle of the night. But this storage unit smells bad, and now that I've gone through the box I can't stand being next to my objects anymore. I have to get out of here or I'm going to die.

Chapter
32

I find an all-night diner, order a Western omelet, a side of fries, a Coke, two chocolate cream donuts, and a bottomless cup of coffee. Fuck everything, I'm going to eat. I hide in a back booth and stuff myself silly. I growl at the waitress when she tries to remove my plate. (There were still several bites left!) Once I'm sufficiently stuffed, I go back to the storage unit, wrap up in a blanket, curl up next to my boxes, and finally fall asleep.

I wake up with a start. It's raining. My ass is ringing. It's my cell phone; I'm sitting on it.

"Where are you?" Tommy cries when I pick up.

"New Jersey," I wail.

"It's worse than we thought"

I hear him yell to someone. "Do you have money for a cab?" he demands.

"No," I sob.

"Call one anyway. Come over to my place, sweetie. I'll pay him when you get here. Okay?"

I nod, my eyes overflowing with tears.

"Okay, sweetie?"

"Okay," I croak.

I'm sleeping on Tommy's red leather couch. His three

horrendously fat cats are kneading my chest like they've just graduated from some bizarre massage school where the technique is to step lightly, lightly, lightly, then dig their claws into the victim's flesh while wiggling their furry asses in your face. Tommy stands in the doorway, a shoe box under his arm.

"She's awake," he says. Kim peers out from behind him. She comes over to me and kneels down by the couch.

"We were worried sick about you," she says. "Are you okay?"

I nod. "How long have I been asleep?"

"Four hours," she says. "Why were you in New Jersey?"

I open my mouth to lie and then shut it. "Can we talk about that later?" I say.

"Of course."

"Can I bring out my surprise now?" Tommy yells.

Kim laughs. "She might not want to do it."

"Do what?" I say, raising myself to a sitting position and scattering cats across the room.

"Marijuana," Tommy says, shaking the box. "Lots of marijuana."

"And cookie dough ice cream," Kim says, poking me. They're the best friends I've ever had.

My eyes are glazed, cookie dough ice cream drools down my chin, and cat hair is sticking to my face as if I too had sprouted whiskers. Judge Jeannie is over, and Tommy leans over to turn off the television when I stop him.

"Greg's coming on next," Kim admonishes him.

"Yummy," Tommy says, and we all giggle. We make fun of Deborah Green and her light blue blazer.

"He's off his game," Kim says, cocking her head and looking at Greg. It was true, he wasn't wearing his signature smile.

"It's all my fault," I say. "We had a fight."

Tommy mutes the television. "Hey!" I say. "They're bringing on the panelists now." Once a week they invite the local business community to the show to discuss legal issues. I loved to listen to Greg espouse legalese. It was a surprising turn-on. Even if he did hate my guts now.

"Spill!" Tommy says, staring at me. I look around the floor. Kim busts out laughing.

"You're pretty," she says.

"I'm talking to you, Zeitgar," Tommy says, pointing at me. "Spill the beans. What did you fight about?"

"Salt and pepper shakers," I cry. God this cookie dough ice cream is good.

"Salt and pepper shakers?" Kim says. "I could go for something salty."

"Me too," I yell, standing up. "Do you have anything salty, Tommy?"

He grabs my pant legs and pulls me down to the floor. "Not so fast, Missy. You and sexy legal man fought over salt and pepper shakers?"

"He is sexy, isn't he?" I say, looking at the television. There are three panelists on, two men and a woman. There's something familiar about the woman. I point her out to Tommy and Kim. "Is she someone?" I ask. Kim and Tommy giggle. I do too, although it's not really funny. "I mean it," I say laughing. "I know that woman."

"She has a big nose," Tommy says, looking at the television.

Follow the nose—Come on! Where do I know her from?

"What does Greg have against salt?" Kim shouts. "Is he a vegan?"

"Vegans don't eat salt either?" Tommy asks.

I turn up the television. The familiar looking woman with the big nose is talking now to Deborah Green. "Well, why don't we play the video and we'll talk on the other side," Deborah says to Greg and the panelist. Greg flashes his signature smile. I smile back and blow a kiss to the television.

"Salt is good!" Tommy yells at him. Do I know her from a temp assignment? And then they show the video.

"Oh. My. God," Tommy says. "Who is that chick?" Kim asks.

"Whoever she is, she looks horrible in that wig," Tommy admonishes wagging his finger at the TV. I don't even try to speak. My insides have turned to cement.

"That's a wig?" Kim says, moving closer to the TV.

"Get back," Tommy yells. "You'll go blind."

"Look, Look. Is she stealing?" Kim squeals. "She is. Oh my God. She's switching the watches. She is so busted."

"You can't really see her face," Tommy says.

"There she goes."

"Melanie. Earth to Melanie. Don't you think you've had enough of that?"

I look down. I've sucked the joint down to the nub, and now it's burning my fingers.

"She's outta there!" Kim repeats, pointing at me running out the door of the jewelry store.

"Cool, she's going to chase her!" Tommy yells. "Get her. Get her."

The video stops.

"Damn," Tommy says. "I wanted to see them cuff her."

I hold up my wrists and stare at them.

"Well," Deborah says. "That was exciting."

"But she got away with it," the bird woman is saying.

"What kind of thief did we just witness?" Deborah asks Greg.

"She knows what she's doing," Greg says. "She's prepared."

"Why do you say that?" Deborah asks, blinking her eyes at him.

"Is she flirting?" I yell. Tommy moves the shoe box full of pot away from me.

"Well, let's watch it again," Greg says. "First of all," he narrates over the video, "she walks in and goes directly to the item she wants to steal. She uses the distraction of your phone call to her advantage and watch this—she's removing the second box out of her bag. Now this is in black and white, but my guess is she's even matched the colors of the boxes perfectly." He looks to bird woman for confirmation, and she nods her head. "Furthermore she's wearing a disguise. This is a premeditated lift no doubt."

"I managed to grab her wig," the woman says, holding up my black wig. "She had blond hair."

"Oh, that should do it!" Tommy shrieks. "Just round up every blonde in Manhattan!" He tugs on my hair. "One of you did it," he shouts, pointing at us. Kim howls with laughter. It's infectious, so I join in.

"I admit it," I scream. "I did it. I took Trina's soap dish and then before I knew it I was a jewel thief too!" I have them literally rolling on the floor holding onto their sides.

"So that's it?" bird woman complains. "She steals an eighteen hundred dollar Omega Seamaster watch and gets away with it?"

Kim and Tommy continue howling, but I stop dead in my tracks. It's slight, but the smile on Greg's face shifts. And then, ever so slowly, I see him lay his right hand casually over his left. He's trying to hide his watch. He looks up into the camera and stares directly at me.

This is how I die. Trina Wilcox challenges me to appear on the Judge Jeannie Show. *I can't wait for my good name to be exonerated and my face to be professionally made up. "What about makeup?" I say to Audrey, the petite redhead who lets me into the building and ushers me into a small blue room called the Green Room. I was dying to get some color on my face. "What about it?"*

she answers impatiently. "When do I get it done?" I ask politely. She snorts. "We're a small claims court that happens to be televised," she announces, "not Extreme Makeup." *A bowling ball flips in my gut. "But—but I didn't wear makeup," I stammer. But before I can yell "Loreal!" she disappears into the hall. Why didn't you tell me to bring makeup just in case? I scream at the Saint of Cosmetics. Just in case, just in case, just in case? Haven't you ever heard of just in case???? Okay Mel, breathe. Breathe. Visualize your mother ship. There she is on the horizon, just beyond the fog. Go to her! Go to your mother ship! Suddenly a torpedo whizzes by—heading straight for—no, God no! My mother ship has been blown to smithereens. I start to pace. My father is a pacer. I wonder if he still paces. I wonder if the Florida sun has eased his tension to the point where he no longer needs to pace. Does he pace on the sand? It would be very difficult to pace on sand—shut up! Shut the fuck up! This is not the time for thinking you need to act. Do something. Do something.*

Okay. It's okay. This is New York. Even the men wear makeup. There has to be makeup somewhere in the building. By God I will sniff it out. I look at my watch. Ten minutes! I have ten minutes. Okay, okay, okay. I step out into the hall. I can see a few skinny men running around in black. Behind one of those doors has to be makeup! I ease down the dark hall, feeling along the wall until I reach the next door. As I'm reaching out to turn the knob, a girl with a headphone breezes right by me, opens the door, and walks in. I follow.

This room is actually a pleasant color of green. And lively. There are new suede couches, colorful paintings, fresh flowers, piping hot coffee, and glazed donuts. Trina Wilcox is sitting in a chair having her makeup done. I open my mouth to scream but nothing comes out. Trina smiles at me with her perfectly lined, soft pink lips. I can feel tears building up behind my eyes, and my mouth tastes salty. I pray to the Saint of Water Works, "Turn them off, turn them off! We've got a leak—we've got a leak!" but to no avail. I'm sobbing now. The next thing I know, Audrey zips up be-

hind me, grabs my arm, and before I can scream "Mascara!" she hustles my sobbing, makeup-less face into the hallway, through a door, and into the courtroom.

The audience is absolutely still as Judge Jeannie swoops into position. Cameras are everywhere, and I can't stop crying. I think of every horrible thing I can to make myself stop. War. Colds. The stench in the subway. Men. Skinny women who can eat whatever they want without gaining weight. My mother. My brother. My sister-in-law. My stepfather. Someone is screaming. Startled I look up. It's Judge Jeannie. She's pounding her gavel. "Bring in the victims," she says. The doors open, and everything I've ever stolen is carried in by scantily clad Victoria's Secret models. There are close to a thousand of them and they're all sporting the stomachs and thighs of my dreams. Gravy boats, candles, sweaters, and assorted cutlery float by me displayed on lacy, colorful, push-up bras. Out of the corner of my eye I spot a male model among them. It's Greg Parks. The Omega Seamaster is wrapped around his neck like a dog collar.

"Thief!" Judge Jeannie yells, pointing at me. "Thief, thief, thief," the audience chants. I don't know who put the paper bag on the podium where I stood, or why—but I did know that a) if it came to a fight Judge Jeannie was going to kick my skinny white ass and b) I was not going to keep crying on national television. I put the bag over my head. I think I hear Kim and Tommy shout my name, but everything is kind of muffled with a paper bag over your head. It smells like a sandwich; this must have been someone's lunch. "Take that bag off your head now!" Judge Jeannie fumes. I don't, of course; I stand there crying into it. I hear the audience gasp first and feel Judge Jeannie's hands around my neck second. "Remember," I gasp as she strangles me on national television, "the camera adds ten pounds."

Chapter
33

"I'm sorry, he's not here right now. Would you like to leave a message?"

I sigh. Greg had been refusing my calls all week.

"Margaret, it's Melanie Zeitgar. Do you know where I can find him?"

"Melanie? The clockmaker?"

"That's me." "Well hello, dear. Are you calling from Europe? How is your one-woman show going?"

"I'll fill you in later. Do you have any idea where I can find Greg?" There is silence on the other end of the phone. "Please," I say. "Please."

"He's finishing up a training at Bloomingdale's," she says. "And then he's off to the television studio."

"Thank you, Margaret. I owe you one."

Keep walking, I tell myself. *Don't take anything*. Not this scarf. Not the plastic blue watch falling out of the bin. And definitely not the gaudy rhinestone brooch sitting right there on the edge of the bin. *Greg's right*, my little voice says. *You're an addict*. The urge to steal courses through my veins like steroids through an athlete. But I don't dare. Greg Parks is somewhere in the building. I walk out of Accessories and head to the elevators. That's when I see her. She can't be more than eleven or twelve years old. She is lingering around the display cases of jewelry wearing a white cap, pink shirt, and jeans with rhinestones. She had a small pink and white knapsack. No baggy clothes, and she has no problem making eye contact with the clerks.

But she can't fool me. Maybe it is the flushed look on her face, maybe it's the way she is scanning the items with her eyes—or maybe shoplifters give off scents other shoplifters can pick up—regardless, I know in an instant. She's using the buy one/steal one method. She picks up a necklace or box of earrings in one hand and places it in her basket while slipping the item she really wants into her pocket with her left. I feel like I've gone back in time and I'm watching home movies of myself. Only there's a big difference this time. This time—this "me" can be stopped. This "me" has a chance.

I approach the cosmetics counter around the corner and ask for a supervisor. The salesgirl rolls her eyes at me and seems reluctant to call a supervisor until I tell her I work for Greg Parks, the Loss Prevention Consultant for Bloomingdale's. She's still clueless so I name drop *Side Court TV*, and within minutes the head honcho, Barbara Stockman, is summoned to my side. I recognize her from the presentation I did with Greg. Obviously, she recognizes me too. "Melanie," she sings. "I was wondering where you were. Come on, the training's just started."

"Barbara," I say, "I'm not here for the training. I've spotted a shoplifter in your store."

Barbara's eyes widen. "Who?" she says, looking around.

I nod my head toward the girl who is now walking briskly away.

"You're sure?" Barbara asks me.

"I'm sure," I say.

She calls security. I watch the security guards follow her.

Barbara offers me a cup of coffee and asks me to wait with her in her office. A few minutes later the guards return with the girl. She glares at me through Barbara's open door. "I hate you!" she yells at me. "I hate you."

I meet her defiant gaze and she holds my stare, but a slight quiver of her lip reveals she's scared to death. This might just be the last day she'll ever steal. *You'll thank me someday*, I want to say. But I know she won't believe me. And she'd never believe it if I told her I'd give anything right now if someone had just done the same for me.

"He's already left, dear," Barbara tells me a few minutes later when I ask after Greg. "They're taping a live show today."

"Oh," I say, trying to hide my disappointment.

"Would this help?" Barbara asks, handing me an envelope. "What is it?"

"It's a guest pass to today's show. Greg was kind enough to give me a pair, but I'm afraid we're all going to be tied up for a while," she says, glancing at the girl in the hall. "Why don't you use them?"

I smile and take the envelope even though I have no intention of bothering him during the show. "Thank you," I say.

"No," Barbara says. "Thank you. Call me if you ever need a job," she says with a laugh. "We could certainly use someone with your sharp eyes."

On my way home I pass a homeless man dropped and rolled in the dirt like a corn dog at the county fair. He has one wrinkled hand wrapped around a tin cup and the other resting on a beautiful yellow lab with big, sad, brown eyes. The dog is nuzzling the old man, who according to the sign is a blind Vietnam Vet in need of help. Although the homeless man is a good ten feet from the deli, the owner is trying to shoo him away with a broom. He brushes it near him and the dog winces as particles of dust get caught in his eyes.

"Hey!" I yell at the man with the broom. "Stop that!"

Both men look up at me; the deli man stares directly at me and the blind man looks a little to my right.

"He's a bum! He upset my customers!" the deli man shouts.

"Well I'm a customer too," I say. "And you're upsetting me."

The homeless man spots a window of opportunity and grabs it. "Spare a dollar, pretty lady?" He lifts his cup and turns his face in my direction.

"How do you know I'm pretty?"

"I can smell you. You smell pretty."

I sniff my wrist. I do smell a little bit like apples.

The deli man huffs and spits on the ground next to him. "I work sixteen hours every day," he yells. "Get a job."

I step near the deli man and square my shoulders. "If you don't stop harassing this man I'm calling my lawyer," I threaten. A thin dark-skinned woman with long braids sticks her head out of the deli door and speaks to the deli man in quick, low tones. He grunts, gives me a dirty look, and shuffles away.

I kneel down next to the old man. "May I pet your dog?" I say.

The lab sniffs my hand. "Do you have a dollar?" the man asks again. "We're hungry," he adds, placing his hand on top of the lab.

"I'm not going to give you any money," I say honestly. "But I'll get you anything you like from the deli."

I take a red plastic basket and fill it with peanut butter, jelly, and bread. I realize halfway down the aisle that I'd better check and see how much money I have on me before loading it up any more. I rummage around my purse, feel-

ing for my wallet. That's funny—where is it? I rummage
around again. I set the basket down and hold the purse in
the light. Where is my red leather wallet? I know it was here
this morning. I know it because I had to use it twice—the
last time was at the diner in New Jersey. Oh no, could I
have left my wallet there? Now what do I do? I can't aban-
don this old man. And I'm so done with stealing. I swear.
But this isn't for me. That man and his dog are getting a
sandwich if it's the last thing I do.

The peanut butter will be easy to stuff in my jacket, but
I hadn't counted on a loaf of bread. I stick the small jar of Jif
in my rain jacket and looked down at myself. The jacket is
bulky so you really can't tell. The deli man is busy cutting
thin slabs of roast beef and his wife is at the counter arguing
with a teenager who is trying to buy cigarettes.

"No good for you. You too young," she admonishes him,
waving the cigarettes.

"I'm twenty-one!" he shouts back, waving his ID at her.
"Now give me the goddamn cigarettes."

I use the distraction to grab the bread, head to the front
of the store where they are still arguing, and pick up the
New York Times. I have enough change in my pockets for the
newspaper. I lay the *Times* on top of the bread and walk toward the register. I place the money for the *Times* on the
counter next to the young man who is still ranting and raving.

"For the paper," I say.

"Thank you," the sweet old man says as I make him a
peanut butter and jelly sandwich.

"You're welcome," I say, sitting down and making one for
the dog and myself. "What's his name?" I ask as the dog
smacks on the peanut butter.

"Charity," the blind man says. We sit for another few
minutes eating our sandwiches in silence. I wonder how he
ended up here, living on the streets. He was an American, a
senior citizen, a soldier. Why were we stepping over him

like he was garbage? Look at Charity sitting next to the old man with his paws on him protectively, loving him unconditionally. He's a better man than we are. We should all be ashamed of ourselves.

"Where do you sleep?" I say after a bit.

The old man rolls his head from side to side. "Cops keep me on the move," he says. "But I get by."

I nod again. Then I see the dog chewing on something. It appears to be a red leather wallet.

I reach for it. The dog growls and the old man grabs my hand. "That's my wallet," I say. In a flash the old man snaps my wallet from me and looks me directly in the eyes. "Hey!" I yell. The man starts to run. Faster and swifter than a blind man could any day. And Charity isn't guiding him, he's running behind him. But he does drop my wallet. Only it's empty. Cash, coins, credit cards, driver's license—everything. It's all gone. He didn't even take the peanut butter or bread with him. I pick them up off the ground and turn around. The deli man is standing at the door watching me.

"You stole that," he says, pointing a shaking finger at me. "My wife says you only buy paper. I'm calling the police." I follow him back into the store and try to explain the situation. I show him my empty wallet. He points to a security camera in the corner of the store.

"Got you," he says.

"Look. I'll get the money. Just let me—"

"Too late. I call police. I sick of thieves. I sick of you people who steal from me. Every day someone want to take my fruit—here is out here—is free. Ha! This is not free," he says, picking up an orange and winging it at my head. I look behind me and he grabs the loaf of bread. Then he starts shaking it so hard all I can think is "Don't Squeeze the Charmin." "I pay for this. I sweat for this. You—" he says, screaming at me now as a small crowd draws—"who do you think you are?"

Tears fill my eyes. "No one," I whisper. "I'm no one."

That's why you steal, a little voice informs me. I hold the empty wallet up again. "He stole my money, don't you see?"

The deli man backs up and looks at me. "He steal your money—you steal my bread and Jiffy. What's the difference?"

"I—I—" I say. I can't think of a good answer. I'm shaking with anger because the old man tricked me and stole my wallet—but he's right. There is no difference between me and him or me and a cat burglar or me and any other lowlife thief.

"What else you take, huh?" the deli man screams. "Something else? In your purse? In your pockets?" His anger goes way beyond the loaf of bread. Years of rage are converging on his face, which is overheating, threatening to blow any minute. He's sweating and his breath becomes labored and grows gravelly as he begins circling me like a shark. His wife approaches timidly from behind.

"Rob," she says in a quiet voice. "Rob, you take it easy now."

"Call the police," he screams at his wife. "We're not letting her go."

"Robbie," she says, her voice gaining a little bit of strength. "She will pay us. You take it easy now." She is speaking to him like he is a jumper on a roof and she's his only savior, perched on the edge right beside him. It occurs to me then that I should be afraid of him. It occurs to me he's having a nervous breakdown. It's quite possible that he is going to snap like a twig, pull out a gun, and shoot me. He's advancing on me now, backing me up into a wall of chips. A few shoppers have stopped to watch. I think of all the horrible crimes in which crowds watched the person being stabbed or raped or mugged, not moving a muscle like they were watching dinner theatre. And those victims weren't even thieves. I wouldn't stand a chance. And now I suddenly, violently, have to pee.

"Please," I say, my voice leaking out with a croak. "Leave me alone."

"Give me your purse," he yells. "And empty your pockets." This is not good. This is not good, not only because this man is a sizzling grenade with his pin about to pop, but it's also not so good because if memory serves me right there just might be a teeny, tiny pack of gum in my purse. And one in my pocket. Or two. Two at the very most.

I've never been so ashamed of myself in my whole life. What have I done? I was never supposed to hurt anyone. I had rules. I wasn't even supposed to steal from mom and pop shops; how could I forget that? Even if the peanut butter and bread was for the old man and the dog, who was the gum for? I didn't give it away; the packs are right here, in my purse, in my pockets. Why do I keep doing this? Shame whittles through me like a raw nerve throbbing outside the skin. I want my mother. But of course she would be ashamed of me too. "Call my mother," I yell. "She'll kill me," I add. "She'll be so ashamed."

"Your mother!" the deli man shouts. "How old are you?"

He advances again, this time he's two inches from my face. I can see the stubble on his face.

"Thirty," I whisper. "In two days." I put my hand in my pocket and pull out the packs of gum. I turn my purse upside down. The other pack of gum tumbles out along with tampons, dental floss, matches, and a can of Friskies. I see the man's hand go up, and for a split second I think he's going to hit me. And what's even stranger—part of me wishes he would. I want him to hit me. I want to be punished. If this were Singapore they'd take the butcher knife from the back and chop off my hands. I could take a hit. But instead of hitting me, his hands clutch at his heart.

"Robbie, no!" his wife screams, running up from behind. She barely gets her arms around him as he crumples to the ground.

Chapter
34

"CPR," I say, dropping to my knees and taking his wife by the shoulders. "Do you know CPR?"

She shakes her head. Her eyes are large, brimming with tears; she's spraying fear like a wild animal. "His heart," she whispers. "Doctor says too much stress."

"Call 911," I say, pushing her toward the phone. He's already on his back. I tilt his head, pinch his nose, and put my cheek down to his mouth. He's not breathing. I try and find a pulse. No pulse. Three breaths, fifteen compressions. It's been well over two years since I breathed into Annie the CPR mannequin, and I pray the rules haven't changed too much. This time I drop the Saints and go right to the source. "Please, God," I say as my hands pump down on his heart. "Help me."

On the third round, I have a pulse. And then air. He's sucking in glorious air. His wife is leaning over us crying.

"Robbie," she says. "Robbie."

He opens his eyes. I'm leaning toward him, listening for the breath. He spits in my eye. But I don't care. He's alive and the paramedics have arrived. I roll away from him and put my head in my hands. The paramedics approach me. His wife and I both yell that it's Robbie who is in trouble.

"You did CPR?" one shouts at me.

I nod. "Did I—did I do something wrong?" I squeak.

"You saved his life," he says.

I remain on the floor as they take him out in the stretcher. She wants to go with him in the ambulance, but she has to close the store first.

"I'll help you," I say.

She hesitates only for a second and then nods. While she's locking up the register, I usher everyone out of the store. The police arrive.

"He's in the ambulance," the wife says to the officers at the door.

"We got a call about a theft," the officer says. "Were you robbed?"

The woman looks at the cop and shakes her head. "No," she says. "My husband was confused. And then he had a heart attack. But it's okay. Everything is okay."

"I'm sorry," I whisper when they're out of sight.

She grabs my hands. "I'm not," she says. "You saved his life. And maybe—just maybe you learn lesson?"

I start to cry. "But it's my fault," I tell her. "I made him mad. If I hadn't—"

She interrupts me by putting her hands on either side of my face. "He's been mad for twenty years," she says softly. "But it's over now. And no matter what else, you are a good girl. And you are wrong. Your mother would be proud."

I give her my phone number, and she promises to call and let me know how he's doing.

I run out of the deli clutching the envelope in my pocket. The studio is only ten blocks away and I run as if my life depended on it.

"Taping has already begun," the guard says as I enter the building and try to get past him.

"Please," I beg holding up my guest pass. Tears are streaming down my cheeks, and I know I have to do this before I lose my nerve. "You have to let me in."

Just then I see Deborah Green round the corner. "Deborah!" I yell. "Deborah."

She disappears into an elevator. It's too late. I turn around and head to the exit.

"Yes?" I hear from behind me.

I turn around to find Deborah waiting impatiently.

"Deborah," I say. "Thank God. You have to let me up."

She puts her hands on her hips. "And why do I have to do that?" she says.

When I tell her, her snippy attitude evaporates and you can see her adding up the ratings in her head. Seconds later, she hustles me into the elevator.

I'm waiting behind the wings. I can see wonderful, beautiful Greg sitting at the commentator's desk. Deborah Green swivels her chair to face the camera. "We have a special guest today," she tells America. "In fact, Greg—she came all the way here just to see you." An assistant gives me a little nudge and I walk out onto the stage and into the bright lights. "Have a seat, Melanie," Deborah says kindly.

"Is it okay if I stand?" I ask. I don't trust my legs, which are shaking something fierce. Greg meets my eyes and then closes his for a second. When he opens them he has his television personality on.

"What can I do for you?" he asks professionally.

Lies are perched at the tip of my tongue, but the truth beats its wings against my chest and tumbles out like boxes stacked precariously in an old attic. "I need you," I choke. "Help me."

"Go on," Greg says quietly, intensely.

"I'm a kleptomaniac," I say. "I steal everything I can get my hands on."

"Well this is quite a confession," Deborah cuts in cheerfully, but Greg puts his hand out and stops her.

"Let her talk," he says and nods at me.

I take a deep breath and let it all out. "Socks. Lipstick.

Jewelry. Scarves. Tampons. Gravy boats, sandals, cordless phones, books, cutlery. Teddy bears, silk panties, cashmere sweaters, pens, boas, diamonds!"

As I speak everything disappears including the cameras and Deborah's gaping mouth and the beautiful image of Greg burned in my brain. "Soaps, candles, candies, pillows, place mats, paintings!" I close my eyes and continue babbling until I feel someone's arms around me. Greg holds me while I shake and cry. No matter what happens, he's here now, touching me.

"Shh," he says as a litany of stolen items roll out of my mouth. "Just stop."

"I can't," I moan. "I can't stop."

Greg takes my head in my hands and pulls back enough so that I can look in his eyes. "You've just taken the most important step," he says. "You've confessed your shameful secret, and you've admitted you need help. How do you feel?"

"Like shit," I say.

"You're the most beautiful piece of shit I've ever seen," Greg says. It's the most disgusting and most romantic thing anyone has ever said to me. And then he kisses me in front of a live studio audience.

Later that night we sit on his Pottery Barn leather sofa and I cry into his lap for a full hour.

"Feel better?" he asks, playing with my hair.

"No," I mumble.

"Would you like to steal from me?" he says.

I sit up. "What?"

He gestures around. "Take anything you'd like. I have way too many things."

I start crying again.

"I'm sorry, I'm sorry," he said. "It's a joke."

I make a mental note to return the penguin. "I need another tissue," I say and excuse myself.

In the bathroom I take a good look at myself in the mirror. I'm still shaky and I could use a little makeup, but otherwise, it's me looking back. I've confessed my shameful secret to the world and it didn't come to an end. Next to stealing, it's the best feeling ever. I splash water on my face and reach for the hand towel hanging over his sink. I hold it on my face, inhaling its clean, comforting scent. When I go to put it back, I notice the object it had concealed while hanging.

"That's what you want to take?" Greg says when I carry the mother of pearl soap dish into the living room.

"Where did you get it?" I ask.

"Steve Landon. He gave one to everybody in the firm last year for Christmas. Somehow I ended up with two, so you're welcome to it. What? Why are you looking at me like that?"

I turn it over. Made in Taiwan. $19.99.

"Do you want to play with that soap dish or do you want to have last-person sex?" Greg teases me.

I toss the soap dish behind me like a bridal bouquet.

We kiss madly on the couch and then roll onto the floor. Greg gets on top of me and begins unbuttoning my blouse. He plants a kiss on me after undoing each button. Then he works his way back up. My neck, my cheeks, my lips, and when he opens my blouse and takes off my bra, my nipples are so erect I either have to enlist them as soldiers or make love to him. It isn't anything like it was with Ray. Physically I enjoyed sex with Ray—but there was always a part of me playing an act or twisting just the right way so my thighs wouldn't look chubby and sucking in my stomach—there was an entire Olympic judge panel in my head every move I made. (The East German judge always gave me a 3.5, the bastard.) But with Greg, he already knew the worst of me and he still liked me. I was even venturing to think maybe he was in love with me. But enough talking. Greg is about to enlist a soldier of his own, and we wouldn't want to miss that, would we?

But let me be the first to tell you that he's going down on me. South Town is no longer a ghost town and I didn't even have to draw him a map. Oh God, oh God, *Oh. God.* But as incredible as this feels, I want him inside me. I pull him up and he doesn't hesitate (by the way he has a lovely penis—I'm gobsmacked), and seconds later we're doing it. We're having unbelievable last-person sex that I pray won't be anywhere near the last. He must have been thinking the same thing, for we've done it a total of three times and now we're in his shower giggling and kissing and soaping each other in places we'd never met up until today—and then if two orgasms aren't enough (the third time I faked it—what can I say—two is my limit) now he's shampooing me.

But after all the sex and the shampooing, I get a lecture. We're sitting at his dining room table and he's made a pot of coffee. He has a list of psychiatrists for me to call in the morning. He says they'll encourage me to join a support group. AA for shoplifters. He tells me there is even a Web site—kleptomaniacs.com. And if that's not strange enough, they now treat kleptos with Naltrexone—a drug used to reduce the cravings in heroin addicts. So I guess it is an addiction. And that means—there's help.

"And I'm sure they'll tell you—you're not to go into stores alone for a while—and when you do you should have someone with you who knows about—your proclivity to take things," Greg says, taking my hands across the table. "I'll follow you everywhere," he adds. And although I was already three-quarters of the way there, I fall the rest of the way in love with him right then and there. Nothing could ruin this moment.

"Do you think your family saw the show?" Greg asks suddenly. A look of horror crosses my face like a line of geese waddling across a crowded freeway. "Sorry," Greg says, squeezing my hand. "One day at a time, right?" I nod. The thought of telling my mother makes me wish I smoked.

Sex, lies, and admissions. It's a wonder we're all not dead. At least now everything is out in the open. "And maybe after you've taken some time to confront your addictions and face your lies," Greg says, looking into my eyes, "you can really concentrate on your clocks."

CONTRACT WITH SELF

I, Melanie Zeitgar,
Oh, fuck it.

Josh Hannigan is much friendlier now that Trina has dumped him. He actually listens to my request with an open mind. "I can't give you your own opening," he says "but I will let you rent the studio for a few hours. Will that do?"

I grin. "Cuckoo," I say, and I'm off to make beautiful art. I buy twelve clocks at a Target in New Jersey and then take a cab to my storage unit. Time flies as I lovingly glue every one of my stolen items onto my clocks. The first clock has a scarf, sunglasses, and a hat. The next one gets six bars of soap-teeth and candle-hair. The third one I call Juan's, and I glue on every cactus salt and pepper shaker I ever stole from the Three Musketeers. It's Christmas, it's Mardis Gras, it's good-bye. Everything gets glued on except for the Omega Seamaster watch that I apologetically took back from Greg. That I place in its replacement box and mail it back to the store with an anonymous typewritten note. *Sorry,* it says. *Returned to you by: The Saint of Kleptomaniacs.* There's no need to give bird woman any more to go on than that.

My favorite is the grandfather clock. I've made it look like a woman with rhinestone-earring eyes, a wide cherry red lipstick mouth, and a floppy hat. But the best thing about it is the mother of pearl soap dish covering her vagina. I call it, "Ode To Trina."

This is how I live. I attend a support group for shoplifters three times a week. My mother, who has finally recovered from the shock that her daughter is a kleptomaniac, now brags about me to her friends. "Melanie gives speeches at high schools throughout New York and New Jersey on the addiction of shoplifting. She's going to be featured in Oprah's O magazine next month. Isn't that wonderful?" I think it helps that I'm also dating Greg Parks—her hero. I've begged him to do something to make my mom hate him, but he refuses to give up his image as most charming boyfriend ever, so I will have to deal.

I'm not completely redeemed of course. My family now requires a receipt for every gift I've bought them since the unveiling—but I'm okay with that. I haven't stolen anything since the deli man's heart attack—but I'm certainly not cured. Like Greg said, it's a day at a time type of thing. Trina went wild with rage when she came to my show and saw "Ode to Trina." She would have ripped it to shreds if Greg and Zach hadn't been there to pull her off. "Family heirloom?" I whispered to her as they dragged her away. "I didn't realize you hailed from Taiwan." I added that I had a very good list of psychiatrists if she wanted any referrals.

The opening, which I called "Saint of Kleptomaniacs," was a surprise hit. I guess I have the Saints to thank for that. The wonderful, helpful, silly little Saints who I was also putting to rest for now. I've started learning about the real ones—and there are almost as many as the ones I've made up. I'm still a vicarious Catholic, but I'm actually enjoying learning about Saint Katherine, Saint Joan of Arc, Saint Jude, Saint Elmo—where there's a want, there's a Saint. And guest what? They weren't all perfect. They were wonderfully flawed, complicated humans struggling to make sense out of their lives. Some of them were even reformed sinners. Now that's my kind of Saint.

The End
But hopefully, just the beginning

Want more Mary Carter?
Then please turn the page for an exciting sneak peek of

MURDER IN AN IRISH VILLAGE

the first book in her Irish Village mystery series
written as Carlene O'Connor!
Now on sale everywhere!

In the small village of Kilbane, County Cork, Ireland,
Naomi's Bistro has always been a warm and welcoming spot
to visit with neighbors and share a cup o' tea. But murder
has a way of killing business. . . .

Nowadays Siobhán O'Sullivan, along with her five siblings, runs the family bistro named for her mother. It's been
a rough year for the O'Sullivans, but it's about to get
rougher. One morning, as they're opening the bistro, they
discover a man seated at a table with a pair of hot pink bar-
ber scissors protruding from his chest. With the local garda
suspecting the O'Sullivans, and their business in danger of
being shunned, it's up to feisty redheaded Siobhán to solve
the crime and save her beloved brood.

Chapter

1

Siobhán O'Sullivan hurried through lush green fields, adjusting every so often for the bumps and dips of the terrain, imagining that from high above, Kilbane, County Cork, Ireland, must look like an ocean of green, rendering her a mere speck at sea. Before she knew it, she had passed the majestic remains of the ruined Dominican Priory, its Franciscan bell tower rising proudly above the town. Sheedy's cycle shop wasn't far now.

She hugged the medieval walls encircling the town, marveling at how something once constructed to keep violent marauders out could just as easily trap them in. She placed her hand on the ancient stone, relishing the way its rough peaks scraped against her fingertips. It was damp to the touch despite the midday sun. One of the few walled towns in existence, it had endured some of Ireland's most turbulent times and survived. These days Siobhán took solace wherever she could get it.

After ten straight days of lashing rain, the sun was laughing down on them, creating good cheer even in the begrudgers. Shopkeepers swept their footpaths, green thumbs tended gardens, and other folk simply turned their faces to the generous swath of blue sky. Children squealed, and kicked balls, and raced their bicycles through swollen puddles. Shoppers bustled along Sarsfield Street, calling in to the market, and the gift shop, and the chipper, and the hardware store. And, of course, to Naomi's Bistro. They would call out to one another—hello, hi ya, and how ya—and everyone would answer they were grand.

Siobhán had less than an hour before the lunch service at the bistro would begin. Given that children were tasting their first week of summer freedom, and it was a Friday to boot, they were going to be jammers. She picked up her pace, as the shop was just over the hill. If her siblings found out she was sneaking out several times a week to visit a pink scooter, they would declare her a right nutter.

Cows lifted their heads and chewed lazily as she panted by, sheep bleated, and swallows streaked through the sky. Patches of gorse set the neighboring fields aflame with their bright yellow heads, emitting the slightest scent of coconut. By the time she arrived at the shop, Siobhán was out of breath. She'd better stop eating so much brown bread at the bistro or she would have to buy a colored track suit and join the race-walking ladies in the morning. Surely their wagging tongues burned more calories than their aerobics. Siobhán laughed to herself and pushed the door to the shop open, hoping the jangle of the bell would disguise her labored breathing.

She looked at the counter, expecting to see Séamus Sheedy break out in his customary grin. Instead, there stood Niall Murphy. His dark hair, normally cut short, hung almost to his chin, giving him an unruly appearance. He seemed taller, too, or at least more filled out. Even before the bad business with Billy, Siobhán had always felt on edge around Niall. Maybe it was his eyes—technically brown, but so intense, his pupils so enormous that she always thought of them as black. She wasn't prepared for the shock. What was he doing here?

It was impossible to look at Niall without a thousand dark memories swarming in. Just when she thought she was on the mend, there he was again, the sniper of grief aiming a killing blow at her heart. Instantly, no time had passed at all. No time since that cruel morning almost one year ago when Niall's brother, Billy, got into his sporty red car, absolutely blotto, and slammed head-on into her parents. They died on impact. Billy was charged with drunk driving and sent to prison, and Niall took off for Dublin. Where, for some reason, Siobhán had just assumed he would stay.

She wanted to back out of the shop, but he'd already trained his dark eyes on her. Just then, Bridie Sheedy's head popped out from the other side of Niall. Séamus's wife was so petite Siobhán hadn't seen her at first.

"Hallo," Bridie called out. "How ya?" Despite an obvious attempt to sound cheerful, Bridie's voice wobbled, and Siobhán got the distinct feeling that she had just interrupted something. What on earth was Bridie doing standing so close to Niall? The two of them couldn't be sneaking around, could they? Surely not. Bridie was mad about Séamus, despite their age difference; everyone knew that.

"Grand," Siobhán said, doing her best to avoid Niall's stare. "How are you?"

"Not a bother." A smile broke out on Bridie's face, and this time it seemed genuine. With her head of brown curls and sparkling green eyes, Bridie's presence eased the tightness in Siobhán's chest a wee bit. Her smile didn't waver, but her tiny hand fluttered to her head, where she adjusted a knitted blue flower stuck in her hair, one she'd no doubt made herself. Bride was always a walking advertisement for her homemade wears.

It was odd to see her in here, surrounded by grease, and wheels, and dirty rags. She was normally at Courtney Kirby's gift shop, where she sold everything from jewelry to handmade scarves. And when she wasn't at Courtney's she was perched on top of a stationary bike at spinning class. Siobhán would much rather ride a scooter; it never made sense to her why anyone would want to pedal like mad atop something that was never going to go anywhere.

Bridie picked up her bedazzled handbag, whisked out from behind the counter, and grabbed Siobhán by the arm. She had a surprisingly strong grip for such a little woman. "Would ye mind keeping my secret?"

Siobhán extricated Bridie's clawing fingers from her arm. She was the porcelain variety of pale and bruised easily. "What secret?"

"Don't tell Séamus I was here. I'm begging ye."

"Oh." *Jaysus, she didn't want to be part of that kind of secret.* Was Bridie cheating on Séamus? With Niall? Right here in the shop?

Bridie must have noticed Siobhán's face go scarlet, for she gasped and then laughed. "No, no, pet. Nothing I'll be needing to confess to Father Kearney." She continued to laugh, and Siobhán couldn't help but laugh with her. "Niall was helping me order a gear for Séamus." Séamus was an avid road racer, always darting about town on his bicycle. He used to compete in actual road races and had loads of trophies to show for it. Better than spinning, but Siobhán still preferred the scooters. "A surprise," Bridie continued. "For his birthday."

"Ah. Of course. Not a bother," Siobhán said.

"Grand." Bridie laughed and then kissed each of Siobhán's cheeks. "When are ye going to whittle us a few dainty birds or roses for Courtney's store?" She kept her big eyes on Siobhán without blinking. Siobhán had learned to whittle from her grandfather, who noticed Siobhán had a temper; although her mam was terrified at the thought of putting a knife into her wee hands, her grandfather insisted whittling would be a good outlet for the young hothead. It required patience and concentration, and to everyone but her grandfather's surprise, she was right good at it. She could turn a piece of wood into a tiny singing bird, or a delicate flower, or her personal favorite, a Celtic cross. There was a box underneath her bed with her carving knife and bits of wood. A little here, and a little there, and before she knew it, another marvelous creature would come into existence. But she hadn't felt like whittling since her parents had passed on. It didn't feel right to be so carefree.

Siobhán forced a smile back. "We'll see."

Bridie sang her good-byes over her shoulder and bounced out of the shop. Siobhán had a strange urge to run after her.

Niall darted out from behind the counter and planted himself in front of Siobhán. "What's the craic?"

Siobhán felt her ire rise. *Oh, we've been having some fun, boyo, since your brother slammed head-on into our parents.* "What are you doing here?" she said instead.

Niall glanced around the shop as if the bicycles had ears. "We need to talk."

Siobhán forced a smile. "Here for a wee visit with your mammy?" Nasty woman, that Mary Murphy. Her mam wouldn't want her speaking ill of a neighbor, but she couldn't help it. Mary Murphy hadn't once said she was sorry for what her son had done. Siobhán didn't realize her right hand was curled into a fist until a fingernail dug into her palm.

Niall's face darkened, and an unmistakable look of hate flashed across it as his mouth turned into a slight snarl. "Me mother hasn't been able to work since the town turned against her. You know it yourself. Séamus was good enough to take me on here."

Turned against her? Mary Murphy was the one who had been avoiding contact with everyone. She slipped in and out of Mass, hurried through the shops, and hadn't once come into the bistro since the accident. And here was Niall, blaming the entire town. Did that mean he was back for good? She didn't want to think about that now, and she especially didn't want to think about how her older brother James was going to react when he found out.

This was the problem with positive thinking: the moment she set herself up to be happy, something in her world always came crashing down. He'd ruined her break, the sunny day, her hope. She should just walk out right now, but she didn't want to give him the satisfaction. Without another word, she turned and made her way to the scooters that were lined up at the front window, all shiny and new.

Oh, how she loved the Italian scooters. She stood next to the black one, praying Niall Murphy wouldn't notice when she glanced down the row at her actual favorite, the one in pink. All her life she'd been told redheads couldn't wear pink. But her hair was a darker red, more auburn, and besides, that old notion had changed with the times, hadn't it? Kilbane had mobile phones, and cable television, and iPads, and redheads could now wear pink. Or else she could tuck her hair into the helmet.

Yes, she definitely wanted the pink one. With a basket. That was only practical. She could see herself zipping around town, picking up bread and milk when the bistro ran low, feeling the vibrations of the road in her body, the breeze on her face. Of course, she'd have to be careful in the rain, and she would have to figure out how to keep her siblings off it—

"Aren't you supposed to be in Dublin?" Niall said from behind her. "Starting university?" Siobhán stopped, and turned. Niall was less than a foot from her. Of course, she was supposed to be in Dublin. The whole village knew about her scholarship to Trinity College. After she completed her Leaving Certificate she'd spent two years working at the bistro and saving for University before the scholarship finally came through. Mam and Da even hung her acceptance letter up in the bistro for everyone to see. To add to her luck, her best friends Maria and Aisling had delayed college as well to travel. All three of them would be starting University at the same time, just like she'd always dreamed.

But just a few months before she was to embark on the adventure of her life, her parents were gone. James wasn't stable enough to run the bistro and take care of the three youngest. So it fell to Siobhán. Her best friends, Maria and Aisling, were at Trinity without her. The more time went by, the less they talked. It was too painful to be constantly reminded of the life she thought she was going to be leading.

How one's destiny could change in the blink of an eye. Niall Murphy knew why she wasn't in Dublin better than anyone. Her da's favorite Sean O'Casey quote rose up in her: *It's my rule never to lose me temper till it would be detrimental to keep it.* "I could say the same thing about you," she said. "Why aren't you still in Dublin?"

Niall looked around, even though they were still alone in the shop, then leaned in and lowered his voice. "I was planning on coming to see ye."

"What for?" Couldn't Niall see that she didn't even want to be in the same room with him?

"When can we meet?" He glanced around the shop. "Somewhere private like."

"Never," Siobhán said. Niall stared at her, and she stared back. There it was. She couldn't pretend, couldn't be polite. If he was back in town, that was his business, but she wanted him to stay far away from her and her siblings.

"Don't be like that."

"I have to go." Siobhán headed for the door. Niall blocked her.

"You've turned into a beauty since I've been gone."

Was he hitting on her? Siobhán felt the familiar flush of heat scorch her face. She'd always hated how she blushed at the drop of a hat. When she was younger it was a curse to be so tall, with flaming red hair. But now that she was twenty-two, everything that was once ugly about her had somehow pulled together and blossomed into something beautiful. She still wasn't used to it. It thrilled her secretly, and that in itself was probably a sin.

Imagine Siobhán O'Sullivan succumbing to vanity. Beauty came and went, Siobhán was well aware, but it appeared this was her time, and wasn't it just as much a sin not to enjoy a rose in full bloom? She'd been looking forward to what kind of a splash she could make in Dublin. But she didn't like Niall Murphy looking at her like that, saying those things. Where was Séamus?

Niall brought his face close to hers. She stood her ground despite desperately wanting to back away from him. "Listen to me, gorgeous. It wasn't Billy's fault. He didn't do it."

"Didn't do it?" Fury rose in her as the sight of her parents' twisted white Volvo accosted her once again. "Are ye mental?"

Niall put his hands up, as if surrendering, looked around, and stepped so close she could smell whiskey on his breath. "I have proof."

"Proof?" Instantly she saw Billy's flashy red car zooming around Devil's Curve and barreling head-on into her parents, who had been returning from a weekend in Waterford. When the guards arrived, Billy was found slumped over the wheel, concussed, but alive, and muttering excuses. Later he was found to be three times over the legal alcohol limit.

"Are ye saying someone forced whiskey into him and pushed him into his sporty car? Made him press down harder on the pedal? Ignored all warnings to slow down around Devil's Curve? Is that what you're saying to me?" Her voice was raised now, and she didn't care.

Niall shook his head. He had a wild look in his eye. "There's so much. You wouldn't believe it."

"I don't."

"The proof. It's worth something. You know?"

"I have to go." Siobhán stepped forward, and Niall blocked her path.

"Me mother is in bad health. My brother is rotting away without good legal help." She'd never seen such a look in anyone's eyes before. It was as if he was pleading with her and threatening her at the same time. Like a wounded animal you feared would tear into you the minute you stepped in to help. *Move, move, move.* But she couldn't. Scooters were lined up behind her, and Niall hadn't budged an inch. She was trapped.

"I need you to move," Siobhán said. *Poke him in the eyes.* Is that what she should do if he didn't let her pass?

"Look here. I'd rather give it to you. That's the right thing to do. But he's my brother. And he's locked away for something he didn't do."

"Give what to me?" He wasn't right in the head. Why was she even talking to him?

"I need ten thousand euro." Niall inched even closer.

"Ten thousand euro?" Mad. He was absolutely mad. They barely had a thousand euro in the bank. Not that it mattered. She wouldn't give Niall Murphy the lint from her pocket.

"I figure you must have some money tucked away for college. You said yourself, you won't be needing it now."

"You're despicable," Siobhán said.

"I'm tellin' ye. Yer one would give me twenty thousand euro for it. But I'm trying to do the right thing, can't ye see?"

Siobhán instinctively stepped back, and her backside

bumped into the handlebars of the first scooter in line. Before she could even turn around, it tilted over and knocked into the next, then the next, and with surprising speed and clatter, the scooters fell like a line of dominoes. "Jaysus!"

Siobhán reached out to fix the mess, only it was too late. The lot of 'em lay on their sides. Oh, Jaysus, no. Siobhán crossed herself. Were they broken? Scratched? She couldn't afford one, let alone all of them. Why had she come to the shop today?

"You're fine, you're fine," Niall said. He stepped in front of her and pulled the first scooter up. Siobhán held her breath. Niall fixed it so it was standing again, then brushed off the dirt on the other side. Siobhán reached to right the next scooter, but Niall blocked her. "I'll do it. It's me job."

Siobhán stumbled back. It was his fault she'd knocked the scooters over—standing so close to her with alcohol on his breath, ranting about his brother being innocent, propositioning her with lies for ten thousand euro. "You're sick, you know that? You're sick in the head."

The door opened, the bell jingled, and Séamus Sheedy entered, wheeling a mountain bike into the shop. He was a middle-aged man, on the short side, and a good ten years older than Bridie, but he had an infectious grin and a full head of chestnut hair, and cycling kept him trim. "How ya," he called. His grin halted the minute he saw Siobhán's face. He looked from her to Niall, to the mess of scooters on the floor. "Are ye alright, pet?"

"I'm so sorry," Siobhán said. "It was an accident." Séamus shifted his gaze to Niall, still trying to right the last of the scooters.

"It's alright, petal. You're fine." Séamus parked his bike and approached. "What's the story?" he said to Niall.

"It's my fault. I lined them up too close together," Niall said. "So far just a smidge of dirt is all."

Séamus turned to Siobhán with a smile. "There's no harm done, pet. They just need a bit of shining is all."

"I'll get a rag," Niall said. He turned and, with a final look at Siobhán, went back behind the counter.

Séamus grabbed a set of keys hanging by the register and approached Siobhán. "Why don't we make today the day?"

Siobhán was still shaking; she just wanted to flee. "Pardon?" Even with a key dangling in front of her face, she couldn't make out what Séamus was trying to say.

"Why don't you finally take her for a ride?" He gestured to the pink scooter.

Oh, God she wanted to. She wanted to ride out of town and never look back. She wanted to run the scooter directly into Niall Murphy.

"Lunch service will be starting. I'd better get me legs under me." Siobhán headed for the door. She should have never come in. What a silly, silly, girl. What a right joke she was.

Séamus threw open his hands. "There's a discount on the pink one today, seeing how there's a wee scratch."

Siobhán's hands fluttered to her mouth. "Oh, Jaysus," she said. "I'm so sorry. I'll pay for it."

Séamus put his hands up. "I'm just jokin' ye. But she could be yours for a real good price."

Siobhán shook her head. She couldn't think about scooters right now. She couldn't think about anything with Niall Murphy standing right there. Had he really just tried to extort her for ten thousand euro? She should tell Séamus. He'd fire Niall on the spot. But not now. She couldn't think, or even breathe. She just wanted to get out of the shop. She'd sort it all out later. Séamus was still waiting for her answer.

"I can't. But thank you."

Séamus put the keys back and gestured to them. "The

keys are here, anytime you want to give her a go," he said with a wink.

"Ba-bye, ba-bye, ba-bye." Siobhán flew out of the shop. She tore across the field, pumping her legs and arms faster, and faster, pushing herself to the point of pain. She ran all the way back to the bistro, and was about to fling herself at the door when Sheila Mahoney jumped out in front of her, wielding what appeared to be a razor-sharp blade.

Connect with  Us

Visit us online at
KensingtonBooks.com
to read more from your favorite authors, see books
by series, view reading group guides, and more.

 Join us on social media

for sneak peeks, chances to win books and prize packs,
and to share your thoughts with other readers.

facebook.com/kensingtonpublishing
twitter.com/kensingtonbooks

Tell us what you think!

To share your thoughts, submit a review,
or sign up for our eNewsletters, please visit:
KensingtonBooks.com/TellUs.